MW01658471

To Evonne,
Best wishes.
Scott Sandahl

# WATER RIDE

## A Rick Blaze Novel

BY

SCOTT

SANDAHL

ANCHOR HOUSE PRESS

This is a work of fiction. Names, characters, places and incidents are the product of the author's imagination. Any resemblance to actual events is purely coincidental.



ISBN: 0-9721727-0-X

Library of Congress Number – 2002092259

First printing 2002

Printed in the U.S.A. by
Anchor House Press
P.O. Box 1240
Port Aransas, Texas 78373
361-749-2305
www.anchorhousepress.com

# ACKNOWLEDGMENTS

Thanks to my wife, Luann, who has been my cheerleader, sounding board, editor, book doctor and inspiration. I would never have finished, much less published, this book without your support. Thanks also to my sons, Chris and Cody, for their help and encouragement.

# FOREWARD

This book has been written over the past few years, well before the events of September 11. I was told that those events preclude the publishing of this book. However, I think Americans love to read about other Americans and visualize how we would react in a certain crisis. I believe *Water Ride* captures the essence of the American spirit and what makes the United States the greatest country in the world. The greatness comes not from technology and weapons, but from the inner soul of our citizens. Our country started late compared to the other powers of the world, but we have left the others behind as we have met every test and overcome each obstacle with our indomitable will.

# Chapter 1

Randy Flanagan heard voices in the alley. If he had learned anything about this part of Chicago, it was to avoid people that did their business in alleys at 2:15 in the morning. He stared straight ahead and crossed the alley opening. A familiar voice caused him to stop and peer into the alley, ignoring his better judgment. In the dim light Randy could see the Mafia boss, Danny Portofina, facing three other men.

Portofina said, “What’s with this? You said we was going to work together.”

The man in the middle, facing Portofina said, “I ain’t working with the likes of you. I’m personally gonna pay you back for messing with my family.”

Then he drew a gun from his coat and fired three quick shots at the single man. Portofina slumped to the pavement and the gunman stepped closer and fired three more shots into the bloody body.

Randy froze in horror. He saw the man fall and then be shot again. The gunman turned to leave the alley and stood face to face with Randy. Even at thirty feet in a dimly lit alley, Randy recognized the man. Gino Carlucci was the biggest and baddest of the Mafia bosses in Chicago. Everyone had seen Carlucci's face on television and in the newspaper scores of times. Now Randy had seen this man gun down another man in cold blood. Carlucci sneered at Randy and lifted the gun, ready to eliminate this intruding witness. As Randy saw the gun begin to rise he forced his mind to tell the rest of his body to run. He dove behind the next building as a bullet zinged past the spot where his chest had just been.

Randy hit the sidewalk hard and grunted as his body protested the blow. His only thought was to run. He rolled to his right and came up moving his legs faster than they had ever moved before. Another bullet whistled by and Randy darted behind a line of parked cars. A bullet broke the windshield of one car and others plowed into the sheet metal. Randy's mind began to function and he concentrated on the layout of the neighborhood. He knew the alley ahead led to several vacant buildings. If he could get to the buildings Randy felt certain he could lose his pursuers.

Taking a deep breath and running as fast and low as he could, Randy darted across the sidewalk and down the alley, leaving the sounds of errant bullets behind him. Another quick right turn and Randy had left the older, slower men well behind. He kept running and changing directions until he was totally worn out and just a little bit lost. The building across the street was vacant and the front door stood open a little. Randy slid through the door and climbed the stairs, passing several limp human forms lying on the floor. These wretched people were no threat to Randy and he knew it. The winos and bums were passed out from their night of drinking and would not wake for many hours.

As he sat in the corner of one of the dark and musty rooms

Randy tried to recall everything that had happened and desperately attempted to decide what to do next. Would they figure out who he was? Or was the real question how long would it be before they figured out who he was? The more his mind settled down and began to function properly the more Randy knew the answer. He had heard many tales at Murray's Restaurant about how the Mafia would relentlessly pursue anyone who was a threat to them. Right now Randy was possibly the greatest threat Gino Carlucci had ever had and it would be easy for Carlucci to place Randy on the street at the time of the shooting. Carlucci probably got a good enough look at Randy to describe him to Murray Sloan. Murray would not think twice about identifying Randy. After all, he had given up his own cousin a year ago to some bookies. Murray would not risk the wrath of Gino Carlucci. Nobody who did that lived very long.

Although all he wanted was to drive to his parents home and go to sleep, Randy was beginning to realize his life would never return to the way it had been. As the only child of a loving middle class couple he had enjoyed the protective umbrella of his parents. Even though Randy had become independent in the last few years he had known his parents would always be there for him. They could not help him now, he thought. In fact, they were in danger as well. This thought hit Randy hard because he had to act fast now. It was not just a matter of hiding. He had to do something to protect his parents. The Mafia never thought twice about using someone's family as leverage to get what they want.

All his life Randy had been told by his parents to do the right thing. As much as he hated the idea of going to the police Randy knew it was the right thing to do. So he left the vacant building and walked toward the police precinct building that he remembered to be about a half mile away. If Carlucci had already identified Randy then he would also know about the bright yellow Volkswagen beetle that Randy drove. Everyone at Murray's knew about the car. So the car is the first thing I have to give up, thought Randy. What else will follow?

Earlier that evening Randy Flanagan had been waiting tables at Murray's Restaurant, a shady cafe on the east side of Chicago. Even though the clientele at Murray's left a lot to be desired Randy enjoyed his job. By day he was in his freshman year at the University of Chicago and by night he mixed and mingled with a completely different crowd of people. Randy longed to be the first person in his family to graduate from college, but found having to work until early in the morning six days a week to be a major drain on his enthusiasm.

At least the work was interesting, not so much from the actual work of waiting tables, but more from the people he waited on. The early crowd was mainly people from the neighborhood, many of whom owned a small business in the area. They were generally tolerant of his youth and encouraged his dream of being a college graduate. A fifteen per cent tip was the most he could expect from these frugal people and he really had to work hard in order to earn this level of reward. He considered their advice on business and life in general to be an extra benefit of the job and he respected most of these people immensely.

The late crowd was completely different. As the decent folk of the early crowd began to leave Murray's the rougher crowd of the streets drifted in. Street toughs, drug dealers, bookies, pimps and even some suspected Mafia types flowed through the door after eleven o'clock. This was a loud and boisterous bunch. They mingled with each other with wariness as they tried to mix business and pleasure. Randy had learned that these people liked to feel important and a twenty to thirty-per-cent tip was the reward for making each customer feel like the most important person in the restaurant. He knew that respect was earned by standing his ground, so he walked a fine line between being a good waiter and common butt-kisser.

At eighteen years old Randy had finally grown to a solid one hundred eighty pounds on his five-foot-ten-inch frame. His brown hair, brown eyes and quick wit made him popular with his classmates, especially the girls. Randy was an only child and that made him both independent and most comfortable when he was alone.

Randy's fellow waiter Richie Lombardini passed by and said, "This is murder, man, it's only ten and I'm already dragging ass. Saturday nights are always busy, but this must be some sort of record."

"Yeah, I'm dragging too, Richie, but it's from all the tips in my pocket," replied Randy.

"Okay, rub it in. So what if you always make more in tips than I do," smirked Richie, "At least I drive a better car than you do."

"I'm saving for college. Maybe when I get my degree and get a good job I'll drop by Murray's and let you wait on me. If you don't drop anything I'll give you a ten per cent tip. That would be a record for you, Richie," replied Randy with a laugh.

Richie grimaced and said, "That's real funny, Randy, real funny."

"Hey, you two punks stop jawing and get back to work," the owner, Murray Sloan, said.

Randy and Richie laughed and went back to their jobs. Keeping the people waiting for a table happy was Murray's main job, so Randy, Richie and the other two waiters managed for themselves. The next few hours passed quickly for Randy as he tried to keep a smile on his face and a bounce in his step.

At 1:30 a.m. a man Randy had never seen walked up to the door. Murray looked extremely nervous as he scoured the room for an empty table. Two men who were about half through eating jumped up and fairly ran over to Murray.

"Mr. Portofina can have our table, Murray. We was just leaving," said a man Randy only knew as Larry the Lizard.

"Thanks, Larry," said Murray with relief.

"I'm Larry Lazzarri, Mr. Portofina. Have a good evening," Larry said as he passed by the man.

Mr. Portofina nodded at Larry and followed Murray to the table. Randy and Richie had cleared the table and watched the man make his way through the restaurant. Other customers would sneak a look at the man and quickly look away. Randy noticed this and marveled at the respect and obvious fear the others had of this Mr. Portofina. He was large, but that was not the reason for the fear. It was the look of total disregard for anyone in the room and the eyes that seemed to glare at everyone, yet no one in particular. Randy bent over and asked one of the more friendly bookies who the man was.

The bookie replied, "That's Danny Portofina. He's the head of one of the Mafia families here. You sure don't see guys like him out by themselves very often. They usually have their goons everywhere, you know, for protection. Go try your charm on him, Randy. You might get a great big tip or you might get a fat lip. That's the way it usually goes with people like him."

The bookie laughed and turned back to his friends, who were also laughing.

Randy grinned and walked over to the man.

"Good evening, Sir. Can I get you something to drink?" Randy said as he put the menu on the table.

"Bring me a beer and then scram, kid. I'm waiting for someone and I don't need nothing else from the likes of you," said Portofina.

Randy didn't have to be told twice. He brought Portofina a beer and went back to his other tables.

Danny Portofina popped his knuckles and drummed his fingers on the table as he waited. He was clearly agitated and his eyes scanned the room continuously, like he was expecting trouble. Around two o'clock the place had cleared out a good bit and Portofina still sat by himself. He grunted, threw a twenty-dollar bill on the table and got up to leave. Portofina acted like he didn't want to go outside, but after a short pause at the door he stepped out. Randy was leaving as well. His deal with Murray Sloan was that he would work six days a week as long as he got off at two so he could get a few hours of sleep before classes. This deal applied to Saturday nights as well so Randy could go to church with his parents.

Randy closed out his tickets and removed his apron. At 2:15 a.m. he left the restaurant and headed for his car.

# Chapter 2

Randy Flanagan walked into the police precinct building at 4:00 a.m. The on-duty officer peered over the raised desk and eyed the young man who stood before him.

"What can I do for you, son?" asked Sergeant Pete Newell. "You look like you've been through the wringer tonight," he continued.

Randy looked at Newell with a weariness that touched every part of his body and said, "Do you know about the shooting over by Murray's?"

"Sure, that's all anyone around here's talking about. It's not often a Mafia type like Danny Portofina gets blown away. Now we have to go out and try to catch someone who just did us a big favor. What's it to you anyway?" asked Newell.

Randy took a deep breath and said, "I saw who did it."

"Oh, really," said Newell, "then why is it you're just now coming in?"

"They saw me and I had to hide. Then I had to decide if I was going to report it."

"And just why wouldn't you report a murder, son? That would be against the law," said Newell.

Randy looked Newell straight in the eye and said, "I saw Gino Carlucci gun down Danny Portofina in cold blood in the alley next to Murray's at about 2:15 this morning. Would you have the guts to come in and report it if it were you?"

"So how come you have the guts to do it?" asked Newell, ignoring the question.

"Carlucci saw my face and probably has been able to identify me because I worked at Murray's. I need your protection and so do my parents," blurted out Randy.

Newell stood up and said, "I think you're shooting straight with me, son. You can stop worrying. We'll take care of you. So, first things first. What's your name? Mine's Pete."

"Randy Flanagan."

"Okay, Randy, come over here. Park yourself in this room here and I'll get a detective to take your statement."

"What about my parents?" asked Randy. "They are in danger, too, don't you think?"

"Just wait here a minute, Randy."

Randy waited in the room for only about ten minutes and then he heard a commotion outside. Then three men came in.

The first man said, "I'm Detective James Albright, this is Detective Williams and this is Detective Whittle. I understand you have quite a story to tell. Let's hear what you have to say, Mr. Flanagan."

Randy began to tell the events of the evening and within thirty minutes had related the whole story.

Detective Albright said, "Randy, if your story is true, we can put Mr. Carlucci behind bars for the rest of his life. That, along with the murder of Danny Portofina, would put a serious dent in the organized crime activities in this city. However, you are in a very serious spot. Do you know what I'm talking about?"

"Yes, Sir, I think so. I think they will try to kill me and maybe my parents."

"Randy, that's exactly what I'm talking about, but we can protect you and your parents. I'll send some men over to your parents house immediately and we'll put you in a safe house," said Albright. Continuing he said, "Detective Whittle, can you take care of these matters?"

"Sure, I'm on it," said Whittle as he left the room.

"Can I call my parents and tell them what has happened?" asked Randy.

Albright pointed to the phone on the wall outside the office and said, "Sure, go call them now. Tell them to lock the house and that we are sending someone over soon."

Randy made the call and had to fight back the tears as he wondered how his life was going to change.

# Chapter 3

Randy watched the news on the TV at the safe house. He was the man-of-the-hour in Chicago and even in the national news. Gino Carlucci had been arrested and placed in a maximum-security jail. There was speculation about why Danny Portofina was in Murray's alone and about why Carlucci would do the killing himself. The police officers that took turns guarding Randy generally thought that Carlucci had convinced Portofina that if they met together alone their differences could be patched up. Carlucci's men had then killed Portofina's men outside of Murray's. Their bodies had been found in a dumpster a mile away. Carlucci and two of his men had remained outside until Portofina gave up waiting and left Murray's. He was then forced into the alley and shot. The only reason anyone could think of for Carlucci to risk doing it himself was that Carlucci's son had been executed five years earlier and it was generally thought to have been some of Portofina's men who did the job.

After a week in the safe house Randy had only seen his parents twice and missed the routine of his pre-Carlucci life. All his plans and dreams had gone up in smoke. The FBI was being brought into the case and had already discussed the witness protection system with Randy.

After four months of moving around to various safe houses and always having at least two FBI agents with him at all times Randy was beginning to actually look forward to the trial. He wanted to get that part over and begin his new life, wherever and whatever it turned out to be. The trial was to start in three days and the pressure seemed to be building on all those around him. The agents seemed edgier and didn't chat with each other or with Randy like he had grown accustomed to.

Agent Sam Brown said, "Randy, get your stuff. We are moving to a hotel two blocks from the courthouse. It will make the trips to and from the courthouse a lot safer."

"Sure, Sam, whatever you say," said Randy with resignation.

He had learned early on that the FBI was not looking for advice or opinion from him. Having no advance notice of a move was completely in character for the Agency as well. Randy, Sam and Agent Paul Grendel went into the garage and got into one car while three other agents were getting into an identical car. The garage door opened and the two cars quickly moved into the street and left in opposite directions. After winding through Chicago for an hour Randy's car pulled into the covered garage of the hotel. The three men rushed into the freight elevator and up to the seventh floor. Sam Brown knocked hard on the door to Room 732. After a pause the door opened and Randy saw two agents he was familiar with.

"The room's clean, Sam," said one of them as they passed by.

Paul went through the suite again, double-checking as he

always did. “Yeah, it’s clean,” he said.

“Your room is over there, Randy,” said Sam, pointing across the room.

“Thanks, Sam, I’ll just make myself at home. Then we can go swimming,” replied Randy.

“Funny, Randy, only I forgot my suit,” said Sam gruffly.

Randy laughed and went to his room. This would be the only privacy he would get. Randy had been in the bedroom for about an hour when he heard a knock on the door.

“Shift change,” yelled Sam.

Randy started toward the door to greet the new shift. He recognized Arnie Williams and Don Winthrop and said, “How do you like my new digs?”

Williams continued walking toward Randy and the others, but Winthrop stopped, pulled out a silenced pistol and opened fire on Sam, Paul and then Williams. Winthrop caught the three surprised agents so off-guard that none of them were able to get off a shot. Randy froze for a second at the horror of seeing Sam with a glazed look and blood flowing from a head wound, Paul lying face down and Williams crumpled over a chair. Realizing that Don Winthrop was really after him and he would be dead in about ten seconds, Randy ducked back into the bedroom and slammed the door. There was no lock so he propped a chair up against it.

Three bullets zipped through the door, right by the doorknob. Randy knew that would not keep Winthrop out for long so he looked for a weapon. The only thing he could find was a brass lamp. Randy picked it up and was ready to use it as a club when an idea popped into his head. A story his dad had frequently told about pranks he pulled on his sister with electricity popped into Randy’s head. With Winthrop outside beating on the door and the chair about to give way, Randy unplugged the lamp and jerked hard on the cord, causing it to pull loose from the socket and come out the base. This left two bare ends. Randy held the bare ends apart and plugged the cord back in. The chair was just about to fall away so Randy pushed the door closed as the killer was backing off to hit it again.

Winthrop heard the chair fall and started to turn the door handle. Randy put both ends of the cord against the metal knob. There was a lot of sparking and finally the circuit breaker flipped, shutting off the power. Randy heard a sound like a large object hitting the floor and no more banging on the door so he kicked the chair away, went through the door and saw the man lying on the floor. Apparently Winthrop had firmly grasped the doorknob when the electricity was applied to the knob and he could not get loose until the power shut off. He was only stunned and still had the gun in his hand.

As Randy stared, Winthrop groaned and started to move. Randy kicked him in the face as hard as he could and that put the agent out. The gun fell out of Winthrop's hand and Randy picked it up and hit him on the head with it. Randy had seen so many movies where the unconscious villain woke that he was not going to take any chances. Randy removed Winthrop's handcuffs and cuffed the man's hands behind his back. Using handcuffs from two of the dead agents Randy cuffed the now stirring man's feet and then his hands and feet together. Randy grabbed his bag and ran out the door and down the stairs of the hotel. He went out the back of the hotel and took off running down the street. He knew he shouldn't run because it would attract more attention but he just could not stop myself.

After running for blocks, Randy stopped at a cafe to decide what to do next. He was in quite a fix because even if he did not testify the Mafia would kill him and it was obvious the FBI could not guarantee protection from such powerful and ruthless people. In addition, Randy had very little money in his pocket, no transportation, and was smart enough to know it was not safe to go to his parents' house. He didn't want to get any of his friends involved so he decided to risk using the FBI for assistance. Randy thought of all the agents he had met during the four months he had been under their protection and one kept coming to mind-Bill Whetland. Randy decided to go with his gut feeling and called Agent Whetland from a pay phone.

After going through several levels of secretaries a voice said, "Agent Whetland."

"Bill, it's Randy Flanagan."

"Randy, are you all right?"

Randy answered, "Yes, I'm fine. I guess you know what happened."

"Yeah, pretty much. Look, Randy, just tell me where you are and I'll come get you," Whetland said.

"Not so fast, Bill. I need to think about this because obviously no one can really protect me from Carlucci's men," Randy answered. Continuing he said, "I need some time to think. Give me an hour and I'll call you back."

"Randy, it would be better to let us pick you up. I know we look bad, but you don't have any protection now," pleaded Whetland.

"No way, Bill," Randy said before hanging up.

# Chapter 4

Randy went to a small café and sat for an hour, sorting through his limited options. He finally returned to the pay phone.

"Agent Whetland," the voice said, exactly as before.

"Bill, it's Randy."

"So, are you going to let me pick you up?" quizzed Whetland.

"No, Bill, but I still want to testify. I want that slime ball Carlucci to rot in jail. He's killed a lot of people and really screwed up my life," said a determined Randy.

"If you are not coming with me, does that mean you have some other plan?" asked Whetland.

Randy replied, "Yes. I'll hide out on my own and then come in at the last minute."

"You know, Randy, I can't recommend this decision, but I understand. Is there anything I can do for you now?" asked Whetland.

"I need protection for my parents, money for the next few days and an agreement from the judge to allow me to testify for one day only," replied Randy.

"I can do all three, I think. I'll dispatch additional men immediately to protect your parents and I'll bring you money personally. I feel sure that under the circumstances the judge would agree to one day's testimony," said Whetland.

"Great. Thanks, Bill," replied Randy.

Randy had devised a plan to get the money without having to meet any FBI people and related the plan to Agent Whetland.

Randy had instructed Bill Whetland to drive slowly along IH 55 on the upper deck with his flashing lights on at 6 a.m. When Whetland saw a blinking flashlight on the road below he was supposed to throw a Pepsi can out of the window. Randy saw the flashing lights approaching above and blinked his newly purchased flashlight on and off. A blue can came flying over the rails and landed a hundred feet away. Randy scrambled over to the can.

As he pulled out the thousand dollars in small bills, Randy chuckled, "I should have asked for ten thousand."

The next day was the day before the trial and Randy stayed in his new motel room watching TV. The TV was making him seem like a hero and everyone else a bunch of idiots.

"We interrupt this program for a special report," the voice said.

Randy saw a fire raging in a neighborhood, one that kind of looked like his.

"An explosion, probably a bomb, has gone off at the house of Dave and Edna Flanagan, parents of Randy Flanagan. Our sources report that the Flanagan's and two FBI agents assigned to them for protection were in the house. All are feared dead," continued the voice.

Randy screamed, "You bastard!" and broke down into

tears.

Randy didn't hear another word on the TV. He stomped around the room, cursing, crying, until he finally collapsed on the bed. His body shuddered as the emotion overwhelmed him. Randy lay there for several hours until he had no tears left. Now, hate began to consume him.

Randy looked into the mirror, his eyes narrowed and his jaw set and declared out loud, "Gino Carlucci, you will surely spend the rest of your life in jail because of me. I have no relatives, the Mafia after me, no protection I can trust, and nothing to live for except the chance to put you away for good."

Randy had to figure a way to get to the courthouse alive and testify. He decided a disguise was his only hope. Later that night Randy went out shopping. He found a resale shop and purchased a suit, briefcase, gray hair color, glasses, a hat and a fake moustache. He went to the resale shop because he wanted everything to look used and besides, the resale shop even carried the hair color and fake moustache in the costume party area.

The next morning he put it all on, took a cab to the courthouse and just walked in like one of the many lawyers involved in the case. Randy was starting to sweat and tried to calm down with slow, easy breathing. As his eyes darted around the room Randy was relieved that no one was paying any attention to him.

He walked up to Agent Whetland and said, "Bill, it's me, Randy."

"Holy cow, Randy. We've been really worried about you. I thought you would call," said Whetland. "You don't testify for another hour."

"I want to testify now and I think the judge would like to hear my testimony before anything else happens," said Randy with a calm that belied his inner feelings.

Whetland and six of his fellow agents stayed with Randy in an office behind the courtroom until word was sent that the judge would allow Randy to testify immediately. Randy testified for four hours and was excused. Agent Whetland escorted him back to the office where Randy put his disguise back on.

Whetland said, “Randy, please let me help you. I know you think these people will be after you the rest of your life and you’re probably right, but I think we can protect you better that you can protect yourself.”

“Thanks, Bill. If everyone was like you I could trust the FBI, but obviously Carlucci has even infiltrated you guys so I’ve got to do this myself,” replied Randy.

Randy walked out of the building and jumped in a cab. After driving for a while he paid the cabby in advance and when they hit a stop light under one of the elevated trains, Randy stepped out, ran up the stairs and got on the first train. All he had was the suit he wore to the trial and about $700 left from the money Agent Whetland had given him. Every so often he changed trains to be sure no one was following him. At least no one could know where he was going because at that time he had no idea myself.

Late in the evening he got off the trains and found a small motel to stay in until he could decide what to do with the rest of his life. That night, as Randy sat in the motel room, the complete shambles of his life hit hard-no family, no identity except the one the Mafia was looking for with a vengeance, very little money, no car and absolutely no clue as to where to go next.

As he lay in bed ideas kept running through his mind, none of them feeling right until he thought of how so many people had gone to Montana to get away from everything, society included. Some were living by themselves, but others were forming militias and had their own societies in the wilderness. He had read about this a year ago in *Time Magazine* when he was in the dentist's office. So many of these people were living on the edge of society that maybe someone out there could help him with a new identity. The chance of the government or the Mafia finding out about him was certainly reduced since the various militias had a great distaste for both. The next day he bought a backpack, toiletries, a US map, and a few clothes. He caught a cab to the edge of town and began hitchhiking toward Montana. Since he was reasonably clean cut he was able to catch rides fairly easily, especially the closer he got to Montana. At the truck stops he found all the magazines he wanted that catered to the militia crowd.

# Chapter 5

As the eighteen-wheeler rolled west along Interstate 94 Randy tried talking to Earl, the trucker who had picked him up in Wisconsin. Since Earl was not very chatty, developing a life plan became the main activity, but planning deteriorated into a pity party. Randy just could not get past his current situation long enough to think about next month, much less next year.

"After two days of testimony and eight hours of deliberation the jury has returned a verdict in the Gino Carlucci case. Mr. Carlucci, perhaps the most powerful Mafia boss in Chicago, has been found guilty of murder. The whole case was built around the testimony of Randy Flanagan. Officials have stated that Mr. Flanagan will not be available for comment. The sentencing phase of the trial will begin tomorrow," said the radio announcer.

Earl noticed Randy's interest and said, "I'd hate to be that young man, wouldn't you?"

"Yeah, I guess he'll have to lay low for a while," Randy replied.

"Lay low," Earl snorted, "he might as well put his head between his legs and kiss his ass goodbye. Those Mafia thugs will track him down like a dog."

"You really think so, Earl?"

"I know so. They already blew up his parents and wasted several FBI agents. They'll find that kid and blow him away. You can make book on that," Earl said.

"Wow, I'd sure hate to be him," muttered Randy.

"Me, too. Me, too."

Two days later Randy had caught a ride going all the way to Billings, Montana. That was where Randy decided to start his new life. Earlier in the day the radio had announced that Gino Carlucci had been sentenced to life imprisonment. Even though Randy knew a life sentence was not really for the rest of a person's life, at least Carlucci would be put away until he was a very old man. Somehow this news had given Randy a resolve to make something of his life. Other than to hook up with some militia group for a while, Randy didn't have much of a plan, but he did have hope now and that was enough to keep him going.

Randy gave the trucker a wave as he stepped out of the truck and onto the sidewalk in Billings. Since finding a militia group was not as simple as looking in the Yellow Pages, he walked around town and got a feel for the city. As the neighborhoods got a little rougher he saw a military surplus shop and decided to push the issue there.

Randy looked at the man behind the counter and asked, "Say, do you know of any militia groups in the area?"

"Why do you want to know?" growled the man.

"Oh, I was just wondering," replied Randy.

The man got in Randy's face and snorted, "Those groups don't like people wondering about them. They don't like people asking about them. Maybe you should get your young ass out of here before some of them come in. They're not as nice as me."

"Sure, mister, I'll leave," said Randy sheepishly.

"Too late, boy. Here comes some now," sneered the man.

"What's up, Lew?" asked the first of the three men dressed in camouflage fatigues.

The man behind the counter replied, "This boy wants to meet some real militia types."

"That so, boy?" asked the man.

"Well, I guess so," stammered Randy, not sure how to get out of this.

The man glared at Randy and said, "I'll meet you, boy. Here's how we shake hands in the militia."

The man delivered a sharp blow to Randy's stomach and followed it with a backhand to the side of Randy's head. As he staggered toward the door in a vain attempt to get out, the other two men pummeled Randy. As he heard all four men in the store laughing, Randy gathered up his strength and ran toward the man who had delivered the first blow. With his shoulder in the man's gut, Randy drove him back until the back wall stopped them. The man slumped to the floor but his two friends were instantly on top of Randy, kicking and hitting any piece of Randy's body they could find. Randy felt blackness overtaking him, but tried to resist. His senses surged when he heard a gong-like sound and felt one of the men fall away. Through his one open eye Randy could see a small, but obviously tough man pulling the unconscious man away, dropping a cast iron skillet and flailing at the other with a nightstick he had removed from the shelves. Randy was able to sit up and notice the leader of the group coming up behind his savior.

"Behind you," Randy yelled.

The man spun around, crouching low and extending the nightstick out as far as possible. The wood stick crunched into the approaching man's shins, dropping him to the floor. The little man delivered a vicious kick to his attacker's head and the fight was over.

The victor pointed the nightstick at the man behind the counter and said, "You don't want in this do you, Lew?"

"Naw, why don't you guys just leave so's my place don't get busted up anymore," growled Lew.

The man helped Randy get up and they went outside.

"I'm Nate Reilly," said the man, holding his hand out.

"Randy Smith. Glad to meet you. Thanks for saving me."

"Smith, huh? We've got a lot of Smith's around here. What got you into trouble back there?" asked Nate.

"I just asked about militias, that's all," replied Randy.

"That's enough to get some people riled up around here. What do you want to know about militias?" inquired Nate.

Randy looked around to be sure they were alone and whispered, "I'm in trouble and I hoped to be able to hide out with some militia group. I'll earn my keep."

Nate looked at the swollen and bruised young man with sympathy and said, "There's all kinds of militias up here. If you want to hide out and you're willing to do your share of the work you're welcome to come with me. We call ourselves the Seventh Infantry of Montana."

Randy grabbed Nate's hand and shook it, "Thank you, Mr. Reilly. You won't regret this. I'll work hard."

"Call me Nate and I'll call you Randy. Fair enough?" said Nate with a grin.

"You bet, Nate."

# Chapter 6

"So where are we heading or is it a secret?" asked Randy as they headed north in Nate's old pickup.

Nate replied, "It's no secret where the Seventh is at. Our compound is a few miles outside of Roundup, about fifty miles north of Billings. As I told you, there are a lot of different militias. Many are anti-government and very radical. Like those three guys you met up with. We're not like that. Ours is more a way of life. We like to be left alone, but we follow the laws of the land. We live in a military style because that's what we like. Self-sufficiency is our goal."

"That fits in with my situation pretty well," exclaimed Randy. Continuing he said, "What do I need to do to get in? Do you need to know more about me?"

"Not really. We're very trusting when we take someone in. But I must warn you, Randy, it only takes one person at the compound to get you thrown out. We're not big on second chances for newcomers, so keep your nose clean and everything will be all right. You follow what I mean, son?" asked Nate.

"Yeah. Sounds great to me," replied Randy.

Randy was surprised when they pulled up to the compound. It just looked like grassy plains with a few large barns and some other small out buildings. There was not any house or barracks to be seen.

Nate noticed his surprise and said, "The actual living areas are underground. It might take you a little while to get used to it."

"Well, Nate, I feel safe for the first time in many months. That's the most I can hope for right now. I don't care where we sleep," replied Randy.

Nate looked at the still swollen young man and chuckled. "I like you, my boy. I think we'll have a grand old time while you are here."

Nate introduced Randy to the group of about fifty people. They were mostly around thirty-years-old, like Nate, and were friendly for the most part. Nate parked the truck in one of the barns along with about fifteen other vehicles. They went through a door and down some stairs, about twenty feet down Randy guessed. The living quarters were constructed of corrugated metal drainpipe. The pipe was about ten feet in diameter and had concrete poured in the bottom to form a flat walking surface. About every fifteen feet there was an intersecting pipe on the right and left that looked like living quarters for each family. After passing ten of these intersections Randy saw a thick padlocked door on each side.

"What are those doors to?" asked Randy.

Nate replied, "Arsenal on the left, supplies on the right."

"I sure don't want to get those two mixed up," said Randy.

"Nah, I guess not," chuckled Nate.

The hall then opened up into a much larger room, still

circular but a good twenty feet in diameter. Randy could see this was the eating and meeting area. On one wall there was a bulletin board with duty schedules and other information on it. Nate gave Randy some food and one of the women tended to his bruises. Randy really did feel safe now, like he could really get a good night's sleep for the first time in a long while.

Randy fell into the daily routine easily and energetically. He was used to working and it made him feel good to contribute to the good of the compound. He and Nate really seemed to get along well. Even though Nate was about ten years older he seemed to really understand Randy and his situation, in spite of the fact that he didn't know any of the details.

After a week Nate told Randy it was time to start the physical training. The first thing they did was assemble a survival pack for Randy. Every member of the compound had their personal survival pack and always kept it close. It was designed to keep you alive under any circumstances. For the next two weeks Randy did exercises and ran long distances through the fields, carrying the survival pack on his back. They worked on self-defense techniques and more aggressive styles of combat. Randy was fairly athletic and loved the challenge to hold his own with the older, more experienced men of the compound. His body was muscular and now packed 190 pounds on his frame. He also learned how to use objects around him as weapons to give himself an advantage. Because he was so slightly built, Nate had become a master at this and Randy recalled with a laugh how easily little Nate had bested the three larger men in Billings. One thing that Randy noticed right away was that every action and movement was designed to disable or maim your opponent. This was not clean fighting for sport. It was dirty street fighting with victory the only criteria.

Every couple of weeks a group of men would go on

survival hikes for two or three days. They would subsist almost entirely on food they found or killed and used the contents of their survival packs for shelter, warmth and light. Randy liked these hikes best when Bob Lany was along. Bob always had a few cans of Wolf Brand Chili stashed in his survival pack and he would share with Randy when they got really hungry. When the other men would scold them, Bob would lean back, take a big spoonful of chili and just smile.

In another few weeks Randy was allowed to join in the training at the gun range. This was completely new to Randy because he had never even held a gun except to hit his would-be assassin on the head in the Chicago hotel room. At first the guns and the damage they did made Randy a little nervous, but he quickly got over that feeling and began to actually enjoy the power the guns projected. As he became proficient with the guns he developed a confidence in his ability to take care of himself.

After three months Randy had become accepted as a full-fledged member of the Seventh Infantry of Montana. When he asked why they were the Seventh when there was no First through Sixth, Nate laughed and told Randy they wanted outsiders to think there were a lot of Infantries up here in Montana.

"So it's kind of like starting your checks at 1001 instead of 1," said Randy. "Makes you seem a little more than you really are."

"Yeah, you could look at it like that," replied an amused Nate.

One night when Nate and Randy were out on a survival hike by themselves an urge came over Randy to share his problems with Nate. It was really hard having everything bottled up inside, so Randy related the story as Nate listened intently, never interrupting the boy's tale.

When Randy was finally through, Nate said, "Randy, that's

about the saddest tale I've ever heard. I don't think you realize how special a person you are to be able to deal with all this mess. You're something, my boy."

"Thanks, Nate. You saying that means a lot to me," said Randy.

"Well, it's true. It really is."

# Chapter 7

As much as Randy enjoyed being with Nate and the others he felt like he needed to be out in the world on his own. Drifting around the country until he found a place that felt right appealed to Randy. What he needed now was a new identity. He remembered how the FBI had promised him that and much more. Perhaps he could get them to just give him the new identity and then he would be able to live a normal life somewhere. The next day he approached Nate about borrowing the truck for a trip to Billings.

"What do you need to go to Billings for? Seems like you're just asking for trouble," said Nate.

"I need to get out in the world a little. I'll be careful," promised Randy.

"I'll go with you, then," replied Nate.

"Come on, Nate, give me a little rope. I won't hang myself," prodded Randy.

"You aren't up to anything, are you?" quizzed Nate.

"Nate, I just want a little freedom. You can understand that."

"Oh, all right," Nate said, giving in.

"Thanks, Nate, I'll bring you a present from Billings," said Randy.

Nate threw the keys to Randy and said, "Just be careful."

As he drove to Billings Randy felt bad about misleading Nate, but he didn't want to get Nate involved any further in his problems. When he arrived in Billings Randy went to a pay phone and called the FBI office in Chicago.

"Federal Bureau of Investigation," a voice said.

"I would like to speak to Agent Bill Whetland, please," said Randy.

"Who's calling?" asked the voice.

"Just let me speak to Agent Whetland," pushed Randy.

"I need to log in all calls by name."

"Fine, this is Rolf Markowitz," answered Randy.

"Thank you."

"Agent Whetland," said Bill Whetland.

"Bill, this is Randy Flanagan."

"Randy, how in the world are you? I think about you every day and hope you're okay," asked Whetland.

"I'm fine, sir. I want to get a new identity. You know, driver's license, social security number, all that stuff. I don't want any more help, just that. You think up a name and use the address here in Montana where I'm staying," replied Randy.

"I can do so much more for you, Randy," said Whetland.

Randy tensed and said, "No. Just the identity. Mail it to me and then I'll leave the area."

"Okay, okay, whatever you say. Just give me the address," said Whetland.

Randy gave Whetland the address and started to hang up.

"Hey, Randy, how about if I use that Rolf Markowitz name you gave the receptionist?" chided Whetland.

"Please, Bill, anything but that name," laughed Randy.

Bill Whetland walked across the floor to the new identity division.

"We've found Randy Flanagan and agreed to give him a new identity. Can you handle it?" Whetland said to Agent Ross Milloy.

"Sure," Milloy answered, "just give me the info. It'll take about a week."

Whetland replied, "Great. When you get it, mail the package to Randy at this address here."

"Mail it to him?" quizzed Milloy. "Isn't that kind of odd?"

"Just do it, Milloy."

"Sure, Whetland, anything you say."

Milloy walked down the hall and handed the information to his assistant, Mike Upshaw. Walking away he said, "Mike, take care of it right away. I don't want Whetland on my butt about this."

"Sure, boss," replied Upshaw.

Upshaw looked at the information and smiled. Christmas was coming early this year. He could almost feel the fifteen thousand burning a hole in his pocket. Upshaw said he was taking a break and left the building. He found a pay phone and dialed a number he had memorized.

"Yeah. What do you want?" said a husky voice.

"I need to speak with Rocco," said Upshaw.

"That's me. Who's this?"

"Upshaw. I got an address on Flanagan. Is it worth 15 g's to you?"

"Sure," said Rocco, "give it to me."

Upshaw read out the address and hung up the phone.

Three days later the people of the Seventh Infantry of Montana filed up the stairs and into the barn, ready to begin a new day. The fifty Infantrymen gathered in the barn, ready to break into their groups for the day. Men appeared in each of the two barn doors, both holding a shotgun.

One of the men yelled, "Everyone get over in that corner."

He pointed the shotgun to one corner.

Jimmy Garcia was closest to the man and he walked right up to him and said, "You're in a heap of trouble, mister."

The man slammed the shotgun butt into Jimmy's stomach and yelled again, "Get over to the corner and drag this guy with you."

The Infantrymen gathered in the corner, trying to make sense of this.

Nate stepped forward and said, "What do you want?"

"We want Randy Flanagan and we know he is here," said Rocco, the man who was in charge.

Nate eyed the two men. They were obviously not from the area. Both were large, dark haired, dressed in suits and around fifty-years-old. To say they were ugly and mean was putting it mildly.

"We want Randy Flanagan. If we get him nobody else has to die," growled Rocco.

"We don't know any Randy Flanagan," said one man. Rocco stepped up to the man and slammed the butt of the shotgun into his face.

"Anyone else have a better answer?"

No one said anything, but most of the Infantrymen were pretty sure these guys were looking for Randy Smith, who was standing in the back, trying to hide.

Rocco grabbed a young girl and said, "Maybe you need

some incentive to give up Mr. Flanagan."

He put the barrel up to the little girl's head and began to squeeze the trigger lightly.

"I'm Flanagan," said Randy from the back.

"Get your ass up here, you no-good snitch. I'm here to teach people that you don't testify against Gino Carlucci and live," hissed Rocco.

The other man kept his shotgun trained on the group while Rocco prodded Randy toward their car.

"Looks like a blown opportunity for us, Randy," said Nate Reilly.

Randy looked at Nate and wondered what he meant.

The other man glared at Nate and said, "Shut up, you turkey or I'll blow a hole in you."

Randy turned and gave Nate a glance. Nate smiled and winked at him. Randy wracked his brain to figure out what Nate was trying to tell him. What did a blown opportunity mean?

"We're going to go for a little ride, Mr. Flanagan. Mr. Carlucci didn't want us to just shoot you right away. He wants us to take it kind of slow so you get to suffer plenty," said Rocco.

As they drove down the road toward the front gate Randy suddenly figured out what Nate meant. He pretended to be sick at his stomach and doubled over, bracing himself against the seats.

When the car turned away from the group Nate ducked down the stairs and grabbed a box with long wires and several switches on it. Just as the car drew even with a bush about fifty feet from the gate Nate flipped one of the switches. There was a loud thunder-like sound and the earth beneath the car erupted, sending the vehicle arching upward. It turned back toward the ground and nose-dived into the trench that now existed where a flat road had been.

Nate looked at his fellow Infantrymen and said, "I thought we mined that road to keep people out, not to keep them in. Let's get down there and see if Randy is okay."

Randy felt the tremendous blast beneath the car but he didn't fly around the vehicle like Rocco and his partner did. Triggered by Nate's blown opportunity comment, Randy had remembered the day Nate pointed out all the mined areas of the compound and wedged himself between the seats. This had saved Randy the brutal beating the other two men took. At least he was conscious, which was more than he could say for Rocco and company. Randy was crawling out the car door when Nate and the others arrived.

"Randy, are you okay?" panted Nate.

Randy looked up and said, "I guess it wasn't a blown opportunity after all. Thanks, Nate, you saved my life."

"I'm just glad you figured out what I meant. I guess we're on the same wavelength," replied Nate.

"Yeah, but now what do we do?" asked Randy.

"First we check out these two turkeys and make sure they are harmless," said Nate.

By now several of Infantrymen had pulled the unconscious men out of the car. Rocco and his partner were tied up and put in a corner of the barn while everyone tried to figure out the next move.

Randy was helped back to the living quarters where he cleaned up and was treated for some small cuts and bruises. Randy was amazed at the way he was treated by everyone at the compound. Even though he had put them in danger he was still one of them and if you are one of them they will do anything for you. Outside of his parents, Randy had never felt that someone cared about him like these people did.

After he rested a while Nate came into his quarters and

said, "Randy, we need to talk. Who were those guys and how did they find you? We need to figure all this out so we can decide what to do with them and how to help you."

Randy looked Nate in the eye and said, "Nate, I'm really sorry I got you and the others involved. I know those two were from Gino Carlucci's operation. They made that really clear to me in the car. The only way I can figure they found me was through a leak in the FBI. When I went to Billings the other day I called the Chicago FBI and asked for a new identity. I told them to send it to this address. That was a big mistake. It must be from that because I haven't told anyone else where I am. I guess I really blew this."

Nate replied, "What's done is done. So why did you want new identity papers?"

"Nate, I've been thinking I should move on. Travel the country a little and see if I can start a normal life somewhere. I like it here with you and the others, but this is probably not the long-term solution for my life."

"Yeah, I kind of figured your stay was short-term. I guess you can't stay here anyway since the FBI and the Mafia both know where you are."

"You're right about that, Nate. I don't have any choice now. I better get my things and hit the road. What about those Mafia guys? How can we get them to leave you alone?" asked Randy.

Nate laughed and said, "I think they will believe you are gone. Nobody in their right mind would stick around here with these types showing up."

"I guess not," chuckled Randy.

"Now, about you leaving. I wish you had told me about your plans because I can help with a new identity. I thought you trusted me," scolded Nate.

Randy recoiled. "Of course I trust you, Nate, but I wanted to take care of this myself. I know I blew it, but as far as trust goes, you are the only person I truly trust."

"Yeah, I know. Look, Randy, I've got plan. I want you to take my truck to Billings and I'll give you the number of a guy that can fix you up with a new identity. I'll send a note from me so he'll know you're not a cop or something. It'll take about a week so you can hide out in Billings. When you get the papers leave the truck at the military shop where we met and hit the road. You can't ever have contact with us because someone will probably be watching. I hate to see you go, but you'll do just fine," said Nate.

"Thanks. I think it's a great plan and I really appreciate your help. I still have the five-hundred dollars that I had when I arrived here. Will that be enough to pay for the papers?" asked Randy.

"Hardly, but don't worry about that. We'll kick in some dough. After all the hard work you have done around here we owe you something," replied Nate.

"I know you don't owe me anything, but I don't have much choice about letting you help me some more," Randy sighed.

"Right on, boy, right on," Nate said, slapping Randy on the back.

The next day Randy had his gear in the truck and was ready for the good-byes. He shook hands with or hugged every member of the group.

Nate walked up and said, "Here's your going-away present, Randy. We're going to miss you."

Nate handed him an envelope, obviously full of cash.

Randy's eyes filled with tears and he said, "You all are great and I'll treasure the memories of the time we spent together. Now, I better get on the road before I rust out Nate's truck even more than it already is with my tears."

Randy put his survival pack and other gear into the front seat and got into the truck.

Before he started to drive off he yelled, "Give those two thugs a kick in the ass for me when you decide to release them."

Nate smiled and yelled, "Sure thing."

A day later Nate and a few other men drove Rocco and his partner out into the countryside and put them out.

He glared at Rocco and said, "Randy is long gone. Don't ever come around here again. It won't do you any good and we won't be this nice next time."

With his fellow Infantrymen pointing their guns at the pair, Nate got out and gave each one a kick in the butt.

"Randy asked us to do that. Personally, I think he was way too easy on you. Now get going," growled Nate.

# Chapter 8

Rick Blaze leaned back in his executive chair and thought about his life. Now in his early forties, he tended to do that often now. His life had taken some wonderful turns after initial hard times had made him question his ability to succeed. He certainly could not ask for any more success than he currently had. Rick was not a greedy person and being comfortable financially with a great family was completely satisfying.

Just when Rick was about to achieve total serenity, a knock on his open door instantly returned his thoughts back to the present. Larry Thomas was standing in the doorway to Rick's office with a glare on his face.

"What can I do for you, Larry?" asked Rick.

"You can get my stupid phone to work, that's what you can do for me. For all the money my company pays you I would think I could expect my phone to work like you told me it would," spat out Thomas.

Rick mentally moved Larry Thomas to number one on his all-time worst tenants list.

Pasting a fake smile on his face, Rick replied, "I'm sorry you're having a problem. Why don't we go to your office and see what the problem is?"

Larry Thomas looked a bit nervous and said, "Can't you just fix it without coming into my office?"

"You haven't told me the problem so I have no idea what I have to do to fix it. Your changing the programming on the phone set caused the other problems you have had with your phone. I have to come in your office to reset the programming if that is the problem again," Rick told Larry, his fake smile beginning to disappear.

"The stupid phone keeps sending my callers to voice mail instead of to your receptionists like your lease says it will. I'm really getting tired of all these problems and you being in my office so much. I have some really confidential documents and I assumed I would have some privacy when I leased an office from you. I need to put up some papers before you come in so give me five minutes and then come see me," Thomas said curtly.

He then turned and headed down the hall to his office.

Five minutes later Rick walked down the hall to Suite 415 where Worldwide Water Solutions, Inc. had an office. He knocked and Larry Thomas opened the door, clearly even more agitated from having to hide whatever precious documents he possessed. Rick walked over to the phone set, pushed a few buttons to check the forwarding program and discovered, as he had on various other occasions in the past two weeks, that the forwarding was set to busy/no answer instead of to no answer only.

Rick reset the phone and said, "Larry, the forwarding was changed again. The stupid phone did just what you told it to-go to voice mail when your phone is busy. If you would leave the forwarding alone the phone would work like it is supposed to."

Larry roared, "I didn't touch this damn phone and you better make sure it works right from now on or you could be in big trouble. If your phone system causes me to lose a deal my company could be out a million dollars and you will be responsible. Our corporate lawyers will have a field day with you."

Rick took a deep breath, trying to control his temper, and said, "Someone changed the forwarding on your phone, Larry. This is the fifth time the same thing has happened and I know it's not my staff and it's certainly not me. That leaves you or one of your co-workers. If it will make you feel better, I'll have one of my employees' check your phone settings from the front consoles every day for a while. We can see your phone programming, but we have to come to your phone itself to set or change it. As for your corporate attorneys, I would strongly advise you to never threaten me again like that if you plan on being here when your lease is up for renewal."

Rick turned abruptly, walked through the door and strode purposely down the hall.

"You talk to me before you come in here and mess with anything," yelled Larry while slamming the door.

Rick entered the reception area and stopped at the front desk.

"Sandra, I want you to check Larry's phone programming every morning. Let me know if he screws it up again," said Rick, rolling his eyes.

"Sure, Rick, you can count on me," said Sandra.

Rick was back at his desk, thinking about what an asshole Larry Thomas was. In his twelve years as owner of Austin Executive Suites he had seen quite a few people like Larry who thought the best defense was a great offense. Rick took comfort in the fact that these tenants were usually reviled by everyone they came in contact with. It was also comforting that Austin Executive Suites never seemed to have more than one of these characters for a tenant at any particular time lately. That could not be said of the first five-to-seven years of the Executive Suites.

Rick had been hired as manager of Austin Executive Suites when the business was about a year old and in a lot of trouble from the real estate bust that had hit the country and especially Austin in the mid 1980's. The next year saw the owner flee to his native Belgium, leaving Rick as the manager of a company that owed tens of thousands of dollars in back rent and had no owner. The building owner, United Life Insurance, took over the struggling business and Rick stayed on, mainly because job opportunities were few and far between. The only thing United knew about executive suites was that they had no interest in owning one. They were also not quick to just shut down Austin Executive Suites since it was paying some rent and the building was then only half full.

After a series of painful meetings United made a proposal that changed his life. Throughout these meetings Rick had not been able to understand the tactics of United Life Insurance's Austin manager, a mean-spirited woman named Sandy Fellows. Sandy seemed to think the object of the meetings was to punish someone for the failure of the business to pay the full rent owed, in spite of the fact that few businesses were able to meet their rent obligations in the depressed economy. Even though Rick had not signed the lease or owned any part of the company and had no liability to United, he bore the wrath of Sandy's misplaced fury.

Finally, when all progress had stopped and Sandy's anger was at a peak Rick had stood up, looked her in the eye and calmly said, "You can go straight to hell, lady."

That was when Sandy threw a bound proposal on the table.

"What's that?" Rick had asked.

"My bosses told me to give this to you," Sandy had replied tersely.

United proposed to give the business to Rick in exchange for a long-term lease to be reviewed yearly and upgraded to a lease rate of 120% of the current market rate. Rick jumped on this deal even though he was not certain whether he had made a great business decision or had made a deal that would cost him what little assets he had acquired.

He was buoyed by the support his family showed, particularly by his wife, Kathy, who was ready to put her college education to work and signed on as the leasing manager. Now, twelve years later, the business was a resounding success due to the efforts of Kathy and Rick and the doubling of Austin's size over that time period.

Austin Executive Suites was what its industry called a shared tenant business. The floor of the building that the Suites occupied had sixty individual offices, a large reception area, two conference rooms, a kitchen and an operations area. The offices were leased to a combination of small one or two person businesses and large national or multi-national companies needing a presence in Austin. Most of the companies leased one office, but several would lease two or three so Austin Executive Suites represented about fifty companies at any one time. Two receptionists answered the phones for the fifty companies and kept track of the occupants as they came and went throughout the day. The operations area contained fax machines for the tenants use, office supplies for sale and a secretary that did word processing and sorted and delivered the mail to each office. Two copiers were located in the hallways and tenants could use them by putting in a code. Austin Executive Suites had its own telephone switch and in-house voice mail system, which Rick had become very proficient with. His understanding of and abilities with the phone switch gave the business a competitive advantage over the other executive suites in Austin. When an office was leased to a new tenant Rick was able to install and program their phones and voice mail immediately, instead of waiting for an outside technician to arrive days later. Rick even leased a block of telephone numbers from the local phone company so he could assign a number to a new tenant when they executed the lease. The Suites were very well appointed and projected an air of professionalism.

One important aspect of a shared tenant business such as this was that the tenants get along and understand that no one else was more important than any one else. One or two tenants pushing the limits of fair play could cause havoc if not dealt with immediately. This job fell to Rick and sometimes caused friction between him and the offending party. It usually did not get as bitter as between Rick and Larry, but was a source of irritation sometimes. Rick and his staff were firmly committed to the issue of fair play and that applied to all tenants, whether they liked the tenant or not. The concept of executive suites was fairly new but was becoming very popular with companies wanting to establish a presence in a particular city but not wanting to commit to long-term office leases. Executive suites offered short-term leases and the ability to add or subtract offices as the business climate in that town called for. This type of setup allowed the tenants to concentrate on business and let Austin Executive Suites run their office for them.

# Chapter 9

Elbert and Mattie Wheeler lived on a farm outside of Fort Davis, Texas. It was an area more remote than most people could stand to live. Fort Davis was in the middle of nowhere and the Wheelers farm was 20 miles from there.

Elbert looked at Mattie and said, "Are you doing any better, Mattie?"

"Oh, Elbert, I feel just awful," she replied weakly.

"Hang in there, girl, it'll get better."

Elbert gazed at Mattie lying on the bed. They both were in their seventies, but had enjoyed relatively good health. Every few years one of them might get the flu, but they quickly recovered. This was something entirely different. Elbert thought the oddest thing was how he and Mattie had started feeling bad at almost exactly the same time. They both had a fever, muscle cramps, and splitting headaches. Elbert saw Mattie clutch her stomach and begin to shake.

"God help me," she cried.

Elbert rushed to her side, trying to ignore his own pain. He held her hand and whispered, "Mattie, it's going to be all right. I promise."

An hour later Mattie's convulsions were getting worse and her face reflected the intense suffering. Elbert struggled to help her, but by now was almost helpless himself. They had not called anyone or gone to the emergency room because they thought at first that the flu had stricken them. They had ridden out that illness several times at their farm. Now that decision seemed perilous as the speed of their deterioration was evident. It had been less than two days since the symptoms began and now Mattie's body was racked by convulsions so violent her muscles were being pulled loose from the bones. Elbert knew he had to call Doc Aleshire in Fort Davis before he began to hurt like Mattie.

He struggled to get up and Mattie shrieked, "Don't leave me, Ellie. Don't leave me."

"I got to call the Doc, Mattie. I'll be right back," gasped Elbert.

He tried to pull himself along the floor but only succeeded in moving about five feet. The shaking was getting worse and his body was wracked with pain. Elbert could see the phone in the kitchen and knew he would not make it. Dragging his body around to face Mattie, Elbert tried to claw his way back to his now unconscious wife. Her hand was dangling over the side of the bed and with one last thrust he was able to grab it.

The pain was unbearable and he was just able to mutter, "I love you, girl."

It was a blessing as Elbert joined Mattie in the next world.

Five days later Sheriff Ray Jenkins finally showed up to investigate Brad Wheeler's concerns that his parents were not answering the phone for any of their every-other-day chats when he called from Tennessee. Sheriff Jenkins knocked on the door and went in when there was no answer. He immediately knew the answer to the son's questions from the smell that greeted him. He had smelled several-day-old death before, but thankfully not very often. Bracing himself, Jenkins went through the house until he came to the bedroom. There, he saw the grotesquely deformed bodies of Elbert and Mattie Wheeler. Mattie was lying on the bed and Elbert was on the floor beside her, still clutching her hand. As he looked into their faces he saw pain and suffering greater than he had ever imagined. The Sheriff ran outside, barely resisting the urge to vomit. As he sat in his patrol car trying to recover from the alarming discovery, he noticed an eerie calm over the entire farm.

For a productive and self-sufficient farm such as the Wheeler's there was a complete lack of movement and noise. This prompted him to begin walking around and quickly led to the realization that all the animals were dead as well. He went back to the car and called for the local medical examiner and the town veterinarian to come immediately. In about an hour the examiner, the vet and several locals showed up, the locals curious about the conversations they heard on the police scanners. To Sheriff Jenkins it seemed like some of these people did nothing all day but sit around listening to their police scanners.

After a short time one of the onlookers, Ed Richter, went back to town and made a telephone call.

"Worldwide Water Solutions, can I help you?" the receptionist answered.

"Yes, I would like to speak to Larry Thomas," the caller replied.

"May I tell Larry who's calling?" she responded.

"Just tell him it is a friend," Ed firmly said.

"Just a minute please."

"Larry Thomas here," the terse voice announced.

"Larry, this is Ed Richter".

"Hello, Ed. Do you have anything to report?"

"Yes, Larry, the results are in and they are positive."

Larry asked, "How far has the investigation gone and what do they think?"

"They just arrived at the scene and are completely baffled so far. I'll continue to monitor the situation and report back soon."

Larry impatiently asked, "Did you inject the neutralizer?"

"I sure did. It was three days ago, just like I was told. If you guys are right there will be no trace of what we did," Ed replied.

"Good job, Ed. Keep a low profile and monitor the developments. Goodbye." Larry hung up and immediately placed a call.

"Hello, this is Rene."

Larry said, "Rene, this is Larry Thomas from the Austin office."

"What information do you have for me, Larry?"

"Initial reports indicated the test was a complete success; however, I will know more in a week," Larry replied.

"Keep me posted, Larry," Rene answered and then hung up.

# Chapter 10

As his chauffeured car wound through the streets of Baghdad, Safreed al Habid thought, If this plan works I will be a hero to Iraq and our leader Saddam, but the risk is being executed for any number of reasons-treason, incompetence or secrecy.

As a General in the Iraqi Army and former battalion commander of the Republican Guard during the Gulf War as well as the Iran-Iraq War, Habid enjoyed the attention of Saddam whenever he needed it. In his current post of Director of the Chemical Weapons Program Habid had great power as well as a tremendous ability to operate in complete secrecy. This ability was crucial to the execution of his plan because he knew that if Saddam was informed of his plan too soon many other people would also be told, thereby reducing the chance of success to virtually nothing. Habid also had to dodge the frequent attempts of the UN Inspection Team to find his main operation. However, the magnitude of the plan was so great that the upcoming invasions of Saudia Arabia and Kuwait would be nothing in comparison. At every meeting of the Iraqi power structure Saddam would state his intention of invading Kuwait again and adding Saudia Arabia to his control. Habid feared another rash attack resulting in yet another crushing defeat would doom Saddam to exile or worse. Saddam would never have more control over the Middle East unless the United States was kept out of the fight. Habid had devised a plan that would be crippling, both physically and mentally, to the greatest foe of Iraq-the United States of America. The goal of Iraq gaining control of the entire Middle East could then be met. With such a large percentage of the world's oil under Iraqi control, Saddam would become the most powerful and feared man in the world, with Safreed al Habid as his right-hand man.

Habid thought of the many war room sessions that had been so frustrating to attend. The plan to occupy Kuwait and Saudia Arabia with a two-pronged attack was solid enough. Even though the economic embargo had never been lifted, Iraq had immediately begun to rebuild its military after the Gulf War, foregoing the general population's needs almost completely. Iraq's allies and America's enemies were only too happy to sell planes, missiles, tanks and other military supplies to restore the Iraqi army to its once formidable level. This had been accomplished in just five years since the Gulf War and Saddam did not want to wait long to flex his muscles again. By overpowering Saudia Arabia and Kuwait in one quick strike, Saddam thought he could take away the United States' ability to have any land-based operations in the area. He insisted that the United States would not have the power to stop him once he had control of the Saudia Arabia bases that the Americans operated out of. Whenever Saddam made this point Habid had disagreed by saying the United States still had many aircraft carriers and long-range missiles. Habid had pushed his luck several times with strong arguments disputing this shortcoming in Saddam's plan. Saddam had glared at Habid enough for Habid to know it was time to back off. But Habid could not just sit back and watch the United States destroy Iraq again so he had devised his plan to take the Americans out of the fight. He would tell Saddam at just the right moment, when the plan was in full motion and assured of success. Habid relished the thought of being able to jump past the idiot relatives of Saddam in the hierarchy of power and rank in Iraq. Habid's thoughts returned to the present as the military staff car pulled up to the school building in downtown Baghdad.

A gate opened by remote control, revealing a concrete ramp going underground. Habid's car went down the ramp and parked in a reserved space. There was nobody around, just boxes stacked up and some wrecked military vehicles. Habid pressed a remote control and his car began to descend. The elevator clanged to a stop and the driver backed the vehicle into a space and watched as an identical vehicle drove onto the elevator. The elevator returned to the top level with a clang. A military aide approached Habid and saluted. Habid returned the salute and got into the golf cart-like vehicle the aide was driving. A three-minute ride brought Habid to the entrance to the Baghdad Chemical Weapons Plant. This operation was about forty feet below the surface, completely encased in ten feet of concrete and further protected from missiles and bombs by the school on the surface. Many times the UN Inspection Team had combed the first level beneath the school for clues to the existence to a chemical weapons plant and every time they left empty handed.

After passing the security check Habid went to his office. He called his most trusted aide, who was also his cousin, Tesar Aboud, for an update on his part of the plan.

When Aboud arrived, Habid asked, "Are the canisters ready to ship?"

Aboud replied, "Most certainly. They are well-packaged and disguised. They can be shipped any time."

"Good! Your exact orders are in this envelope along with the shipping instructions, complete with the labels, routing and proper clearances for the border guards. Be ready to leave tonight. I am most anxious to proceed with this project, cousin," said Habid.

"I will return to the plant tonight at 11:00 and begin the journey. I understand your requests for the highest security, cousin, but I still must be sure that Saddam knows about this. Several men have already died and thousands more will perish if this chemical is released. I do not want to be the man responsible," Aboud said with a trace of doubt in his voice.

Habid bellowed, "Of course Saddam knows about this operation. He also knows the importance of secrecy. I will show you my orders if you feel you cannot trust your own cousin and superior."

"Oh no, cousin, I truly believe you. Pardon any doubts I may have had," said Aboud sheepishly.

"Good. Now, go about your business," replied Habid, relieved that his bluff had worked.

# Chapter 11

Rick Blaze was watching CNN again and as usual the current topic of another possible Middle East war made him nervous and more than a little paranoid. Most Americans had hoped that the devastating defeat of Iraq less than a decade earlier would keep their interests in Kuwait and Saudia Arabia safe, but now Saddam Hussein seemed to be flexing his muscles again. At least that was what CNN wanted everyone to think. The United States military and the United Nations continually maintained that Iraq was not a threat anymore.

In spite of the economic sanctions and United Nations inspections Iraq was struggling to rebuild its military to possibly be more powerful than ever. Satellite photos had shown some activity, but it was not clear what Saddam was up to. The greatest fear was that Iraq would gain possession of missiles much more accurate than the Scud missiles that had almost no effect during the Gulf War.

The United Nations had let Iraq sell oil to supposedly buy food and medical supplies and to rebuild the schools and hospitals that had been demolished. The world was giving the Madman of the Middle East the opportunity to prove that he had learned something from his devastating loss. The current thinking was that Saddam must rebuild his country or risk revolt. After all, he had led his country to the most devastating defeat in its history. Surely he could not maintain control by further plundering the people for the sake of the military. What Saddam was doing was the great debate of the year. The United States military had bases in Kuwait and Saudia Arabia, but much of the naval backup had left the area to deal with other hot spots around the world. CNN warned that America could be caught off-guard, but military leaders suggested that CNN leave the Middle East strategy to them. This great debate had raged for a couple of years, but seemed to be getting more fervent.

Rick tended to side with CNN on this issue. His experience told him that people rarely change and he could see no reason for Saddam to change from being a vicious dictator to a benevolent leader. Rick was beginning to get a bad feeling about a possible new encounter with Iraq. This feeling had caused him to pass up visits to convenience stores to cut the odds of running into some crazy Iraqi convenience store manager who was ready to bring the war to America. In his brain he knew they were probably just as glad to be in America as he was, but his heart said-be careful. They are unstable and taught to hate Americans from birth. Rick thought Saddam would have no greater pleasure than to pull off some terrorist stunt in the United States, especially considering how Americans had portrayed Saddam as a complete buffoon. The CNN reporter was discussing the need for heightened security at all major U.S. airports and speculating on possible terrorist acts that the staff at CNN had been able to dream up. Again Rick's heart took over from his brain and he felt an overwhelming need to be prepared for any emergencies he could foresee. This could be fun and relatively inexpensive in addition to providing a comfort level for the paranoid side of him.

Rick got a pad of paper and began to outline the Rick Blaze Emergency Preparedness Plan. He started writing as fast as his hands could go. This was not really a new idea for Rick. He frequently ran a survival plan through his head. He also frequently wondered how his life might have turned out if he had not met Kathy and had kids. He could picture himself chunking everything and living in the woods. Kathy had grounded him and given him the confidence to sign the deal with United Life Insurance for ownership of Austin Executive Suites.

After struggling for the first four years of Rick and Kathy's ownership, the occupancy level and profits of Austin Executive Suites had increased each year. The last five years had seen all sixty offices stay full virtually every month and be a wonderful financial provider for Rick and Kathy's family. They had been able to purchase a nice house in an upper-middle-class part of Austin and in recent years had invested their money in properties that the family could enjoy. They had a lot on Lake Travis, north of Austin, that was their family weekend getaway. Rick, Kathy and the boys had restored the old cabin into a modest but comfortable home and the addition of various boats and water toys made the place seem like a poor man's Club Med to the family. A small stock windfall had enabled Rick and Kathy to purchase a house in Port Aransas. As they had done with the cabin, the Blazes' had restored the old fishing hut into a comfortable, if cramped, Gulf Coast beach getaway. The family joke was that the wood frame structure was a one-bedroom house that slept twelve. The living area had sleeper sofas and a trundle bed used by Davis, Mack and their friends.

Rick's mind was busy with the ideas and possibilities that

were running through his brain. Now it seemed his heart and brain were finally working together. He wondered if his family would think he was going a little crazy or that he was being incredibly smart and resourceful. Rick decided he would be happy if they would just indulge him and so he began to expand his emergency outline. He worked for thirty minutes and was pleased with the progress he had made. The plan was taking shape:

1. Money-cash
2. Weapons
    a. Handguns
    b. Rifles
    c. Shotgun
    d. Knives
    e. Stun guns
        i. A pair of 100,000-volt guns
    f. Mace and Pepper Gas
        i. Pepper gas for each pack and vehicle
    g. Ammo, Clips, Holsters, Etc.
        i. Ammo and clips to be stockpiled
        ii. Purchase holsters for concealment
3. Survival gear-equipment

    Backpack with various items as:

    Utensils, ropes, flashlight, thermal blanket, tools, wire-various sizes, radio-battery, crank and solar powered, first aid supplies, over the counter drugs for allergies, headaches, etc., toiletry items, reflective thermal blankets, rain poncho, electrical tape, duct tape.
4. Survival gear-MRE's, canned goods
5. Communications-phone equipment and walkie-talkies

6. Vehicles and Escape Routes
    a. Maps
    b. Rick's Chevy Blazer
    c. Family Boat-1952 Chris-Craft 42 ft. Commander
    d. Mack's 1972 Cessna 172 Skyhawk airplane
7. Base of Operations during Emergency
    Prepare weekend hideaway on Lake Travis-secure and stock food and water

The trick now was to accumulate the items, organize them and have them ready in case they were actually needed. Rick was pleased to note that he already possessed many of the items on the list, particularly the guns and knives and he had always kept a sort of survival pack in his car. His bank account was always in good shape these days, thanks to Austin Executive Suites so the cost was not an issue. Rick decided to go shopping the next day for the items he needed to complete the plan.

# Chapter 12

Rene Charlton was a microchemist with a flair for the dramatic and a passion for riches. His public relations efforts did a wonderful job of covering up the cunning and ruthless manner in which he operated. His top employees were well paid, but expected to provide life-long loyalty. It was the rare top-level employee that left Worldwide Water Solutions, Inc. without falling victim to some bizarre accident. None of the accidents were ever traced to Worldwide Water or Rene Charlton, but they served the purpose they were intended to.

Rene was born, raised and educated in France. His fascination with chemistry, especially toxic compounds, led to his Masters degree in Chemistry. He decided at the age of twenty-four that his fortune could best be accumulated in the United States. He seemed to have a knack for developing antidotes and neutralizing agents for a wide range of microbiological enemies to the human body. The greatest potential for financial reward for these talents could best be achieved in the country where capitalism was the way of life and panic and government ineptness worked hand-in-hand to create wonderful opportunities for someone who was smart and not bounded by any set of moral compunction. Obviously, to Rene anyway, the United States was the country that fit his plans and goals perfectly.

Charlton had made some money working as a graduate assistant at the University of Paris. He worked closely with Professor Jacque Ringling developing an experimental drug designed to counteract the effects of the Hepatitis A virus. They were fairly successful, but could never overcome some serious side effects. Without the knowledge of Ringling Rene sold the formula to a French pharmaceutical firm that did not mind releasing drugs that were not completely safe. With the profits from his first foray into the world of business he moved to the United States.

After ten years of working for various companies and learning their secrets he was able to start his own company-Worldwide Water Solutions, Inc. His capital investment was derived from his wages and ample supplements from selling company secrets to competitors at each place of employment. Suspicion usually followed Rene, but no proof ever seemed to turn up. Rene chose to concentrate his efforts on water treatment because he felt that water problems always became an emotional issue to the people involved and this meant higher prices and profits to Rene. Over the years Worldwide Water grew at a rapid pace, eventually becoming a true worldwide business by continually being able to solve the riddles of contaminated water. Rene was never sure which was more important, being able to clean up the water and cure the illnesses caused by the bad water or his ability to convince people that it was reasonable for the solutions to be so expensive even if they really were not.

As Rene's business and fame grew he made friends all over the world, many of whom were also unburdened by the restraints of strong morals and integrity. It always seemed like the lesser the concern for one's fellow man the greater the amount money one had available to hire someone like Rene to further his cause. In the last five years Worldwide Water had branched out into the field of causing the problem instead of solving it. This had led Worldwide to add several governments and terrorist groups to its client list. Rene had developed the reputation for discretion and success. The ability to organize and execute his plans was held in the highest esteem by his customers of the terrorist bent. The terrorists of the world had their own underground communications network. Word spread quickly through the network when a valuable asset such as Rene Charlton was identified.

# Chapter 13

Tesar Aboud pulled out of Baghdad at about 11:30 PM with his top-secret cargo. His plain cargo truck was loaded with wooden crates covered with Iraqi writing proclaiming the contents to be repair parts for military vehicles. The papers his uncle, Safreed al Habid, had prepared for him matched the crates' information to the last letter. This was important to pass the scrutiny of the border guards who were sticklers for paperwork, yet often short on common sense. If the paperwork was in order the chances of incurring the wrath of some higher-up were lessened greatly. Aboud had great confidence in Habid's ability and high standing in the regime and knew that he was lucky indeed to be chosen a part of such a secret mission. If Aboud could continue to please uncle Habid a great future in the Iraqi army was in store for him. These thoughts ran rampant through Aboud's head as he headed toward the border.

Aboud could picture himself as a Colonel someday, possibly to be known by name to Saddam himself. However, thoughts of possible flaws in the plan began to creep into Aboud's head. What if some over-zealous border guard looking for a promotion himself decided to look in the crates and saw the metallic canisters that did not resemble vehicle parts at all? What if he tried to open one of the canisters? What if he was successful and unleashed the deadly chemicals each canister contained? Aboud's mind was now spinning with the visions of the disaster he could be held responsible for. The canisters could be easily traced back to his lab at the Chemical Weapons plant. He knew that if a guard opened one of the canisters he and the guards would be quickly infected and die a painful death in short order. Trying to calm himself, Aboud developed a backup plan to get Habid on the phone at the earliest point that a problem arose. Habid would take care of any problem involving his favorite cousin.

The hours passed and Aboud finally reached the border between Iraq and Syria. He handed over the papers to the guards and silently prayed to Allah for success. As the guards studied the paperwork and inspected the crates Aboud tried to look calm and natural although his growing anxiety was gnawing away at him. The guards had no reason to doubt either the validity of the papers or the contents of the crates and they certainly did not possess the energy to bother with this one truck. They waved Aboud through the checkpoint after only a thirty-minute wait. Aboud was greatly relieved, knowing he had no great reason for fear and was just overreacting. Buoyed by the ease of the mission so far Aboud was again adorned with a Colonel's uniform in his mind.

# Chapter 14

"Worldwide Water Solutions, may I help you?" the receptionist at Austin Executive Suites said.

"I need to speak to Larry. Tell him it is Ed," replied Ed Richter.

After about 15 seconds Larry Thomas came on the line, "Ed, give me an update," he curtly said.

"The locals here in Fort Davis do not have a clue about the cause of death for the Wheelers or their animals. Also, many of the investigators and other visitors to the scene have drunk water from the Wheeler's tank and no one is getting sick. The neutralizer is working perfectly, just like you said. I'm going to stay here for another week to monitor the situation further. After I leave here I'll come to Austin so we can discuss this in greater detail and prepare for the next job."

"That's great, Ed, just follow the plan and lay low. I don't want anyone to notice you are there so they won't notice when you leave. Call me before you leave in a week. I think the next step will be right up your alley."

"All right, Larry, I'll talk to you next week," Ed said before hanging up.

Larry hit the top speed dial button and waited for an answer.

"Hello, this is Rene," the voice said, answering his private line.

"Rene, this is Larry Thomas. I have a follow-up report on our experiment and I think you'll be pleased. Everything is going perfectly and I expect to have my man back in Austin in a week."

"That's wonderful, Larry. I knew you were the man to trust with this job. Keep me informed and wait for further instructions. It appears that our foreign associates are succeeding in their mission so you can expect a delivery from us in about a week," Rene responded.

"I won't let you down, sir. You'll always be able to count on me," Larry proudly exclaimed.

"Yes, I believe you are right. Now, I must attend to other matters. Goodbye, Larry," Rene answered.

When Larry heard the phone click on the other end he breathed a sigh of relief. He knew he had done well, but Rene was so powerful and possessed such a temper that Larry frequently envisioned a sword hanging above his head, ready to fall on Rene's whim. Another thought was eating at Larry. He was not comfortable with the access that Rick Blaze's staff and the cleaning crew had to his office. The mail was delivered to his office every day and the cleaning crew came in every night. In addition, that damned Rick Blaze had the habit of knocking and then coming into the office with his master key. This irritated Larry and caused him to quickly cover up papers and cut short phone calls. Larry decided to visit Rick and solve this problem immediately. He walked down the hall to Rick's office and stood in the doorway with the glare that always got Rick's attention.

Rick was on the phone, but he knew Larry would stand there and stare at him until he hung up. This tactic usually worked for the few tenants with the rudeness to pull it off. Rick quickly got off the call and addressed the fuming person.

"What can I do for you, Larry?"

"You can do something about the endless parade of people through my office. I have trade secrets and important papers in there and I don't want you or anyone else in my office. That's what you can do for me," Larry bellowed.

Rick calmly replied, "Larry, the cleaning crew has to get in and my people only come in to deliver the mail to you. None of us has any interest in the contents of your office. I also want you to know that all of our other tenants feel perfectly comfortable with the arrangements here."

Larry firmly pressed on, "I don't want you, any of your people or the cleaning crew to be able to get in my office. I want the locks changed immediately. If you don't do this I'll have it done myself."

"All right, I'll have the locksmith come in this afternoon and change your locks. You'll have to come to the operations area and pick up your own mail. You'll also have to empty your own trash and I'll charge you for the cost of changing the locks. If you get tired of the office being dirty I'll occasionally get the day porter to vacuum the office while you are there. Is that good enough for you?" Rick questioned.

"Yes, that is exactly what I want, including you not being able to get in."

"I need to have emergency access, but I'll respect your request for privacy," Rick shot back.

Larry's face began to turn red and he yelled, "I don't care what you think you need, I don't want you in my office. If you can't stay out I'll have my lawyer get some kind of court order."

"Larry, why don't you just move out if you are so unhappy? I'll be glad to let you off the hook on your lease. I can lease your office in a few days to someone who'll appreciate our services."

"I don't have time to move and I've given out the phone number to a lot of people already. I'm going to stay and so you might as well go along with me," Larry snorted.

Rick breathed out deeply and said, "Okay, I'll have the locks rekeyed so nobody can get in. You've pushed me as far as possible on this one. I suggest you try to be happy with this situation and get off my back. I don't enjoy being pushed around and threatened. You have gone as far as you can go. I'm trying to honor my commitment to do the best job possible for you and all my tenants, but in your case you're making my job very difficult. I suggest you get out of my office now and let me call the locksmith."

"Great, let me know when it's done," Larry sniffed and then walked briskly back to his office.

Rick picked up the phone and called Ace Locksmiths, who had been doing the locks for Rick for ten years. Paul Lochridge answered and agreed to come by that afternoon. Rick sat back in his chair and mentally ran through all the foul names he could think of for Larry Thomas. Rick hoped no other tenant decided to accost him today, for he didn't think he would be able to keep his temper for very long. He tried to never take his problems with one tenant out on another, but Larry's behavior was hard to get out of his system.

Rick decided to resort to his favorite style of running the

business-management by walking around. Never one to sit still very long, Rick walked the halls often, looking for problems to take care of and trying to generate goodwill with his tenants. As he walked past the operations area Rick saw Dave Savage at the copier, fuming and looking like he was ready to deliver a kick to the machine. Dave was one of those people who just seemed to have a difficult time with any type of machine. Rick stopped and noted how animated Dave was.

"What's the problem, Dave?" asked Rick.

"This copier keeps eating my documents," Dave sputtered.

"That's no good. I'll take a look at it," said Rick.

"I doubt you can do anything. It needs the repairman. It's really screwed up," replied Dave. Continuing he said, "You know, Rick, I always have problems with this machine. I think you bought a bad machine."

Rick grimaced as he took the insult. Sometimes he got tired of it being his fault, no matter what really happened. He opened up the copier and pulled out several sheets of wadded paper. Rick identified the original problem and knew the rest of the mess was from Dave just feeding in more paper to be copied when he knew one had jammed.

"See. It's a total mess. This is just a piece of junk," said Dave.

As Rick cleared the paper out he thought about how reliable this machine actually was. A small grin came across his face as he closed the copier doors.

Knowing the copier would now work, Rick looked at Dave and said, "Dave, I need to be sure you are operating this copier correctly. Watch me closely and let's see what happens. You enter your code like this."

"I know how to enter my code. This is not my fault,"

replied Dave.

"I'm not saying it is, Dave, but watch this next step in particular," said Rick, trying to look serious. Continuing, he said, "You have to press this green start button just right. Like this."

Rick put his finger on the green button and gave an exaggerated downward push along with a dip in his hip and a wiggle in his butt. The copier churned and out slid a perfect copy. Rick repeated the movement and another perfect copy slid into the tray.

Rick said, "Now you try, Dave."

Dave mimicked Rick's move and the copier again did its job.

"Hey, that worked great," said Dave, beaming with delight. "Thanks, Rick."

"You're quite welcome, Dave. Just keep doing it that way and the copier will be your best friend," replied Rick, concealing his amusement.

He walked down the hall and turned to watch Dave merrily making copies, clearly enjoying his newfound prowess. Rick felt a little guilty at making Dave look somewhat foolish, but at least Rick's spirits were lifted.

About mid-afternoon Paul Lochridge showed up to change the locks. Rick called Paul in his office and instructed him to put Suite 415 on its own key.

As Paul started out Rick said, "Paul, wait a minute, I want to make one change. I need you to give me a copy of his key, but tell him there are no more copies. I don't like asking you to lie, but I'm very uncomfortable with not being able to get in if there is some emergency. Can you do this for me?"

Paul looked at Rick, sighed and said, "Yeah, I can do that. You must feel pretty strong about this. I'll take care of it for you.

This guy must be a real smuck."

"He is. Thanks, Paul, I really appreciate it." Rick thought, I should do anything I can to get Larry and his company to leave. They'll always be a pain in the rear.

But he knew he had to treat them as well as any other tenant. Customer service was how he had built the business and he could not just turn it on and off, depending on the tenant. The exceptions to this were if they were not paying their bill or if they were doing something illegal.

The next day Rick took off work for a few hours to go shopping. He was trying to keep his mind on his survival packs and off of that jerk Larry Thomas. Rick picked up some ammunition for the Ruger .357, Glock .40 S & W, and Colt .45 handguns, the .270 rifle and the 12-gauge shotgun he owned. Next he went to Al's Military and Security Store. He had always wanted to go in this store, but never seemed to make the time. As Rick walked through the store he wished he had made the time earlier since it was such an interesting store. Some of the more intriguing items to Rick were the electronic surveillance products. He had always liked electronic gadgets and some of these were irresistible, even if unneeded.

A man walked up to Rick and said, "I'm Al. Anything I can help you with?"

"I'm browsing, but I'm going to buy a few items," replied Rick.

"This here is a nifty device. We just got it in. It's a listening device that looks like a regular electrical wall outlet. The wall outlet part even works. You can pick up conversations in the room over an FM radio," explained Al.

"That is pretty neat," Rick said while examining the device.

"Yeah, but I guess you would have to be listening all the

time to catch everything," said Al.

"What if you rigged it up to some voice-activated device to activate a tape recorder?" asked Rick.

"I guess that would work," Al said.

"Well, I'm going to give it a try," Rick replied.

Rick bought the electric wall outlet that was also a FM radio transmitter, a small radio receiver and a voice-activated tape recorder. If he could make them work together he would have a great listening device and it would cost less than fifty dollars. Rick had no particular use for these devices, but could not resist the urge to hook them up and see if it really worked.

As Rick walked out the door, Al shouted, "Let me know how it works."

"Sure," said Rick with a wave.

Driving back to work, Rick's first thought was to take the parts home to his shop, hook them up and listen in on the family. Spying on the family seemed to betray their basic ideals of trust so perhaps a better target could be found. Immediately Larry Thomas came to mind. This idea still violated Rick's basic ideal of personal and professional trust, but since he really didn't care what Larry was talking about he could chalk this up to being a real-world science experiment. Rick had never done anything like this to any of his tenants, but this idea seemed like great fun with very little downside.

Then it hit Rick that Larry was certainly a candidate to skip out on his lease agreement. Other tenants had done just that by moving their stuff out late at night. For the most part the only people who did this were out of money and did not want Rick to be able to seize their computers and furniture. His lease agreement gave him this power and the tenants never doubted that Rick would hesitate to change the locks on their office. Rick didn't think that Worldwide Water Solutions was running out of money, but a griping, overbearing person like Larry would move out in the middle of the night just to make Rick mad. Even though Rick had offered to let Larry break his lease and move out immediately, Larry would not get nearly the pleasure out of this as if he stiffed Rick and just disappeared. If Larry was thinking about anything like this it would be on Rick's terms.

It was now a game of cat-and-mouse and Rick decided the cat needed more information. The listening device would tell him what was actually going on and if Larry suspected anything the worst he could do was to move out on Rick's terms or bring in his all-powerful corporate lawyers. In either case Larry would be gone and that would be cause for celebration. If Rick did not misuse any of the information the lawyers would probably drop the matter. Rick headed back to Austin Executive Suites to finish out the day and plan the job. At the end of the workday he headed for the elevator.

"Say, Rick. I saw Dave Savage doing some kind of dance with our copier. Did you have something to do with that?" asked Sandra mischievously.

Rick grinned. "Did he look happy?"

"Why, yes. He did."

"Then let's leave it at that," Rick answered as he entered the elevator.

"Hi, Rick, how was your day?" asked Kathy as he walked in the door.

Rick replied, "Oh, it went pretty well. I went shopping for some items for my survival pack and some ammo for the guns. Besides that it was pretty quiet."

"No tenant uprisings today? You know, if they do get too out of hand you can take the guns down there and straighten them out. If that system works we can put on a seminar on tenant relations at the next executive suite convention. We can also show how handy your survival pack comes in when the power goes out," Kathy said with only a trace of a smile.

"Very funny. Someday one of our tenants or one of their customers is going to freak out like a postman and start spraying bullets around and we all will be wishing for a gun. Anyway, I'm having fun with my precautions. In fact, I might just have a new hobby. Speaking of my new hobby, I think I'll run over to the indoor gun range after dinner."

"Okay, but don't stay long. I certainly can't have you shooting up all of our precious ammo. You really need to leave some for the rest of us," Kathy scolded.

"I'm glad you're so concerned with our ammo levels. On another subject, where is Mack? I had hoped to see him at dinner tonight."

"He's flying. What else is there to do? All he can think of is getting up in that plane. I hope we didn't blow our job as parents by getting him that plane. It still seems like we went overboard by getting a seventeen-year-old boy an airplane," mused Kathy.

Rick thought, here we go again, but out loud he responded, "I know it looks like we are spoiling him, but check the facts. He has wanted to be a pilot since he was 5 years old, he started lessons at fourteen and had fifty hours in before he could legally solo at sixteen. Then he had another forty hours in before he got his license at seventeen, passed the written test with a high grade, is perfectly happy driving a cheap car to help pay for the plane and is such a great kid. Having two partners in the plane keeps the cost lower than what we spent on Davis' car when he turned sixteen and they hardly ever use the plane. Anyway, I don't care what other people think, he's worked hard and earned the privilege of having a plane."

"Does the fact that you love flying around with him count as a reason too? If so, you need to add it to the list," Kathy teased.

Rick looked at her seriously and said, "Yes, that might have something to do with it. I really like being up in the old Cessna with him. If I'm really nice he lets me fly some."

They looked at each other and laughed.

"You men! Everything you do has to be dangerous. I thought it was bad enough flying around everywhere and landing on a runway, but now you are always putting the floats on and landing on Lake Travis," Kathy moaned.

Rick thought back to his forty-first birthday when Mack and Davis totally surprised him with a set of used floats for the Cessna 172 they had owned for over a year in partnership with two friends. They had even hired a Herve Villachez look-alike to dress up like Tattoo on the TV show *Fantasy Island* and yell "Boss, de plane, de plane." Whenever the talk at a party turned to old TV shows and then inevitably to *Fantasy Island*, Rick always said his fantasy was to land in the seaplane that delivered the guests to the Island.

The only problem with the floats was that the Cessna was designed to have either permanent floats or the regular tires, not both. Rick's challenge now was to adapt the floats to their plane and make them removable. For the next two months Rick and the boys had spent hours researching the weights and center of balance of float planes and regular Cessna's. Finally, Rick had commissioned a local machine shop to build an aluminum framework to hold the two floats together and modify each float with a channel for each rear wheel of the Cessna to roll into. The front tire rolled into a cradle in the framework. The tires were secured to the cradle and the two floats by strong nylon webbing. They needed a runway that was close to a body of water and the small strip on the north shore of Lake Travis would be perfect. On a calm Saturday morning Mack flew to the landing strip and Rick and Davis met him there with the float assembly. They put the floats on the edge of the lake and rolled the Cessna's rear tires into the channels in the floats and then the front tires were guided into the cradle. The tires were secured with the webbing and the job was done. Fortunately it was still calm on Lake Travis and they sped across the lake. Mack lifted the plane gently out of the water and then let it settle back down. He repeated this several times to get the feel of the plane with the added weight.

Rick said, "Can you do it, Mack?"

Mack replied, "Sure, it feels stable."

Mack increased the throttle to full power and the plane accelerated. He pulled back on the yoke and the Cessna slowly lifted off the water and climbed into the air.

"Happy birthday, Dad. Your present is complete," said Davis.

"This is the neatest thing," cried Rick above the noise.

"Yeah, it's real neato, Dad," laughed Mack.

"Now let's see if you can land this thing, Mack," said Rick.

Mack circled and checked for boat traffic. He slowly let the plane drop until the plane was just above the water. Mack pulled back the yoke and the plane held its altitude for a second and then settled into the water. The three Blazes let out a simultaneous yell and Rick patted Mack on the back.

"There's our lake lot," said Rick, pointing to the shore. "Let's run it up on the beach."

They were able to idle the plane up to the beach, just like

they did with their jet skis. Rick never ceased to get a rush out of landing, taking off and taxiing around the lake. In fact, they spent so much time doing this that the other partners were making noises about how little they got to use the plane. A few lake landings with the partners, however, made the fact that the plane was only a four-seater the biggest issue.

Rick's mind floated back to the present when Kathy asked, "Did you go to the Bahamas for a while?"

"Yeah, it was great, but I'm back now," Rick replied.

Rick and Kathy sat down for dinner and discussed the more mundane things of the world like politics and local gossip. After dinner Rick left the house to go to the gun range.

"I'll be back in a couple of hours," Rick called back.

As he pulled out of the driveway Rick headed not toward the gun range, but in the direction of Austin Executive Suites. When he pulled up to the building, Rick noticed that the light in Suite 415 was not on, indicating that Larry Thomas was not in his office. He went up to the fourth floor and checked the Suites for late night workers. A few were there, but they were all busy at their desks.

Rick went to the telephone and mechanical room to get some tools and then retrieved the key to Suite 415 from his office. He went in the office, his heart starting to beat faster, and began to unscrew one of the electrical outlets. Rick didn't know which circuit breaker controlled this circuit and could not just start shutting off breakers because so many tenants left their computers on all the time. He didn't want a rebooted computer or an interrupted file download to alert anyone to a possible problem or cause him to look around the Suites for help.

Because of this, he had already decided to replace the outlet with the listening device with the wires hot. If he was careful it was no big deal to work with hot wires. He had done it before, but those times it was because he was being lazy. Now he was more than a tad nervous and his hands were getting clammy.

Rick worked steadily, trying to keep the thoughts of Larry walking in the office out of his mind. Within ten minutes he had removed the outlet and replaced it with the electrical outlet/listening device. In five more minutes he had picked up his tools, turned off the light, and gone back to the phone room.

Now, his pulse was starting to slow and his hands were dry. Rick tuned the radio to the proper frequency and began to work on the custom patch cord he felt would make the system complete. He took an external speaker with cable and cut the speaker off. Next, he took a microphone with cable and cut the microphone off. Paying attention to the polarity, he spliced the two cables together and plugged the ends into the radio receiver and the tape recorder. The theory was that when a sound occurred in Suite 415 it would be transmitted over the frequency to the radio, causing the sound-activated tape recorder to begin recording.

Rick felt everything was ready and headed home, excited about tomorrow's day at work.

# Chapter 15

Tesar Aboud left the Iraq border and continued his secret journey to meet the unknown contacts his uncle, Safreed al Habid, had set up. He ventured through Syria until he reached the city of Latakid on the Mediterranean Sea and found the dock area that was his final destination. At the proper dock Aboud met his contact, Captain Alphonse Mobatu of Algeria, a swarthy, evil looking man whom Aboud was not inclined to trust. Aboud's job was not to trust, but to follow instructions; in particular the instructions Habid had provided him. So Aboud helped Mobatu's men carefully unload the crates from his truck and place each crate in another crate that was just large enough for the smaller one to fit in. The new crates were stamped with writing that Aboud recognized to be French, but he had no idea what the writing said. He was impressed with the care and diligence that Mobatu and his men exhibited. They were clearly well trained and most likely well paid.

After all the crates were unloaded, recrated and loaded on Captain Mobatu's boat Aboud returned to his truck and started back to Iraq. As he was pulling away from the dock he saw

Mobatu's boat already leaving the dock and heading out to sea. Aboud loved being a part of such an efficient and intriguing operation and hoped his perfect execution would make him privy to the rest of the plan. Surely Uncle Habid would reward him with a commendation or a medal. Aboud worked his way back through Syria to the Iraqi border, passed into Iraq, and headed toward Baghdad.

He stopped to sleep for a few hours in the cab of the truck, ate some of the rations Habid had provided and continued the journey home. Returning the cargo truck to the vehicle compound, Aboud was relieved to be back, yet excited to report in to Habid. He hailed a cab and was driven to the school above the Baghdad Chemical Weapons Plant, where he passed security at the special elevator in the east wing and descended the forty feet to the Plant's level. It was now mid-afternoon and he hoped to find Safreed al Habid in his office. As luck would have it Habid was working at his desk and, glancing up, waved Aboud into the office.

"Welcome back, cousin, I have already received confirmation that your part of the plan has gone splendidly," Habid said pumping Aboud's hand furiously.

"Thank you, cousin, your planning and instructions were perfect. I know our leader Saddam will be glad to hear of our success. I would be pleased to accompany you to tell him the news," Aboud blurted out.

Habid cautioned, "Now, Aboud, you know we must be very careful. This is a secret shared by only a few and must be protected from those who would not agree with us. You will meet with Saddam when the time is right. Until then you are needed back in your lab."

"Will Saddam be informed that it was I who developed the chemical?" quizzed Aboud, who was beginning to get a little suspicious of the secrecy.

"Of course, Aboud, I will tell him everything. I will tell him that it was you who found that a low-level exposure to one of the very antibiotics that is used to control the E. coli 0157:H7 strain acts as an accelerator," said Habid.

"Well, cousin," replied Aboud, "I learned of the possible effects of using low-level amounts of the antibiotic norflaxin from the Japanese. They found that if treatment of the E. coli by norflaxin was suspended shortly after initial treatments that a latent virus in the E. coli's DNA could be triggered that greatly increases the vero toxins to a level never before seen in any E. coli samples."

"Yes, yes, Aboud. I know all that. Even though I am not as educated as you in chemistry I am capable of understanding the concepts."

"Sorry, cousin. I just do not want to take credit for the Japanese research. However, it was I who adapted the findings and used other accelerators to create the E. coli strain that is so concentrated and deadly that it is effective with almost any dilution levels and is impervious to normal water treating techniques," responded Aboud.

"Aboud, you have done a wonderful job and you will get the proper credit. Your career in the Iraqi army is assured," said Habid. Continuing he said, "Our other technicians have been able to duplicate your work and this will allow you to take a different role in our quest to control the Middle East. Who knows, some day you may have my job."

"Thank you, cousin, I hope I have not offended you in any way with my comments," replied Aboud.

"No, cousin. I understand your concerns and you will most certainly get what you deserve. Now return to your lab and work on the next project."

Aboud bowed and returned to his private lab. He opened a packet indicating his next task and began putting on his clean room suit. The sample he removed from the packet needed immediate analysis, so he set right to work. He opened the sample vial and moved to his microscope. In less than a minute his body began to itch, his skin tightened and started to contract and crack. Aboud's breathing was labored as he struggled to activate the water bath and chemical wash. He activated both devices with the panic switch but nothing happened. By now it was too late anyway. His body had been completely taken over by the deadly virus and his life slowly sapped away.

One of the technicians heard the audible panic alarm and ran to the lab. He saw the crumpled body of Aboud and knew there was nothing that could be done for the poor man. More of the technicians arrived and surveyed the scene. It became obvious to them that Aboud had been murdered. Even though the panic alarm had sounded and Aboud was under the nozzles, no water or chemicals were on the floor. Someone who knew what they were doing had tampered with the emergency devices.

Word of the tragedy quickly reached Safreed al Habid's office, including the finding that one of the exhaust valves in the helmet had been reversed. This had allowed the outside air to be drawn inside the helmet.

Habid ran to the lab, peered in, and declared, "Whoever is responsible for this will be found and shot!"

The technicians began to back away as a group, terrified at the thought of being in front of a firing squad. Someone always paid for a crime in Iraq, but it was not always the real criminal.

Habid continued his rampage. "I want a statement from everyone on duty detailing your whereabouts today. I will avenge my cousin's death."

Habid turned and stormed back to his office, acting shocked, but thought, a pity, cousin, but it had to be. Some must die for others to claim the glory.

# Chapter 16

Rene Charlton brought up the map of the United States on his computer and scanned the red dots that marked the major cities that drew a large part of their drinking water from an upstream lake. There were a lot of cities to choose from, but Austin always seemed to jump out as the easiest and most emotional target to start with. No one would expect Austin to be where it all starts and he could count on the panic factor to have people lining up to fill his pockets with money. Although money was always a great motivator to Rene it ranked way above anything else, including power. He had learned to speak the language of power as he dealt with a growing procession of government and terrorist types that thrived on power and would pay any amount of money to get it. Rene found the money flowed more freely if a customer thought Rene shared their delusions of grandeur. Rene did not care who ruled the world as long as he could manipulate that person with brains and money. A growing file system containing potential extortion and blackmail information was the newest weapon in the ever-growing arsenal of Rene Charlton. As Rene studied the map on the computer screen he marveled at how well the operation was coming together. He knew a few setbacks were to be expected, but so far there was only smooth sailing. As he thought of sailing he decided to check the progress of the shipment coming from his partner in Iraq. Rene hit the speed dial key to call his special operations group in Paris, France.

A voice answered, "Worldwide Water Solutions, may I help you?"

"Yes, this is Charlton and I need to speak to Devolt."

"Yes sir, Mr. Charlton, I'll patch you through to Mr. Devolt immediately. He is in the field, but I should be able to reach him," the voice continued.

Rene thought, I had better be able to reach him for all the money I spent on high tech communications equipment.

A minute later another voice came on the line. "Hello, Mr. Charlton, this is Devolt. I can give you a complete update."

"Go ahead, Kirk, I'm anxious to hear it."

"Well, I'm here at the plant in Toulouse and things are going very well. We received the shipment from Mobatu yesterday and finished the repackaging this morning. The shipment certainly looks like a load of computer equipment headed for the United States. All the specifications have been very precise. The canisters fit the atmospheric pressure-compensated trunks as well as the trunks fit into the padded cardboard boxes indicating the contents as CPU's, monitors and printers. This will look like just another upgrade of your computer system in America. The boxes have been delivered to the airport and the cargo shipment for the States leaves tonight. The items should be ready for you to pick up tomorrow afternoon. I've shipped the one canister packaged as a printer to the Austin office and it should also arrive tomorrow. I have my people stationed at the airport to keep an eye on the shipments until they are in the air. After that point I believe my duties on this project are complete."

Rene replied, "Kirk, you've done very well, as usual. There will be a substantial bonus in this for you, not to mention a promotion. Contact me if there are any changes or problems."

"Yes sir, Mr. Charlton. No news will be good news."

Rene hung up the phone. He ran the steps of his plan through his mind, decided he had a wonderful plan and it was time to get the world's attention.

Rene hit another speed dial key and heard the receptionist say, "Worldwide Water Solutions, may I help you?"

"Larry Thomas, please."

"May I tell Larry who is calling?" replied the receptionist.

"Yes, this is Rene Charlton," Rene said indignantly.

"Hello, Rene, Larry here."

"Larry, everything is going perfectly. Your shipment should arrive tomorrow, so you need to be ready to act immediately. I want to hear the plan as you understand it. I can't afford for anything to go wrong."

Larry took a deep breath and spoke, "I'll have Ed Richter pick up the shipment at the FedEx office. That way there'll be no chance of it being lost around Austin. Ed will take the canister to his hotel room in Georgetown, outside of Austin. I'll meet him there and we'll unpack the canister, remove the tape covering the dispersion membrane holes and immediately place the canister in the floating degenerative suspension module. I understand that I will have only two minutes to do this or face the risk of the chemical escaping through the dispersion membrane holes. Next, I place the suspension module in the storage container and pull a vacuum on the container with the vacuum pump. By watching the vacuum gauge I can be sure the container is airtight, then I put the container in the suitcase designed for it. This will keep the maids or anyone else from suspecting anything.

"Ed and I will store the suitcasc for two days until Saturday. On Saturday Ed and I will rendezvous at the hotel, drive to Executive Airport, load the suitcase in Ed's plane and take off at 10:00 PM. We will file a flight plan to Oklahoma City as a cover and have an unplanned stop outside of Waco at a small airfield I have found. We will report minor trouble with the flaps, land, and appear to make repairs. After taking off again we will appear to fly toward Oklahoma City, duck under radar level and return to the Austin area. We should arrive over Lake Travis about 1:00 a.m. On the last leg I'll remove the floating degenerative suspension module from the suitcase and prepare it for the drop. Ed will circle the plane about one-half mile upstream from the dam and I'll drop the module out the plane's window. We will continue to fly under radar for a while and fly on toward Oklahoma City. The module will float on the water's surface and the degenerative process will begin. After approximately one hour of the canister being exposed to the water the chemical will begin to leak out. Because the chemical is released on the surface and drifts toward the bottom the dispersion process is more thorough than if it was released on the bottom.

"The chemical will reach the City of Austin water treating facility in about twelve hours and will be released through the City's water system in another twelve hours. Within the next twenty-four hours the initial flu-like symptoms will appear and the City's leaders will be somewhat baffled. In the next twenty-four hours the skin will begin to deteriorate, massive stomach pains will begin, muscles will start cramping and the headache pain will resemble a full-time migraine. In the next twenty-four hours death will begin to overwhelm the city and panic will take over. There will be a mass exodus out of the city and no one will be able to figure out the problem. At this time your Iraqi contact will release a tape to CNN in Baghdad claiming responsibility for the mass murder and promising continued attacks on the population. While the nation becomes totally concentrated on its problems, Saddam will launch his plans. While Saddam is waging his attacks we will continue to attack the cities we have identified as the best targets, crippling the entire country either by disease or by panic. Ed and I will wait at our Oklahoma City office until I hear from you. That's the plan as I understand it."

"Excellent, Larry. I knew you were the man for the job after the success you had with the mustard gas in Iran. You may proceed with the plan as you detailed it. I'm looking forward to the results. We all will profit handsomely. I'll contact you in Oklahoma City. Goodbye and good luck," Rene replied.

Larry heard the phone click and breathed a sign of relief. If Rene was pleased, Larry was pleased.

Two hours later the receptionist called Larry and informed him that Ed Richter was in the lobby and wanted to see him.

"Send him down the hall and I'll meet him," replied Larry.

"Ed, come in," said Larry.

"It's good to see you Larry. It's great to get out of Fort Davis. Boy, what a dead place! Those two geezers we toasted were the only thing interesting that has happened there all year. I was about to go out of my gourd, all that sneaking around and lying low. I'm ready for some real action," Ed blurted out.

"Well, Ed, you're going to get your wish. We should receive a shipment tomorrow at the FedEx office. The delivery instructions are for FedEx to keep the package at their office for pickup. As soon as I get notice that it has arrived you'll go pick it up and take it to your hotel. I trust your reservations were in order?" Larry replied.

"Yes, the hotel in Georgetown is perfect. It's remote and close to the airport. Executive Airpark is a nice little airport and the staff seems very trusting. I don't think they would ever entertain the notion that we're pulling something on them," Ed responded.

"Good, just wait around here until FedEx calls, then we can get rolling. I have the floating degenerative suspension module locked in the cabinet there. I also have a small amount of the neutralizing agent, both in vial form and syringe for individual cases. The suspension module is designed specifically to go through the window of your Cessna 172. I don't see why you insist on using that old airplane of yours. Rene would provide us with anything we wanted."

Ed replied, "I know my Cessna like the back of my hand and I trust the machine. It has wonderful low speed control and stability-just what we need for flying under radar and making airdrops into lakes. It takes a little longer to get from city-to-city, but that is not really an important parameter."

"Okay, okay, I believe you. Whatever you feel most comfortable with, especially since I'll be flying with you," Larry shot back. Continuing, he said, "The drop is scheduled for Saturday night, actually early Sunday morning for the drop itself. I'll have my important papers boxed up and with me. The rest of this stuff will stay so it doesn't look like I split town, even though I did. Now, I've got work to do so you can just hang around or explore Austin. Just be sure to check in every hour."

"All right, Larry, I think I'll hang around here. I wouldn't mind checking out the receptionists here a little. They're a nice change of scenery from the Fort Davis country girls. So I'll be on the floor when you need me," Ed said, turning to walk out the door.

Just before he got to the door Larry cautioned, "Ed, be careful around the owner up here. His name is Rick Blaze and he seems to be everywhere. You know, one of those mother hen types, always checking everything out. He doesn't take shit off me like most people do. In some ways he reminds me of Rene-someone not to mess with too much.

"Okay, what's he look like?" asked Ed.

Larry replied, "What's sort of spooky is that they somewhat resemble each other. You know, the same height and build, dark hair and complexion. They have one other thing in common. When they're mad the veins in their neck pop out and their face turns red. If you get that far with either of them, you've gone too far. Anyway, just be careful around him. I don't want him keeping watch on us anymore than he already does."

"Okay, I'll just avoid him."

Ed left the office and Larry got back to the papers on his desk.

Rick had a fairly uneventful day and greatly appreciated the time to catch up on paperwork. His mind kept wandering toward the bugging device and tape recorder that was hopefully recording conversations in Larry Thomas' office. While the invasion of privacy still bothered him, Rick was getting more curious about what Larry was doing and if he was an asshole to everyone or just to Rick. Rick's curiosity was aroused even more when that Ed guy showed up to talk to Larry. After spending some time in Larry's office Ed had spent the rest of the afternoon hanging around the Executive Suites, mainly in the lobby area. When Rick noticed the guy hovering around the receptionists he had gone out to make him leave the employees alone. Talking to the receptionists was a common way for tenants to kill time; however, it was distracting for his people trying to answer the phones for over fifty companies as well as keeping track of the tenants as they came and went. Kathy had always spent a lot of time training the receptionists to maintain an accurate in and out sheet throughout the day and Rick was not about to let her training be compromised by idle chatter with bored tenants.

Rick introduced himself to the man standing by the main desk. "Hi, my name is Rick Blaze and I'm the owner of the Executive Suites. Is there anything I can help you with?"

The man stared at Rick for a few seconds, seeming to recognize something about Rick. Finally, he said, "I'm Ed and I work with Larry Thomas at Worldwide Water Solutions."

"What's your last name Ed?" asked Rick.

"Let's just leave it at Ed."

"Oh, like Madonna or Cher?"

"No, like what's it to you," replied an agitated Ed.

"Well, Ed, we keep track of our tenants. It's just a service most companies want," replied Rick calmly.

"It's Richter, Ed Richter. Are you happy now?"

"Ecstatic. Now, again, is there anything I can help you with?" quizzed Rick.

"I was just getting to know the staff here. I don't see why that would be a problem."

"I didn't say it was a problem. I want you to meet the staff here. I will have to ask that you refrain from just shooting the breeze with them. It takes a lot of concentration to do their job properly and I want them to represent Worldwide Water in the best possible way. I'll be glad to give you a tour of the Suites and introduce you to the rest of the staff," Rick said, not meaning it at all.

He thought that this guy was a perfect companion to Larry-a real butt.

Ed tersely replied, “No thanks, I’ll just go to the kitchen for a while. Is that okay with you?”

“It sure is, Ed. Have a good day,” Rick said, turning away.

As the rest of the day wore on Rick kept wondering what the world was coming to. It was bad enough that the United States had to keep dealing with those crazy Iraqis, but more and more he was dealing with people like Larry Thomas and this Ed guy. If people would try a little harder to get along and be pleasant, this would still be a great country to live in. Kathy had nailed it on the head, Rick thought, when she said that if everyone used good manners most of our problems could be quickly and fairly solved. Anyway, Rick noticed it was five p.m., time to head home. He closed the door to his office and walked to the telephone and maintenance room. Rick looked at the recorder and saw it actually had recorded something. He popped out the tape and replaced it with a blank one. The recorder he had purchased used the full size cassettes, making it possible for him to listen to the tape in his Blazer.

# Chapter 17

Rick drove out of the Executive Suite parking lot and headed toward home. He inserted the cassette tape into the tape player and wondered what kind of mundane dribble Larry was so eager to keep secret. The listening system seemed to work fairly well, although sometimes it would cut in and out, making the conversation somewhat choppy. In addition, the device only picked up Larry's side of a telephone call so Rick had to guess the caller's conversation. The first two calls were rather trivial, just people wanting to buy water conditioning and filtering equipment.

Larry quickly dispatched each of them with a booming, "I'm not the Culligan Man and we don't do little systems."

Immediately after each of these calls Larry could be heard muttering something about where these people were getting his number.

Next, Rick heard Larry say "Hello, Rene, Larry here," followed by "I'll have Ed Richter pick up the shipment at the FedEx office. That way there will be no chance of it being lost around Austin. Ed will take the canister to his hotel room in

Georgetown..."

Rick listened in horror as Larry spelled out the entire plan. Could it be possible that an attack on the United States and other countries by Saddam Hussein was being planned and initiated in one of Austin Executive Suite's offices? Rick could not concentrate on his driving and he was almost home so he pulled into a deserted parking lot. The tape was now picking up a conversation between two men, but Rick had missed the first part of their conversation while his head was spinning with the details of the insidious plan he had just heard. He ejected the tape and just sat there for a minute, trying to collect himself. Surely this was some kind of sick joke or fantasy warfare plan, like the fantasy football leagues that were so popular. Yes, maybe that was the answer; Larry was part of some stupid group playing out their version of how this upcoming Middle East War could go. This was a possibility, but Rick didn't get the feeling from the tape that Larry was anything but serious.

"Stop it!" Rick exclaimed out loud, trying to get his runaway mind back into reality.

"Just listen to the entire tape and everything will be clear and you can calm down," Rick muttered again to himself. He picked up his cell phone and called Kathy.

"Hi, Kathy, it's me. I need to run a couple of errands so I'll be a little late."

"Okay, Rick, just go spend another hour at Al's Military and Nuclear Weapons Store. Dinner won't be ready until seven anyway. Even if you miss it you can have a can of your beloved Wolf Brand Chili," Kathy replied, enjoying the needling.

Rick impatiently shot back, "It's Al's Military and Security Store and that's not where I'm going anyway. I'll be home in an hour. See you then."

Kathy said, “Okay, see you.”

Kathy wondered what was bugging Rick, after work he was usually in a mood to play. I’m sure he will tell me when he gets home, she thought.

Rick took a deep breath, pushed the tape in and hit the rewind button. He listened intently to the conversation being replayed, finally getting to the end where Larry said, “Ed and I’ll wait at our Oklahoma City office until I hear from you. That is the plan as I understand it.”

As Rick listened to the conversation between Larry and Ed that followed he began to believe that this was real and he had to do something about it. Since the drop was Saturday night he didn’t have much time, only three days. Rick wondered who this Rene person was that seemed to be in charge and who apparently resembled Rick enough for it to bug Larry.

Even with this dire information in hand Rick had to chuckle at Larry’s description of his face turning red and the neck veins popping out. Kathy frequently told him those same characteristics caused people to be scared of him. The fact that Rick was five-foot-ten and about two hundred pounds of muscle compounded the image. Rick’s active life, especially all the basketball games with Davis and Mack, and the frequent water skiing that Rick loved, kept him in excellent shape and created an image of him that caused people to overestimate his height. Even people who were around Rick a lot would swear he was at least six feet tall.

Snapping back to his current problem, Rick searched his mind for a solution or at least some plan of action. Rick could hardly believe that his ominous feelings about the Iraqis terrorizing

America were actually coming true and he was the one who had to stop them. In a perfect world all Rick would have to do was to tell the police or the FBI about this, play the tape and let them handle the situation. But Rick's world was not perfect, especially concerning any law enforcement agency. How ironic it was that Rick had spent the last twenty years avoiding any trouble with the law, even to the point of never speeding or getting a parking ticket, and now he was embroiled in a plot to destroy America. The more he thought about the situation the more Rick knew the time had come to tell Kathy about his secret past. He had hoped that she would never have to know and, thus, to worry about his past coming back to haunt the Blaze family.

Rick knew in his heart that he had to do something about Larry's plan and that he could not do it alone. He must take her into his confidence and let her help him decide what to do. She was the only person he could trust and he needed that trust now. Rick looked at his watch, noticed that it had been an hour and a half since he talked to Kathy. He started up the Blazer and headed home. He searched his mind for the best way to tell Kathy; mainly though, for the best way to start the conversation at all.

# Chapter 18

Rene Charlton looked at his watch. It was precisely the time to place his call to Safreed al Habid at his office in the Baghdad Chemical Weapons Plant in Baghdad. As the call was going through Rene thought about how well things were going for him.

A voice answered in Arabic and Rene said, “Habid?”

“Yes, it is I, Rene. How are you?” Habid answered in English.

“I’m fine and our operation is going very well. We are in receipt of the shipments and our field people in Texas are preparing to execute their part of the plan. The drop will be Saturday night and you will begin to see some effects show up on a wide scale Tuesday night or Wednesday morning for sure. We can’t calculate exactly how fast the chemical will move through the treating plant and distribution system. I’m positive CNN will give complete coverage to the events in Austin. You can time your actions by their reports,” Rene explained.

“Excellent, Rene. I will be a hero here and you will be an

important part of the New World order as it develops," Habid pompously replied.

Rene dove into the subject closer to his heart than the New World Order. "That's great, Habid, but I must also ask about the money."

"You have already received fifty-million dollars and I will wire another fifty million to your account today as our payment schedule calls for. When I am convinced that you have completed the first stage of the plan in Austin I will wire ten-million and we will proceed to the next targets. At ten-million dollars a city you should have quite a fortune if you pull it off," explained Habid.

"I *will* pull it off, Habid. You can count on it," Rene replied, thinking about how much more money he was going to make than Habid ever imagined.

"I will count on it then. We must be more careful with our communications next week. When Saddam and the world see what is happening Saddam will most likely watch me more closely. He will initially be mad that I did this without his knowledge, but he will quickly realize the beauty of the plan and see the multiplying of his power. But, knowing how he operates, he will have someone keep an eye on me," Habid cautioned.

"All right, I'll await your instructions. Good luck with your end of the plan."

"Yes, thank you. I will be in contact. Goodbye," Habid said, hanging up the phone.

Rene leaned back in his chair and commended himself on his skills in manipulating people. What an exciting time this was going to be.

# Chapter 19

Rick pulled into the driveway, still not sure how to start the conversation. Should he pretend that everything was okay, eat dinner and then tell her or just go straight into it, trying to relate the events as coherently as possible? Finally, he decided to just go straight into it, since Kathy would know something was wrong and push him to tell her right away. She always knew when something was bothering him. He walked through the door and Kathy was immediately chastising him for being late.

"I know I'm late and should have called back, but I need to talk to you right away. This is very serious and I think dinner will just have to wait," Rick answered.

Kathy said, "Can't we talk about this at the dinner table? Mack is here and we're ready to eat."

"No, this is something we need to talk about right now, in private. Just the two of us," Rick replied.

"Okay, if it's that important, I'll tell Mack to go ahead and then meet you in our bedroom."

Rick went into the bedroom and waited. When she came in

he closed the door and told her to sit down.

Kathy looked worried and said, "What's this all about? Are you having an affair or something like that?"

"No, it's not anything like that. First, I have a tape I want you to listen to and then I have quite a story to tell you. You won't like how I got this tape, but that's not the issue. I used some of the electronic devices that I got at Al's Military and Security Store to record conversations in Larry Thomas' office. I thought it would be funny to know what secrets he thinks are so important. I know it was wrong and I shouldn't have done it, but I did and now I have to deal with what I found out."

Kathy slowly said, "Okay, let's hear the tape."

Rick started the tape player and said, "You'll only hear what is said in his office so anyone on the other end of the phone with Larry won't be recorded."

As the tape played Rick could see a puzzled frown spread across Kathy's face. She seemed to be having a hard time concentrating on the last part of the tape.

When it was over she looked at Rick and said, "This is one of your big jokes, right?"

"No, I'm afraid it's not a joke. In fact, it's the most serious thing I have ever heard," Rick said.

Kathy scolded, "You're certainly right that you shouldn't have done this, but it looks like the world will owe you a debt of gratitude. Now all we have to do is turn the tape over to the authorities and let them handle the matter. I hope they'll take it seriously, especially since you made the recording illegally. You may even get some recognition out of this. I know you don't like publicity, but this is really something you should be proud of doing."

Rick took a deep breath and replied, "Kathy, I'm afraid it

won't be that easy. The big problem is that I can't take the tape to anyone and if I just mail it in no one will take it seriously."

"Why can't you take the tape in?" Kathy interjected.

"I'm going to tell you why. It's a long story, but it will answer other questions you probably have about me. I had hoped to never have to tell you this story because it'll put you in more danger than you can imagine. I wanted to leave Davis, Mack and you out of this forever, but I can't deal with the tape unless I tell you the truth about my past. First of all, my name is not really Rick Blaze. I mean it really is now, but I changed my original name to Rick Blaze."

"Why on earth would you change your name?" Kathy asked.

"Well, it's like..." Rick began.

"Wait a minute. You're trying to pull one on me. Rick, you're always trying to *get* me, but this time there's nothing funny about it," scolded Kathy.

Rick responded, "No, I'm serious. Something happened a long time ago that caused me to change my name. It's why I never talk about my parents or childhood."

"You said your parents died in a car wreck," said Kathy.

Rick looked straight into her eyes and said, "They were blown up in their own home."

"You mean like a gas explosion?"

"No, like with a bomb. To stop me from testifying against a Mafia guy," answered Rick solemnly.

Kathy gasped and asked, "Here in Texas?"

"No. I was actually born in Chicago. That's where it happened," said Rick.

"Rick, I don't know what to say. This is all so shocking."

Rick said, "I'll tell you the whole story."

Continuing he said, "I grew up in Chicago as the only child of a nice middle class couple. My name was Randy Flanagan. I had a wonderful childhood, filled with love and attention. All that changed one night when I was eighteen. I witnessed a Mafia killing and my testimony put the head of a Mafia family in prison."

Rick went on to relate the story of Randy Flanagan and how he became Rick Blaze in Billings, Montana.

Rick said, "After getting a new identity and false identification papers from a guy in Billings, I started hitchhiking south. Along the way I read about Texas and it seemed like a good place to be. The descriptions of Austin made it seem like a neat place to live so that's where I headed. It took me a couple of months to get here because I wanted to earn some money whenever I could. When I got to Austin I actually had some money in my pocket, about a thousand dollars. I found a cheap place to stay, near the bus routes, enrolled in Austin Community College and went looking for a job.

"You know the rest of the story. I went to work for Austin Executive Suites and rose up to manager. We met, married, and had two great kids. I told you I was an orphan because I thought it kept my story simpler. The guilt about lying to you was overcome by the fear of the Mafia or government locating me. That would put you and subsequently, Davis and Mack, in jeopardy and I could not bear to allow that to happen, but now Davis, Mack, you and I are in a terrible situation. Now, you know the whole story."

"Do I, Rick? I don't know what to believe anymore," cried Kathy.

"I'm sorry, Kathy. I thought it was in our best interest to keep it all a secret," apologized Rick.

"We need to decide what is in our best interest *together*. I also need to be able to trust you. I don't know if I ever can again," she sobbed.

"You can trust me. You really can. Other than this I've never lied to you," said Rick.

"Other than this? You lied about your real name. You lied about where you are from. You lied about your parents. What wouldn't you lie about?" Kathy asked.

"I love you. I wouldn't lie about that," said Rick. "I was just trying to protect you and the boys. I've been straight with you on everything else. I wish you could forgive me," he continued.

"I wish I could too, Rick. It may take a while. You know we are going to have to talk about this a lot more," Kathy said.

"Yeah, as much as I hate to rehash the same things over and over again, I promise to devote as much time to discussing this as you want," replied Rick.

"Well, that's a good start, but I guess it doesn't solve our current problem," said Kathy.

Rick sighed and said, "No, it certainly doesn't. We know about this horrible plan and I can't go to the authorities. If I just walk up to the police with this wild story the first thing they will do is check me out thoroughly. I don't think my false identity can stand up to that scrutiny."

"But don't you think that after all these years the Mafia will have stopped looking for you?" Kathy interjected. Continuing she asked, "Even if they are looking, how on earth would they put all this together to identify you?"

"I can guarantee that they're still looking and will always be looking. Part of their power comes from the fear of retribution, no matter how long it takes. I made one little slip up while I was in Montana and two Mafia goons showed up looking for me within days. I was lucky to escape and I don't want to press my luck anymore. Besides, Gino Carlucci is still in prison, thinking about me every day, I'm sure," Rick replied.

Kathy asked, "Well then, just what do you propose we do?"

"This may sound crazy, but I think we can stop their plan cold here in Austin by pulling that canister out of the lake after the drop and disposing of it. When nothing happens maybe they will think the chemical doesn't work and give up or at least put off their plan. I'll continue to monitor Larry's conversations to see what their reactions really are."

"You're crazy," Kathy yelled. "You heard about how deadly the chemicals are. You can't risk all of our lives like that."

"Whatever I do, I'm risking all of our lives in one form or fashion," Rick countered. Continuing, he said, "Look, Kathy, I know this is all really scary, but we have to do something. The way Larry and Ed are handling the canister and the hour that it must float in the lake before it starts releasing the chemicals gives us time to retrieve it. Since the canister is being dropped out of a plane from low altitude we will be able to pinpoint the canister quickly and they won't be able to see us because they will be heading for Oklahoma City. We know the approximate spot of the drop so we just take the boat out near the area, keep the lights off and listen and watch for the drop. When the drop is made I'll just go pick up the canister with one of the Jet Skis and put it into some kind of air-tight container."

"You can't just ride out there and throw it into some kind of sack. You have to find it in less than an hour, have the right size container and protect yourself from the chemicals in case the canister starts leaking sooner than they think," Kathy scolded.

Rick replied, "You're right, it will be a little harder than I said, but I think I can do it. If I don't find the canister within 45 minutes we will have go to the authorities. We can take the cell phone with us and call from the boat."

"You promise that we will call the police after 45 minutes?" asked Kathy.

Rick replied, "Sure. I promise."

"So what is the rest of your plan, Rick? It sounds like you have already thought this one out."

"I'll use one of the powerful flashlights and you can use the Qbeam floodlights on the boat. I can wear my water-skiing dry suit, gloves and some kind of air mask. Since they are dropping the canister out the window of a Cessna like Mack's we know it can't be any larger than a shoebox. I can certainly rustle up some kind of air-tight container that size," he answered.

"Just what will you do with the canister then?" Kathy asked.

"I haven't figured that out yet, but I will. So, what do you say? Shall we save the world? It'll certainly look good on our resumes," Rick prodded.

"It's so irritating when you get flippant about serious matters," Kathy said, adding, "I don't know if I want to go along with this crazy scheme."

"Kathy, we have to do something. We agree on that."

"Doing something doesn't have to include jumping into the water to retrieve a dangerous chemical so it won't kill everyone in Austin," replied Kathy.

"I don't think we have a lot of choice," answered Rick.

Kathy looked Rick in the eye and said, "Rick, I think we are better off taking our chances with the Chicago Mafia than with Saddam Hussein and these Worldwide Water Solutions people."

Rick sighed as a wave of understanding came over him, "Maybe you're right. I need to think of the people of Austin. I just didn't want anything to happen to you and the boys."

"The police will help. I'm sure of it."

"I guess the FBI would be the appropriate agency to contact," Rick surmised. "Since it is a national plot, they would eventually get jurisdiction."

"Maybe I could take the tape in. I have no secret past to be exposed," Kathy offered.

"They would know you didn't make the tape. Then I would be in the middle anyway. It's better if I do it," Rick explained.

"Okay, Rick. This is the right thing to do."

"Yeah, it is."

# Chapter 20

The next day was Thursday and Larry Thomas arrived at Austin Executive Suites at 8:00 a.m. Ed Richter arrived shortly thereafter and went immediately to Larry's office.

"Hi, Larry, are you ready for the action to really heat up?"

"Yeah, I'm ready to actually do something instead of just talk about it. The canister should be ready to pick up at FedEx at 10:00. I want to pick it up and get the next step over with. Transferring the canister to the floating degenerative suspension module is the only part of the plan that makes me nervous," Larry said.

Ed replied, "Me, too. Do you think we can trust those scientific boys back at the home office to check all this stuff out thoroughly?"

"Sure, I trust them. They are so scared of Rene that thoroughness will not be a problem. But I still believe in Murphy's Law too much to stop worrying."

Larry and Ed picked up the package at the FedEx office

right at 10:00 and drove to Ed's hotel in Georgetown. Ed already had the other equipment inside and ready for the task at hand. They gently unpacked the canister and eyed the tape they must remove to expose the discharge membrane. Neither said anything, but they both were thinking about the numerous times they had been warned about having only two minutes to remove the tape and get the canister sealed into the floating degenerative suspension module. As they put on rubber gloves, treated paper clean suits and special air masks Ed could not help thinking about the horribly disfigured bodies of Elbert and Mattie Wheeler in Fort Davis and the grotesque expressions on their faces. He knew he would be safe if he was careful, but still, things could go wrong.

He and Larry opened the FDSM, as they had decided to call it. They had tried to come up with a catchy anachronism, but none had come to mind. With the FDSM sitting on the table with the hatch open, Ed held the canister while Larry removed the tape. Ed then carefully placed the canister into the FDSM, hesitating for only a few seconds to note the Iraqi markings on the canister. Larry closed the hatch door and secured it quickly, letting out a sigh of relief as the latches snapped shut.

The FDSM unit consisted of a center tube that housed the canister and an orange float attached to each side of the tube. The FDSM was then placed into the thick plastic storage container and a hose was connected from a valve on the container to a vacuum pump that Ed had set up nearby. They turned on the vacuum pump and let it run until the gauge on the pump indicated a moderate vacuum had been pulled inside the container. They shut off the valve on the container, removed the hose and placed a cap on the valve end. Larry made a note of the gauge reading and they watched to be sure that the vacuum level remained the same. This would indicate that the container was airtight and safe to put in the special suitcase for storage. The gauge did not change so they began to relax a little.

"Let's wait about thirty minutes and recheck the gauge before we put it in the suitcase," Larry ordered.

Ed replied, "Good plan, I could use some fresh air. I'll be back in a few minutes."

Ed returned in about twenty minutes and he and Larry spent the next ten minutes staring at the gauge. Seeing that the gauge had not changed at all, they put the container into the specially designed suitcase and secured the locks.

Ed said, "They have some lockers at the airport that this will fit in perfectly. I think that'll be the safest place to keep it until Saturday and it'll be there with the airplane when we are ready to go."

"That sounds like a good idea. I didn't want to leave it at the hotel, in my car or at the office. I'm going back to the office now. I want to let Rene know about our progress," Larry replied.

Larry returned to his office and called Rene. "Rene, this is Larry. Everything is going smoothly, the canister has been transferred and the unit is in storage waiting for our Saturday flight."

"Excellent, Larry. I look forward to seeing the results of your work early next week. It will be fun watching all the so-called experts in Austin and around the country try to figure out what's happening. I wanted to ask you about your precautions with the neutralizing agents we sent you."

"I'm keeping the syringes and vials of the neutralizing agent on my person at all times," Larry replied.

"Perfect," Rene said. "I'll rest easier with you in possession at all times. Speaking of the neutralizing agent, we have made some slight improvements to the formula and I need to get this updated formula to the lab at Oklahoma City. I was going to fax it to them, but I worry about their security sometimes. I'm going to fax the formula to you tomorrow and you can personally deliver it to Oklahoma City. That way I can be sure that only the right people see it."

"I'll be glad to deliver the formula," Larry said. "I'm honored that you trust me so much."

"You've earned the trust, Larry, as well as the money you shall receive. I'll fax the formula to you at 10:00 tomorrow morning. I want you to be at your fax then and when the document is received, to keep it on your person until you deliver it."

"Yes sir," Larry answered. "I'll be at my fax at 10:00 tomorrow and when the formula is received I'll keep it with me until I reach Oklahoma City."

Larry knew it made Rene more comfortable if he repeated the instructions and he had to admit that their miscommunications were few and far between because of this.

# Chapter 21

Rick took a deep breath as he strode into the Austin FBI offices. He approached the person manning the information desk.

"I need to speak to an agent, please."

"What for?" the man asked gruffly.

"I have information about a plot against the United States," Rick said.

"Oh, really? There's a lot of that going around these days. This isn't something you made up in that pumpkin head of yours, is it?" the man asked.

"May I speak to an agent?" Rick asked, ignoring the man's comments.

"Yeah. We have to listen to every crackpot that dreams up a subversive plot," the man replied.

"I guess there is some reason you're not taking me seriously," Rick offered.

"We get about a dozen plots against the United States every week, especially when CNN is on the rampage."

"Oh, I see."

"Still want to see an agent?"

"Yes."

The man nodded toward some chairs and said, "Have a seat."

After a thirty minute wait a tall thin man approached Rick.

He extended his hand and said, "I'm Agent Parker. What can I do to help you?"

"I'm here to help you," Rick replied nervously.

"Come to my office and we will talk, Mr...."

"Blaze. Rick Blaze."

Once inside Agent Parkers office, Rick laid a copy of the tape on the desk.

"What's this?" Parker asked, not making a move to pick up the tape.

"I taped one of the people that lease an office from me. It details a plot to contaminate water supplies all over the United States." Rick explained.

"And why did you tape your tenants?"

"I was afraid they were planning to skip out on the rent. I wanted to see what they were up to," Rick said.

"So you were lucky enough to discover an insidious plot," Parker observed.

"Yeah. I guess you could say that."

"Well, this is our lucky day then. We can mobilize the FBI and scurry around checking this out. I bet you would enjoy watching that, Mr. Blaze," Parker said with a deadpan look.

"Are you going to listen to the tape?" Rick asked, trying to keep focused on the issue.

"Sure. But first I need to get some information on you. Fill out this form. I'll be back in a minute," Parker instructed.

"You're not taking this seriously, are you, Agent Parker?"

"Look, Mr. Blaze. We get these subversive plots all the time. It's usually someone looking for attention or trying to get revenge on an enemy. If there really were something going on, we would know about it. But, we'll check you and your story out. It's part of the job."

Rick filled out the information form as the agent left and eventually returned with a cup of coffee. He slid the form across the desk and stared into Parker's eyes.

Parker picked up the form and glanced over it. "We'll run a check on you and listen to the tape. Will you be at your work number today?"

"Yes. Is that it?" Rick asked incredulously.

"Yeah, I'll be in contact with you," Parker said as he stood up.

Rick followed the agent back to the lobby. Parker shook his hand again and led Rick to the front door.

Rick drove to Austin Executive Suites and spent the rest of the workday on Thursday trying to figure out what to do about the lack on interest from the FBI. He had immediately phoned Kathy upon leaving the FBI and she was astonished at their reaction. Rick didn't tell her, but he was beginning to get a gnawing feeling that he was going to have to do this himself.

The phone rang at four o'clock. Rick picked up the handset and his receptionist said it was Robert Parker.

"Agent Parker. I was hoping to hear from you today," Rick said.

"Mr. Blaze, there are some problems with this plot you have uncovered. First of all, there are no known chemicals that are strong enough to get through a city's normal water treating system. Second, Worldwide Water Solutions checks out okay. Third, we do have some concerns about you. I would like you to come in tomorrow morning so we can discuss the results of our background check. Will that work for you?"

"You're not going to talk to Larry Thomas about this?" Rick asked incredulously.

"We'll continue to look into it. Will you be here tomorrow or do I need to send someone after you?"

"I'll be there."

Now Rick knew the FBI was probably not going to believe him or the tape. He also was the object of their concern instead of Worldwide Water. Rick resolved to continue his plan to stop Larry Thomas until the FBI changed their direction. The more he thought about his possible upcoming trials, the more he knew he could not risk failure by trying to do the job all by himself. The only people he could trust besides Kathy were Davis and Mack.

At nineteen and seventeen-years-old they were more men than boys and he really needed some men on his side. Besides, they had talents that could come in handy. They were both smart and athletic and had thrived on the basics of shooting, self-defense and survival that Rick had exposed them to. Kathy had participated in most of this learning process and Rick knew she would always be able to do whatever she had to. She knew which end of a gun was the business end and once, when she had felt threatened by a couple of men posing as prospective tenants, she stuck her Mace in their face and backed them down.

Rick also had a strong feeling that it was time to level with Davis and Mack about his past. Davis attended the University of Texas at Austin and always joined the family for dinner on Friday nights. Rick decided to immediately tell Davis and Mack then. He really needed to find a good way to get Kathy to go along with the new plan. Since no good way was coming to him, Rick decided to concoct his plan on the way home. Besides, it was five o'clock now and he needed to listen to today's recording from Larry's office. Maybe something would happen to Larry's plan and it would be called off. Or maybe it would really turn out to be a big joke after all. Perhaps the FBI would take him seriously.

Rick went into the maintenance and phone room and replaced the recorded tape with a fresh one. He then went out to his Blazer, got in and drove to a deserted church parking lot a few blocks from the office. As Rick sat there listening, he heard Larry and Ed talking about going to FedEx to get the package, worrying about the dangers involved with their upcoming tasks, and he knew for sure that all this was serious. Rick heard Larry and Ed open and close the door and knew this was just before he had talked to them this morning. The next recording was of Larry calling that Rene person again.

A chill went up Rick's back when he heard Larry say, "Everything is going smoothly, the canister has been transferred and the unit is in storage waiting for our Saturday flight."

When Larry's next words were, "I am keeping the syringes and vials of the neutralizing agent on my person at all times," Rick filed that knowledge away as important information to be aware of. The existence of a neutralizing agent also gave Rick some extra confidence in his plan and any problems he might run into. Next Larry said he would be glad to deliver the formula and when Rick heard Larry say he would be at his fax machine at 10:00 tomorrow to receive the formula, he knew he must figure out a way to get that formula without Larry knowing it. The rest of the tape was of no consequence to Rick, just a bunch of trivial calls and Larry mumbling to himself.

Rick sat in the Blazer for a while thinking about how to get the formula. Should he intercept the fax or try to get the formula from Larry after he started carrying it around on him. Rick kicked around many ideas in his head and suddenly he had it! He had an idea that with a little refinement could just work. He started up the Blazer and headed back to Austin Executive Suites. It was now about six o'clock and chances were good that Larry would be gone for the day. He almost always left a little before five and did not usually return, to the best of Rick's knowledge. Rick went into the phone room and retrieved the tone generator he used to track down telephone lines when he installed or moved lines for his tenants. Rick dialed Larry's extension and when there was no answer he felt certain that Larry had left for the day. As he entered Larry's office Rick's heart started beating fast and a light sweat broke out on his forehead.

"Stay cool, stay cool," Rick muttered to himself as he moved to the phone jack by Larry's desk. Rick unplugged the line going to the fax machine, plugged in the tone generator and flipped the switch to tone. This put a tone into the telephone line that could be detected with an inductive amplifier. Rick left the office, remembering to close the door, and headed down the hall toward the reception area. He heard the elevator ding and suddenly he saw Larry Thomas walking toward him. With his pulse racing and his heart pounding Rick tried to look as casual and unconcerned as possible.

"Hello, Larry. What are you doing up here so late?" Rick said, trying to sound like he really didn't care.

Larry gave Rick a dirty look and said, "None of your business."

He walked past Rick and went into his office, slamming the door behind him.

"Nice talking to you, jerk," Rick muttered as he walked toward the phone room. As long as Larry didn't try to fax anything he probably wouldn't notice the tone generator Rick told himself over and over, only half believing it. He decided to track the line down as fast as possible in case Larry found and unplugged the device. He ran through possible explanations for the tone generator and for how he got into Larry's office, but nothing even close to believable came to him. Rick picked up the inductive amplifier and ran it down the pairs of wires connected to the telephone company Dmark terminal until the amplifier picked up the tone being put into the wires by the tone generator. Rick tagged the wire pair and put the inductive amplifier away. He went to the shelves that he kept obsolete and spare equipment on and found the old thermal paper fax machine that he had replaced with a plain paper fax machine a few years ago. Sometimes being a pack rat came in handy, he thought.

Next, he took a telephone cord and cut off one end and skinned the outside cover back, exposing the four wires. Rick used his wire cutters to cut off the yellow and black wires, leaving the green and red wires. He plugged the modular end of the wire into the fax machine, plugged the power cord into the wall socket and verified that the machine had plenty of paper. Rick was now ready for tomorrow, so he went to his office to wait for Larry to leave. He felt pretty sure Larry had not seen the tone generator since he hadn't heard any yelling or screaming, so he decided to call Kathy while he watched the elevators.

"Hello?" Kathy answered.

"Hi, it's me," Rick replied. Continuing he said, "I'm up here at the office. There have been some new developments and I need to stay here a while longer. I'll be home as soon as I can."

"Okay, Rick, but be careful," Kathy said with a touch of worry in her voice.

"You know me, I'll be careful," Rick responded.

"Yes, I know you. That's why I asked you to be careful," she said.

"I really will be careful," he said seriously.

"Call me when you leave the office so I know that you are all right," she replied.

Rick smiled and said, "Okay."

Rick hung up and started thinking through the events to come. Timing was going to be really important so he called the time and temperature number and set his watch to the correct time. While in his office he set the voice mail system time as well. Next, he went back to the phone room and set the phone switch time to two minutes earlier than the correct time to compensate for his plan for tomorrow. On his way back to his office Rick encountered Larry heading for the elevator.

"Have a good evening, Larry," Rick said, knowing how much his niceness would irritate Larry.

"Yeah, right," Larry grunted, clearly irritated.

Larry got into the elevator, leaving Rick standing there smiling.

I'm going to wreck your plan and nail you, Rick thought.

He had one last clock to set-the one on Larry's fax machine. Rick let himself into Suite 415 and unplugged the tone generator. He plugged the fax line in and then reset Larry's fax machine to the same time as the phone system, two minutes earlier than actual time. He also noted the name appearing on the fax machine, something he had forgotten to do before. Rick quickly left the office and headed out to the Blazer, ready to get home and undertake perhaps the most difficult part of the plan. Talking Kathy into letting Mack and Davis help was certainly going to stretch his limited persuasive skills. He could not be sure he had logic and reason on his side and without those he could not be sure his convictions were in order.

Rick pulled into the driveway at about seven o'clock, took a deep breath and walked into the house. Kathy ran up to him, giving Rick such a strong hug that he knew she was really worried.

"You didn't call. I was starting to worry," Kathy said.

"Oh, damn, I'm sorry. I guess my head is so full thoughts that I plain forgot. I'm really sorry," replied Rick, embarrassed at his forgetfulness.

"It's okay. You know how my mind can think of the worst possible thing that can happen," she said.

"Yeah, getting that ability from your grandma doesn't always help," said Rick with a grin.

"True, but that doesn't make it go away. So what kept you?"

Rick kissed her and said, "I found out about a secret fax coming in to Larry and I'm going to intercept it. Now, I think everything is going fairly well, but I need to talk to you about something."

"I don't think I'm going to like this," Kathy said with a sigh.

"I don't think you will either, but it's really important," Rick replied. Continuing, he said, "I'm very concerned about the FBI doing anything in time. They think I'm just another crackpot with a conspiracy theory. Now that they are poking into my past I'm beginning to feel like the bad guy. We need to be ready to act if they don't."

"I see your point, but I have the feeling there is more to it, now," Kathy observed.

"Okay, here is the deal. I think I need Mack and Davis to help me be sure I can pull this off. If I can't find the canister in time the entire city is in danger. It's too big a risk to do it myself and I can't trust anyone else outside of this family," Rick said, trying to sound convincing.

"Damn it, Rick. You're getting us in this way too deep," exploded Kathy.

"I know, but I can't figure out a better way."

"Well, you had better, because you are not going to get our sons involved in this mess," Kathy retorted.

"Kathy, I don't want this anymore than you do, but I have to have some help. The only other person I can think of to help is my old friend from the days in Montana, Nate Reilly."

"Well, get Mr. Reilly down here."

"It's not that easy. They try to be out of communication with the rest of the world. I have to be careful that I don't lead the Mafia to them again, too."

"Do what it takes, Rick, just don't involve Davis and Mack," Kathy said firmly.

Rick replied, "The only way to contact Nate is by letter and even then he might not read it. I can't put Randy Flanagan on the return address. On top of that he couldn't get here in time. I really need the boys for this. I don't have a choice."

"I just don't like it at all," replied Kathy, wavering a bit.

"Kathy, I'll do everything I can to protect them. I'll also try to contact Nate in case I need more help in the future," promised Rick.

Kathy let her head drop and said, "Okay, Rick. I hope you know what you are doing." After a pause she added, "If something happens to one of the boys, I hope our marriage can stand it."

"I'll take care of you and the boys," Rick promised.

"I do think Davis and Mack will have to know the whole story. We can't ask them to help without knowing why we have to do it this way," Kathy said.

"Yes, I totally agree about telling them the whole story. It's time for me to trust all of you," Rick replied, relieved that this went over. Sometimes Kathy really surprised him and this was one of those times.

"I'll talk to Mack and Davis when Davis gets home tomorrow night. Now, I think it would be a good idea to get as much rest as possible. Let's see if we can get our minds off this for a while and get some sleep."

"Okay," Kathy said soleumly.

# Chapter 22

Rick reported to the FBI at eight Friday morning. He asked for Agent Parker and was immediately greeted by the agent. Instead of the previous days look of contempt, Parker's face showed concern and total seriousness.

"Sit down, Mr. Blaze. I wanted to talk to you about the routine background check we run on informants such as yourself. Your check indicated some discrepancies. According to our two possible scenarios you are either one-hundred-twelve-years-old or came into this world at age nineteen. Either one seems suspect."

"I can explain the problem," Rick answered.

"I was hoping you could. By all means, enlighten me."

Rick spent the next forty-five minutes detailing his life as Randy Flanagan, the Mafia problems, and buying a false identity.

"That's quite a story, Mr. Blaze," Agent Parker said as Rick finished. "It's almost as good as the one you told yesterday."

"Did you ever give any consideration to the possibility that I'm telling the truth? That there really is a plot against the United States?" Rick asked point blank.

"Not really. But, you do need to stay here while we check out this new tale. All we really know for sure is that you are not Rick Blaze," Parker replied curtly.

"I need to be out of here by nine-thirty. I have an appointment," Rick said, noting that it was already nine and he needed to be at Austin Executive Suites for the incoming fax.

"You need to worry more about the FBI than anyone else, Mr. Blaze," Parker huffed.

"Look. I'll give you a choice. You can let me go take care of my business and come back this afternoon or I'll call my attorney right now and the whole process will slow to a crawl."

Parker glared at Rick. He didn't take well to this tactic, but getting a lawyer involved would complicate matters greatly. Parker eyed Rick for a moment and then waved his hand. "Go take care of your business. Be back at one."

"Thanks," Rick answered as he strode out the door.

Rick arrived at his office at nine-twenty. He followed his ritual of walking all through the suites, making sure everything was in its place and all the floors were clean. As he passed suite 415 a shiver went up his back and he had to gather all his resolve to push the doubts out of his mind. Rick continued his walk and then went to his office.

He unlocked his fireproof file cabinet and thumbed the folders until he came to the one marked Montana. Rick pulled out the sheet with Nate's address and sat down at his computer. It was hard to think of dragging Nate back into his life after the close call with the Mafia many years ago. It was also hard to communicate his problems without revealing too much. This was not something you just blurted out in a letter. Rick completed the short letter that included a private telephone number for Nate to call. This number rang only into Rick's office and went to a secret voicemail box if the call was not answered. Rick addressed the envelope and left the return address blank. Instead of running it through the postal meter he owned, Rick put a stamp on the envelope and took the elevator to the first floor where there was a mail drop.

Rick returned to his office stared at his watch as it turned to 9:45. It was time to start his plan. Rick went into the phone room and checked the fax machine and all the connections. Then, he programmed the fax machine to show the same name and telephone number as Larry's fax. At 9:55 Rick pulled the wires that ran to Larry's fax machine from the Dmark and punched down the wires to his fax machine in their place. This would result in Larry's incoming fax being received by Rick's machine. Larry would not know the phone line was down unless he picked up the receiver and that would block the incoming fax so Rick had high hopes the missing dial tone would not be discovered.

At exactly 10:00 the fax machine started up and Rick was relieved when the cover sheet said there was only one more page to transmit. At the instant the second page was received Rick took scissors and sliced off the top part of both pages, the part that had the sending fax's number and name printed on it. He quickly reprogrammed his fax with Rene's name and number, pulled the wires from his fax machine and replaced the wires to Larry's office, giving Larry's fax its correct phone connection again. Again moving as fast as possible, Rick punched down his fax machine on his own fax line, inserted the fax from Rene, dialed Larry's number and pressed the start button. The fax pages moved smoothly through the old fax machine, giving Rick great relief when the transmission was completed. Larry should have received what he thought was the fax from Rene at almost exactly 10:00, complete with the proper identifying name and number of Rene's machine.

Rick turned his attention to the fax containing the formula to the neutralizing agent and realized he still had a problem. From his limited knowledge of chemistry even Rick could tell the formula was in some kind of code. Nothing was ever easy, thought Rick, trying at the same time to plan his next step. Who could he get to decipher the formula? The person must have math skills, possible computer skills, an inquisitive mind, knowledge of chemistry and experience in decoding. Only people in the government had all these skills and he could not talk to any of them. Suddenly an alternative hit him; he had two sons with all the needed skills except for the decoding experience. Granted, this one shortcoming was probably the most important, but he could still let them give it a try.

Larry Thomas looked at the fax from Rene and sighed. Rene was so paranoid that he never seemed to trust anyone. However, he did trust Larry more than most so that put Larry in a position he was very comfortable with-trusted employee and advisor. When all this shook out Larry would be Rene's right hand man, a very powerful position. Larry stopped his daydreaming and went out into the hall to copy the formula. His fax machine used thermal paper that was prone to fade after some time so he felt more comfortable if he immediately copied any incoming fax. As he put his identifying code into the copier provided by Austin Executive Suites Larry cursed under his breath about having to give Rick Blaze the twelve cents that the one copy would cost him. There was just something about that guy that got under Larry's skin, something Larry could not readily explain.

Larry ran the fax through the shredder and went back into his office. He folded the formula several times, placed it into a protective pouch and slid the pouch into a pocket in the special belt he wore around his waist and under his shirt. This special belt also carried the vials of the neutralizing agent Larry always carried on his person. Larry started organizing the files and papers that he was planning to take to Oklahoma City after the canister drop was accomplished. Nothing of any importance would be left in the office, but it would not look like he completely cleared out. Hopefully, he would not have to return and the assumption would be that they were scared off by the deadly water problems of Austin.

Rick left for lunch at 11:30 and headed for the container store. He was working under the assumption that the FBI might not help. He hoped he would find something to put the canister in that was airtight and solid. He found some Tupperware style containers of various sizes that should work. They were air tight, but could be easily opened and thus would need to be secured with duct tape. Rick purchased several sizes of the containers with the hope that he could put the canister in several layers of containers, each providing yet another layer of security for the deadly chemicals. Rick was now set for action. All that remained was to get Mack and Davis into the plan and be sure the boat and Jet Skis were fueled and ready. There would be plenty of time for the boats and Jet Skis tomorrow.

Arriving at FBI headquarters promptly at one, Rick was immediately greeted by Agent Parker.

"I checked out your Chicago Mafia story and there are some problems," said Parker.

"Oh, have there been other people claiming to be Randy Flanagan showing up at FBI offices?" asked Rick indignantly.

"No, but we do have a shortage of information and no

pictures."

"What does that mean?"

"It means there was a fire in the Chicago office fifteen years ago and the Flanagan files were destroyed," Parker explained somewhat sheepishly.

"Great, this gets better and better. So, since the files were burned up you think I'm lying," Rick observed.

"Not really. We checked the local newspapers archives and confirmed that the story you told is true. The picture in the paper could be you."

"Okay, so now what? Are you going to check out Worldwide Water and their plan?" Rick asked hopefully.

"Sure, it's in the mill."

"In the mill? You're not getting it. The canister drop is early Sunday morning," Rick barked, his face beginning to turn red.

Ignoring this outburst, Parker said, "We would like to rebuild our files on the Gino Carlucci case. I want to set up a series of interviews with you and others that were involved. Carlucci is still in prison and recreating the files will be useful at future parole hearings. Besides, your help may get you off our possible subversive list."

"Why on earth am I on the possible subversive list?" Rick asked incredulously.

Parker spoke as though the answer was obvious. "Leaving the protection of the FBI to join a Montana militia and securing a false ID doesn't look particularly good, Mr. Blaze."

Rick took a deep breath to control his anger. "If I was a subversive, why would I come in here and tell you my story?"

"We'll get to issues like that soon enough. Are you willing to cooperate, Mr. Blaze?"

"Yeah, sure. Can I go now? I have a business to run," Rick answered wearily.

"Yes. You can go now. But, I should warn you, we'll be watching," Parker replied.

"Yeah, the wrong people," Rick retorted.

Rick left the FBI offices resigned to the fact that he was the object of their attention instead of Larry Thomas.

Rick returned to Austin Executive Suites determined to thwart Larry Thomas and Worldwide Water. His biggest challenge today was to convince the boys to help and get everyone, including Kathy, to fully understand the plan. As people came and went from his office that afternoon, Rick tried mightily but often failed to concentrate on whatever problem they brought up. He quickly realized that the best way to deal with his lack of concentration was to write down the person and the problem and deal with it on Monday. All he could really think about were the things he had to do and the things that could go wrong. He was playing with his family's safety and the lives of many people in Austin.

Rick was being hit with pangs of guilt that maybe he had not done enough to convince the FBI and perhaps people would die because of it. As all this raced through his mind he struggled to regain his perspective and review his situation from a rational point of view. He left his office and went into the kitchen area to get a soft drink. As he engaged in some idle chitchat with a few of his tenants and sipped a Pepsi Rick's perspective did indeed return. Feeling sure he really had no choice now, Rick again believed totally in his plan.

Rene Charlton placed a call overseas to the private number at the Baghdad Chemical Weapons Plant.

A voice answered in Arabic and Rene replied "Habid? This is Rene."

"Oh, hello, Rene. I am glad you have called. I was wondering if all was going well."

"Yes, my friend, all is going very well," replied Rene.

"The drop will be tomorrow night, so I would suggest that you make your announcement at a time corresponding to our Sunday morning," Rene continued.

"Are you sure you can count on your people in Austin? They will not let you down at the last minute, will they?" Habid questioned.

"They are my best people. I trust them completely, or at least as much as I trust anyone. Larry and Ed will carry out their orders exactly as I have instructed them and then they'll move on to the next city to get ready to accelerate the plan when I tell them to," said Rene.

"Wonderful," cheered Habid. "I will put the finishing touches on the announcement speech I am preparing for Saddam. This will be a great victory for Iraq and a terrible defeat for the United States. You and I will reap the rewards of this victory. We make quite a team, Rene, quite a team."

"Yes, Habid, we'll be the victorious team. Our partnership will go down in history," Rene said, all the while thinking about how much better it would turn out for Rene than Habid. Continuing Rene spoke, "I must go now, Habid. I have many things to oversee. I will watch CNN for Saddam's speech."

"I must go now also. May Allah be with you and your men. Goodbye," said Habid.

# Chapter 23

Rick pulled into the driveway and was pleased to see that everyone was at home. Kathy's car was in the garage and Davis and Mack's cars were out front. He felt a surge of happiness at having his whole family together. It was getting harder and harder to get them all together in the same place at the same time. Rick bounded in the door to greet his family and saw them all in the living room. He kissed Kathy and hugged each of the boys.

"So how's school going, Davis?" Rick inquired.

"Fine, Dad. I'm making good grades and having fun."

"And the job? Is it still fun?" questioned Rick.

"Yeah, working at the movie theater is really fun, as far as jobs go. The hours work out great with my schedule," Davis said.

"Mack, how about you? What was your day like?"

"Great, Dad. After school I went out to the lake. It was windy so I practiced some crosswind landings in the lake while I still have the floats on my plane. I really get a kick out of water landings, especially when I can see the faces of the people watching."

"Well, Kathy, are you ready to fill the boys in on our adventure?"

"Rick, I'm ready for you to fill them in, but I wouldn't call it an adventure. I would call it a nightmare," Kathy answered.

"Mom's right," Rick said. "We are involved in a nightmare. I'm afraid that I have inadvertently gotten us involved in quite a mess. The only way I can think of solving the problem and being responsible citizens calls for us to take a terrible risk."

"What gives, Dad?" Davis quizzed.

"Yeah, Dad, what is going on?" Mack asked.

"Okay, here it is," Rick said. "I was messing around with some electronic surveillance stuff at the office and discovered a plan by one of our tenants to poison the water supply of Austin and other cities in order to help the Iraqis defeat the United States or at least distract us. They plan to start with Austin by dropping a canister of some chemical weapon into Lake Travis tomorrow night. The chemical will be released into the lake slowly and get into the water supply. Apparently people will begin to get sick within about a day and possibly die within three days."

"That's a sick plan," interrupted Davis, "but I don't see what the big problem is. Really all we have to do is let the police know what is going on and they'll stop it."

Rick responded with a sigh. "Yes, it would seem to be that easy. However, I've tried going to the FBI and because of certain details from my past, they are not taking it seriously."

"What's in your past that would freak out the FBI? You never even get a parking ticket," huffed Mack.

"I'm sure you have noticed that I have quite an aversion to dealing with any police. I've never explained why, but now I feel I must. I've been carrying around a secret that even your mother didn't know about until recently. This is a story that can't go beyond the four of us. It is a life-and-death matter that will never go away as long as I'm alive."

"Come on, Dad, spill the beans. You're creeping us out," Davis blurted out.

"Okay, here it is," Rick replied, "Here's the whole story. My name is not really Rick Blaze. At least it didn't use to be. I had to change my name and disappear from my life as I knew it when I was about Davis' age."

Rick went on to relate the whole story of his past, taking over an hour to cover all the details. The boys listened with wide-eyed amazement, not knowing whether to believe this wild tale. It would be like their dad to tell a whopper every now and then to see if they would believe him, but he always made sure they knew in the end that he was just having fun with them. He was not giving any indication that this was just a story he made up. Eventually Davis and Mack seemed to believe Rick was not only telling them the truth, but also that it was hurting him very much to tell it.

Finally, Rick said, "Well, that's the real story of my life before I met your mother. It's why I don't trust the police and why I have absolutely no family. I know in my gut that the Mafia will find me if I give them half a chance. I don't think they are actively looking for me still, but I think they'll always keep their eyes and ears open to find someone like me that did a lot of damage to one of their families. If there's one thing that will get opposing Mafia families to work together it's to do away with a person that has ratted out a top Mafia member. Now the FBI is more concerned with my false identity and the time I spent with a militia than the plan I discovered. I can't think of a way to stop it without involving the three of you."

Still not completely sold on the story Davis said, "This is all a bunch of hooey, isn't it, Dad? I mean, it sounds so ridiculous.

You're just an ordinary person, not someone involved with some Mafia."

"Yeah," Mack chimed in, "you had us going for a minute there."

"Boys," Kathy said, "I'm afraid your father is telling the truth. I didn't want to believe it either, but it's true."

"Well, then, what really is our name?" quizzed Mack.

"Our name is Blaze. Nothing is changing. We're all the same people with the same names," replied Rick.

"We're the same people, only now we are being hunted by the Mafia and we have to risk our lives to save everyone in Austin. Isn't that what you mean, Dad?" scoffed Davis.

Mack blurted out, "We aren't the same people at all. I don't know who we are."

Rick got up and hugged the two boys.

He said, "We're the Blazes. We're a family. That's who we are and who we always will be."

Kathy joined the group and said, "Your father's right. We're the same family we were yesterday.

Davis said, "Okay, if we're going to do this as a family, we need to know what to do."

"Yeah, tell us what you need us to do. We all want to help you and we certainly don't want anything to happen to the people of Austin," said Mack.

"Thanks, guys," Rick replied. "Here's what I need from you. The chemical drop will be at 2:00 a.m. Sunday morning from a Cessna like Mack's into Lake Travis. I know precisely where the drop is planned to occur. The chemical canister is designed to float and then begin releasing the chemical after an hour in the water. I want us to be waiting for the drop and grab the canister. I'm hoping that when nothing happens these people will give up this terrible idea. Maybe if it isn't easy they will stop pursuing this venture. So here's my plan, such as it is. We try to get a good night's sleep, get up about mid morning and go to the lake house. We'll check the fuel levels in the boat and Jet Skis and make sure they are running good. I have a container to put the canister in and a map marked with the planned drop area. I've also acquired several high-powered flashlights. I'll be the one to handle the canister once we locate it, because I have some protective clothing to wear. In order to stay in touch with each other I have four walkie-talkies on the same frequency, but I must remind you to be careful because they are not waterproof."

"Hey, Dad," Davis interrupted, "what are we going to do with the canister once we retrieve it?"

"Well, Davis, I thought we might take a family vote and send it to whoever we are most mad at. I'm just kidding of course," Rick replied after a pause and a grin. Continuing he said, "Actually, I'm not sure what to do with the canister. I guess I'll worry more about that once we get it. Maybe the FBI will believe me if I give it to them."

"One would think that would get their attention," said Kathy.

"Assuming we pull this off," Rick continued, "I have one more project for the two of you."

Davis jumped in with his comments. "How about if we put on our blue tights and red capes and do something like ridding the world of all nuclear weapons?"

"Yeah, and then we could find a cure for the common cold," chimed in Mack.

"No, I'm sorry, boys," Rick retorted. "Those things will have to wait a couple of weeks."

Kathy rolled her eyes and said, "Can't any of you be

serious about anything?"

"We could, Kathy, but then we would not be our lovable selves. Besides, I get it from Mack and Davis. It's their fault," Rick chuckled. "Anyway, what I have for you needs to be done right after we get the canister. There is a neutralizing agent for these chemicals and I've intercepted the formula. However, the formula is in some kind of code and I thought two smart computer wizards like you could decipher it."

"I bet we can figure it out, Dad," Mack said eagerly.

"What we really need to figure out is how Dad is getting all this stuff. I didn't think he was this sneaky. I have to wonder if he's spying on us too," Davis teased.

Rick replied, "Most parents don't really want to know everything their kids are doing. If we did know everything both of you would be grounded all the time and your mother and I would have never had a moment alone. Now, I think it's time for us to get some sleep and be fresh for tomorrow. Here's a copy of the formula for each of you, but don't look at it until tomorrow. Goodnight, boys. See you in the morning."

"Good night Mom and Dad," Mack and Davis replied.

"Good night. I love both of you," said Kathy.

"Love you too, Mom," they said as they bounded off for their rooms.

The phone rang in the hotel room in Georgetown.

"Hello, this is Larry."

"Larry, Rene here. How is everything going?"

"Well, Rene, all things are going well. Ed and I are just going to take it easy today and go to the airport after dinner and get everything ready. We'll make the drop at precisely 2:00 a.m. and be on our way to Oklahoma City. There's no way for us to fail. It's just too easy and nobody has a clue about what we are up to."

"Good, Larry, just keep it that way. Habid is going to make his announcement Sunday morning and he has a lot riding on this plan. I sure wouldn't want to have that crazy idiot Saddam mad at me," cautioned Rene.

"Me either," replied Larry. "I think it could be really bad for your health."

"I can see you realize the consequences he faces if something goes wrong. I have complete faith in you and Ed, Larry. Good luck tonight. Give me a call in the morning after you arrive in Oklahoma City."

"Okay, Rene. Don't worry about us. We'll have the people of Austin in panic and terror according to plan."

# Chapter 24

Saturday morning came and the Blaze family awoke after a restless night of little sleep. They milled around, barely speaking and all of them tried to act like it was just another day. After lunch they drove out to their house on Lake Travis. It was a small two-bedroom cabin that the Blazes had purchased as their weekend getaway. They spent the afternoon checking the boat, the Jet Skis, and all the other equipment. Everything was gassed up, oil checked, batteries charged, and the gear stowed on the Chris-Craft. The boat was old, but in excellent shape. It was a 42 foot 1952 Chris-Craft Commander that Rick and Kathy had restored to the former glory of the boat that was top of the line in 1952. It was a wood boat that now gleamed after hours of sanding and coat after coat of polyurethane finish had been applied. The old engines had been replaced with a pair of new, more powerful engines that enabled the old boat to hit a very respectable 25 knots. Air conditioning, microwaves and most electronic equipment had not existed in 1952 so Rick had rewired the boat and installed a more powerful generator to accommodate the new amenities. The galley had been upgraded to specifications that made life at sea much easier than the original owners enjoyed. The staterooms retained the look of 1952 with the deeply grained wood and highly polished brass fixtures.

Since Austin Executive Suites had provided the funds for the boat, the name *Suite Deal* had been painted on her transom. Rick and Kathy loved to cruise around Lake Travis, exploring coves and spending relaxing and romantic nights aboard the splendid old boat. Now the boat would be called on to perform her most important task. As the platform to launch the search and recovery of the canister, the Chris-Craft had to perform flawlessly. It had to carry the gear, tow the Jet Skis and be the communications center for the operation. Rick rechecked the oil, charged up the batteries completely and started the engines up every hour just to keep them warm. Davis and Mack wanted to take the Jet Skis out and ride around for a while, but Rick didn't want to risk one of the boys getting hurt or one of the Jet Skis breaking so he made them stay around the house.

Kathy prepared sandwiches and snacks and filled the boat's refrigerator with the food as well as some assorted drinks. She also did the bulk of the worrying for the family. Being the only female in the household for all these years had been hard, but she had long since gotten used to it. The three men in the family seemed to deal with their fears and worries by turning everything into a joke. At times the jokes were funny and tension relieving, but frequently the lack of seriousness got on Kathy's nerves.

The hamburgers smelled good and the family ate well, especially Mack and Davis, who always seemed to eat well. Rick had always found it relaxing to cook burgers outside on the grill and it did seem to be at least a little relaxing now. Rick replayed the plan for what seemed like the millionth time and the family retired to their rooms to get what rest they could. At Rick's instruction three alarm clocks were set for 1:00 a.m. He reasoned that the boat was ready and it would take about 15 minutes to get to the drop location, leaving them about 30 minutes to wait. Rick thought it would be best to cut the time a little close instead of waiting for an hour or more for the drop. They were nervous enough and waiting long periods of time would just make it worse.

At 1:00 a.m. the alarms all went off and the family jumped out of bed and into their clothes. They hustled out to the *Suite Deal* and after Rick started her up the boys released the dock lines and secured the ropes towing the Jet Skis. As they moved toward the drop zone Kathy insisted that they all join in a prayer. Although they had not been a particularly religious family, this night a prayer seemed completely in order. They held hands, bowed their heads as Kathy said a short prayer asking for protection and safety for her family. A renewed sense of confidence seemed to surge through each of them. Was it God's power or just their adrenaline that was flowing into their bodies? They didn't know and each had their own idea, but all were ready for the task at hand.

As Kathy kept the *Suite Deal* on course, Rick and the boys put on the dry suits they used for cold water skiing and Jet Skiing. These suits were worn over regular clothes and kept the person completely dry. They also had waterproof boots and used the long plastic gloves that Rick had bought. Although Rick was to be the only one to touch the canister he wanted the boys to be as protected as possible. As they neared the spot that Rick had picked, all the boat lights were turned off and the final preparations were made. The lake was still so they did not drop the anchor. The boat was shut off and Rick and the boys got their walkie-talkies and lights ready. Rick had a painting respirator and the Tupperware containers already on his Jet Ski.

Rick said, “It’s 1:45 a.m. so we should hear the airplane shortly. When it gets here I want everyone to be quiet and listen for the splash of the canister. Also, follow the path of the plane if you can. I think he’ll fly fairly low so his drop will bc accurate. If we hear the splash we can head straight toward the spot. However, if we don’t hear it we’ll start searching in concentric circles like I described earlier.”

As Rick finished talking a dull roar could be heard in the distance. They all recognized it as the familiar sound of a Cessna 172 only instead of Mack flying over this sound underscored the seriousness of this deadly game they were playing. The four of them watched and listened as the airplane flew over the boat. As they strained their eyes and ears the Cessna flew level for a short ways and then started a sharp climb.

“Okay,” Rick yelled. “Let’s go. We have to assume that the drop was made just before he started climbing. Kathy, go to the bow and shine the floodlight toward that spot. That’ll give us a point to start our circles from.”

Rick ran toward the Jet Skis and saw that Mack and Davis were already starting theirs. Rick put on his respirator and followed the boys toward the spot. He glanced at his watch and saw that almost five minutes had already passed. They quickly arrived at the spot Kathy had lit up and started making circles around the spot. Each of the bikes was about five feet apart, allowing them to cover about fifteen feet at a pass. They had decided that this would allow them to cover enough area in half an hour to be sure they found the canister. They circled and circled and found nothing. Rick looked at his watch and was shocked to see that thirty minutes had already passed!

He got on his walkie-talkie and said, “We’re running out of time. We need to expand our circles. Let’s move to ten feet apart.

We've got to find it."

"You don't have much time left," Kathy yelled.

"I know, I know," Rick replied.

For ten more minutes they circled without finding the canister and then suddenly Davis called out, "I think I see it!"

He was speaking into the walkie-talkie, but Rick and Mack heard him plainly without the electronic device. Rick went over to join Davis and saw what was obviously the canister. He glanced at his watch and saw that forty-five minutes had passed. He waved the boys off and grabbed the Tupperware containers from the back of the Jet Ski. Rick was thankful that the lake was so calm that night. He was able to pull up beside the floating canister. He leaned over and let the canister gently float into the smallest container. Rick quickly closed and sealed the lid and pulled it out of the water.

"I have it," he yelled.

Rick then put the container inside of the larger container, sealed it, and continued to do this until the canister was inside of five Tupperware containers. With a great sigh of relief Rick and the boys headed back to the boat. Aboard the boat Rick wrapped the outside container securely in duct tape to prevent it from opening. As soon as he finished this task he sank to the deck of the old boat and breathed a huge sigh of relief.

Rick looked at Davis and Mack and said, "I'm sure glad that I brought the two of you along. I don't think I would have found it by myself."

"Glad to help," replied Davis.

"Yeah, no problem," said Mack.

As they headed back to the lake house Kathy, Mack and Davis all stared at Rick and at virtually the same time said, "Now what are you going to do with the container and the chemicals?"

"Well," Rick replied, "I need to keep it away from people and water so I guess the best spot would be in our shed at the lake. I'll take it to the FBI later. Has anybody got any better ideas?"

Hearing no better ideas Rick decided on the shed. They arrived back at the dock and started unloading. Rick went immediately to the shed and placed the containers inside. Next he burned the gloves he had been wearing since those had come the closest to the canister. When everything was put back in its place they all went back to bed and slept soundly for the first time in days.

# Chapter 25

Sunday morning dawned in Oklahoma City and Larry Thomas was in high spirits. He even looked forward to calling Rene Charlton this morning.

"Hello?" said Rene.

"Rene, this is Larry."

"So, I assume the drop went as planned?"

Larry proudly stated, "Yes, perfectly. I must give you credit for a simple, yet foolproof plan. The city of Austin is in for quite a surprise."

Rene impatiently said, "Yes, it's a good plan, but there's much more to do. I must go now, Larry."

"Do you want me to prepare for the next drop?"

"We'll talk about that later in the week, after we see how things go in Austin," replied Rene.

"Yeah, okay. Talk to you later," said Larry as he hung up the phone.

Rene dialed an overseas number and waited for someone to answer.

When the answer came in Arabic Rene said, "Habid, it's Rene."

"Ah, Rene, my friend. How goes our little project? A success, I trust," said Habid al Safreed.

"My man in Austin reports a complete success with the chemical drop. We should see the results in a day or two," replied Rene.

"Perfect! I knew you and I could do great things together, Rene. Now that you have done your initial part I have to take the next step in my operation here. I will leave you to your own business. Goodbye, Rene."

"Goodbye, Habid."

Habid dialed a number known to only a few in Iraq.

"Hello, this is Habid al Safreed. I must speak to him immediately. It is vitally important. Saddam will surely have you shot if he thinks you kept the information I have from him for even a few hours."

"Then speak to him you shall. One hour from now," said the man.

One hour later Habid strode purposely into the current palace that Saddam Hussein was staying at. Saddam had thirty or so palaces scattered throughout Iraq, but Habid was one of the few to always know which one he was residing in.

A grand door opened and an aide beckoned Habid to come in.

"Habid, what brings you to my chambers with talk of such importance?" asked Saddam with interest.

"Your Excellency, I have initiated a plan to bring the United States to its knees and divert its attentions away from our occupation of Kuwait and Saudia Arabia. This plan is already in action and the results will begin to be seen tomorrow."

"You have started this plan of yours without my approval?" bellowed Saddam.

"Yes, but I have good reasons. I did not think we could carry out this plan unless it could be done in complete secrecy and by someone bold enough to think it up and take it on."

"Habid, tell me your plan. If it is a good one I may not kill you for your deceit."

Habid responded, "I have developed a deadly chemical weapon that is so easy to deploy that it cannot fail. I have made alliances with a company in the United States that is owned by a Frenchman. This company has taken delivery of the chemical I have developed and is injecting it into water sources in various cities. The chemical is potent enough that in even small quantities a city's entire water source can be infected easily. In two days the people who drink the water will be very sick and one day later they will begin to die. As this happens all over the United States the leaders will begin to worry about their internal problems and not be so concerned about what we are doing."

"This *is* a good plan, Habid, one I will be glad to take credit for myself," Saddam ranted. "When will the plan be ready to start? I am anxious to see many Americans die."

Habid replied, "We made our first attack two days ago against a city called Austin in the state of Texas. The people of Austin should be finding themselves very sick as we speak and tomorrow they will begin to die. I am calculating a death count of at least 100,000 from this first attack alone. Other cities will be attacked within the week. I doubt that the Americans will ever be able to figure out how we are contaminating the water supplies, so they will not be able to stop us."

"I will go to CNN immediately with a prediction of mass retribution against the United States," Saddam boasted, "then I will have the whole world in fear of me. And you, my friend Habid, will rise to great power in my regime. I am very proud of you."

"Thank you, your Excellency. I will always serve you and Iraq."

Sunday passed quietly for the Blaze family. They talked little about the previous day's events, although the boys were interested in the methods Rick used to accumulate all his information. They were proud of their father for his cleverness as well as for his trust and faith in the two of them. They were also proud of their mother for going through such an ordeal so stoically. Sometimes she really was "one of the boys". Mack and Davis were eager to begin deciphering the formula for the neutralizing agent and so the family returned home to the city Sunday after lunch.

Davis and Mack went up to Mack's room.

"So, Mack, what do we know about deciphering a coded formula?" asked Davis.

"I suspect we know very little. I hope we don't let Dad down on this. He's counting on us," replied Mack a little nervously.

"He just wants us to give it a shot. So let's see if we can come up with anything. Most codes seem to be based on mathematics or some kind of letter or word substitution. I doubt these guys are some kind of code wizards," said Davis.

"Yeah, they probably just came up with something easy so these field guys could deal with it," replied Mack hopefully.

"Crank up that supercomputer of yours and let's see what the Internet has to say about codes," said Davis.

After a couple of hours Davis said, "Let's stop for a while.

My eyes are starting to cross. Besides, I have some homework to do before class tomorrow. Email me if you make any progress."

"Okay, I'll keep after it. I don't have any homework to do," said Mack.

"You never have any homework to do. I don't see how you make straight A's and have a 98 average when you don't do any work," said Davis with a touch of envy.

"I have homework. I do it at school. It doesn't take very long, especially if you don't waste time yakking with your friends and tormenting the teachers," said Mack indignantly.

"Are you saying I wasted time when I was in high school? Actually all that yakking and tormenting was very entertaining, just like school is supposed to be," replied Davis.

"I think Principal Mason has a different view of the purpose of high school," Mack said.

"Hey, Mason and I got along great, especially when I made first team all-district in basketball," Davis huffed.

"Wow, it's been almost a week since you mentioned you were first team all-district. You're slipping Davis."

"Yeah, well, I'll catch up next week," replied Davis with a smirk.

Mack changed the subject by saying, "I'll scan the formula into my computer and give you the hard copy so you can work on it too."

"Okay, good plan, bro," replied Davis.

# Chapter 26

Monday morning Rick went to the FBI at 8:00 a.m. The agent manning the reception desk eyed the Tupperware container wrapped almost completely in duct tape.

"I'd like to speak to Agent Parker," Rick said flatly.

The man dialed a number on his phone, asked for Parker, and replaced the handset.

"Parker's not in right now. I can have him call you."

"I really need to speak to him. He'll be interested in what's in here," Rick replied, holding out the container.

"Well, if it's that important I can have Agent Parker materialize right here in front of us," the man said with a smirk.

"That's real funny. Please have him call Rick Blaze. He has my number."

"I'm sure he does."

Rick left the FBI disgusted, as usual. He was not about to leave the container with anyone except Parker for fear they would open it carelessly. He drove to Austin Executive Suites muttering about the use of his tax dollars.

Rick hoped the worst was over and that Larry and his group would give up their crazy idea when it didn't work. As he walked around the office he noticed that all the talk was about a possible confrontation with Iraq. There were rumors on every television channel of a statement from Saddam some time today. Monday afternoon a buzz went around Austin Executive Suites about a news flash on CNN at 3:00 PM Saddam Hussein had a message for the United States and he wanted everyone to hear it. The next couple of hours went by slowly as everyone waited to see what the madman had to say this time. Finally, it was 3:00 PM and time for the news flash. As all eyes were on the TV set in the main conference room, Saddam threatened all the people of the United States with an attack unlike any the U.S. had ever experienced. The frightening thing was that Saddam seemed so sure of himself, like he really could pull this off. Rick thought that perhaps Saddam was talking about the attack he had just thwarted. Hopefully, there was not another awful plan being launched against the United States.

Rick called Kathy to get her reaction. "Did you see the CNN report?"

"Yes," she replied. "Is he talking about the canister we picked up?"

"I think so. I guess we will know more soon," Rick answered.

"At least the FBI will believe you when they analyze the contents of the canister," Kathy said hopefully.

"Yeah, if they ever see it."

"I thought you were taking it there this morning."

"I did, but Parker wasn't there and I couldn't leave it with the guy at the front desk. They might have opened it right there and killed everybody in the building," Rick explained.

"What are you going to do?"

"I'm waiting for Parker to call me back. Then I'll take it to him."

That night there was a lot of talk on the news about Saddam's bold threats, but nothing was actually happening. This was especially true in Austin, where there were no sicknesses, no panic and no fear. Basically, life just went on in Austin. This was wonderful news to Rick and his family, but puzzling to Larry, Ed, Rene and Habid. The telephone lines fairly burned up with speculation, anger and especially desperation on the part of Habid. Surely, they thought, something would happen tomorrow.

Tuesday came and still no illnesses. Also, Rick did not get a call from Agent Parker. He left several more messages for Parker. Wednesday came and still no illnesses. Austin was just rolling along like there never was any threat at all. Rick watched the national news closely for any sign that Larry had struck somewhere else. Mack and Davis kept making progress on the neutralizing formula and Kathy prayed that her family would never have to take such a chance again. Wednesday afternoon Rick's phone rang.

"Blaze, this is Agent Parker. What can I do for you?"

"Have you figured out that the tape I brought you describes the attack Saddam is talking about?"

"Actually, at last count there are 131 conspiracy plans that fit the bill. That's why it took me a couple of days to get back to you."

"I have the canister that we fished out of the lake. Coincidently, the situation was just as the tape described. Do you want your lab guys to take a look at it?"

"Oh, yeah. The Tupperware container. From the front desk agent's description, I thought you were bringing me brownies."

"Yeah, right."

"Why didn't you leave it here?"

Rick sighed and said, "I was afraid one of you non-believers would open it improperly and kill everyone in the building."

"Good point. You can never be too careful with stuff in a Tupperware container. I have to caution my wife about that all the time," Parker snickered.

"Maybe I should go to the newspaper or one of the TV stations," Rick offered.

"No, don't do that. Bring it down and we'll take a look at it. I promise the lab guys will be careful," Parker responded.

After hanging up, Rick rushed to the FBI office. He turned the canister over to Parker only after the agent again promised to open it in a safe environment.

Thursday arrived and things began to change. At 8:30 Thursday morning Rick was dismayed to see Larry and Ed walk off the elevator at Austin Executive Suites. They were clearly in foul moods and barely spoke to the receptionists.

Rick instantly thought, I had better check the tape recorder and microphone setup. He went into the phone room and was relieved to see the tape recorder turning as Larry and Ed spoke. Rick desperately wanted to know what was being said, but didn't dare stop the recorder for even a second. He would have to wait until Larry left the office.

Rick went back to his office and called Kathy, "Hi, Kathy. I'm afraid I have bad news. Larry and Ed just showed up here."

"Have you found out what they are up to?" Kathy asked.

"No, I'm going to have to wait until they leave, then I can check the tape."

"What're you going to do if they are here to try again?"

"I don't know, I guess I'll just wait until I see what their plans are," Rick said. Continuing, Rick said, "Let's have lunch together. We've gotten out of that habit the last couple of weeks. How about our favorite Italian food place?"

"Okay, I'll meet you there at 11:45," Kathy replied.

"Great, see you then."

Rick left his office and walked around the Suites. It was the best way to see what was really going on and, besides, he never could sit at a desk for very long at a time.

He stopped and chatted with the receptionists. "What's with Larry and Ed? I thought they were going to be gone for a while."

"They were supposed to be gone for at least a couple of weeks," Sandra answered, "but Larry grumbled something about a problem and said they would be here for a few days. Boy, he's in a worse mood than usual."

"Well, thank goodness Larry would never take a bad mood out on any of us," Rick said as he walked away, leaving both receptionists laughing.

# Chapter 27

Larry dialed the phone and waited as it rang several times.

Finally Rene answered, "Hello?"

"Rene, this is Larry,"

"Well, what have you found out about the problem?"

"Nothing so far. There's no evidence of any of our chemical in the water. I took several samples this morning and it's like we never dropped the canister. I really don't think the chemical ever got into the water so either we missed the water, which I can't come close to believing, or the canister did not release the chemicals properly. We know the chemicals work once they get into the water. The Fort Davis experiment proved that."

Rene said, "Those are the same possibilities we are exploring. We have run exhaustive checks on the Floating Degenerative Suspension Module and it works perfectly every time."

Larry replied, "Just because the FDSM works in the lab doesn't mean it will always work in the field. Maybe there's something in the water in Lake Travis that interferes with the degenerative membrane process."

"We thought of that and we have duplicated the water from the Lake Travis samples you sent us earlier. It makes no difference. You must have missed the lake and dropped the canister on land," Rene accused.

"There's no way we missed the lake. We were only five hundred feet above the lake," Larry retorted.

"Look, Larry, all I know is that you and Ed screwed up the mission and we're in big trouble. We must get back on track as fast as possible so here is the new plan. I want you and Ed to repeat the process with a new canister that will arrive tomorrow. However, this time I don't want you to use your cute little airplane drop scheme. I want you to follow the same time schedule and make the drop in the same place, but I want you to take the FDSM out in a boat and stay within sight of it until it sinks."

Larry replied, "Okay, but why don't we just dump the chemical into the lake and let it start dispersing right away?"

Rene answered, "It's very important that we release the chemicals at the proper rate. Otherwise the chemicals won't be spread evenly throughout the lake. Now, Larry, I don't want any more of your questions. I just want you to follow your orders. You're on shaky ground right now and you know how I frown on failures. There is one more possibility that I have thought of that must be considered. Someone may have found out our plan and is working against us. You need to be prepared for this in the event someone shows up at the next drop, which will be this Sunday at 2:00 a.m. Am I making myself perfectly clear?"

"Yes, Rene, I understand what I have to do. The job will be taken care of this weekend," replied a worried Larry.

"Good, don't fail me again," Rene said and slammed the phone down.

"So what does Frenchy think about all this?" Ed asked.

"He thinks we had better not fail again," Larry said.

"Well, what's our plan?"

Larry explained briefly.

Ed snarled, "We didn't miss the lake! I'd bet my life on it."

"You may be betting your life on the plan working right this time," Larry said. "Rene is pretty upset. Since he is in so tight with the Iraqis he has to be wondering if Saddam is planning some kind of retribution if we fail again," Larry continued. "We'll stay on the lake until we see it sink with our very own eyes."

"Wait a minute," Ed exclaimed. "I don't want to be near that damn thing when it starts releasing the chemical."

"Relax, Ed, we'll be in the boat. It's not an airborne chemical. Rene also suggested that we be prepared in the event of someone else interfering."

"No problem with that," scoffed Ed. "I always carry my 9mm with me."

"Yeah, me too," added Larry. "Go see about getting a boat for the mission. It only needs to be a small one," Larry continued.

"Habid, do you have any last words before you are executed?" bellowed Saddam. "You have made me the laughing stock of America."

Habid meekly replied, "Please, Excellency, give me one more chance. I know the plan will work. My operatives are going to make sure it happens this weekend. I have just talked to the headman and he assures me the plan has no chance of failure this time. By this Tuesday your threats will have come to pass. You will be the great leader of Iraq and the world."

Saddam thought for a minute and said, "Yes, Habid, I will

give you one more chance. But this is the last one. There will be a bullet with your name on it if you fail."

"I understand, your Excellency," Habid said with great relief.

Rick and Kathy met for lunch at one of their favorite lunch spots. Lunch had always been a time of escape from the day-to-day problems of the business. It was a time that no one except the waitperson interrupted.

They chatted about mundane things for a while and then Kathy said, "How are you feeling about revealing your past to us? Are you wishing you had kept the secret going?"

"No, actually I'm quite relieved," replied Rick, "It's been a big load on my mind."

"I'm glad you are relieved, but I have to wonder if there are any more secrets you are keeping from me," Kathy continued.

"Only your Christmas present," Rick said with a laugh.

"I'm serious," she said. "You make a joke out of everything."

"I'm sorry, Kathy, I'll be serious. I really don't have any more secrets. I swear to God. You know I don't do that very often," Rick said.

"Okay, I guess I'll believe you," Kathy said with a sigh. Continuing, she said, "You know, I've been very impressed with your cleverness in the last week. I kind of thought you were a little nuts when you started all that survival gear stuff, but it turns out you had good cause for concern. Did you learn to be suspicious and paranoid while you were with that militia group or are you just naturally this way?"

"A little of both, I suspect. I think the militia group advanced the paranoia and suspicion. But they also gave me some tools to deal with anything that actually panned out. I learned a lot about weapons and fighting, as well as survival techniques. It was actually quite fun because they seemed to have an unlimited supply of ammo for all kinds of guns. We would just go out and shoot up a bunch of targets."

"So why exactly did you decide to leave?" asked Kathy.

"I didn't really buy into their philosophy completely. They had their points, but they went overboard on their solutions. I just wanted to be a normal person with a normal life. I guess I had what I wanted until all this mess started," Rick answered.

Kathy reached across the table and held his hand and said, "We'll get back to normal. I know we will."

"That makes me feel better because you're usually right," said Rick.

# Chapter 28

"Holy crap, Blaze. That is the most powerful toxin my lab guys have ever seen," Parker blurted out when Rick answered his phone.

"Are you starting to believe me?"

"Yeah. I listened to the tape again. This has moved to top priority."

"Larry Thomas and his buddy, Ed Richter, are back in Austin. I think they are going to try something else. I'll check the newest tape when they leave."

"Call me if you find out anything. We'll be watching Mr. Thomas closely."

"I intercepted a fax of a neutralizer serum. It's in some kind of code. Do you want me to fax it to you?" Rick asked.

"Yeah, we'll take a look at it."

Parker gave Rick his fax number and hung up. Rick immediately went to the operations area and faxed the formula.

The afternoon dragged on at Austin Executive Suites and

Rick was given to wild speculations about Larry's next actions. Finally, at about four Larry and Ed left the office, which was a relief to everyone, especially Rick. After Rick retrieved the latest tape and put in a new one, he left the office for the day. He placed the tape in the Blazer's tape player and listened to Larry's conversation with Rene and then with Ed. The rest of the tape was just idle conversations and crude remarks about what the people of Austin were in for. When Larry remarked that he hoped Rick was a big water drinker, Rick felt his whole body tense. As he replayed the part of the tape with the new plan on it, Rick searched his brain for a way to end this madness forever.

Counting on the FBI still seemed to be a risk, at least until they actually did something. He felt he needed to assume the FBI would not stop this latest effort and hoped he could foil yet another attempt. Slowly an idea began to form in his head and this one would not involve his sons and would keep Kathy far away from trouble. It did involve a larger risk for him, but that could not be helped. He drove home, made a copy of the tape, and dropped it off at the FBI office. Returning home, he began to explain his thoughts to Kathy.

"Okay, this is how I see it," Rick said. "They're going to take the canister out to the same spot at the same time, only this time they'll use a boat and stick around to make sure the canister sinks correctly. They're pretty scared of this chemical so they will back off as far as possible."

"Yes," said Kathy, "that's what they are going to do. The big question is what are *you* going to do?"

"I have a plan," Rick answered.

"I was afraid of that. Tell me what it is so I can go ahead and call the loony farm," replied Kathy.

"Okay, here it is. We don't need the boys for this one.

We'll just take the *Suite Deal* out like we are on an evening cruise and anchor a little ways from the drop spot. We'll try to look as innocent as possible. A little before two a.m. we should see their boat approaching the drop spot. At that time I'll have my dive gear on, slip into the water and swim toward them. When they start to back off I'll have a good bearing on the exact spot. I can just swim up under the canister, grab it with some tongs and put it into the same type of containers we used before. By the time I grab it about 15 minutes will have passed and they'll just think the canister sank a little early. They'll go home and wait and nothing will happen and they'll give up."

"Rick, the FBI said they were taking this seriously now. Let them take the chances."

"If they apprehend Larry and get the canister then there is no problem. I just want to be ready in case the FBI screws up."

"Aren't you just a little concerned about being in the water with the canister?" Kathy asked. "After all Larry seems to be quite scared of it."

Rick replied, "I'll have my protective clothes on and the canister shouldn't release anything for another 30 minutes and, besides, I won't be drinking the water. I should be quite safe. So? Are you with me on this?"

"I can't think of a better alternative, so I guess so. I do want one promise from you," Kathy said.

"Okay, what is it?"

"If this doesn't stop them I want you to promise to bring in more outside help. I know that has a risk, but I feel very strongly about this."

Rick sighed and said, "I'm not about to argue about one of your feelings, so I promise to bring in outside help if this does not end it. I did send a letter to Nate Reilly and I hope to hear from him soon."

"I was thinking more about another law enforcement agency."

"Okay, I'll do that, too."

Friday was a busy day for Rick because he had to get more containers and check out his scuba gear. He didn't have a lot of scuba time under his belt, but he had plenty to do this job. Fortunately Lake Travis was one of the best diving lakes in Texas, being both clear and warm. He also scoured many stores for tongs large enough to grasp the canister. He finally found the perfect ones at an industrial supply house. They were designed to handle large items in chemical and plating vats. Then he returned to the container store and bought another set of Tupperware containers.

Rick knew his next problem was to keep Mack and Davis out of the action. They both would be home this weekend and could not be kept from finding out what Rick and Kathy were up to. He would just have to insist they stay away.

Friday afternoon Rick went back to the office and was pleased to find two FBI agents at the receptionist's desk asking for Larry. Sandra indicated that Larry and Ed had not been in all day.

After the two agents left, Rick settled into his desk chair and noticed his phone set indicated a voice mail message on his private line. As he listened to the message his heart leaped.

"Hey, boy, this is old Nate. Sure was good to hear from you. I'll call you back at three."

Rick looked at the time on the phone set and it said 2:45. He would get to talk to Nate in 15 minutes. It seemed more like an hour when the phone rang at exactly three.

"Hello? " said Rick.

"Hey, boy, it's me."

"Nate, it's great to hear from you," gushed Rick.

"Likewise, er, Rick, isn't it?" asked Nate.

"Yeah, it's Rick. Rick Blaze."

"So, what's up? Your letter was pretty cryptic."

"Before I tell you about that, have you all seen any more of those city boys looking for me?" asked Rick.

"No, I guess they knew you moved on and decided not to mess with us anymore," answered Nate.

"Good, that's real good," said a relieved Rick.

"So what's your predicament?"

"I stumbled across a plot by Saddam Hussein and a company in the U.S. to put a deadly chemical in some city's water supply. This stuff will kill anyone who drinks the water," said Rick.

"Is this that stuff Saddam was yakking about on CNN?" Nate asked.

"Yeah, I think so."

"Well, nothing came of it."

"That's because I stopped it."

"Well, good for you, boy," said Nate proudly.

"Yeah, but they are going to try again this weekend. I hoped that if I stopped them they would give up. I'm afraid that if I stop them this weekend they'll keep trying. I guess that's why I need help."

"And you certainly aren't going to the police, are you?" Nate asked.

"Actually, I tried with the FBI and they initially were more concerned with my past. The agent I'm dealing with says he's taking it seriously now, but I haven't seen any real action."

"They have a bad track record with you, boy," Nate said. He paused and continued, "How about if I drift on down to Austin in my pickup? I'm not too keen on flying and I couldn't get there in time to help you this weekend anyway."

"That would be great. I'll look forward to seeing you, Nate," replied Rick.

"I'll call you when I get close to Austin. Just remember one thing-I'm a lot older than the last time we hooked up."

"I'll bet you're as tough as ever, Nate."

"See you soon," Nate said and hung up.

Rick leaned back in his chair and allowed himself to feel better about the events in his life. Now he would not have to go it alone.

Friday night Rick arrived home and saw that Mack and Davis' cars were both in the driveway. He had his mind set on keeping the boys out of trouble, but knew it would be hard.

Opening the door, he shouted, "Hey everyone, I'm home."

Kathy, Mack and Davis all ran into the room immediately.

"Okay, Dad, what's going on? Mom won't tell us anything. She says you are in charge of all covert activities in the family," Davis fumed.

Mack said, "Yeah, Dad, what excitement have we got planned for this weekend?"

Rick took a deep breath and began, "Here's the deal. They're going to try again, only this time they are using a boat. I think the FBI finally decided to do something. However, just in case, I'm going to be on the scene to help. I don't need you guys for this, so go have fun."

"Are you nuts? I wouldn't miss this for the world," Davis said excitedly.

"Me either," Mack chimed in.

"Here's the best deal I can give you. As long as you

promise to stay back at the house and man a walkie-talkie in case we need help I will let you go to the lake this weekend," Rick announced.

Davis said, "Let Mack and me talk about it for a minute. Come on, Mack, let's go in here and discuss this."

They left the room and Kathy came running over to Rick and whispered, "I thought you were going to keep them out of it."

Rick replied, "This is the best we can hope for. They're not going to just let us go out there alone. This way we know what they're up to."

Davis and Mack came back into the room and Davis said, "Okay, Dad, you win. At least we'll be there if you need help."

"Good. I appreciate your cooperation, boys. Now, how's the deciphering going?"

Mack replied, "Great. We've completely deciphered the formula. It wasn't really that hard once we got into it. They basically switched numbers for letters and vice versa. Once we figured that out all we had to do was figure out which letter represented which number and which number represented which letter. That took a while, but it was fun."

"Fun? That was torture," howled Davis. "My friends ragged on me endlessly about wasting my time."

"You didn't tell them what it was, did you?" asked Rick nervously.

"Of course not. They're goofy. I just told them it was for my trade secrets class in the business school and they believed me," laughed Davis.

"Anyway, here's the decoded formula," Mack said, handing over a piece of paper.

"Thanks, guys, you did great," Rick answered. "Now, let's all get some rest. We have another late night tomorrow."

When the boys left the room, Rick turned to Kathy. “I talked to Nate Reilly today. He’s coming down here.”

“That’s great, Rick. But, you and Nate can’t save the world.”

“I know. Maybe he can help, though.”

Kathy shook her head as she left the room.

# Chapter 29

The Blaze family headed for their Lake Travis house Saturday morning. The activities of the previous Saturday were repeated with the addition of the diving gear to the inventory of the *Suite Deal*. Rick and Kathy decided to take a nap Saturday afternoon in hopes of catching up on some of the sleep they had lost. Mack said he and Davis were going to take the Cessna up for about an hour. As Rick lay in bed he could hear the engine fire and the Cessna glide across the waves on her floats and finally rise into the air. He felt an overwhelming sense of pride in those boys. They were certainly all he could have ever asked for in two children.

Rick and Kathy slept for several hours and rose just before dinner. Davis and Mack had returned and were watching a football game. Rick wished that were all the family had to do this weekend. After dinner Rick fired up the Chris-Craft and he and Kathy set out for their preset spot near the drop zone. They engaged in idle chatter mixed in with long periods of silence.

At first, Larry Thomas didn't notice the two cars following

them. Ed was strangely quiet and Larry glared intently ahead, concentrating on his task. The traffic on Highway 183 was light at midnight and the two cars of FBI agents trailed well behind. Larry began to relax a little and run through the precautions he would normally take. He checked his mirrors constantly and changed lanes often. When he drove through one intersection just as the light turned red another car followed from well back. While running red lights was quite common in Austin, the car's action sparked Larry's interest.

Taking no chances, Larry turned into the next strip mall and wandered throughout the parking lot. The car did not follow, but another similar vehicle appeared. Larry pulled back onto Highway 183 and stopped at the first green light. He waited until the light turned yellow and floored the accelerator pedal. Two cars flew through the red light in pursuit.

"Why are they after us?" Ed shouted above the roar of the engine.

"I don't know, Ed. We just have to lose them," Larry replied as he swerved from lane to lane, dodging the few cars on the road.

As they approached the intersection of Highway 183 and Ranch Road 2222, Larry barked, "I'm turning left. What vehicles are coming?"

"An eighteen–wheeler and a couple of pickups."

"Who's going to have the green light?"

"They are, I think."

Larry saw the red light ahead and a large freight truck nearing the intersection. He slowed, allowing the two FBI cars to close. As the truck barreled through the intersection, Larry tromped the gas and swerved in front of the eighteen-wheeler. The drivers of the two cars reacted immediately to Larry's acceleration and their cars leapt ahead. The first car was hit broadside by the truck. The driver of the second car wrenched the wheel to the right and put his car into a spin. On the second revolution the rear bumper hit the truck's rear tire and flipped the car upside down on the road.

"That took care of them," Ed muttered as he looked out the rear window.

"Yeah. We can't afford to botch this job. Keep an eye out for anyone else."

At one o'clock Rick started to get into his dry suit and protective gear. He didn't feel as fully protected against the chemicals as he had been the last time. Before he put on his scuba gear Rick went to a cabinet and took out a bag. Reaching into the bag he gave Kathy a walkie-talkie and a cell phone.

"Use these whenever you feel the need. I trust your judgment. I want you to keep this near you at all times," Rick said as he handed her a Ruger Blackhawk .357 Magnum revolver.

"Why would I need a gun?" Kathy exclaimed.

"I don't think you will, but I like to cover all the bases," Rick replied. Continuing, he said, "You know how to use that gun. Just point and pull the trigger."

At that moment they could hear the sound of an approaching motorboat.

"That's my cue. I guess the FBI's still not taking this seriously," Rick said as he pulled on his scuba gear. He moved to the platform on the transom and filled the Tupperware containers with water so they would not be buoyant.

He placed the containers and the tongs into his diver's bag and said to Kathy, "I'll be right back. I love you."

"I love you, too. Be careful," she said as Rick slipped into the water.

Rick moved slowly on top of the water so he could see where the motorboat was heading. At least Larry was helping by being prompt and accurate. He was going to exactly the spot Rick had calculated from what Larry had said on tape. Rick slipped under the water and headed toward his rendezvous with the canister. When he heard the motorboat come to a stop Rick rose to the surface. He was close now, within about 50 yards. In the moonlight he could see two men in the boat and Rick knew it must be Larry and Ed. One of the men leaned over the side of the boat and placed something into the water.

Rick saw a small glimmer of moonlight reflecting off the canister just before the man released it. The two men quickly started the boat to drive away. Rick noticed they were careful to stay upstream from the deadly package. He waited until they were about a hundred yards away and started to dive under the water when he heard the motor stop. He resurfaced and was somewhat surprised that they decided to stay so close to the canister. He had no choice but to follow through with the plan, but he would have to be very careful.

Rick dove under the water and swam strongly toward the canister's location, trying hard to stay on course. A compass would have been a good idea, he thought. As with last Saturday night, luck was with Rick because there was little current and hardly any waves. He felt he should be directly under the canister and wished he could use his light, but he was sure Larry and Ed would see it. Rick slowly circled about five feet under the surface and finally he saw it! Reaching into his bag, Rick pulled out the industrial tongs and reached them toward the canister. Feeling the canister in the tongs' grip, Rick pulled slowly downward. He kept descending until he was about 20 feet under the surface.

Using his buoyancy vest to stabilize him at that depth, he

began to place the canister into the various sized Tupperware containers. This accomplished, Rick breathed a sigh of relief and checked his watch. The canister had been in the water less than thirty minutes. Rick felt some of the tension leave his body as he realized his task was virtually complete.

Suddenly he heard the motorboat come to life and begin to move. Rick quickly realized that the boat was moving toward him instead of away. Rick wasn't sure what to do, so for a minute he did nothing. In that minute the boat arrived directly on top of him. Now lights were shining down and he had to act fast. If he took a breath of air the diving gear would release air bubbles and give him away. Rick held his breath and furiously kicked away from the probing light beams. The harder he kicked, the faster he needed to take a breath and finally he could hold it no longer. He breathed. The light beams didn't move so he guessed they had not seen the bubbles.

His heart leapt as the boat started up again. It was coming in his general direction so he turned off to the left and took another large breath. The boat kept coming, but then passed by him. Rick thought that in his haste he had turned in the direction Larry and Ed had come from so he surfaced to get his bearings. To his horror Rick saw he was heading right toward the *Suite Deal* and so was the motorboat with Larry and Ed in it. They must have known something was wrong and decided to check out the only other boat in sight.

Rick began to kick furiously toward the Chris-Craft, his lungs beginning to burn and the containers dragging down his progress. The boat was pulling away from him, but then slowed as Larry approached cautiously, allowing Rick to gain some ground as Larry and Ed decided what to do. Rick was within about thirty yards and could see the small boat approach the larger one. As they came together one of the men jumped onto the rear platform and began to climb onto the deck. The other man began to move the small boat away from the Chris-Craft, apparently to appraise the situation from a distance.

Rick moved closer and could see the lights still on inside the cabin. He hoped Kathy had seen the approaching boat and had the gun ready. Rick moved to the opposite side of the *Suite Deal* from the other boat and approached the platform as silently as possible, knowing he didn't have time to remove his dive gear. He released the bag containing the canister and it descended toward the bottom. Rick removed his diver's knife and scrambled onto the platform and over the transom. He saw Larry Thomas about to enter the cabin. Rick's heart was beating harder than he thought possible as the semi-automatic pistol glistened in Larry's hand.

Rick yelled as loud as he could, "Kathy, look out. Get the gun."

He began to run at Larry, but with his gear on Rick could not move fast enough. Larry was pointing the gun straight at him. Rick veered to the side and ran past Larry, trying to get behind the cabin. One shot was fired and Rick realized he had changed directions just in time. Larry followed Rick around the cabin wall.

"I recognize that voice. It's you, Blaze. You sorry bastard. I'm going to put an end to our differences right now," snarled Larry as he pulled the trigger again.

Larry was trained for this and the bullet hit its mark and Rick toppled over the side.

Kathy heard the shot and picked up the Ruger revolver. She rushed from the cabin onto the deck. She saw Larry turn in her direction.

"Rick, where are you?" she frantically called.

"I shot him and you're next," Larry growled.

He began to raise his gun and Kathy darted back into the cabin.

"Stay away! I've got a gun," she cried, trying to remember Rick's instructions. Oh my God, has he killed Rick? she thought.

Kathy tried to put that thought out of her mind and concentrate on the killer stalking her.

"Stay back," she cried again. Why doesn't he say anything, maybe he went away, she thought, but she knew better.

She knew he was out there somewhere, taking his time, waiting to surprise her. Kathy backed through the salon area until the door to the master stateroom stopped her. With her arms outstretched and the gun shaking violently Kathy listened for any sound that would give away her attacker's position. She couldn't hear anything. She thought about calling for help, but the radio was near the cabin door and she could not move. Her legs seemed to be frozen and she pressed harder against the stateroom door, trying to get further away from the danger. Kathy felt the boat rock just a little and thought the killer might have left. Suddenly, Larry burst through the door, staying low and moving fast. Kathy pointed the Ruger toward the moving object and pulled the trigger. The gun leapt upwards and she fired again, before she could even aim. She saw the man spin around and stagger back onto the deck.

"Get the hell out of here. I still have plenty of bullets left," Kathy yelled, not really sure how many bullets she really had left.

Damn the luck of that woman, Larry thought as he looked at the blood run down the crease in his arm, I'll just break out a window and shoot her in the cabin.

He moved toward the cabin side and tried to look through the window. The curtains were drawn so he drew back the semi-automatic to break the glass. A hand wrenched the gun loose and a fist crashed into his jaw, sending Larry reeling toward the bow. Another blow landed and another as Rick poured out all his anger on the bloody man. Rick had Larry on his back on the deck and was delivering blow after blow to the already unconscious man.

Kathy heard the scuffle and ran onto the deck.

"Rick, stop. You're killing him. Stop," Kathy screamed.

"He tried to kill me and you. He deserves it," Rick panted, still striking Larry with all his fading strength.

"You can't just beat him to death. You've got to stop."

Rick stopped, but it was as much from the sound of the motorboat starting up as from Kathy's pleading. His mind quickly shifted to Ed in the motorboat. Rick looked around for Larry's gun and could not find it.

"Give me the gun. Ed's still out there," Rick barked at Kathy.

She handed him the revolver. Rick turned to face the oncoming boat. Ed was idling toward the *Suite Deal*, apparently being cautious in his approach. A bright light flashed in Rick and Kathy's eyes as Ed pointed his search light in their direction. As Rick moved to the bow to avoid the blinding light he heard another sound coming from Ed's direction.

It wasn't a boat. Rick was sure of that. It was a roaring sound coming from behind Ed's boat. The sound became more familiar and Rick recognized it as the sound of a small airplane, a Cessna probably.

"Kathy, I think they're coming after us with their airplane too. Get inside the cabin," cried Rick over the ever-increasing noise.

"I'm staying right here with you," Kathy replied firmly.

Rick realized he didn't have to shout because she was right behind him, pressing against his back.

"Stay low and keep your eye on the boat. I think it's more of a danger than the plane," Rick ordered.

Rick was confused when he saw Ed drop the searchlight and turn away from the *Suite Deal*. Surely he knew his help would be arriving. As the silhouette of the oncoming aircraft appeared Rick's heart seemed to skip a beat. The plane had floats hanging under it.

"Kathy, it's Mack's plane. I'm sure of it."

As Rick and Kathy watched in amazement they saw the Cessna float plane skimming across the waves, bearing down on Ed and his boat. Ed turned and froze at the sight of the spinning propeller moving at him. The searchlight dangling from his left hand illuminated the whole boat and made Ed appear to be standing on a sacrificial altar. The landing light from the plane further illuminated Ed and gave Rick and Kathy a perfect view of the impending event.

Ed stood frozen with fear as the he could now see the spinning propeller heading right for him.

"Oh my God, Rick. Mack's going to hit that guy," shrieked Kathy.

"I think he is. I hope it doesn't crash the plane."

Rick, Kathy and Ed all stared at the speeding plane, their bodies tensed for the impact. But just before the prop would have sliced Ed to shreds the plane climbed about three feet out of the water. As the plane rose all three could see a figure clinging to one of the floats. The light from the boat reflected off what appeared to be an aluminum baseball bat held with one arm by the figure. As the plane passed over the boat the figure swung the bat and hit Ed squarely in the ribs. Ed howled with pain and fell to the bottom of the boat.

When the plane passed by Ed could only think of one

thing-get the hell out of there. The boat was still running and he threw it in gear and pushed the throttle all the way forward and headed to the safety of the other side of the lake.

Mack settled the Cessna into the water and idled over to the *Suite Deal*. Davis and his old Little League bat were back in the plane's cabin now and the two boys were greatly relieved to see their Mom and Dad standing on the deck, apparently okay. Mack shut the engine down and Davis stepped back onto the float, leapt into the water and pulled the plane over to the boat with a rope. Davis scrambled onto the platform and halfway up the deck before Mack could get out of the plane. In a short couple of minutes the family was standing together on the Chris-Craft's deck.

Rick exclaimed, "That was the craziest stunt I have ever seen. Where on earth did you dream up that scheme?"

"Gee, I wonder," said Davis.

"Yeah, Dad, I wonder where we got the ability to think up some crazy plan," Mack chimed in.

Davis asked, "What's with the bloody guy over there?"

"Oh, he's just a guy I know from work," Rick laughed.

It finally hit Kathy that Rick was supposed to be dead and she hugged him and said, "I thought Larry shot you."

"Well, he did, but I was turned sideways. I felt the bullet hit from the back and then go through my side. I guess the unlucky bastard hit my scuba tank first and the bullet deflected off that," Rick explained.

Kathy looked at the wound in his side and shrieked, "You are shot. There's blood all over."

Rick tried to calm her and then looked at the wound for the first time.

He felt his side and said, "I don't think it's too bad. It just grazed me. It looks a lot worse than it really is."

Kathy recovered her poise, looked at the gash closer and said, “Yes, it is a graze wound. I can patch it up.”

“Great,” said Rick, “I don’t have time to go to the hospital.”

Like you would anyway, she thought. “Well, now what do we do?” asked Kathy.

“I’m going to tie this guy up and get some answers from him when he comes to,” Rick said with determination. “The first thing we need to do is get the canister. I dropped it before I came on board. Hopefully, it sunk straight down. My scuba tank is down there, too. I let it go before I climbed back on board after being shot. Then we need to get out of here.” Rick continued, “We sure don’t need any more company out here. Davis, you and Mack take the plane back and wait for us at the dock. I’m going to make sure Larry doesn’t go anywhere and then I’ll dive for the canister.”

Rick had brought his survival pack on board so he opened it and found several items to secure Larry. Rick thought of the movies had seen where the people tying up someone did such an obviously poor job that the bad guy escaped easily. He decided that his abilities with rope and tape, honed from his early years, would serve him well now. Rick took ¼ inch cord and wrapped it around Larry’s wrists and ankles several times and then wrapped the cording between the wrists and ankles, tightening the cord so there was no chance of Larry wiggling out. He then tied the wrists and the ankles together so Larry could not move. Rick took some pleasure in putting a piece of duct tape across Larry’s foul mouth. He had wanted to do something like that ever since he had met Larry. Muttering something about wanting to keep blood off his boat, Rick taped gauze over Larry’s arm wound.

With Larry secure, Rick donned Kathy’s scuba equipment and slid into the waters of Lake Travis. The scuba gear was easy to find and he shoved it on the rear platform. He dove straight down and was relieved to see the Tupperware container sitting on the bottom directly below him. Rick lashed the container to the platform and climbed into the boat. Kathy had stowed the scuba gear and was looking at Rick with great impatience.

"Rick, get your butt into the boat and let's get out of here," said Kathy.

"Yes, ma'am," Rick said as he plopped onto the deck. "Fire this thing up and head her toward home."

After resting a few minutes, Rick went through Larry's clothes, finding the case with two syringes of neutralizing serum and a copy of the encoded formula. A small black address book, a cell phone and a pocketknife also turned up. Rick put all these items in his survival pack and closed it. Kathy had the boat halfway home now and Larry was secure, so Rick went below to change clothes and tend to his wound. He put on some dry clothes and washed out the bullet crease in his side. He applied a large Band-Aid and pronounced himself fine. Kathy brought the boat into the dock and Davis and Mack attached the lines. The boys carried the still-unconscious Larry into the house and not so gently dropped him onto one of the bedroom floors. Larry was starting to regain consciousness so Rick walked over and hit him with another fierce right-hand blow.

"Why did you do that?" asked Kathy. "Isn't that kind of cruel?"

"He deserves that and more. Besides, I'm not through with him yet."

Actually, Rick had a plan that needed Larry to be out for a little while longer. Digging through his survival pack, Rick removed the two syringes of neutralizing serum. While Kathy and the boys watched incredulously, Rick removed one of the syringes from the case and jabbed it roughly into the vein in Larry's arm. He then just pulled it out without injecting any serum. Kathy was beginning to fear that Rick had lost his mind, not that she could blame him. Even though Larry had tried to kill them, Kathy could not let Rick do the same to Larry.

"Rick," she said, "you're acting a little crazy here. I think you should back away and settle down."

"Relax, Kathy," Rick replied, "I'm okay. Everything I did has a reason, you'll see."

"Okay, I'll believe you for now. Let's take a look at your wound." Kathy peeled back the bandage and exclaimed, "What a surprise. You did a terrible job on this. Do you want it to get infected? If it does, you won't be able to keep up your superhero antics."

"All right, Nurse Kathy, fix me up," Rick replied with a grin.

Shortly after Kathy finished with Rick's wound Larry began to come around. After Rick had heard Larry thrash around for a while he entered the room and grinned at the distressed figure on the floor. As he reached down and quickly pulled the duct tape from Larry's mouth, Rick felt a sense of satisfaction at the pain the tape removal caused. Larry yelped with pain and then began a barrage of curse words aimed in Rick's direction.

"Now, now, Larry, if you can't keep a civil tongue in your head I'll have to put the tape back on," Rick said.

"What are you going to do with me?" Larry stammered. "And how did you find out about our plan?"

Rick replied, "I'm not going to share with you how I know about what Rene, Ed and you are up to, but I'll tell you what I'm going to do with you. I'm going to sit here while you tell me everything about this scheme you all have hatched up. I already know a lot so I'll be able to tell if you are lying."

Larry screamed, "You won't have to worry about me lying because I'm not going to tell you anything."

"Before you make up your mind completely, Larry, I want to tell you about your reward for talking," Rick said while walking over to a table. He picked up the neutralizer serum syringes, held them for Larry to see and said, "If you tell me the whole story and I'm convinced you are telling the truth, I'll let you have one of these. If you're thinking you don't need one, then I would advise you to look at your right arm."

Larry looked at his right arm and saw the needle mark and the bruised skin around the hole. He panicked and asked, "What the hell have you done to me?"

"Well," Rick responded, "you know the old saying-a taste of your own medicine? I've injected you with the chemical in the canisters. You know I have two of them now. I guess you have about three days to think about talking to me."

"You're crazy," Larry cried, "You wouldn't just let me die."

"Just watch me," Rick said with a deadly serious voice. "I'll just let you think about it for a while."

Kathy and the boys were listening at the door and Rick motioned to them to leave. They all went into the other room.

"Do you think he's going to buy it, Dad?" Davis asked.

Mack chimed in, "Yeah, Dad. Whatever he does, that was a really cool idea."

"I think the word is cruel, not cool," Kathy said.

"I just hope it is cruel enough to work," replied Rick. Continuing he said, "Let's help Larry make the right choice. Boys, you go around the house and close all the heat vents. I'm going to crank the thermostat up to about 90 degrees. Hopefully he will think the fever is beginning to set in."

Ed Richter jumped onto the dock and ran to his car, holding his side as he ran. He dove into the car and sped away as fast as the car would go. After driving for about fifteen minutes, Ed pulled over and dialed his cell phone.

Ten rings later a voice finally answered, "Hello?"

"Mr. Charlton, this is Ed Richter."

"Ed, what are you calling for? Larry should be the contact person. Where is he and why are you calling?" Rene asked.

"I don't know where Larry is or if he is even alive. Someone knew about our plan and was there to intercept us," Ed blurted out. "They also had two cars tailing us on the way to the lake. We lost them, though."

"Was it the police?" Rene asked.

"I don't know what's going on. The cars that followed us looked like cops, but it was an old wood boat that grabbed the canister. I saw a man and a woman. The man looked like the guy who runs the place we lease our office from. We tried to get the canister back. Larry went on board and there was gunfire. I never saw Larry again."

Rene said accusingly, "Didn't you go to help? That *is* your job."

"Yes, I started over to the boat to help Larry, but some kind of airplane flew right over me. The propeller almost cut me up. As it went over me something or someone hit me in the side. I think some of my ribs are broken. I decided to get away so I could tell you what happened."

"So, you're sure the canister was removed from the water?" Rene quizzed.

"Yes, yes, I'm sure. I don't know how, but someone

removed the canister from the water," Ed replied. "What should I do?" he asked.

Rene replied, "Find Larry. If he's alive, either free him or kill him. He knows too much. Call me as soon as you know any more. It appears we have serious problems, but apparently not only with the police. This is very curious, very curious indeed."

Our plan has been compromised, Rene thought. What are the motives of the interlopers and just who are they? Should I cancel all our plans or accelerate them? What am I going to tell Habid to keep him on the line?

An hour had passed and Larry was covered in sweat. He was having difficulty breathing and felt like throwing up.

That bastard really did inject the chemical into me, he thought.

The door opened and Rick walked in. Larry could see Kathy and the two boys standing just inside the door.

"I'll talk," Larry cried, "You win, I'll talk. Give me the syringe."

"No syringes until I hear the story and decide if it's true," said Rick. Continuing he said, "I'll just step outside and get my tape recorder."

He went out of the room and turned down the heater so he would not begin to sweat also. Rick returned to the room with a small hand-held tape recorder. He set it down by Larry and said, "Get on with it."

"My company, headed by a man named Rene Charlton, acquired the chemicals in the canisters from someone overseas. I'm guessing it has something to do with the Iraqi announcements lately. Austin was the first city to be poisoned. There were to be nine other cities hit as soon as the plan worked in Austin. It takes three days for the chemical to kill and the neutralizer solution will work almost immediately. Rene has said the payoff was from a foreign government, but he always has a special look in his eyes that makes me think that there is more to it. He has spent a lot of time and money on the neutralizer serum, kind of like it has a big part in his plans."

"Who is this Rene Charlton?" asked Rick.

Larry replied, "He's a Frenchman. He was educated and worked in Europe and then moved to America. After a while, he started Worldwide Water Solutions. I came on board shortly after he started the company. Can I have the serum now?"

"Not yet," Rick said, "What cities are on the list?"

"They were all picked for their orientation to a nearby lake. Austin is first, then Oklahoma City, following that is Chicago, New York, Boston, New Orleans, Seattle, Houston, San Francisco and finally Washington, D.C.," Larry said.

Rick asked, "Why did you start with Austin, and if this is an Iraqi plan, what is the goal?"

"Austin had the perfect setup of a lake system being used for the city water supply. The water treatment plants would disperse the chemicals all over the city very efficiently. My guess about the Iraqis is to distract the U.S. and keep us out of the Mid-East."

Rick scoffed, "Rene and Saddam don't know very much about Americans. The worst thing you can do is make us mad and this will definitely make us mad."

"What are you going to do with me after you give me the neutralizer?" Larry asked.

"I guess I only have to worry about that if I give you the neutralizer," Rick retorted.

"You promised to give it to me if I told you the truth and I have," Larry screamed.

"Calm down, Larry, and let's finish our little talk before we discuss the serum. Tell me what you think will happen now that you haven't returned, the canister is not in the water supply and Ed Richter has run home to Rene?" Rick asked.

"Ed is free? What happened to him?" Larry asked, surprised that this is the first time he had even thought of Ed.

Rick answered, "Ed drove off in his little boat. I'm guessing that he and old Rene are wondering about you now."

"Didn't Ed try to help me?" Larry moaned.

"Oh, he had some ideas about coming to your rescue, but my sons introduced Ed to our aluminum baseball bat. I think Ed decided not to play ball with us and went home. His ribs are probably a little sore right now, but I guess he's better off than you," Rick scoffed. "Now, Larry, what about your predictions for the immediate future?"

Larry blurted out, "I don't know, I really don't."

"Take a guess," pressed Rick.

Drawing a deep breath, Larry said, "I think Rene will keep pursuing the plan. He's not the kind to give up, especially if there's a lot of money involved. That's all I know. Please give me the neutralizer."

"Well, Larry, I'm through with the questions. I think you have been a good boy and told me the truth. However, I'm not going to give you the neutralizer," Rick said with a smirk.

With panic in his eyes Larry cried out, "You can't just let me die. You promised. Aren't you a man of your word?"

"Normally I'm a man of my word, but this is a special case. Let me explain about one of my character traits. I like to play by the rules; however, if someone is using a different set of rules and forces me into the game, then I get to use *their* rules. In this game I now get to use *your* rules. That's why I have decided not to waste the neutralizer on you," Rick explained.

He turned and walked to the door with Larry screaming and begging behind him.

"I hope you remember this moment the rest of your life, however short it may be. This is how thousands and even millions will feel if Rene's plan is carried out," Rick replied. After a pause he smiled and said, "By the way, I never injected you with the chemical. I just poked a hole in your arm. April Fools, asshole."

Rick left the room, laughing at the stream of profanity coming from Larry.

As Rick walked into the living room Kathy said, "What's all the commotion about?"

"Oh, Larry blew a gasket when I told him about our little trick. He didn't seem to appreciate how clever it was," Rick answered with a smile. Continuing, he said, "He did tell me quite a bit about their plans. They have ten cities picked for the chemical drops and it appears to be part of an Iraqi plan to keep our armed forces away from the Middle East. I get the impression that Larry thinks there is another angle that he has not been privy to."

Davis asked, "What are you going to do with Larry?"

"I'm going take him to the FBI and hope they don't charge me with kidnapping," Rick said.

Kathy looked surprised and said, "Finally you are making sense. The FBI will believe you when Larry and a second canister are in their hands."

"I hope so," Rick said.

"Rick, are we in any danger now? I mean, what if the guy in the boat recognized you? Will the FBI protect us?" Kathy asked.

"That's a good question. I doubt the FBI is going to protect us. They already let me down in that area twenty years ago."

"So what should we do?" Kathy asked pointedly.

Mack chimed in, "Yeah, Dad, I think this is getting pretty dangerous."

"I bet those guys would love to pay you back for messing up their scheme," Davis observed.

"All right, I agree. We need some help. As you know, I have contacted my old friend Nate Reilly from the militia group in Montana. He's on his way to Austin this very moment. He should be here in a few days. Nate's the only other person who knows my complete story. I also have an idea about someone else that we can trust. He may be retired, but I think he will still help. I'm thinking about Bill Whetland, one of the Chicago FBI agents who helped me. He was the only one I trusted then; I hope I can trust him now. I'll try to get a hold of him tomorrow. In the morning I'll take Larry to the FBI. These are the best things I can think of to do. Has anyone got a better idea?" Rick replied.

"Not really," said Kathy, with Davis and Mack nodding their approval.

"Okay, let's get some sleep. Tomorrow promises to be a big day," said Rick, trying to sound like everything was going to be all right.

Rick and Kathy lay in bed, not talking at first. It was hard to grasp what had happened to their lives lately and now they were trying to sleep in their own cabin with a man tied up in the other room. Kathy had just never pictured her life including this scene.

After a while she snuggled up next to Rick and said, "Rick, I know you have been thinking about all the angles lately. What do you really think will happen if the Mafia locates you?"

Rick paused and then replied, "They seem to be very direct people with long memories. I think they'll dispatch one of their best hit men to kill me immediately. I don't know if they would go after you and the boys as well, although I think probably not."

"When we are sure the FBI believes you, could we disappear like you did before?" Kathy asked.

"I've thought about that, but it would be so much harder for the four of us to disappear than for just me. Also, the methods of finding people are so much more advanced now as well. I just don't think we would be able to pull it off," Rick said.

They just laid there in silence for a while until the exhaustion finally caught up and they drifted off to sleep.

# Chapter 30

"Habid, you are certainly destined for the firing squad. You have made me look like a fool. You will pay with your life for that!" roared Saddam.

"I know it looks bad, your Excellency, but I have news from America. My contact and agent there has explained to me that someone discovered our plan and was able to disrupt it. However, this person can't stop the new plan. The remaining nine locations will be attacked at the same time within the week. No one will be able to stop us now. The delay in the results you have promised will be long forgotten once the holocaust has begun. Please allow me to live so that I may glorify your position as the most powerful man in the world," pleaded Safreed al Habid.

"Most powerful man in the world," replied Saddam, "I like the sound of that. I will give you one more week to succeed or you will surely die and it will not be an easy death."

Habid replied with obvious relief, "Thank you. Your mercy is overwhelming."

Ed Richter's cell phone chirped.

"Ed, this is Rene. What more do you know?" said Rene Charlton.

"Mr. Charlton, I think I'm on to something. I have been poking around various Lake Travis marinas and restaurants. Rick Blaze, the owner of Austin Executive Suites, has an old wood Chris-Craft and his son flies a Cessna 172 with floats. It's got to be Blaze. I just found out where his place is on Lake Travis and am heading that way," Ed replied.

"Ed, I've been in contact with my partners in this venture and I need some immediate results. I must step up our efforts and attack nine other cities within a week. Can I count on your help after you deal with this Blaze guy?" Rene asked.

"Yes, sir, I'm a professional and I like to always finish a job I start," said Ed.

"Excellent. Go to Oklahoma City as soon as you free or kill Larry," commanded Rene.

Ed was relieved when the phone line went dead. Talking to Rene always was unsettling to him. At least Rene still wanted Ed on the team, which would give him a chance to redeem himself. It would also give him a chance for some revenge against the people who almost hit him with that airplane and left his ribs black and blue.

It was about midnight when Ed Richter found the Blazes cabin. He saw the cars in the driveway and knew some, if not all, of the family were there. The cabin was dark so Ed decided to move closer. He parked on the road and walked down the driveway. The cabin was old and small, no problem getting in, Ed thought. He moved to the back door and examined the lock. The dead bolt caused Ed to curse under his breath. He was going to have to wait until the family woke up, break the door down, or break a pane of glass in the door. Ed decided to get it over with immediately. He held his 9mm Beretta in his left hand and broke a pane of glass with his right elbow. He reached in and twisted the dead bolt open.

Ed slipped quickly into the house, knowing the noise of breaking glass eliminated any chance of being undetected. He opened the first door he came to. Rick was halfway out of bed and stopped when he saw the Beretta pointed at him. Kathy started to scream, but seeing Ed with his finger over his lips caused her to hold back any noise.

"Where's Larry?" Ed asked, getting right to the point.

"Larry who?" asked Rick innocently.

"Look, Blaze. I know it was you in the boat and your son in the plane. What have you done with Larry?"

"He's in the other room. Take him and go," Kathy pleaded.

"Show me where he is," Ed ordered.

Rick and Kathy walked out of the bedroom followed by Ed. Davis and Mack were in the hall and Ed waved his Beretta at them. They fell in line behind Rick and Kathy. Rick opened the door to the third bedroom. Ed peered over Rick's shoulder and saw Larry bound and gagged on the floor.

"Untie him," Ed ordered.

Rick began to untie Larry. When the ropes fell off, Larry drove his right fist into Rick's temple. Rick staggered back, but stayed on his feet. Larry ripped the duct tape off his mouth and glared at Rick.

"You meddling fool. You'll pay dearly for what you've done, Blaze," Larry barked.

"Why don't you two just leave and you won't get in any deeper with the law," Rick said.

"Not on your life, which, by the way, is about to end. Give me the gun, Ed."

Against his better judgment, Ed moved into the room and extended the gun towards Larry, grip first. Sensing an opportunity, Rick rushed directly at the Beretta. Ed's hand was on the barrel and Larry's fingers touched the grip when Rick hit the gun with his outstretched hands. The gun bounced across the bed and slid into the corner of the small room.

"Get out," Rick yelled to his family.

Davis, Mack and Kathy backed into the hall. Ed dove over the bed in a desperate attempt to be the first to the gun. Rick started toward the gun, but changed his direction when Ed toppled over the bed and landed in the corner. Rick dove out the door as Ed came up with the Beretta. One bullet whizzed over Rick who started rolling sideways, out of the line of fire.

"Get the shotgun!" Rick screamed.

Davis ran to Rick and Kathy's closet, grabbed the 20 gauge, pistol grip, pump shotgun they kept for snakes and intruders. He desperately tried to remember where the shells were kept. They never kept a loaded gun in the house. Kathy and Mack followed Davis into the bedroom and Rick half-rolled, half-crawled in behind them. Kathy went straight to the shelf where the shells were kept, but Rick grabbed the shotgun and worked the slide.

Ed and Larry heard the sound of the slide clicking and decided not to take on a shotgun. They broke the window with a chair and scrambled outside.

"I'm not through with you, Blaze," Larry yelled as his feet touched the ground.

Rick loaded the shotgun, moved down the hall, and peered into the bedroom.

"They're gone," he said.

"Rick, what are we going to do? They know who we are," Kathy asked.

"I don't know, Kathy. I don't know."

"Are you going to call Agent Parker?" Kathy asked hopefully.

"Yeah, I guess so."

Rick dialed the now-familiar FBI number and asked for Parker. Since it was five o'clock in the morning the last thing he expected was for Parker to be at work.

"Blaze. What's going on?" Parker asked.

"Oh, Parker. I didn't expect you to be there."

"We tailed Thomas last night, but he evaded us. He put four agents in the hospital. That's why I'm here," Parker answered tersely. "What are you calling about?"

Rick recanted the evening's adventures, leaving out only the part about faking the injection. He figured Parker would frown on that tactic.

"I'm sending an agent out to pick up the canister. Where are you?"

Rick gave Parker the address and quick directions to the cabin. Then he asked, "Do you think we are in any danger?"

"No, I don't think they will bother to come back and mess with you. It would be pretty stupid."

"Yeah, right," Rick replied doubtfully.

The agent arrived around six and took possession of the canister. He listened to each of the Blazes version of the events and took pictures of the broken window and tracks outside the cabin. He was gone by seven.

The next morning Rick decided to try an idea he had been

kicking around. He got out his survival pack and removed his notebook and Larry's cellular phone. Rick dialed the number Larry had always called to reach Rene. This had been easy to obtain since the telephone switch at Austin Executive Suites printed out all the outgoing long distance calls that were made. The printout told the time, number dialed and the extension of the phone that made the call. This printout came in very handy when a tenant denied making a call that they did not want to pay for. By looking up all the outgoing calls from Larry's office it had been easy to compare that with the recordings of Larry's conversations and deduce which calls had gone to Rene.

Rick dialed the number and a voice said, "Hello?"

"Is this Rene?" asked Rick.

"Yes, it is. Who are you and how did you get my private number?" Rene replied.

"I'm the one who keeps messing up your plans and I got this number from Larry Thomas," Rick answered.

"Yes, Larry and Ed told me about you, Mr. Blaze," Rene said calmly.

"Look, Rene, let's put our cards on the table. I know about your great plan. I know which cities you are attacking and I know your methods. I have some of the neutralizer solution and I know about the test you did in west Texas," Rick answered, deciding to leave out the fact that he had the formula.

Rene asked, "What do you want? Money?"

"I want you to stop your plan. If you don't I'll turn over everything to the authorities," Rick said.

Rene paused for a second and decided on a course of action.

He coldly said, "You can't stop me, no matter what you do. All you have done by calling is speed up my operations. Thousands and maybe millions will die and you can't stop it. Furthermore, I will track you down and eliminate you. Larry knows who you are and he will surely be on your trail as long as he is alive. Nobody pushes me around and those who try get squashed. Your days are numbered, my friend."

The line went dead and Rick felt a wave of nausea come over him. It was like he had made a $100,000 bet on red in Las Vegas and black had just come up. Rene was not going to back off and Larry would probably turn up again.

Rene bitterly thought about how Blaze really had changed his plan. He was going to take the money from Iraq to poison the lakes and kill millions of Americans. However, he had also planned to miraculously develop an antidote and sell it to the stricken cities for at least three times what Habid had already paid him. His warehouse was full of boxes of the neutralizer solution and he was set up to run the product through his coding machines so it would look like they had just come off the production line.

He did not worry about retribution from Iraq because the Americans would surely decimate the country that had struck them at home. When things got personal the Americans seemed to get vicious. Iraq would be just a sandbox full of rubble shortly. Now, however, he would have to just keep the Iraqi money and stop there. With this Rick Blaze around it would be too great a risk to be the white knight riding in with a cure to the disease he had created. He would immediately dump the chemicals in the nine other lakes and watch the results. He would have the Iraqi money and be able to sell his services to other terrorists around the world with this on his resume. He would also fulfill his promise to eliminate Blaze. Rene dialed Ed Richter's cell phone.

"Hello, Ed here."

"Ed, this is Rene. Let me speak to Larry."

"Yes?" Larry said.

"Larry, we must speed up our plans. I want all your drops made as soon as possible. I have told the other three teams to get moving immediately. You and Ed get to Oklahoma City and make your next drop."

"That's a good idea, Rene. I'll get right to it."

"Oh, and by the way, Larry, as soon as the drops have been made return to Austin and eliminate this Rick Blaze. Be sure to eliminate anyone else he has talked to. I'll send the proper equipment to Austin. It'll be at airport in Georgetown."

"Yes sir, Rene. I understand and you can count on me. What about the FBI or whoever was following us?"

"Avoid them. Just deal with Blaze."

Rick knew he needed help, but he didn't think he could fully count on the local FBI office. Nate would be able to help, but not on the scale Rick needed now. There was one person he thought he could trust who could help. He would have to reach back into his past again, but it was all he could think of. The only person Rick trusted at all who was in some form of law enforcement was Bill Whetland. Bill was the FBI agent from Chicago that Rick had come to know. Whetland seemed to be the only person who appreciated Rick's dire situation. When Rick decided to forego the witness protection program and hide out on his own, Agent Whetland didn't approve, but seemed to understand.

Normally at nine o'clock on a Monday morning the Blaze house in Austin would be empty, but today was different. At Rick's request, all four gathered around the kitchen table.

"Well," answered Rick, "I decided to call one of the FBI

agents who protected me back in Chicago. His name is Bill Whetland and he's the only person besides Nate Reilly I can think of to help." Continuing Rick said, "We need to get a plan for ourselves right away. We're in real danger and I think all we have accomplished is to delay Larry's operation."

"We do have the neutralizer solution and the formula," said Mack.

"That's true, Mack," Rick replied. "We need to keep after this and stop Larry and Rene any way we can. However, our main priority is to stay alive. We must assume that Rene will want some kind of revenge. I get the distinct impression that Larry will be the one coming after us and he certainly has his own personal motivations from the treatment we have given him. I do think their first actions will be to get the chemicals into the different water sources around the country and then they will come after us.

"We can't return to our normal lives until this is over. We can't return to our home, our business or even your schools. I've dragged all of you into this and I'll do everything in my power to protect you, but we must be very careful. I think we have time to pick up things we need at home and I need to get some stuff from the office. I'll contact Agent Whetland and see what he recommends. I know it will be tough for you boys to miss school, but I can't risk you being found."

"Gee, Dad, I didn't think I would ever hear you tell us not to go to school," said Davis.

"Yeah, that is pretty strange around this family," said Mack.

Rick said, "I hope we can resolve this in a week. Until I know what Agent Whetland or Parker will do I think we need to keep our pressure on Larry and Rene."

"Rick, that's a terrible idea," interrupted Kathy. "You just told us that they are trying to kill us and now you want to go after them still. I think you're risking too much. We need to hide and let Parker or this Agent Whetland do their job."

Rick replied, "In this case I think the best defense is a good offense. I think we are better off knowing where they are than waiting for them to find us."

With a touch of resignation Kathy asked, "Then what is your new plan? I'm sure it is a doozy."

"Okay, here's what I'm thinking," Rick answered. "We need a central communications point that is safe. Kathy, I want you to go to our little house in Port Aransas. Since hardly anyone knows about our Port A property I think you will be safe there. It's always been our escape from the pressures of our lives and should be the perfect place to hide from Larry and Rene. You can take the computer from home and the backup fax machine from the office."

"And just what are the Three Musketeers going to do while I'm hiding in Port A?" asked Kathy.

"We are going to go to Oklahoma City in Mack's plane. I think that is where Larry and Ed were going next," Rick replied.

"Why are you using Mack's plane?" asked Kathy.

"Well, it's faster than driving and I can take stuff on his plane that's hard to take on commercial flights," answered Rick.

"You mean like your guns?" Kathy said.

"Well, yes, among other things," replied Rick. Continuing he said, "Look, Kathy, I know it sounds dangerous, and it is, but we can't just drop this until we know the FBI is going to do something and time is very short. So are we all together on this?"

They all looked at each other and nodded. Rick began to spell out his new plan.

"Mack, we need to get the floats off your plane and be ready to travel as soon as possible. Can you be ready in a few hours?"

"Sure, I can have the floats off and everything ready in a couple of hours. Then I'll get it gassed up and be ready to go to Oklahoma City."

"Great," replied Rick. "Check out all the airports in the Oklahoma City area. That will help us find where they are keeping their plane. Davis, I need you to take Mom in your car to the office, get the fax machine and return home. Load the fax machine and the computer into Mom's car and help her pack some clothes. I'll call Whetland, go to the office for a few minutes and then meet you back at home. Davis and I will come out to the airport to hook up with Mack as fast as possible. Everyone needs to be very careful and keep all doors locked. I think we have plenty of time to do all this before we have to worry about Larry showing up, but never assume you are safe. Now, let's get everything closed up here."

They went about loading up the cars and preparing the house for their departure. Rick went into the bedroom and began the search for Bill Whetland. He called information in Chicago for the FBI office number. As he dialed the number he said a silent prayer, hoping that this was the right thing to do.

"Federal Bureau of Investigation, may I help you?" the voice said.

"May I speak with Agent Bill Whetland please?" Rick asked.

"There's nobody here by that name. May someone else help you?" the voice answered as Rick's heart sank.

Recovering he said, "Is there someone that has been in the Chicago office for a long time that I can speak to?"

The receptionist answered, "Yes, I can let you talk to Dave Wannerly. He's one of our senior agents."

"Thank you very much," replied Rick.

After a few moments a voice came on the line, "Agent Wannerly here. Can I help you?"

"Yes," replied Rick, "I'm looking for an agent I knew about twenty years ago named Bill Whetland. Could you help me find him?"

"Bill Whetland retired about ten years ago, but as far as I know he still lives in Chicago. That's all the information I can give you. Is there anything I can do for you?"

"No, but thank you for your trouble. You've been very helpful," Rick said.

After calling information again Rick had the numbers for three William Whetland's in the Chicago area. He was greatly relieved when the lady who answered the second number said her husband did work for the FBI.

Rick said, "May I speak to him, please."

"Sure, I'll get him," she said.

"Bill Whetland here," a voice gruff said.

"I would like to know if the name Randy Flanagan means anything to you?" Rick asked.

"I still think of that name fairly often. Why are you asking and who are you?" replied Whetland.

"I'm Randy Flanagan and I have a big problem I'm hoping you can help me with," Rick said.

Whetland answered, "As you must know I'm retired now, but I'll certainly do whatever I can to help you. I've always felt bad about the way things turned out for you. Tell me what's going on."

Rick related his tale and fears of being found by the Mafia.

Bill replied, "I think you are wise to still be concerned with the Mafia. They are stronger than ever and are always interested in righting any wrongs against them, no matter how long it takes. Gino Carlucci is in jail, he would be in his seventies now, but he still is in control of his mob. He would like nothing better than to have you killed. Now, tell me what kind of fix you are in and maybe I can help."

Rick recanted the whole story, trying not to leave anything out. Finally he said, "That's the story. Where do I go from here?"

Bill replied, "That's quite a tale. You don't seem to have any real proof, other than the recordings that you made and I don't think they would count because of the way they were acquired. I want to help you, but I'm sure you understand how crazy this all sounds."

"I have the canisters."

"Yes, but that doesn't mean you didn't make them yourself."

Rick was beginning to get worried that Whetland didn't believe him and said, "I know how crazy it sounds, but there is no way I would risk my identity by calling you if it wasn't true. Why would I make this up and go to the FBI?"

"Okay, say I believe you. What do you expect me to do?" asked Bill.

"Go stop them," Rick retorted, beginning to lose patience.

"Look, Randy, I can't just call someone and tell them the story and say stop the bad guys," replied Bill. "I'll talk to this Agent Parker."

Rick took a deep breath and said, "Okay. Then what?"

Whetland replied, "Give me a little while to check things out. Where can I reach you?"

Rick replied, "I'll call you. How long do you need to check things out?"

"Give me a few hours," replied Bill.

"Okay, I'll call you in a few hours," Rick said and hung up.

Rick gathered up his survival pack and various clothes and headed to the office.

# Chapter 31

Rick arrived at Austin Executive Suites and called a quick meeting of his staff.

"I'm going to be out of pocket for about a week," he said, "You can leave messages on my voice mail, but I won't be checking it consistently. I need to count on all of you to take care of the place while I'm away. If anyone calls or comes looking for me just say I'm out."

Rick concluded the meeting and gathered up his phone equipment and the Executive Suite Association directory.

As he walked out, Rick said to Sandra, "If you see Larry or Ed or anyone else from Worldwide Water Solutions call my voice mail and leave any information you get on them."

Rick left and headed home. He pulled into the driveway and saw Davis hauling the computer out to Kathy's car. Rick found himself praying again, this time to protect his wife and kids and give him strength and wisdom. Rick had never been much of a praying person before, but it sure seemed to make him feel better.

He went inside and told Kathy, "I have to make some calls

and then we need to leave."

"Okay," she said, "I'm all ready. I figured the fax was to distribute the neutralizer formula so I got a copy of it from Davis."

Rick laughed and said, "You fit right into our little espionage ring."

"Yeah, I guess so. It kind of gets the adrenaline flowing," she replied. Then she asked, "Did you reach Bill Whetland?"

"Yeah, I talked to him."

"You don't sound too excited about reaching him. What did he say?" she asked.

Rick replied, "He doesn't seem to know whether to believe me or not. I guess I don't blame him. The story sounds kind of lame, especially from someone you don't know. He's retired now, but he's checking some things out and I'll talk to him in a couple of hours."

"Well, at least he's not just blowing you off," Kathy said hopefully.

"Yeah, I guess you're right," Rick said. He then went into the den to make some calls. First he called directory assistance in Oklahoma City for the number of Worldwide Water Solutions.

He dialed that number and the receptionist answered, "Worldwide Water Solutions, may I help you?"

"Could I speak to Larry Thomas please?" Rick asked.

The receptionist said, "He's not here today and I don't know when to expect him. Mister Richter will be returning to the office shortly. Would you like to have him call you back?"

"No thanks," said Rick, getting all the information he needed about Larry and Ed. "Say," continued Rick, "this is an executive suite isn't it?"

"Yes," replied the receptionist.

"Well, I'll be looking for an office shortly. Could you tell me the name of your operation?"

"Sure, we are Sherman Oaks Executive Suites," she said.

"Thanks, I'll come by sometime soon," replied Rick. After a pause he said, "Maybe you can help me. Mister Thomas wanted me to deliver some boxes to the airport his company uses. I wasn't sure if it was the municipal airport or one of the smaller feeder airports. Would you have any idea where they keep the plane?"

The receptionist replied, "I get calls from Wiley Post Airport. It's a small airport outside of town."

Rick said, "Yeah, that sounds like the one. Say, if you don't mind, could you not mention this to Ed or Larry? I want to keep their business and they might think I'm bad for forgetting which airport they said."

"Sure, no problem," she said.

Rick hung up and went back to Kathy. "I think we should be on our way," he said.

Kathy replied, "I think so, too. I'll miss you."

"I'll miss you, too," said Rick.

"Take care of our boys," she said.

"I will. Be sure you keep Bertha and some Mace with you," he said, referring to the 20-gauge pump shotgun they had brought from the cabin.

"Okay, I will. I love you."

"I love you, too."

They kissed and Kathy got into her car and headed for Port Aransas and the Texas Gulf Coast. Rick and Davis locked the house, got into the Blazer and headed to the airport. Along the way Rick stopped at his bank and cashed a check, figuring that cash would come in handy at some point. He also stopped at the FBI office for an update. Parker assured Rick that they were fully on the case now, especially since two of his agents had been seriously hurt in the car chase with Larry. Rick was relieved that the FBI had actually been following Larry, but their results didn't comfort him at all. He was more determined than ever to continue his personal quest to stop Rene's plan.

Rick and Davis arrived at the airport and saw Mack topping off the Cessna's tanks. After it was towed back to the hanger area they loaded it with their bags and Rick's survival pack. Rick went to the back of the Blazer and removed a sack.

"I want each of us to carry these things," he said.

He handed out a pocketknife, a bottle of Tylenol and a can of pepper spray to each of them.

"What's the Tylenol for?" asked Mack.

"Headaches," replied Rick. "I've noticed I seem to have more of them these days."

Rick parked the Blazer in the Cessna's hanger and said, "Let's go to Oklahoma City."

Mack asked, "Where do you want to land?"

"I want to land at the municipal airport. We can rent a car there. Larry and Ed's plane is at another airport."

"How do you know where their plane is?" asked Davis.

"I just know these things," Rick said with a grin.

Mack finished filing the flight plan and they took off. During the several hours flight they talked about sports, computers, airplanes and girls-anything except the task at hand. They needed this break to be just people, just a father and his two sons living a normal life, not The Three Musketeers, as Kathy had taken to calling them, out to save the country.

They landed at the Will Rogers Municipal Airport and tied down the Cessna.

"Are you going to tell us why we are in Oklahoma City now, Dad?" asked Davis.

"Sure," replied Rick. "We're going to rent a car, get a hotel room, call Bill Whetland and when it gets dark we are going to incapacitate Ed and Larry's plane. Hopefully, that will keep them on the ground for a few days."

"We know where the plane is, but there are probably lots of Cessna's at the airport. How will we know which one to go after?" asked Mack.

Rick responded with a laugh. "We'll just call the airport and ask them. We will, of course, have to ask them just right."

They found a small motel between the two airports and checked in. Rick's first call was to the Wiley Post Airport.

"Hi, this is Pete Johnson with Global Insurance Company. We had a claim filed by an Ed Richter with a company called Worldwide Water Solutions. I know the aircraft is a Cessna 172, but I didn't get the identification number. They wanted to process the claim fast and now I can't seem to catch up to them to get the information. I thought you might have the number handy and then I could finish with the claim."

The airport employee answered, "Sure, we have it right here." There was a pause and he came back on the line, "Yep, I got it. The number is NQ3446."

"Thanks a million. I owe you one," said Rick. After Rick hung up he showed Davis and Mack the paper with NQ3446 written on it. They shook their heads and laughed.

Davis said, "What about honesty is the best policy?"

"Today I'm going with the saying the end justifies the means," said Rick.

Next he dialed Bill Whetland's number. Again Whetland's wife answered and Rick asked for Bill.

The same gruff voice said, "Hello."

"Hi, Bill, this is Randy Flanagan."

"Oh, hello, Randy. I'm not really sure what to tell you. I talked to some people and there is some uneasiness about this Rene Charlton fellow, but no real evidence he's doing anything wrong. I also checked out Larry Thomas and Ed Richter and they have no records, but are known as troubleshooters for shady people. They have skills that most people don't need in their line of work. They're not people to mess with. But, most importantly, Agent Parker says he has everything under control."

Rick said, "What do I do now? Just sit around waiting for them to carry out their plans so you'll believe me?"

Bill replied, "I know this is difficult and you think I'm not helping, but I need more to go on. After all, I'm not an agent anymore; I'm working from the outside. If you want to talk to another agent here or in Austin I'll be happy to set it up for you."

"No, I won't risk talking to anyone else," Rick replied. "I already have enough people after me. I don't need to worry about the Mafia, too."

Bill said, "Give me some more time. Get back to me tomorrow morning and maybe I can give you more help."

Rick thought a minute and replied, "I'll call you in the morning. I'll also fax you a copy of the neutralizer formula that I intercepted. They encoded the formula so I had my sons work on decoding it. The boys succeeded in breaking the code, but I'll send the encoded version as well so your people can check to be sure my kids are right."

"Okay, Randy, that sounds like a good idea. Are your boys in the military or some branch of the government? That's usually where people learn to break codes," Bill inquired.

Rick laughed and said, "No, actually one is in high school and the other is in college. They're very smart and extremely good with computers."

Bill responded, “We really do need to see both versions, just to be sure.”

Whetland gave Rick a number to fax the formula to and they hung up.

Rick then called Kathy.

After a few rings she answered, “Hello?”

“Hi, it's me. How are you doing?”

Kathy said, “Just sitting here worrying about the Three Musketeers.”

Rick replied, “We’re fine. We haven’t gotten into a lick of trouble. No swashbuckling or anything like that.”

“Very funny. Is there anything I can do? I feel kind of helpless just sitting here,” Kathy said.

Rick replied, “Yes, I need you to fax a copy of the encoded neutralizer formula and the decoded version that Davis and Mack came up with to Bill Whetland. I think that will give us some credibility and also put the formula in someone else’s hands.”

Kathy didn’t even want to think about why that could be important. She got the fax number from Rick and confirmed that she had both versions of the formula with her.

Rick said, “I guess I had better go now.”

“What have you and the boys got planned for tonight?” Kathy asked.

“I tracked down their plane and we’re going to make sure they can’t use it for a while,” Rick answered.

“Oh, God, please be careful, Rick. I’m worried that we’re really pressing our luck messing with these people,” Kathy blurted out.

“Don’t worry, we’ll be careful. Anyway, we have our plan. You know, the best defense is a good offense,” Rick said.

Kathy replied, “You know how much your little sports

sayings mean to me."

"Yeah," he said, "I still don't get why your whole life doesn't revolve around sports like it does for the rest of us normal people."

Kathy chuckled and said, "Since you like sayings so much, how about this one-you are full of crap."

Rick laughed and replied, "That's my girl. Always direct and to the point."

"Well, you better go do your dirty work and get it over with," she said.

"Okay, I'll call you in the morning. I love you."

"I love you, too, and you *will* call me when you get back from messing up their plane."

"Okay," he said.

It was about eight o'clock and Rick thought it was dark enough to sneak out to the plane unseen. He hoped Larry and Ed stuck to their normal timetable of two o'clock flights. Rick and the boys got into the rental car and drove to Wiley Post Airport, northwest of Oklahoma City. They pulled into the parking lot and surveyed the area. It was quiet, very little activity. From their car they could see about fifteen airplanes tied down. As their eyes adjusted to the darkness the airplane numbers became readable.

Suddenly Mack called out, "There it is-NQ3446. Over there on the right. It's a white Cessna 172 with a red stripe."

"Good job, Mack. I see it. Now, I just need to sneak over there and disable it," said Rick.

"How are you going to damage the plane?" asked Davis.

"I'm going to stick a screwdriver through the front cowl opening into the oil cooler. When I see oil coming out I'll know they can't fly it, at least not tonight," replied Rick.

As he dug into his survival pack to get a screwdriver and flashlight Rick hoped the plan would be as easy as he made it sound.

"Davis, when I get out I want you to get behind the wheel in case we need to leave fast. Keep it running until I get back," said Rick.

He then slid out of the car and into the darkness. As he approached the airplanes the light was brighter, making him worry about being seen. He slipped from one plane to another until he reached Ed's Cessna. Rick peered toward the office and saw no one. He crept around to the front of the plane, checked the office again, and jammed the screwdriver repeatedly into the oil cooler. For good measure he pulled out his pocketknife and began to cut the alternator belt. As he sawed against the belt Rick failed to notice the office doors open and two men walk out. Finally, he cut through the belt and looked up to check his path back to the car. The two men running toward him caught his eye immediately. They were carrying a box and some other gear that they apparently didn't want to put down so they were unable to run fast. Rick bolted around the right side of the Cessna, but as he started to go around the tail Ed and Larry were there to cut him off. Rick turned around and stopped under the right wing.

"You've messed with us for the last time, Blazc," barked Larry.

He put down the canister and drew his handgun.

"If you fire that, the law will be here and start asking questions like what's in the canister. You'll be in jail and I really will have messed you up," said Rick.

Larry snarled, "Maybe I'll just club you to death with it."

Ed yelled, "Larry, you go to the right and I'll go to the left."

As Ed passed under the left wing Rick gave a mighty heave to the right aileron. The upward motion of the right one resulted in a downward motion of the left aileron, catching Ed squarely on the head. Rick quickly pumped the aileron up and down several times until Ed's knees began to give out. It was not enough to knock him out, but it certainly slowed him down.

While Rick was standing under the wing he saw Larry dive under the fuselage and come up gun-first on the other side. In one smooth motion Rick's right hand swept the foot-long Maglite flashlight from his back pocket and swung it across the side of Larry's head. Larry went down in a heap.

By now Ed was back on his feet and yelling, "I don't care about the police, I'm going to blow you away."

Ed ran around the tail section of the Cessna, oblivious of anything except Rick. As Ed rounded the tail section a horn blared right behind him. He turned to face Rick's rental car bearing down on him. Davis pointed the car right at Ed, freezing Ed in his tracks. At the last moment Davis veered to the right and swung his door open. The door shuddered as it hit Ed squarely. Ed crumpled to the ground and lay there motionless.

Davis spun the car around and Mack yelled out his window, "Dad, get in."

Rick had frozen in disbelief at his boys coming out of nowhere to take Ed out again. When he heard Mack yelling Rick began to run to the car. Just then Larry was coming to and reached out, tripping Rick. Rick rolled once, reached into his pocket and pulled out the pepper spray he had insisted each of the Three Musketeers carry. He emptied the contents into Larry's face. Rick sprang up and ran to the car, chuckling at the howling coming from Larry. Davis sped off into the night, leaving Ed and Larry to explain what was going on.

"Gee, Dad, do you think we killed that guy?" asked Mack.

Rick replied, "I don't know. I doubt it. Those two seem to be pretty tough and Bill Whetland says they have been doing this kind of work all their lives."

Davis laughed and said, "I bet they are getting tired of being done-in by some rookies."

Mack chimed in, "Yeah, I bet they haven't run into people like us before."

"We need to be very careful. These people aren't playing around. They truly want me killed and they are capable of doing it. We can't get over-confident," warned Rick.

"Aw, Dad, let us have our fun," pouted Davis.

As they drove back to the motel the main topic of conversation was about whether Ed would rather be hit by a baseball bat or by a car door. It was good for a laugh and certainly took an edge off the deadly game they were playing. After they arrived at the motel Rick called Kathy to update her. He decided to tell her as little as possible about their confrontation.

"Hello?" Kathy answered.

"Hi, there," said Rick.

"How did it go?" she asked.

"Fine. We put the plane out of commission for a while," answered Rick.

"Any problems?" she quizzed, sensing that she was not getting the full story.

"Well, we did run into Larry and Ed," Rick replied reluctantly.

"I knew you weren't telling me the whole story, Rick. Don't make me pry it out of you," she scolded.

"Okay, they did surprise me when I was working on their plane. There was a confrontation and they attacked me. Fortunately

I was able to get away with Davis and Mack's help. I'm afraid their lumps and bruises will give them a little more incentive to find us again," answered Rick.

"Whose lumps? Did any of you get hurt?" Kathy said, barely sounding under control.

"Ed and Larry ended up with all the lumps. I hit Larry in the head with a flashlight and sprayed him with pepper spray and Davis hit Ed with the car door as he drove by. It was pretty exciting, but the Three Musketeers triumphed, you know, just like in the movies," replied Rick, knowing that, as usual, he had told Kathy the whole story.

"I keep praying that you all don't turn into the Three Stooges. It seems like you have a knack, or should I say *flair*, for this kind of work," Kathy said. Continuing, she asked, "What do you have on the agenda now?"

"I'll talk to Bill Whetland in the morning and see where to go from there," replied Rick.

Kathy said, "Call me as soon as you finish talking to him. I sure would like to turn this mess over to someone else."

"Sure, I'll talk to you soon. I guess we better hit the sack now. Tomorrow could be another long day."

Larry gritted his teeth and dialed the number. His jaw was swollen and his eyes still red. Ed had bruised ribs and a broken nose. They were both in a foul mood and now had to tell Rene about their failure.

"Hello, this is Rene."

"Hi, Rene, Larry here. We, ah, had another problem."

"What is it this time? Why is it so hard to fly over a lake and drop a canister out the window?" asked Rene.

"Well, that damn Rick Blaze damaged our plane. It will

take several days to fix. We could rent one and do the job tonight," Larry said.

Rene asked, "Are you sure Blaze did it?"

"Yes, we caught him in the act."

"Then can I assume that he has been dealt with?" Rene asked.

Larry replied, "No, actually he was able to damage the plane and get away. He has someone helping him. I don't know who it is, but they seem to come out of nowhere when Blaze is in trouble. This time they drove up, hit Ed with the car door, and picked up Blaze and escaped."

"Where were you all this time, Larry?"

"Well, I was there. He got the drop on me and hit me with something and sprayed me with pepper spray," Larry reluctantly said.

"What is going on here?" Rene bellowed, "Why is this person giving two experts so much trouble?"

"I don't know, Rene. He seems so unconventional and resourceful. We are trained to deal with people who are trained like us, but he's just so unpredictable," Larry said.

"Are you saying that you can't deal with him, Larry?" Rene asked.

"No, I think we just need to approach it different. We can take care of him. We will right after we make the drop," promised Larry.

Rene paused for a second and said, "Okay, Larry, here is the new plan. Forget about making your drops. Just go after this Rick Blaze and anyone who is helping him. There is some reason that it is only Blaze showing up. The FBI has made some inquiries about me and even tried to meet with me, but I have stalled them. Be sure you only call me on the secure line. If we get rid of Blaze I will feel better about this mess. I want him disposed of as fast as possible. Do you understand me?"

"Yes, I understand. What are you going to do about our ten city plan?" asked Larry.

"The other teams are not having any problems. They all made their drops last night. Seven cities will be enough to please our partners in this venture. Just get rid of the meddlers-kill Rick Blaze!" said Rene firmly.

"Yes, sir. Have you sent my gear out?"

"Yes, I sent it to the Austin office instead of the airport. I assumed that would be where you would find Blaze. The UPS package should arrive this morning. Get the job done, Larry. I'm not used to you letting me down," Rene said, slamming the phone down at the end.

# Chapter 32

It was actually a pretty good plan, especially if you had the shear manpower to pull it off. Saddam Hussein had been working on the overthrow of Kuwait and Saudia Arabia from the day the first Gulf War had ended with his devastating defeat. The Americans had let him live and that would prove to be a huge mistake. Saddam was no great tactician, but he did realize that Kuwait fell so easily because of the surprise attack. It would not be so easy to surprise anyone this time, but perhaps it could be done. The reward would be control of 45% of the world's oil supply and if he could add Iran in the future Saddam would control almost 55%.

The assets Saddam had were time and unlimited manpower. He did not worry about rebuilding schools and hospitals. He bought military weapons on the black market instead. He didn't put his manpower to work rebuilding the infrastructure of Iraq; he put it to work digging trenches and tunnels. The trenches and tunnels headed straight for Kuwait and Saudia Arabia. In the first Gulf War Saddam was forced to hunker down his forces in trenches and underground bunkers. This did not help him fight the war, but it did teach him that his forces were nearly invisible to the enemy when they were buried in the endless sand of the Iraqi desert. Even the Americans with their sophisticated satellites and electronics could not pinpoint his locations until something appeared on the surface. To distract the satellites Saddam stepped up military activity in the north of Iraq.

And so the trenching began. They were wide enough for two military vehicles to pass and were covered with sand colored tent material. Like the great construction projects of the past, such as the pyramids, raw manpower kept this endeavor progressing. Day and night the digging continued. The sand that came out of the trench was piled on each side of the trench so that to end up with a trench ten feet deep the diggers only had to go five feet down. They were careful to keep all progress covered with the sand colored tent material.

Year after year they dug. They used bulldozers and backhoes. They used shovels and buckets. For almost five years they dug. Now, the time was right. The trenches were complete. At their end the tunnels fanned out to create many attack points. They stopped only twenty miles from borders of Kuwait and Saudia Arabia. The digging machines were replaced with missile launchers, tanks and hundreds of thousands of troops.

The terribly inaccurate Scud missiles of the first Gulf war were gone and in their place were modern Russian SS-21 Scarab Short Range Ballistic Missiles purchased from corrupt Russian military leaders thirsting for financial power. Saddam had formed an economic alliance with Syria that enabled him to sell much more oil than was allowed under the Gulf War sanctions. Syria brokered weapons deals with the Russian government and Iraq. Through these channels Saddam was able to purchase Kornet laser-guided anti-tank missiles and the deadly S-300 PMU-1 anti-aircraft defense system.

From the security of a Baghdad bunker Saddam Hussein gave the order to start the second Gulf War. The Russian S-300 missiles rained down on Kuwait City and Riyadh and King Khalid Military City. Even the American forces were taken by complete surprise. They had grown complacent; secure in the fact that Saddam would never dare to attack American allies ever again. Even if he tried, the Scud missiles he used had no range and couldn't hit anything. They were dead wrong.

The combination of the proximity and the highly accurate Russian missiles enabled the Iraqis to hit most of their targets. Wave after wave of missiles pounded their targets relentlessly throughout the night. The Americans could not get their planes in the air without taking terrible risks.

At dawn the hordes of troops, better equipped than before, crossed the two borders and flowed like fire ants toward their objectives. They fired on any one they saw. They did not want prisoners; they only wanted the oil, for it was the power. The Kornet anti-tank missiles picked off tank after tank, negating the overwhelming advantage the Americans enjoyed during the first Gulf War in tank warfare.

The Americans were finally able to launch their fighters only to find that Saddam's state of the art SAM's were deadly at this close range. Shortly the limited supply of American military might in the area began to vanish. Kuwait fell easily because of its small size. Saudia Arabia took a little longer. There were more American troops there and it was a much larger country. However, most of the area's troops were stationed within one-hundred-and-fifty miles of the Iraqi border because that was where the threat was. The flaw in this plan was that it also put the troops and equipment within easy range of Saddam's new missiles.

When the futility of continuing the conflict became evident the American military leaders ordered all troops to retreat and evacuate Kuwait and Saudia Arabia. The American Navy's diminished presence in the Persian Gulf and Red Sea were enough to hold Iraqi troops at bay for a while, enabling soldiers from the U.S., England, France and other participating allied countries to escape. Planes were flown to airbases in Europe and tanks were destroyed to keep them out of Saddam's hands.

The unthinkable had happened, Saddam Hussein controlled Kuwait again and Saudia Arabia as well. The Iraqis set up their defense perimeters in the new territories, ready for the counterattack that would surely come.

# Chapter 33

Rick called Bill Whetland the next morning.

"Hi, Bill, this is Randy."

"Hello, Randy. I'm glad you called. I sent the formula you faxed me to the FBI lab here in Chicago and it looks real. I want you to know your boys were exactly right with their decoding work. I'm very impressed. More importantly, the people in our office who decoded it were hard to convince that two kids were able to do it. That tells me you have a couple of really sharp boys on your hands."

"Yeah, I already know that. Sometimes it has been challenging to stay ahead of them as a parent. Now, where do we go from here?" asked Rick, trying to stay on the task at hand.

Bill replied, "Well we still do not have any proof that this is really happening or going to happen. I believe you, but no one can dig up anything to go on. This Rene Charlton is a slippery guy. We're not giving up; we just need more time to check into it."

"Bill, they tried last night to make a drop in Oklahoma City. I was able to stop them, but it's only temporary. If they are using other teams for some of the other cities the chemical could already be in some water supplies," said Rick.

Bill asked, "How did you find them last night?"

"Some luck and some skill," answered Rick. Continuing he said, "I used the same information Parker has. I'm running out of leads and I think we're running out of time. The FBI needs to jump into this with both feet right away."

"Do you have any idea what they will try next?" asked Bill.

"I imagine they will hit all the cities as fast as possible and get the hell out of the country."

"Yeah, I agree. Maybe I can convince the higher-ups to nab Charlton and this Larry Thomas character," Bill replied.

Rick took a deep breath to calm down and said, "Okay. But, what should I do now?"

Whetland replied, "Keep out of danger and I'll stay on it. Like I said, I believe you, and that counts for a lot in the FBI. Call me this afternoon and maybe I'll have better news for you."

"Okay, Bill, I'll call you this afternoon," said Rick.

Rick called Kathy and related the conversation to her.

She said, "You know he's in a tough spot. He's retired and doesn't really know you and the local office won't completely take the ball. It's a bad situation and I really don't know the answer. I guess we just have to play this out, although part of me thinks you, Davis and Mack should get in the plane and fly down here to Port Aransas. I'll even be glad to meet you at the airport with swim suits and towels and we can head straight to the beach."

Rick sighed. "That would be great, but you know I can't do that, at least not now."

"Yeah, I know. So what are you going to do?" she asked.

"I'm not sure. I feel like I'm at a dead end. Kind of

helpless, you know. I guess I need to think on this for a while. I'll call you when I figure something out," he said.

"Okay, just be careful."

"I will."

Rick called his voicemail box and sorted through the messages. One message was from his secretary, Linda. She was telling Rick that a UPS package had arrived for Larry. It was fairly large and heavy. He also checked his private voicemail box and was happy to have a message from Nate Reilly. Nate indicated he was several hours from Austin and would call Rick when he arrived.

Rick called the office and asked for Linda.

"Hi, this is Linda."

"Hi, Linda, this is Rick."

"Hey, boss, how's the vacation?"

"Well, it's not exactly a vacation. I want you to do something for me. Close the door, open the box to Larry and check the contents. I'll wait on the phone while you do it. Don't let anyone else see the contents or talk to any one about this."

After several minutes Linda came back on the line. She said, "There is all kinds of military looking stuff. You know, like packs, containers and some sort of guns."

"Okay, Linda here's what I want you to do. Repack the box, pull the labels off and put the box in the mechanical room by the phone switch. Don't tell any one about this, not even our other employees. When Larry or Ed comes looking for the box tell them you haven't seen it. They'll probably check with UPS and find that you signed for the package. When they come back to you tell them you signed for a lot of packages at once and didn't really count them," Rick said.

"But I would never do that, Rick," she protested.

"I know you wouldn't, but I need you to do this. It's really important, Linda," Rick said.

"Okay, Rick, I'll do it. I never liked those two jerks anyway," she replied.

"Great, do it right now. I'll talk to you later. Be sure to leave me a voice mail when you see them," instructed Rick.

"What's that all about?" asked Davis.

"Larry and Ed received a box of guns, ammo and other military type stuff at the office today. I guess they're really coming after us now. I had Linda hide the box. We can pick it up when we get back to Austin," replied Rick.

"And just what are we going to do in Austin?" asked Mack.

"I don't really know," said Rick. "Nate Reilly called. He should be in Austin by now. Mack, you brought your notebook computer, didn't you?"

"Sure, I take it with me everywhere," replied Mack.

"Plug it in the wall jack there and dial up this number," Rick said, writing a phone number, a name and a password on a piece of paper and handing it to Mack.

After a couple of minutes Mack said, "I'm in."

"Good, let me on the keyboard," said Rick.

"What are you doing?" asked Davis.

"We're in the maintenance port of the phone switch and voice mail system at the office. I'm changing the parameters of my private telephone extension to forward any calls to my cell phone," replied Rick.

"So any calls from Nate will come to your cell phone?" said Davis.

"Right. Hopefully it will be soon, too."

"You're just full of good ideas, Dad," said Davis.

"Yeah, I guess so," Rick replied. "Let's go to lunch. After that I'll call Bill Whetland again," Rick continued.

"Yeah, he's been a great help so far," said Davis.

Rick replied, "He might help us. At least he gives me some credibility."

They went to lunch and tried to concentrate on sports. The restaurant had ESPN on and that kept their attention for a while. A special bulletin banner across the TV screen got their attention. The announcer was talking about some kind of possible epidemic illness in several cities in the United States. So far cases have been reported in Chicago, New York and Boston. There was no indication how serious the illnesses would get, but it was affecting a large number of people in each city. Thousands had already made their way to emergency rooms, complaining of symptoms similar to the flu. A link between the cities was being researched. More announcements would be made when there was additional information. The station returned to ESPN. Rick, Davis and Mack sat in the booth stunned. They had failed. People would die by the millions and they could have prevented it. At least they felt like they could have done something different and prevented it.

Rick said, "Finish your lunch. We need to get back to the room."

They quickly scarfed down their food, paid the bill and left. As soon as they reached the motel room Rick dialed Bill Whetland.

"Hello?" Whetland said.

"Do you believe me now?" Rick yelled.

"Yes, I do, Randy, but more importantly, so do some others."

"Have you received reports from any other cities?" asked Rick.

Bill answered, “Yes, Seattle, Washington, D.C., San Francisco and New Orleans. They were all on your list. The others on the list that appear to be all right are Austin, Houston and Oklahoma City. Look, Randy, we, or at least, I, need to talk to you in person. We need your help since you know so much and we need you with us, in person. I’ll be glad to meet you, but I have to turn you over to a current agent. I have one in mind that you can completely trust. His name is Robert Whetland, my son. He’s the number three man in the Washington, D.C. office. He’ll come to Chicago to meet you. Will you do it? I can promise protection, but I know that doesn’t mean much to you.”

Rick paused and finally said, “I’ll come to Chicago, but not to your office. I’ll meet you at Oakwood Towers Executive Suites. They have a conference room we can use. I also want you to promise me that it will be only you and your son and me and my sons. Also, I must be free to go my own way, not under some custody or anything like that. Is that agreed?”

“Yes, we can live with those terms, Randy.”

“Okay, I’ll meet you there at six o'clock. If I can’t get there by six I’ll call you back,” Rick said and hung up.

He looked at Davis and Mack and said, “Look guys, I want you to fly to Port Aransas and be with your mother. I don’t like her being down there by herself.”

Davis protested, “But, Dad, they’re after you. We had come to your rescue twice. You might need us. Besides, you told Whetland that you were bringing us.”

Rick replied, “I feel very strongly about this. I’ll be with the FBI most of the time. I should be safe. I can’t say the same about Mom. I’m going to send you back with the guns and some other stuff from my survival pack. No more arguments, this is the way it’s going to be.”

Davis and Mack knew it was fruitless to argue any more, so they gave up.

Rick drove them to Mack's plane and then headed back to the Will Rogers Municipal Airport. His cell phone rang and as he hoped it was Nate.

"I'm here in Austin, boy. So where do you want to hook up?" asked Nate.

"Well, Nate, it's really gotten complicated. I'm in Oklahoma City now and I have to be in Chicago shortly," replied Rick.

"What the hell are you doing running all over the country?" asked a stunned Nate.

"Nate, have you seen the TV reports about the epidemic illnesses all over the country?" asked Rick.

"Yeah, sure. It's all anyone can talk about. Especially with that damn Saddam taking credit for it. Is this the plot you have been messing up?" Nate asked.

"Yeah, that's it. But I wasn't able to stop it. They weren't deterred by the monkey wrenches I threw in the works," said Rick sadly.

"I bet you did some good," said Nate.

"Well, they didn't hit all ten cities they had originally planned to. They only got seven."

"That's a lot of people that you spared," Nate said.

"Thanks, Nate. I know I did some good. But I still have problems. The people doing this know who I am now and their head guy has vowed to kill me. I also talked to one guy at the FBI who I trusted twenty years ago and he wants me to help them since I know so much," replied Rick.

Nate paused and said, "You sure know how to get in some hellacious messes, don't you?"

"Apparently so, Nate."

"So, the 64 dollar question is what can I do to help you now?"

"I'm not sure. I hate to endanger you. Maybe I should go it alone," said Rick.

"No way, Randy, no way. I'm here to help and that's exactly what I'm going to do," replied Nate firmly.

"Thanks, Nate. I really owe you again."

"Well, it was getting kind of boring up there in Montana anyway. It sounds like you can liven up my life for a while," chuckled Nate.

"I can definitely do that."

"So, tell me what I can do."

"I have to meet the FBI in Chicago and then I'll return to Austin. I worry about my business and those guys looking for me. If you could hang around there until I get back I'll rest easier and I know my employees will be glad to have someone around," said Rick.

"I don't know much about business, but I know how to protect people. I still got that old Colt .45 to do the talking for me," said Nate.

"Perfect. My receptionists are Sandra and Mary and Linda works in the operations area. I'll let them know you're coming. The bad guys are Larry Thomas and Ed Richter. They may be a little banged up and thoroughly pissed at me," replied Rick. Continuing he said, "The business is called Austin Executive Suites and is located at 9400 Technology Boulevard. It's the fourth floor of the building."

"I'll find it, Randy. Don't you worry. Everything will be fine when you get back," reassured Nate.

"Thanks. Oh, and one other thing. I'm now Rick Blaze. I

have a wife and two kids."

"What about them? Are they safe?"

"Yes, they're safe."

"Okay then. I'll see you soon, Rick."

"See you soon, Nate."

Rick arrived at Will Rogers Municipal Airport. He turned in the rental car and checked the flights to Chicago. He was able to catch one that arrived in Chicago at five. Rick had 20 minutes until boarding so he went to the phones.

He called Linda at Austin Executive Suites.

"Hi, Rick, this is Linda."

"Hi, Linda. Have you heard from Larry or Ed?"

"Yeah, they both were here. They got pretty hot about the missing box, but I think they're blaming UPS."

"Great," Rick said. "I need to change our plans a little. Send the box UPS next-day air to me at Oakwood Towers Executive Suites in Chicago. You can call them to get the address. Be sure there is nothing on the box that Larry or Ed will recognize."

"Okay, Rick, I got it. Say, be careful in Chicago. There's some kind of mystery disease all over the country. I know they have it in Chicago."

"Yeah, I heard about it. Is Austin having any problems?"

"No, none so far."

"Good. An old friend of mine, Nate Reilly, will be coming by soon. He will hang around to be sure you all are safe," said Rick.

"Why wouldn't we be safe, Rick?" asked Linda.

"Well, I've had some trouble and most of it revolves around Larry Thomas. I don't think he'll mess with you, but Nate will be there just in case," replied Rick.

"We'll make Mr. Reilly feel right at home."

"Not if you call him Mr. Reilly, you won't. He's just Nate," laughed Rick.

"Okay, Nate it is."

"Great, Linda. I've got to go now. See you soon."

Rick hung up and went to the bar to see what the TV was saying. In a few minutes a special bulletin came on.

The newscaster said, "All across the nation thousands, perhaps millions, have been affected with this mysterious ailment. Seven cities have reported the disease so far. These cities are Chicago, New York, Washington, D.C., Boston, Seattle, San Francisco and New Orleans. The disease starts with a fever and progresses to muscle cramps and severe headaches. Local authorities in these cities are warning citizens to be careful of what they eat and drink. Because the disease affects so many people so fast it is thought to be some kind of bacteria or virus. We will get back to you as soon as there are more developments-wait, our producer is telling me that we will have a network feed of a videotape delivered to CNN in Baghdad. This tape is said to have an address to the American people by Saddam Hussein. The tape will roll any second now."

On the TV screen appeared the face of Saddam. Through his interpreter Saddam said his loyal forces, which reach all over the world, have invaded the United States of America with a chemical weapon. The seven cities reporting mass illness were the targets of this attack. All who drank the water in these cities will die within three days. These millions who perish are a warning for the United States to leave Iraq and the Middle East alone. The loss of Kuwait and Saudia Arabia is a small price to pay for future lives to be saved. America has now seen the global power of Iraq and should bow out of this conflict before any more damage is done.

Saddam continued to ramble on with the interpreter trying to keep up, but Rick had heard enough. He needed to get to Chicago, so he started running for his gate. Rick arrived in plenty of time to board because things in the airport had come to a complete standstill as news spread about the illnesses and now Saddam's mad plan. He boarded and waited for everyone to get back to their jobs. Fortunately his flight was only delayed fifteen minutes so he could still make his six o'clock meeting.

Saddam addressed his cabinet members and others present. "Safreed al Habid is a hero to our country. He was the mastermind behind the development and deployment of the chemical attack upon the United States. Now America will quiver whenever it thinks of the power of Iraq. We have beaten the most powerful country in the world. They will surely not choose to invade or attack our country now. Hail to the most powerful country in the world–Iraq. And hail to the most powerful man in the world-myself. Even though Habid has been the force behind this most devastating of all terrorist attacks, I myself, as supreme ruler of Iraq, must be seen as the one who commands the attack. Whenever it is asked whose plan, whose actions are responsible for this triumph, you all will answer Saddam Hussein. Habid will get his just rewards in my Cabinet and circle of power."

Habid stood at rigid attention as the eyes of Iraq's leaders darted between Saddam and himself. Prouder he could not be, for it was the ultimate honor in Iraq for Saddam to take your idea or actions as his own. This was the culmination of years of work for Habid. This was where his dream reached its zenith. As Habid had risen through the ranks in the Iraqi military he had always visualized himself standing next to and being recognized as a hero by Saddam. It was his moment of complete triumph and he would treasure this moment for the rest of his life. In fact, Habid could very well see that this could be the point that he took the next step up, joining the Iraqi Cabinet. Maybe even sitting on Saddam's right hand seat, the second most powerful man in the world. Yes, Habid could see it all very clearly now.

Rene Charlton watched the big-screen television in his office overlooking New York City. The screen was split into four parts and a different channel was broadcasting in each part. Rene used his remote control to move from channel to channel, listening to the various special reports coming in from all over the country. He laughed as he thought about the stockpiles of pure water stashed at the office and his home. Why, he had even installed a small water tank at his home. No one would think that someone would poison the water of his own drinking supply, but Rene was a cut above everyone else. He covered his tracks and planned everything perfectly. Even though Blaze had uncovered the plan, Rene's cadre of lawyers kept the FBI at bay. Of course, if they showed up at his office with a warrant, Rene would disappear through his secret route out of the building and he would leave the country without having to use his passport. They could block all the roads and airports, but Rene would still be gone. Outsmarting Rene Charlton was something that just didn't happen, Rene proudly thought.

Everyone on the plane was talking about the news bulletin and the message from Saddam. They were on a plane to Chicago, one of the stricken cities, and fears for their loved ones showed. The reality of the United States' vulnerability to terrorism was setting in. Saddam had struck and his further threats were certainly not just another of his bluffs. He really had attacked the United

States. The plane was filled with fright and belligerence. Some wanted to pull back and others, the majority, seemed to feel a nuclear attack was called for. Saddam could not hurt anyone if he and his country were wiped off the map. The term “world’s largest sand trap” was circulating around the plane. Rick felt certain that Saddam had completely misjudged America’s response. We have the habit of winning wars, no matter how they start, Rick thought.

As the past days’ events circulated through Rick’s head one nagging thought kept coming up. Why was the neutralizer serum so important? Why were Rene and Larry passing around an encoded formula? Why did Worldwide Water Solutions develop a presence in each of the cities that were attacked? Finally, it hit him. There was another layer to the plan. A layer that was known only to Rene and possibly a few of his people. Larry had even hinted that there was more to the operation than he was telling. If Rene was in it for the money, which he surely was, how could he raise his profits even higher? Rick’s mind turned this over and over until suddenly a possibility emerged. What if Rene took money from Saddam to poison America and then turned around and planned to sell the neutralizer? He could certainly get more for the cure than for the original deed. If this were the plan Rene would soon announce that he had developed the neutralizer and cranked up production but he would need a lot of money to pay for this. It would be difficult to produce the quantities fast enough so Rick guessed that Rene had large supplies of the neutralizer ready to ship.

The plane was beginning its descent into Chicago so Rick decided to tell the Whetlands in person instead of trying to call. The plane landed at 5:25 and Rick was on the road in his rental car at 5:45. His Executive Suite Association Directory had enough of a map to get Rick to Oakwood Towers Executive Suites with a minimum of wrong turns. He arrived at 6:10 and bounded off the elevator. Even after all these years he recognized Bill Whetland.

Rick walked up to Bill and shook his hand.

"Hello, Randy. This is my son, Robert. Where are your sons?" Bill asked.

Rick replied, "I decided to send them somewhere else. Now, let's get into the conference room before we say anymore. They said a key would be in the right hand drawer of the receptionist's desk."

Rick retrieved the key and opened the conference room door.

Rick spoke first. "I want you to know I trust the two of you. I'll do anything to help. I feel somewhat responsible since I wasn't able to convince Agent Parker to take me seriously."

"I doubt that it would have stopped the attacks and we might not have known what we do now," said Bill.

"Anyway, that's in the past. We have to deal with the present," said Robert.

Rick replied, "I agree. On the flight I had an idea and I want to see what you think. I feel that there is a strong possibility that Rene Charlton is doing a double-cross, or at least had one planned. I think the neutralizer formula was so important to him, yet being circulated around his offices because he is planning to sell it to us. First, he gets paid by Iraq to kill millions of Americans and just when that's working he tells the American people he has a developed a neutralizer serum. Rene says he can provide the serum almost immediately if he receives a large sum of money to pay for his effort. That way he makes his money from Iraq and America. Does that sound completely loony?"

Robert answered, "Actually, that would fit the profile we have developed in the last six hours on Rene Charlton. He's profit-driven and completely ruthless. It would also explain the worldwide shortage of some of the chemicals in the formula. We can't find enough to produce significant quantities of the neutralizer."

"Has there been any noise out of Rene lately?" asked Rick.

Bill said, "No, Randy, er, I mean Rick, he has been quiet as a mouse. His lawyers are giving us the run around and we can't seem to persuade a judge to issue a warrant based on the skimpy evidence. Nothing you acquired can be taken into account in a court."

Robert was thinking about this new theory. Suddenly he blurted out, "He may be afraid to initiate the last part of his plan because Rick found him out. He may have decided to just stick with the Iraqi part of the plan. But he would have the facilities to produce the neutralizer and he would be ready to do it."

"I bet he already has it produced and on the warehouse floor, ready to ship," said Rick.

Robert replied, "I bet he does, too. I really think we're on to something here."

"Yeah, if you guys weren't so law-abiding you could just go get the neutralizer and have it delivered to each city in time to save most everyone."

"Rick, you have a good point in that we can't go through legal channels and get the serum distributed fast enough if the timetable of three days until death is correct," said Robert. Continuing he said, "At this point I need to swear you to secrecy."

Rick proudly said, "I swear that I am under complete secrecy."

"Good," exclaimed Robert, "because we are going to need you for our next step."

Rick curiously asked, "And what would that be?"

Robert replied, "There is a way for us to just go in and take the neutralizer serum from Worldwide Water Solutions. We have a special division that does these things when the nation's security is being threatened."

"When can you do it?" replied Rick.

"As soon as we find out where to go," said Robert.

"Oh, yeah, that would be helpful to know," said Rick dejectedly.

Robert said, "We'll have to track down his production and warehouse facilities."

Rick jumped up and exclaimed, "I bet I can find out! Do you have a cellular phone?"

Robert handed Rick his cell phone. Rick dialed Kathy in Port Aransas.

When she answered Rick said, "Hi, it's me. Did the boys get there okay?"

Kathy said, "Yes, they're here and armed to the teeth. I feel plenty safe. Where are you? Do you know about all the cities Saddam has attacked?"

"Yes," replied Rick, "I know all about it. I'm in Chicago with Bill and Robert Whetland. We think there may be a way to keep these people from dying. I need for you to look in Worldwide Water Solutions' tenant folder. It should be in the box of papers I grabbed from the office."

Kathy replied, "Yes, I've seen it. I looked all through that box several times."

"Great. I'm looking for an address for their production and/or warehouse facilities. Maybe there is a delivery receipt from something shipped from an address other than their offices."

Kathy browsed through the backup documents Austin Executive Suites kept with each month's bills. She exclaimed, "I think I have got it. There is an address that several boxes have been shipped from that is different from their corporate address."

Rick took down the New York address and gave it to Robert.

Robert said, "Give me a couple of minutes on the phone and then we'll be ready to roll."

"What do you mean, we?" asked Rick.

"I'll tell you all about it in a few minutes," Robert answered.

In about five minutes Robert came back and said, "It's all set. The team will be assembled when we get to New York. We checked the address and it is a warehouse owned by Worldwide Water. Rick, you were right on the money, as usual. My people will meet us at the airport and we'll move to the warehouse. We'll enter the warehouse, identify the neutralizer, remove it from the premises and distribute it to the seven cities. Rick, I want you along to help identify the serum. You won't be exposed to any danger. The team will clear the way before you come in. I also want your instincts about these guys in case we have trouble. You really seem to have a feel for how they operate. My dad had agreed, or I should say demanded, that he accompany us. He'll be at your side the whole way. What do you say, Rick, are you in?"

"I'm in," Rick exclaimed.

"Let's go. We're wasting time," said Bill.

They drove to the airport and boarded a white Lear Jet with no markings. Inside, the pilot, copilot and two more agents greeted them. Rick and Bill were introduced to the other men and the jet's door closed. They were in the air a few minutes later. During the flight Rick asked to use a phone to call Kathy. Bill handed him a cell phone and reminded Rick of the secrecy involved.

"Hi, how's it going at the beach?" Rick said when Kathy

answered.

"Fine, Rick, what are you up to?"

"I'm with Bill Whetland and his son Robert in a FBI Lear jet flying to New York."

"Sure you are and I just got back from winning the surfing tournament," Kathy scoffed.

"Kathy, I really am."

Kathy realized he was completely serious and said, "Rick Blaze, I'm continually amazed. At least you should be safe from Larry and Ed with your new FBI friends."

Rick said, "Yeah, this is the safest I have felt in a couple of weeks. How are the boys? Are they driving you nuts yet?"

"Other than feeling like Rambo's mom, I feel pretty good. They won't leave my side. I can barely get away to get to the bathroom. But I have to say I feel completely safe."

Rick sighed and said, "Hopefully we'll get back to our normal life soon."

"I could go for that," said Kathy. She continued, "So what are you flying around on a FBI Lear Jet for?"

"They won't let me say any more about it. I should be back in Chicago by morning. I'll call you then," Rick said.

"A lot of people are really sick now. I hope you all are doing something about that," said Kathy.

Rick replied, "We are. I think things will be okay. I guess I better go now. I don't want to break the government with a large cellular phone bill."

Laughing Kathy said, "Go get some rest so you can save the country."

Rick hung up the phone and laid back in his seat. He began to think about how calm Kathy had been throughout this whole ordeal. She tended to be the excitable one in the family, but was very levelheaded in this predicament. Her support and understanding had really helped Rick get through the stress and uncertainty.

Larry Thomas thought something was fishy about the missing package. He had been trained to be suspicious and his senses were at red alert. He also was unhappy that Rene had sent the gear to Austin Executive Suites. It just gave that damn Rick Blaze another way to meddle with them. He waited until everybody left for the day. At around seven Larry went down the hall to the Operations area. He worked with his lock picks for a couple of minutes and the door opened. He turned on the light and shut the door behind him. Larry moved through the large room slowly and systematically, as he had been trained to do.

The UPS log caught his eye. As he scanned down the list of outgoing packages, one caught his eye. It was sent to Rick Blaze at Oakwood Towers Executive Suites by next-day air. The package weighed forty-three pounds, exactly the weight of his missing package. Bingo, he thought. I know where to find Rick Blaze. Larry continued his search of the room and on Linda's desk was a Post-It note with Kathy Blaze and a phone number written on it. The number was a long distance number and had an area code that Larry didn't recognize. I have both of them now, he thought. He returned to his office and placed a call to a contact in the phone company.

"I need an address to go along with this phone number," said Larry.

His contact promised to call him as soon as he had the information. Larry and Ed headed to the airport. They had to get to Chicago before the package arrived. Rick Blaze would walk right into their hands and their troubles would be over. They could easily surprise Blaze, kill him and return to their plan, to Rene's plan. Larry felt he could earn back his spot as Rene Charlton's top troubleshooter if he eliminated the pesky Rick Blaze and his family. The whole family would have to go because Blaze would surely have told them and Rene had said to kill anyone Blaze had told. Larry didn't have any problem killing women and children, it was just part of the job and something he had done before.

Louise Exner felt horrible. Her fever had climbed to 102 and her muscles ached. Not just ached, but felt like they would tear in half. The splitting headache would not go away. Her husband Jim had just arrived from a business trip in Nevada and had been careful not to eat or drink anything in Boston. He had rushed home when the news of the terrible sickness in Boston had reached him. It seemed to take forever to get back home from Nevada and every time he called Louise at the house she seemed to get worse and worse. Jim tried to call the family doctor, but never could get through to him. On the third try a recorded message instructed callers to go to one of the emergency rooms because the chemical poisoning had afflicted the doctor and his whole staff.

When he landed, Jim witnessed a sight so odd it jumped right out at him-the Boston airport was totally devoid of taxicabs and rental car buses. Very few people were at the airport and most of them were trying to get out of town. When Jim arrived at home Louise was crumpled up on the couch too weak to move, yet in too much pain to sleep. The low moaning was almost more than Jim could take. He could not imagine his life without Louise and was as scared as he had ever been in his life. He swept her up into his arms, surprised at the strength he now seemed to possess, and gently put her in the front seat of his car.

Louise softly whispered, "Jim, they think it is in the water.

Be careful. I don't want this to happen to you. They think it is okay to drink bottled water. Be careful. I love you."

"I love you too, baby. Just hang in there. We will be at the emergency room in a couple of minutes."

Jim intended to park right at the door of the emergency room no matter what the no parking signs said, but seemingly hundreds of cars jamming the parking areas and even the sidewalks caused him to stop a block away. Again, he swept up Louise and carried her to the emergency room. People were everywhere and they all looked like Louise, in a lot of trouble. The staff, or what was left of the original staff, was trying to keep everyone comfortable and kept repeating that they had no cure for the mystery affliction. All they could do was dispense some painkillers and muscle relaxants. To the hospital's credit, thought Jim, they were not making people fill out forms or worrying about medical insurance. They were just handing out the medicine to anyone who showed up. An hour after taking the medicine Louise seemed to rest easier, but Jim knew it was not a cure and he feared for his wife's life.

The plane landed in New York and Rick could see several unmarked vehicles on the apron. They left the plane and Rick and Bill were ushered into one of the vans. They were given black clothes and full-body armor to wear.

"I thought we wouldn't be in danger," Rick said.

Bill replied, "Just precautions. No problem."

After a thirty-minute drive the vehicles pulled up to a warehouse. The lights were out and the parking area was locked with a chain link fence. A big sign proclaimed it to be the home of Worldwide Water Solutions, Inc. A man jumped out of the first vehicle and cut the lock with a pair of bolt cutters. Rick noticed that the man had a ski mask pulled over his face. He thought that was odd for a FBI raid. Everything he saw on television showed the FBI wearing jackets with FBI clearly showing. The vehicles entered the parking area and the lead one drove to the side of the building. Two men with toolboxes jumped out and went to the phone line and keypad for the security system. They worked for less than a minute and signaled to the others. Another ran up with some kind of drill and a large bit. He drilled through the door, completely removing the lockset. The door opened and a force of fifteen armed men ran in. The lights came on and two minutes later one man came out and waved to the rest of the group.

Bill said, "That's the signal. Let's go." He grabbed Rick's arm and led him into the building.

Rick was amazed at how large and spotlessly clean the warehouse was. It seemed to be well organized and plainly marked. That gave Rick an idea.

He turned to Bill Whetland and said, "Bill, see if this makes sense. Everything here is well marked. If you had the product we were looking for would you clearly mark it or would you leave it unmarked and out of the way?"

"I see what you mean. If we're looking for the right thing it will probably jump out at us. Robert, come over here. Rick's got an idea we should consider."

Robert came over and listened to Rick's theory.

He said, "Why don't the three of us search with that in mind. Let's each take a part of the warehouse and do a quick walk through. We can meet at the other end."

"Great," said Rick. "I'll take the loading dock area."

"I'll take the middle," added Robert.

The three men took off in their respective directions. Rick had picked the loading area because he felt they would store the neutralizer in that area for the quickest deployment possible. He walked past row after row of clearly marked products. Nothing looked like the neutralizer scrum. As Rick approached the other end of the warehouse he saw Bill and Robert.

"Any luck?" asked Rick.

"No, none," said Robert.

"Keep looking," urged Bill.

For thirty more minutes they scoured the large warehouse and found nothing. The enthusiasm of before was gone and solemn expressions were on everyone's face.

The group of black clad men gathered around Robert Whetland.

"We have no choice but to begin opening every box in this damned warehouse. Start by opening one box from every pallet. We need to move fast, so get to it," ordered Robert.

The men scattered throughout the warehouse with several operating the forklifts. Rick began to feel helpless as well as a little bit chagrinned. After all, this was his idea. He walked outside, muttering to himself, and inhaled the night air. Standing outside the dock doors he noticed the tire tracks in the dirt and dust on the pavement. The eighteen-wheeler's tire tracks converged from each dock opening into a single path to the front gate. His eyes traced their path out the gate and onto the street. Rick's senses surged when he noticed that the tracks divided. One track turned and went down the street towards the highway. The other track went straight across to another gate. Past the gate was another warehouse.

Rick turned and ran back into the warehouse. It had become quite a mess now, with boxes scattered everywhere.

Rick spotted Robert and Bill and yelled, "I think I've found it."

Bill raised his head and asked, "Found what, Rick?"

"The neutralizer! I know where it is."

Robert walked briskly over to Rick and said, "Rick, this is where you said the neutralizer would be. What are you talking about?"

"Tire tracks from this warehouse lead to another warehouse across the street. It doesn't have a sign or any identification. I bet that's where the neutralizer is," replied Rick, hoping he was right.

"Let's take a look," said Robert.

They went outside and Rick pointed out the tracks. Robert looked unconvinced, but he had no other ideas. He quickly found the leader of the black clad team and motioned toward the warehouse. Five members of the team gathered their tools and moved toward the locked gate. As before, they were quickly inside the warehouse. Rick, Robert and Bill used the same pattern to search the new warehouse.

Rick walked into the dock area and his eyes swept the boxes stacked up fifteen feet high. At first it looked like the other boxes. Rick was encouraged that these boxes also had Worldwide Water Solutions labels. Finally, he spotted several pallets of unmarked boxes inside a chain link fenced security area.

"Over here," he yelled.

Several men, including Robert, came over. Seeing the fence Robert instructed one of the men to get the bolt cutters from outside. Within a minute the man returned and with one snip they were inside the area. Rick opened one of the boxes and removed a set of instructions. He read it quickly and knew this was what they were looking for. The instructions said it must be used within three days of when the symptoms start and it must be injected intravenously. The last part dealt with recovery and obviously was referencing a deadly water borne chemical.

"This is it," he exclaimed.

One of the team stepped forward, took the paper, read it and said, "I agree. This is the neutralizer serum. Let's get it loaded."

As the boxes were being loaded onto the team's trucks, Robert came over to Rick and said, "I knew you had good instincts for how these people think."

"Thanks, Robert," replied Rick.

After about ten minutes a man yelled, "We're ready. Let's roll."

Rick noticed that the men made absolutely no attempt to cover-up their actions. They just left every door and gate wide open. It was almost as if they were showing their disdain for the owner of the warehouses. Everyone moved to their vehicle and sped off into the night. After a while the procession pulled into JFK International Airport. The driver of the lead vehicle never slowed down, even as gates were opened for him. They headed away from the main terminals and toward a cluster of military airplanes and vehicles. Rick counted six medium-sized cargo jets, about the size of a Boeing 737. Rick watched the unloading of the trucks and loading of the planes, marveling at the precision. The FBI team seemed to mesh perfectly with the military personnel that were loading the planes. Rick knew this was not the result hours of training together, but rather of the American spirit at work. The jet engines were already emitting their high-pitched whine when the cargo doors were closed. One man directed the planes onto the taxiways and Rick watched as the planes gained speed. He had never seen airplanes move so fast on the ground. He noticed that the rest of the airport seemed to have shut down. No planes were on the taxiways, no planes were on the runways and he could see airplanes in the sky, but none were on an approach. The rest of the world seemed to stand still as the six planes roared off on their mission to save the lives of millions. One of the military trucks pulled up to the team's truck and the last of the serum was loaded for distribution there in New York. That vehicle was loaded in about five minutes and roared out of the airport.

Bill Whetland turned to Rick and said, "Well, Rick, I know you thought we were moving kind of slow at first, but we're at full throttle now."

Rick replied, "I'm very impressed. In fact, I feel a lot better about sending my taxes to the government. I do have one question, though."

"And what might that be?" asked Bill.

Rick answered, "Well, I noticed that there were no markings on any of the men on the team and no markings on any of the vehicles. Everyone except Bill, you and me had their faces covered and they were very well equipped for some illegal breaking and entering. My question is-who were those masked men?"

Bill replied, "You're very observant, Rick. All I can tell you is they do not work directly for our government."

"Kind of a special task force with unlimited powers?" asked Rick.

"I've told you all I can," said Bill.

Rick could see it was time to let it drop.

Robert came up and said, "Rick, your country owes you a debt of gratitude. You've saved the lives of millions. Unfortunately, you can't tell anyone about this-no books, no interviews and no talk shows. We've let you see things that very few people know about. Your country is now placing a great deal of trust in your vow of secrecy. We can trust you can't we, Rick?"

"You sure can, Robert. Besides, I still have the Chicago Mafia to worry about. They would just love to see me on a talk show," replied Rick.

"You're right about that," said Robert. "Now I can offer you a ride to wherever you need to go."

Rick said, "I guess I need to go back to Chicago."

"Okay, I'll send you and dad back on the Lear."

"Thanks. By the way, what'll happen to Rene Charlton and his people?"

"We will have them in custody shortly. The paperwork we need to arrest Charlton and the others is dragging because of all the chaos. Several of the judges in Washington, D.C. drank the water and are out of action for a while. We do have Charlton under surveillance, so he won't get away. They'll be in jail soon," replied Robert.

Rick said, "I'm still concerned about his people being after my family."

"I think they'll be worrying about avoiding us, not about you anymore. Still, be careful," said Robert.

Rick was even able to get a little sleep on the plane ride back to Chicago. When they landed it was about daylight.

Bill and Rick each caught their own taxi and as they parted Bill said, "If you ever need me again don't hesitate to call."

"Thanks, I won't," replied Rick.

In his hotel room the TV was giving reports of the government's miraculous response to the epidemic. A cure had been discovered almost immediately and had been delivered to each of the afflicted cities. Every hospital in each city had the antidote in its possession and the military was setting up medical units at each high school in the cities. EMS vehicles were pouring in from cities all around the seven afflicted ones and were being dispatched to people who were too sick to leave their homes. Rick marveled at the speed and efficiency with which this was all happening. He swelled with pride. When there was trouble, Americans could always rise to the occasion. He showered and decided he had better call Kathy. He told her as much as he could, but somehow she already knew he was a part of the incredible life-saving effort underway.

"So, if I'm understanding all this and filling in the blanks right, you and your new buddies from the FBI went to the address in New York that I found in Worldwide Water's tenant file and ripped off their stockpile of neutralizer serum and distributed it across the country in a few hours last night?" Kathy asked, incredulously.

Rick felt the pride swelling his chest and said, "Yes, that's about it. The stuff wasn't in that warehouse, but we found it across the street. You know, I've never seen anything like the teamwork that I witnessed last night. It was truly amazing. To have a small part in it makes me feel really good."

"A small part? Didn't you come up with the theory that the neutralizer was stockpiled somewhere and didn't you come up with the address of the stockpile? Rick, I don't think that's a small part. I think you have saved millions of lives with a little help from your friends," said Kathy emphatically.

"Well, you are kind of biased," said Rick.

Kathy replied, "You're just trying to sound humble. You don't have to do that for me, Rick Blaze."

Rick laughed and said, "Okay, you're right. Actually, I feel pretty good about myself right now."

"Good," she said, "so do you think we're safe now? I mean from Larry, Ed, Rene and the Mafia?" she asked with hope in her voice.

Rick answered tentatively, "I'm not sure. The FBI thinks Rene's bunch will go into hiding and I don't think the Mafia could have found out anything."

"You don't sound so sure about Rene's bunch," replied Kathy.

"I'm not sure at all. I think we should assume they are still after us for a while."

"What are your plans now, Rick?"

"Later this morning I'm going over to Oakwood Towers Executive Suites to get the box I had Linda send me. I don't want a box full of guns sitting around there with my name on it. After I get the box I'll head in your direction. I'll call you later with the details. How're the boys doing?" he asked.

"I'm getting kind of worried about them. They keep talking about where it's best to shoot someone. I'm afraid if one of our friends here drops in they will get shot," she replied.

"Just tell them I said to keep the safeties on until they identify the person. And don't worry, they know how to handle guns," said Rick, trying to sound convincing.

Larry awoke the next morning and flipped on the local Chicago TV. He was expecting to revel in the pain and suffering Rene's plan had caused. It didn't matter to him that he was hurting his own country. Larry was a talent for hire and could not afford to be bound by patriotism or any such loyalties. As the reporter spoke Larry was shocked to see the forces at work. Where had the government gotten a neutralizer serum so fast? It was impossible. A thought hit him like a brick. He picked up the phone and dialed.

"Rene, this is Larry. Where did the government get their serum?"

Rene blasted out his answer, confirming Larry's fears. "They stole it from us. Someone came in last night and removed all of the neutralizer serum from the warehouse. No search warrant. No arrests. They just came in and took it."

Larry retorted, "They can't do that. They have to have proof, a warrant. There are laws about that kind of thing."

"Well, someone took the serum and the government ended up with it," replied Rene.

Larry asked, "What're we going to do? Should we leave the country?"

Rene barked, "No. I assume the FBI will have a warrant for me soon. I'm ready to duck out. But, you need to stay on task. I know where they got their information. It must be that Blaze fellow. You can't seem to stop him and now he has destroyed our operation. Worldwide Water and I will survive, but Rick Blaze and his family will not. I want you and Ed to find him and kill him. I'm putting the other three deployment teams on this mission as well now that they are through with making their canister drops. There will be an extra $100,000 to the team that accomplishes the task. Do you understand me, Larry?"

"Yes, sir, I understand perfectly. I also know where to find Blaze."

Larry thought about the $100,000 bonus and how he would enjoy collecting it. Things usually worked out for Larry and it looked like this was another victory for him. The result of all that had gone wrong because of Rick Blaze's interference was that Larry was going to collect a large bonus for killing Blaze and this was a job Larry would have done for free. Actually, this was a job that Larry would do, no matter what the monetary reward. He had a score to settle and he always followed through when revenge was the motive.

Jim Exner's heart jumped when he turned on the television and heard about the neutralizer serum.

"The serum must be administered by shot and apparently begins to work almost immediately," said the news anchor. Continuing she said, "Anyone can get the injection for free at any local hospital, minor emergency clinic or high school in the Boston area. If you are not able to travel, call 911 and give your address. They will dispatch an ambulance to give you the injection. However, authorities have asked us to encourage anyone who can travel to do so. It's much more efficient to give the shots at one of the hospitals or schools. Please leave the ambulance option to those who truly can't move or be moved. Local health department authorities are still warning citizens to avoid drinking tap water for at least another week. Bottled waters are completely safe."

Jim ran to Louise's side and said, "Honey, wake up, Louise. We've got to get you a shot. You'll be all right. Louise, can you hear me?"

"Uh huh, I hear you," Louise said faintly.

She was so doped up on painkillers she did not really have much of a clue of what she was talking about.

Jim was glad that at least she was moving and talking. She was beginning to become somewhat contorted by the awful effects of the chemical as her muscles convulsed and ripped against the bones. Jim picked her up and carried Louise to the car, trying to be as gentle with her as possible. After strapping her in he sped off to the nearest high school. It was only a half-mile away and he was there in a few minutes. As he approached the school Jim could see the thousands of vehicles converging on the site. He would never get the shot for Louise, he thought. But he knew the other sites would be just as crowded. Louise was beginning to moan again and each time she uttered the sound Jim felt a wave of fear come over him. He couldn't lose her. He just couldn't. Jim pulled into the long line and tried to reconcile himself to the hours it would take to progress to the front. If only he had gotten up earlier this morning he could have been at the front by now and Louise would be receiving her shot. As he was in the process of beating himself up, Jim noticed something truly astonishing-the line was moving rapidly. He kept moving up and within less than an hour he was within sight of the people giving out the shots. In another ten minutes a female dressed in military clothes ran up to the car.

"It's my wife. She needs a shot. She's dying," cried Jim.

Without saying a word, the woman ran around to the passenger side, opened the door and gave Louise an injection in the left arm. After applying a quick cotton ball and Band-Aid the lady ran back around to Jim's side.

"How about you, sir? Do you have any symptoms?" asked the lady.

"No, I'm fine," replied Jim.

"Great. Then move along," she said.

Jim yelled back at her as he drove off, "God bless you. God bless you all."

The lady smiled and waved to Jim and then sprinted back to get the next syringe.

Jim looked at Louise and prayed out loud for her to be all right. When he was through he heard Louise whisper, "Amen."

# Chapter 34

Rick knew the UPS deliveryman should show up at Oakwood Towers Executive Suites at mid-morning because that was the deadline for next day air shipments. He hoped the contaminated water had not decimated the local UPS branch too much and thrown off the delivery schedule. To be sure he called the local office and was told deliveries were running almost on time, mainly because the volume of shipments had diminished tremendously the last few days. It was about 10:00 a.m. and Rick was thanking the manager of Oakwood Towers Executive Suites for her help. She had really aided Rick by allowing the nighttime use of the conference room to a non-tenant. He was also glad she was a self-proclaimed "bottled water snob" and had not been stricken by the local water.

"If you ever come to Austin be sure to come by and see our operation," said Rick as he headed back to the Operations Area.

The box had arrived. Rick signed for it and started out the door. Now he just wanted to get back to the car and on a plane. As he turned the corner and headed for the reception area, a man stepped out of the bathroom and pressed something into his back.

A voice said, "Just walk straight to the elevators. Don't talk to anyone. I don't have a big problem with wasting you here, asshole."

Rick grimaced as he recognized Larry's voice. He knew the pressure in his back was from a gun and he knew Larry was dying to use it.

"Well, Larry, you finally got the drop on me. Why don't you just shoot me now and take your box of goodies," said Rick.

Larry snarled, "Because I want you to carry it down for me."

Rick sensed that Larry really just didn't want to attract any attention.

He said, "This box is heavy and is starting to slip out of my hands. If we are going all the way down without resting, at least let me get a better grip. I don't want you to shoot me if I drop it."

"Okay, but no funny business," said Larry.

Rick leaned the box against the wall and moved his hands around. He had timed it perfectly. The box was right next to the red emergency fire alarm lever. As he moved his hands he slid the right one over a couple of inches, grabbed the lever and pulled it down. Larry looked around instinctively as the sirens began to wail and when Rick felt the pressure from the gun in his back lessen he spun around and put the box between himself and Larry. Rick heard a muffled blast and felt the box being driven against him. Larry had fired, but the box contents had stopped the bullet.

Rick recovered his balance and pushed toward Larry, using his twenty-pound weight advantage and superior leg strength to maximum benefit. Larry fired again and once more the box stopped the bullet. Rick drove the box against Larry with all his might, flattening Larry up against a wall. All the air went out of

Larry and the gun fell to the floor. Rick kicked the gun away and dropped the heavy box down on Larry's feet and ankles.

Larry doubled over and fell to the floor. Rick darted down the hall to the stairway. After a couple of flights Rick could hear the door close and someone coming down the steps in a hurry. Taking the steps two and three at a time, Rick was able to descend the seven flights quickly and was out into the parking lot at a dead run. He heard a car start up and instinctively darted away from it. The car was moving now. Moving toward him. Rick turned to look and saw the white bandage across the driver's nose. Then he recognized the evil eyes of Ed Richter.

Larry was now running across the parking lot toward him. Rick took a quick look around and saw a bank of office warehouses less than a block away. He sprinted toward the building, widening the gap between him and his pursuers as Ed tried to negotiate the parking lot and Larry's smashed feet slowed him down. All those basketball games with Davis and Mack were paying off now. The thought of Davis and Mack also made him realize there would not be anyone swooping in to save him this time.

Rick bounded through the first office, yelling "There's a man with a gun after me. Call the police."

The offices cleared out immediately. Rick headed into the back offices trying to figure a way out of this. He spotted the copy room. It had a door that looked like it led to the warehouse part of the building. He ran in and surveyed the room. It was the standard copy room and kitchen combination so common in small offices. He only had a minute to do something.

Rick reached to the shelves and removed a spare copier toner cartridge. He blocked the door open a couple of inches with a box of paper clips. Moving quickly, Rick pealed back the protective strip from the toner box and placed the box carefully on top of the door. He saw a half-full pitcher of coffee on the warmer at the snack bar. Rick grabbed the pitcher and scrunched behind the entry door and waited. In less than fifteen seconds Larry came running down the hall.

He cried, "Ed, over here. I see a door. I think he just went through it."

"I'm right behind you," yelled Ed.

Larry burst into the room, saw the partially open door and charged through it. The toner cartridge fell from the top of the door and covered Larry with a layer of fine toner dust. He yelled and screamed as the toner crept into his eyes. The substance was a fine, insidious powder that worked its way into every opening and would not rub or wash off.

Ed came into the room at that moment and froze, amazed at the sight of Larry being covered in black toner dust. Rick swung from behind the door and slammed the glass coffee pitcher across the side of Ed's head. Ed shrieked as the hot coffee burned and the glass cut. Rick kicked him in the crotch and headed out the front door.

As he ran past the group of people gathered outside Rick yelled, "Those men in there are very dangerous. They have guns. Stay out of their way."

Rick ran as fast as his tiring body could go and quickly reached his rental car. As he jumped into the car and began to drive away he saw people gathering outside Oakwood Towers, reacting to the fire alarm Rick had pulled. He saw two men on the fringe kneeling by something. It was the box. They must have brought it down to show the police. They were pointing at the two bullet holes in the side.

Rick looked to see if Larry or Ed were coming. Seeing that

they were not, Rick squealed the tires as he headed toward the men. He screeched to a halt right by the box. The men jumped back and Rick stepped out and calmly picked up the box and placed it on the front seat.

He looked at the two men and said, "Thanks for bringing this down. I owe you one."

He jumped back into the car and sped off. Rick breathed a huge sigh of relief as he cleared the area. No one was following him, no police and no Larry. He had made a clean getaway, but this was certainly his closest call yet. A gun pointed in your back by your most hated enemy was a feeling Rick never wanted to relive. Yet he had made his escape without the help of Davis and Mack and had done it instinctively. That was truly amazing to Rick because he had never done anything like this. He had run from the Mafia and the FBI many years ago, but he had not had people pointing guns at him. He had a bit of confidence growing in him, but he cautioned himself to not get over confident. After all, it only took one bullet to change things forever.

Safreed al Habid knew what the summons to Saddam's court meant. His plan had failed and he would pay the price. The terror he had created only increased the resolve of the American people, particularly since virtually no one had died from the chemical-laced water. The efforts to administer the neutralizer serum were completely successful and he marveled at the American resolve to save each and every person. In Iraq the military would have received the serum and very little attention would have been paid to the citizens.

The Americans would be able to deal with the tainted water and all Safreed would have accomplished is to stir up a hornet's nest. He walked into the court erect and chest out. He was proud of his efforts, but he had tried and failed. His punishment would be swift.

Saddam bellowed, "Safreed al Habid, you have failed in your mission. You have made me a fool as I boasted on television that the plan was mine. You have caused the United States to double their efforts to stop us. You must pay for your failure. I sentence you to death by firing squad."

He nodded to one of his men who led Habid outside. Habid stood gallantly against the wall of death, as it was called by Saddam's inner circle. He refused the blindfold and any last requests. Safreed al Habid dropped to the ground, a hail of bullets visiting death upon him.

As Rick drove to the hotel his worst fears were confirmed. Rene, Larry and Ed would chase him forever if they had to. The irony almost overwhelmed Rick. He had been consumed with fear for over twenty years that the Mafia would be after him and now the fears were real except that the pursuers were not the Mafia, but a group of international criminals with no conscience and plenty of resources. His next move was clear; he had to get to Port Aransas. His family would be targets as well and he had to protect them. Rick dashed into the hotel room, scooped up his clothes and drove to the airport. He booked the first flight to Austin and called Kathy.

"I don't have much time, so just listen. They're still after us. Larry and Ed showed up in Chicago and almost got me. I'm heading to Port A. I think it's a safe spot for a while. I'm flying into Austin and picking up my car. My friend from Montana, Nate Reilly, should be at the office. He said he would watch the place for us. I'll be with you as soon as possible. Be very careful and keep the doors locked. If I'm not there by bedtime be sure the boys take turns watching. Don't take any chances. I love you. Got to go now."

"I love you, too," Kathy said.

Kathy told Davis and Mack about the call.

"Dad wants us to be careful, but he thinks they'll have a hard time finding us here," she said.

They kept the house locked up and even closed the storm shutters on the outside. The little white frame house was beginning to seem cramped with all three of them inside the whole time. The house was only a little over 600 square feet with one bedroom and one bathroom.

Rick was fond of saying that it was a one-bedroom, one-bath house that slept twelve because they never stayed there without some of the boys' friends tagging along. The original house was built in 1955 and had been through two major hurricanes since then, giving credibility to the strength of its construction.

It originally consisted of a tiny bathroom and a fourteen-by-twenty-four foot room that served as the kitchen, bedroom, dining room and living room. Sometime, probably thirty years ago, the bedroom had been added on in an interesting way. It was about nine-by-fifteen feet and had a sloped ceiling that Rick could barely stand under at the lowest point. Where there had been windows to the outside were now open-framed holes into the bedroom. This was done to help circulation from the one-window air-conditioner that cooled the whole house, but the two openings certainly cut down on the privacy.

Rick and Kathy claimed the bedroom and the boys and their friends slept on the various beds and couches that were crammed in the main room. The house was small and quirky, but the family loved it immensely. It was their getaway, their haven from the stresses and pressures of the world.

Hours came and went as they waited for Rick. With their food supply running low Davis decided it would be best to stock up now, before it got completely dark. He peered out the door, saw nothing and stepped out. He walked the block to the grocery store, bought a couple of bags of food and headed back to the house. As he walked up the steps a man sprang from around the corner and pointed a rather large gun at Davis' head.

"Knock on the door and tell them to let you in," growled the man.

Davis did as he was ordered. Mack opened the door and the man pushed Davis in and pointed the gun at both of them. Another man bounded up the steps and into the house. Both men had their guns trained on Davis and Mack.

"Don't even think of trying anything," said the second man, who sported a scar running across his forehead.

"Yeah, he don't want to hurt you, at least not until your dad gets here. You see, its payback time and I'm the paymaster," croaked the first man, a short and ugly man.

The men made Kathy, Davis and Mack sit in chairs in the bedroom and bound and gagged them.

"Now we just wait until the mysterious Rick Blaze shows up. He won't be able to deal with us as easy as he did with Ed and Larry. The boss thinks they are the number one team, but this will show him who is the best. It will also put a cool $100,000 in our pockets," said Shorty.

Scarface snapped, "Hey, shut up. We don't need to tell these guys about the bonus."

"Yeah, okay, we'll just sit here and wait."

The two men sat down and began to play cards, laughing and cursing at the various hands they were dealt. In about an hour the phone rang.

Shorty said to Kathy, "Answer that. If it's your husband don't say anything that would cause me to get an itchy trigger finger. I might have to take out one of the boys here."

He ripped the tape off Kathy's mouth and put the receiver to her ear, tilting it so he could hear also.

"Hello?" she said.

"Hi. What's up? You sound kind of upset," said Rick.

"No, I'm okay. I guess I'm just tired. We just got back from spending the day at the beach. In fact, we went to two of our favorite beaches."

The man nudged the barrel of his gun into her ribs.

She said, "Are you coming today or tomorrow?"

Rick knew something was wrong so he added a couple of hours onto his arrival time. "I'll be there about 10 tonight. I'll see you then. I love you," said Rick.

"Yeah, all right, see you then," said Kathy.

The phone line went dead and Rick's mind began to race. He knew something was wrong because Kathy would not have spent the day at the beach. That must have been her way of warning him. She had also asked if he was coming tomorrow when she knew he was due to arrive today and she always, without exception, said I love you whenever he did. He was positive there was someone else there. Could it have been Ed and Larry or maybe Rene had sent others after his family? How was he going to deal with this?

Rick recanted the conversation over and over. Why did she say they went to two of their favorite beaches? Maybe that meant there were two people at the house. They must be holding his family hostage, just waiting for him to show up. Then they would all be killed. A deadly calm came over Rick as he vowed to become the hunter instead of the hunted.

Nate Reilly walked into Rick's office at Austin Executive Suites.

"What's up, Rick? You look positively pissed," said Nate.

"I am. I think the bad guys are holding my family in Port A," responded Rick.

"Holy shit, boy. What are you going to do now?"

"I'm going to get my family back," said Rick with a steely glare.

"Well, if you need any help giving somebody a good ass-whipping, I'm your man," said Nate.

"Thanks, Nate. I hate to put you in real danger, but I can't turn down the help."

"What's a little danger among friends? When do we leave?" quizzed Nate.

"As soon as possible. Let's check out that box I swiped from Larry and Ed. Maybe some of that stuff will help," replied Rick.

As he emptied the contents Rick found two silenced Glock 9 millimeter handguns, plenty of ammo and clips, several types of holsters, six smoke grenades, a parabolic listening device, infrared night vision glasses, regular binoculars and a pair of two-way radios with headsets. Fortunately, the two bullets Larry had blasted into the box at Oakwood Towers Executive Suites had damaged nothing. One of the Glocks had a dinged and cracked grip and one box of ammo had absorbed a bullet.

"Hoo, boy. These people are serious. This is really expensive stuff," whistled Nate.

"Yeah, it was nice of them to provide for us so well," replied Rick.

"I know you don't want to hear this and I'm kind of surprised to think it myself, but now that you have connections in the FBI, maybe you should let them handle this," said Nate.

"I haven't had any luck with them protecting me or any of my family. I have to take care of this myself, Nate. Those guys won't do anything to my family until I get there. I'm the one they really want and they won't mess with the bait until I'm taken care of. I'm ready to leave. Are you in?" asked Rick.

"I'm in. Let's roll."

"Thanks, Nate, I really appreciate your help," said Rick.

# Chapter 35

While the United States was dealing with a major terrorist attack on its home soil, the military had put maximum effort into retaking control of Kuwait and Saudia Arabia. The first task had been to put as many assets in place as possible. Submarines churned toward the area, not concerned with stealth, just speed. Airplanes and troops flew in from the United States and foreign bases. Fighters, troop carriers, electronic surveillance planes and bombers flooded into the area. Aircraft carrier groups came from various parts of the world, causing some military advisors to warn of other potential hot spots igniting. These fears were brushed aside as the task at hand was all consuming. This was not a campaign just to free the two Middle Eastern countries; it was a campaign to destroy Iraq.

For all its abilities the United States military could not do miracles, so the logistics of boat speed and distance to travel became paramount in the planning of Operation Desert Fury, as the President had named it. As soon as enough troops and equipment were in place to please the generals the President gave the command to proceed.

Then it started and the name Desert Fury seemed entirely appropriate. The plan was to cut the Iraqi troops in Saudia Arabia and Kuwait off from their supply routes and destroy any radar locations in Iraq. Like the first Gulf War, the Stealth Bombers came over Baghdad at night and rained destruction upon any and all military targets. The Iraqi operators of the new Chinese radar that claimed to be able to detect Stealth aircraft perished without a clue of their impending doom.

After the Stealth Bombers left Baghdad the Tomahawk Cruise missiles began descending, sometimes aimed at the same targets as the Bombers, just to make sure. Hundreds of Tomahawks further reduced the city of Baghdad to rubble. There were no games about trying to separate civilians from the military this time. It was war and Saddam had attacked American civilians at home.

Next came the destruction of cities between Baghdad and Saudia Arabia. An Nukhayb and Karbala were destroyed, then An Najaf and Al Hillah. Almost immediately the supplies to the troops in Saudia Arabia began to dry up. Because of the limited space in the tunnels Saddam had begun the war with minimal ammunition and fuel reserves. Counting on continued supplies from Iraq was proving to be a mistake. His forces could get fuel in Saudia Arabia, but not ammunition for his Russian-made weapons.

The Persian Gulf was now full of American war ships. Their missiles and aircraft pounded Basra and An Nasinyah to the north of Kuwait. Iraqi soldiers in their occupied territories were alone now and most were beginning to realize this fact.

The mobile surface-to-air sites were the next to go. Although they had inflicted minimal damage on American aircraft thus far because of electronic jamming and the high altitude that the aircraft maintained, lower level flights were needed. The Iraqi SAM operators made critical mistakes by turning on their radar trying to take a shot at highflying aircraft. This enabled the AWACS planes to pinpoint their exact location. Before the SAMS could move Tomahawks were programmed and launched, followed by low-level cluster bomb attacks. After two days no SAM sites were operating or at least willing to turn their radar on. The Russian S-300 PMU-1 defense system had proven to be woefully inadequate against the electronic capabilities of the Americans.

The Iraqis tried targeting some American ships with the SS-21 Ballistic Missiles. Their range of 120 kilometers allowed some shots at the Persian Gulf fleet. However, the Phalanx Chain-gun Defense System had been greatly improved since the first Gulf War and only a few SS-21's got by, inflicting little damage. As with the SAM sites, each launch of an SS-21 allowed the Americans to pinpoint the launcher's location and to destroy it within fifteen minutes.

Then, the difficult part began. An estimated 250,000 Iraqi troops were in Saudia Arabia and Kuwait. They were cut off from Iraq, but they were also occupying the military installations that had been built recently to protect against outside attack. The American generals decided the first step would be to free Kuwait. It was smaller and the United States military presence was far greater at that point because of the Persian Gulf. The Kuwait citizens had fled to the coast and were being taken care of by the Red Cross and also troops sent by the United Nations. The Americans had made it clear to all concerned that it was now personal and they would deal with Iraq.

The Iraqis had about 75,000 men in Kuwait and they were scattered throughout the country. Operation Desert Fury pointed its attack at the perimeter and began squeezing in slowly and surely. The Iraqi troops gave ground willingly at first, until they realized they were being herded to slaughter. It was like an old-west cattle drive, when a stray left the herd it was forced back. When the 75,000 troops were left to make their stand together, all hell broke loose. Cluster bombs rained down upon them and helicopter gun ships emptied their magazines from above. Tanks fired shells into the middle, hoping to take out the command posts. The Iraqis had no air support, no reinforcements and were low on ammunition. There was really no one to fire at anyway. The destruction came from well beyond their range.

It was over in a couple of days. The Iraqis surrendered and were disarmed and released to return home. They were sternly warned that satellites would monitor their progress home and any indication of returning to the military would start the bloodbath again.

The same tactic was used in Saudia Arabia although the Iraqis knew what was going on this time. More skirmishes erupted, but the Americans continued their destruction from the air. The Iraqi electronic warfare machine was dead and only the foot soldier with his limited weaponry was left to deal with the wrath of the greatest military power on earth. A few days later what was left of the 175,000 troops in Saudia Arabia trudged back to Iraq unarmed and disgraced. It was hard to get an exact count, but the best guess was that Iraq had lost at least 100,000 and probably closer to 150,000 troops with American losses numbering in the hundreds.

As the American troops celebrated, one common thought flowed through their minds-that Saddam Hussein was buried under the rubble of Baghdad. However, they were realistic enough to know that Saddam would not have risked danger to himself if he could help it. Hiding seemed to be his greatest talent.

Two days after the victory American General Vince Petralli addressed his troops and the world.

"We have achieved a great victory here over a relentless opponent. When I was given command of Operation Desert Fury I received orders not only to free Kuwait and Saudia Arabia, but also to make sure this does not happen again. Hundreds of your fellow Americans paid for this victory with their lives and we shall let their memory guide us in our quest to keep peace in the area. I think that most of the people of Iraq recognize the folly of testing the United States. The one person who can't seem to grasp this futility is Saddam Hussein. He is willing to have thousands of his countrymen slaughtered while he cowers deep inside some bunker in Baghdad. After the first Gulf War we thought that the Iraqi citizenry would rise up and replace Saddam with a new leader. Apparently, either they did not want this or Saddam is too strong to overthrow. In any event, I have been given approval to initiate Operation Saddam Watch. It's a very straightforward operation. If and when Saddam ever appears in public or addresses the Iraqi people in any manner cruise missiles and bombs will rain down upon his location. This will happen until we never hear from Saddam Hussein again."

The cheering from the troops told General Petralli all he needed to know about his speech.

The next day planes flew over all parts of Iraq, dropping leaflets written in Arabic that contained the text of General Petralli's speech.

# Chapter 36

Rick and Nate drove on through the night, formulating a plan to save his family. He used to worry how he would react if he had to fire a gun at another human being. He had wondered if he would be able to pull the trigger in order to hurt another person. At this moment, Rick was not concerned at all about being able to fire at these people holding his family. Nobody was going to mess with his family this way. Rick's face began to redden and the veins in his neck started to bulge out. The rage was hard to contain, but he had to get it under control. He had to be cool, calm and efficient.

It was about eight o'clock when Rick and Nate arrived in Port Aransas following a four-hour drive and a short ferry ride from Aransas Pass. Fortunately, a moonless night would provide them with a cover of darkness. As Rick drove through the town he saw the nightclubs and restaurants coming to life and people out to have a good time, a relaxing vacation. The last time Rick relaxed seemed so long ago. Rick pulled the Blazer into the empty field next to their house. A large clump of bushes ten feet from the house was where Rick parked the vehicle and began to set up his equipment. Nate hooked up the parabolic listening device and pointed it at the bedroom. Voices started coming through the headset.

"Hey, Rick. I got something. I can hear two guys talking," whispered Nate.

"Let me see if I can recognize the voices," said Rick softly.

He heard two men, definitely not Larry or Ed. They were talking to each other and also directing comments to Kathy and the boys. Rick knew they were all in the bedroom. His blood began to boil as he heard the two men discuss how they would take care of this Rick Blaze who kept making Larry and Ed look like fools.

Shorty said, "I'll take a lot of pleasure in popping this guy. Mr. Charlton will be very happy and the bonus will sure feel good in my wallet."

Scarface replied, "You better not mention the boss man's name around these people."

Shorty said, "They won't live to tell anybody."

Scarface replied, "Yeah, well it still is not a good idea."

"Aw, go stick it!" snorted Shorty.

From this conversation there was absolutely no doubt about their intentions.

Rick took off the headset and whispered to Nate, "There are two men, all right, but it's not the two I keep bumping into. It's another team and they obviously intend to kill us all. They even talked about a bonus for the job."

"Man, that's cold. Do you have any ideas? I guess we can either try to take them inside or lure them outside," said Nate.

"They think I won't be here for a couple of hours so I think we should take them by surprise inside," replied Rick.

"We have to be really careful with your family in there," replied Nate.

"Sure do," said Rick as he pondered his next move.

Rick had to get inside and eliminate the two men without hurting his family. The big question was how. He could kick down the front door, but that would give the men time to react and possibly shoot Kathy or one of the boys. There was no way to come in from underneath and all the windows had the storm windows closed. The house was completely buttoned up.

"The attic," Rick whispered. "I can get into the attic."

"How are you going to do that?" asked Nate.

"Look up there at the gable. There was a vent but it kept rusting out and so I covered it with a piece of plywood. I can remove the screws and crawl through the hole into the attic," answered Rick.

"Yeah, but you have to get up there first."

"There's a ladder under the house."

"Okay, you get into the attic, then what?" asked Nate.

"I'm not sure. Give me a minute."

After a couple of minutes Rick whispered the plan to Nate. Rick pulled his ladder out from under the house and leaned it up against the sidewall. The ever-present howling winds of the Texas coast and the humming of the window air-conditioner provided noise to cover his actions. He climbed up the ladder and with a screwdriver from his survival pack removed the two foot square piece of plywood that covered the old gable vent opening. He climbed down the ladder with the plywood. Nate and Rick strapped on the silenced Glocks and put on the night vision goggles. They each wore one of the two-way radios with a headset. Rick thought that if he knocked out the power and wore the night vision goggles he would certainly be the only one who could see in the house. Rick checked the parabolic listening device and determined that the two men were still in the same place.

He and Nate shook hands and began their quest. Nate positioned himself by the main breaker panel and opened the cover. He waited as Rick climbed the ladder.

Rick headed up the ladder with a steely resolve. He climbed through the gable hole and into the attic. Sitting perched above the scuttle hole into the main room Rick readied his Glock and switched on the night vision goggles. It was amazing to be able to see in the dark attic. He took a deep breath and whispered into the headset, “Go, go, go.”

Nate heard the go, go, go in his headset and pulled down on the main circuit breakers. Then he ran around the corner to the front of the house and began to bang on the door.

As soon as Rick heard the banging he kicked the scuttle hole cover away and dropped through the hole towards the floor below.

The two men knew something was happening, but weren’t sure what. No lights and someone banging on the door. Their training kicked in and they instinctively responded. Shorty moved through the doorway into the main room. He crouched and pointed his Glock at the door. Scarface stayed with Kathy and the boys, his Glock sweeping the darkness. As Shorty felt his way toward the door he heard a noise above him and then someone crashed onto him.

Rick was as surprised as Shorty when he landed right on top of the man. Fortunately, Rick had driven Shorty to the floor face first, keeping the man from having a shot at him. Rick pressed the Glock against the lump beneath him and pulled the trigger several times. The 9-millimeter bullets poured into Shorty and mushroomed as they were designed to do. The bullets did their job, shredding muscle and tearing organs. Shorty’s life ebbed out quickly.

Scarface heard the commotion in the main room and hesitated. Should he stay with the hostages or check out Shorty's predicament? This hesitation proved costly as Scarface decided to enter the main room.

Rick rolled off Shorty and tried to focus through the night vision goggles. They were slightly askew but he was able to catch a glimpse of a large man coming into the room. Rick was lying on his back with the Glock extended above him. The man was right on top of him as Rick pulled the trigger. There was almost no way he could miss from this range and he kept pulling the trigger until the slide locked open. The man staggered, but his momentum carried him forward. He toppled onto Rick like a two hundred pound sack of feed. Rick grimaced as the dead weight landed on him. He could tell there was no life in the body and yelled, "Kathy, it's me. I'm okay."

Rick rolled the body off and dashed to the door.

"Nate, it's me, I'm coming," he yelled.

Rick threw the door open and Nate jumped in, Glock ready.

"It's over, Nate," said Rick with a great sigh.

Through his night vision goggles Nate saw the two bodies lying on the floor just ten feet away. With a sense of pride he said, "I guess I trained you pretty well, boy."

"Yeah, I guess so."

"I'm going to turn the power back on. You go get your family," said Nate.

"Take those funny-looking goggles off first. We don't want the neighbors to see you," replied Rick.

Rick quickly untied Kathy, Davis and Mack. The lights came back on as they were pulling the tape off their mouths. They seemed to be all right. They all hugged each other and Rick and

Kathy embraced and kissed for what seemed like minutes.

"Wow, Dad, that was something. Where did you come from?" asked Mack.

Rick replied, "I just dropped in from the attic. I guess they were expecting me to use the door."

Kathy looked at the gun and the funny-looking goggles Rick had pushed back on his head and, though trying to regain her composure, said, "There's something different about your outfit tonight. I just can't put my finger on it."

"Larry was nice enough to let me use his equipment. It was quite helpful of him and you were clever enough to alert me to the situation," said Rick.

Kathy asked, "What about those two men? Do we need to tie them up or get them to a doctor?"

"Kathy, they're dead," Rick said, beginning to shake a little.

"Oh my God, you've killed two men! I just can't believe it has come this far," Kathy replied, starting to cry.

"We're just doing what we have to do," replied Rick, putting his arm around her.

"Hey, anybody want to introduce me?" asked Nate.

"Sorry, Nate. This is my wife Kathy and my two sons, Davis and Mack. And this is Nate Reilly, my friend from Montana," said Rick.

"Very nice to meet you, Mr. Reilly," said Kathy, still breathing rapidly.

"Nate, please."

"Dad, I'm sorry we didn't do our job taking care of mom," said Davis.

"Yeah, we really blew it," Mack agreed.

"Look guys, these two men were professionals. I put you in

danger and it almost cost me everything I hold dear," Rick said, still shaking.

"Rick, what are we going to do now?" asked Kathy.

"First of all we are going to get out of here. Then we can figure out what to do long-term," replied Rick.

Rick went outside and looked around the neighborhood and saw no one.

He said, "I want the three of you to get in your car and disappear for a while. Nate and I will deal with the situation here and police if they show up."

"We can stay here and help, Dad," said Mack.

"Yeah, after all, we let you down. We let those guys get the drop on us," said Davis.

Rick looked at them and said, "You didn't let me down. These guys are professionals, just like Larry and Ed, and you guys are students. You have saved me and I have saved you. That's the way the Three Musketeers work, isn't it, Kathy?"

"Yes, dear, that is the way it works," she said, her voice trembling with fear and relief.

Rick put the guns and goggles inside the house and fairly pushed the three into Kathy's car.

"Drive around or go to Snoopy's or Shorty's for about an hour, then come back. Now go," Rick said firmly.

Davis drove the car off, hoping he was doing the right thing.

Rick was encouraged that no police or neighbors had shown up. He figured the two men used the same silenced Glocks that he had. With the storm shutters closed the house looks the same with or without electricity. He was not sure what to do with the two bodies, but didn't want to be tied up with the authorities and leave his family unguarded. He wanted them to stick together until this ordeal was over. Rick went back into the house. Nate was checking out the two bodies. He pulled their guns away and searched their pockets.

"Rick, you might be interested in this," said Nate, handing him a piece of paper.

Rick was startled when he read a fax from Larry addressed to all field personnel.

The fax said, *I have found the location of Rick Blazes' wife. His sons may be with her or with him.* The fax went on to give the telephone number and address of the Port A house.

It suddenly hit Rick that Larry must have discovered this and where the box was sent to him in Chicago from Austin Executive Suites. Kathy must have left the number to call in an emergency and Larry found it and possibly the UPS shipping records. Damn, we must be more careful, Rick thought.

"This is really getting complicated, Nate."

"It sure is, Rick."

"We need to do something with these bodies," observed Rick.

"Let's just dump these sons-of-bitches in the ocean," said Nate coldly.

Rick recoiled at first but then said, "You know, you might be right."

"Really? I would have thought you would want to give them a proper burial or something like that," said Nate.

"Screw'em," replied Rick gruffly.

"Damn straight," agreed Nate.

Now that they agreed on what to do they had to figure out how to do it. As Rick pondered what to do with the bodies, suddenly an idea hit him. Rick went around the side and put all his gear back into the Blazer. He drove the truck around by the storage shed and loaded several things inside the back. He pulled around front and parked. Nate had taken all identification from the two men and put their stuff into a large trash bag. He did keep their two Glock pistols out, putting them with their ever-expanding arsenal. Together Rick and Nate put two trash bags over each body, one on the head and one on the feet. The two bags overlapped nicely on each body. They wrapped duct tape all over the bodies. By now an hour had passed and Kathy and the boys returned. They looked pretty shaken and Rick felt bad for them.

He said, "This night has been pretty harrowing for all of us. I think we should get a room over at the Tarpon Inn for tonight. We can't stay here anyway since they know about this house."

"Do you think there are more on the way?" asked Kathy.

"Yes, I'm almost sure of it," said Rick. Continuing he said, "You all go over to the Tarpon and get one room. We'll all stay together. Nate and I will deal with these bodies and then we'll meet you there."

Mack asked, "What are you going to do with them, Dad?"

Davis put his hand on Mack's shoulder and said, "I don't think Dad wants us to ask that question."

Davis started them toward the car and Rick said, "I do need to see you all inside for a minute."

They came in and sat down, trying to ignore the fact that there were two dead people in the other room.

"I want each of you to hold one of these," Rick said, handing each of a Glock. "These handguns are identical and I want you to get familiar with them. They are very high-tech guns. They are Glock 9mm semi automatics. They have the safety built into the trigger so to fire all you do is put your finger on the trigger and pull. There is no other safety. These guns have been modified by adding a silencer. This is extremely illegal so no one can see these guns. Get used to their feel and balance," Rick instructed. "Now go," he said. "I'll be there in a couple of hours."

"Rick, are you sure you know what you're doing?" asked Kathy.

"As much as ever," answered Rick.

"That's not much of an answer," Kathy replied.

"I know, but I'm just making this up as I go," Rick said.

"I'm just afraid we're pushing our luck. We've had some pretty harrowing experiences," she said.

"I know, Kathy. We just need to keep our wits about us and continue to persevere."

"Yeah, but I'm really scared, Rick."

"Me, too."

As they drove off Kathy said to the boys, "I've always said I hope you guys turn out to be just like your father, but now I'm not so sure. I have never seen him like this. I just don't know what to think."

Davis said, "It's okay, Mom. He is just doing what he has to do. He's going to pull us through this."

Rick looked up and down the street. It was dark and quiet. Nate helped him hoist one of the bodies over his shoulder. Rick carried it out to the Blazer and chunked it in the back. They repeated the procedure with the second body. Nate threw a plastic tarp tent over the bodies and went back inside. Rick pulled out two dishrags and sprayed them liberally with glass cleaner. Moving as fast as he could Rick wiped down the furniture, doors, cabinets and walls to remove any fingerprints. Nate sprayed the entire container of Resolve carpet cleaner on the blood spots in the bedroom and wiped the spots on the wood floor in the main room with another rag. Next, he rearranged the room to position the throw rug over the remaining bloodstain. Rick and Nate then loaded all the gear into the Blazer and locked the house up. Rick went around the side and screwed the plywood back over the gable vent hole, put the ladder back underneath the house, locked the storage shed and drove off.

They drove slowly to the beach and turned south. For several miles they continued a slow pace down the beach. When they passed the last hotel Rick slipped the Blazer into four-wheel drive, pressed down his right foot and blasted down the beach. He kept the pace up for thirty minutes and suddenly stopped and backed the Blazer toward the water, stopping at the water's edge.

Rick pulled out one of the bodies, an old surf board, some bricks and about twenty feet of 12 gauge interior Romex wire that he had removed from his storage shed. Nate wound the wire around the body and through the holes in about ten bricks. He rolled the body onto the surfboard as Rick stripped off his clothes. Rick began walking the board out into the Gulf of Mexico. When the water got too deep to walk Rick began to swim the board out farther. The water was cold and Rick had another trip to make so he dumped the body off the surfboard and into the Gulf.

He laid on the surfboard and glided back to the beach with the waves and started the process over again. This time was harder because he was tired and cold, but he struggled to get out as far as he had with the first body. Finally, he judged it to be far enough and dumped the second body. He hesitated as it dropped out of sight, feeling a chill that was not due to the cold ocean. Again, he glided back to the beach.

He dried off with some clothes from his bag and put his old clothes back on. Nate drove the Blazer back up the beach as Rick tried to warm up and recover mentally from what he had just done. He longed to be back with his family again. He would not leave them again. They must be together. He was almost comatose with exhaustion, both physical and mental, when they arrived at the Tarpon Inn. Rick and Nate went into the room at the famous old hotel and they all sat together holding hands.

Mack looked up after a while, grinned and said softly, “Blaze’s rule.”

They all looked at each other and joined in, “Blaze’s rule, Blaze’s rule, Blaze’s rule.”

After a while Rick said, “I hate to put a damper on our celebration, but if these guys knew where to find us, you can bet they told Larry and any others that are looking for us. I don’t think they’ll find us at the Tarpon, but we should assume that they are here now or on the way. In the morning we can think about a new plan for getting away. Right now we all should sleep and get our strength back. We are winning the battles, but the war is still on.”

As they lay in bed Kathy asked Rick, “Are you okay? After all, you have had your family held hostage, killed two people and done heaven-knows-what with their bodies. You have no intention of turning this over to the local police and we still have people after us. I just can’t imagine how you are dealing with this so well.”

“I don’t know,” replied Rick. “I just seem to be on some kind of autopilot. I just know what I need to do. I’m sure it will sink in later, but I hope it waits until I get us out of this mess. Speaking of handling things, you’re really holding up well. It’s probably been scarier for you than me. I’m proud of you.”

“Thanks. I’ve certainly never been so scared in my life as tonight,” she said. Continuing she said, “You know, I’m really proud of Davis and Mack. I hope you don’t blame them for us being held hostage. They did their best.”

“Yes, I know. I don’t blame them at all. They are supposed

to be students, not secret agents. Like I said back at the house, we are supposed to take care of each other and that's what has happened. They have saved me and I have saved them."

"We are quite a family, aren't we?" asked Kathy, her voice catching.

Rick replied, "Yes, we are. We really are."

"It's great to have Nate here, isn't it?"

"It sure is."

# Chapter 37

Larry and Ed were in Ed's Cessna, flying south. They had gone back to Austin to get the plane and continue the pursuit of Rick Blaze. Team 2 had followed up on the phone number for Kathy Blaze that Larry had found in the operations area at Austin Executive Suites. The number had been traced to a house in Port Aransas, Texas. Under the assumption that Kathy Blaze was hiding there, Team 2 had gone to check it out. When the assumption proved to be correct Team 2 had contacted Team 1(Larry and Ed), Team 3 and Team 4. Each team had two men and was responsible for the canister drops for their territories.

Team 2 had not checked in at their scheduled time so Larry assumed a problem had surfaced. This probably meant that Rick had shown up to be with his family and Team 2 was not able to handle the situation. Teams 3 and 4 were converging in cars while Larry and Ed flew in. They were not about to let Rick Blaze get the best of them anymore. They were professionals and this was a situation they should be able to handle easily. The fact that it was not going easily was not lost on the men. Their resolve was dampened somewhat by the complete disaster their plans had turned into. At least they had the $100,000 bonus to look forward to when they disposed of the Blazes.

Larry dialed his cell phone and spoke, "Where are you now, Team 3?"

The voice answered, "Arriving in Port Aransas from Corpus Christi. I just talked to Team 4 and they should arrive at the ferry soon. There's still no word from Team 2."

Larry said, "All right, keep an eye out for any of their vehicles. You have pictures of all family members and descriptions of their vehicles from the Texas Department of Motor Vehicles. We will arrive within the next 30 minutes. Meet us at the airport then. Pass this information on to Team 4."

The next morning the Blaze family got up and turned on the TV. The neutralizer serum was working perfectly and the cooperation between government agencies and private citizen groups was unprecedented. It was the American spirit at its best. Rick breathed a sigh of relief when he finally felt sure he had not cost people their lives. He was beginning to wonder if there had been a better way of dealing with the situation yesterday. Was killing the men and dumping them in the Gulf of Mexico the best way? For the life of him, Rick could not think of an alternative that would have worked. If in hindsight he couldn't think of a better way, he knew he could live with what he had done. His family was safe and that was the main thing. Rick felt refreshed and could tell that Kathy and the boys were in pretty good shape. It was time to talk about getting out of there.

"Okay, troops, let's get a plan. I say let's load everything into one car and high-tail it away from here," Rick said.

"I don't want to leave my plane here," exclaimed Mack.

A thought hit Davis and he said, "You know, Dad, Mack

and I could spot Nate, mom and you from the air. I bet those fancy two-way radios you got from Larry's stuff would keep us in touch from about a mile. We could see if anyone was following you or waiting up ahead of us."

Rick replied, "I like your plan, but I would prefer that we be together."

"As much as I hate to say it, I think the boys have a point, Dear," said Kathy.

"Sounds good to me, too," added Nate.

Seeing he was out-voted and actually feeling pretty good about this idea Rick said, "Okay, let's do it that way. Split up the gear. I want everyone to have their own stuff and I want the weapons divvied up as well. Do it quickly and let's get on the way. We'll take my Blazer and leave Mom's car here."

They quickly packed, checked out and drove to the airport.

Rick said, "Mack, since you fly so much faster than we drive you can fly in circles around us. Try to stay around 2000 feet up so our radios will work. If you have to go higher to get a good look that's okay, just stay in touch. We're going straight to the ferry now. You should be up by the time we get across the ship channel. Be careful and don't take any chances."

"Sure, Dad," they said together.

Jim Exner looked at his wife Louise and smiled. Twenty-four hours earlier he knew in his heart he would lose her and now, thanks to the miracle serum, she was recovering at a fast rate. Her fever was almost back to normal and although her muscles were damaged they would be back to normal in about a month.

Jim saw Louise open her eyes and said, "How're you doing, honey?"

She smiled faintly and replied, "A lot better than I ever

expected to feel again. Just being able to talk to you is such a blessing."

"You gave me quite a scare. I thought, well, you know what I thought," Jim said, choking up.

"I was thinking the same thing, Jim," she said.

They embraced and cried together.

After a minute Louise asked, "Jim, is everyone that got sick getting well like me?"

"Most are. The serum seems to work fast on everybody. CNN said an hour ago that all seven cities that were poisoned are reporting very high recovery rates. The biggest problem now is getting water to drink until the chemicals are washed out of the system. Unfortunately the washing out procedure really just means the tainted water runs downstream so those towns below the seven cities are in danger. One report said they think that so much was ingested into the water treatment plants of the original cities that a much smaller danger is seen for the downstream people," replied Jim.

Louise asked, "I guess that's the best we could ever hope for. Maybe someone will come up with a quicker way to clean up the water."

"Well, one of the last reports said a group of scientists are working with the neutralizer serum formula to see if they can use it to clean up the water, either at the lake or at the water treating plant," Jim replied.

"I hope we have enough bottled water to last us until the water is safe," Louise said.

Jim answered with pride, "You just wouldn't believe the efforts private companies and the different levels of government are going to in order to supply all the bottled water that the cities need. The bottled water companies are working overtime to produce as much as possible and selling the water at their cost. Some of the beer companies are bottling just water in the cans and the government is furnishing extra vehicles to move the water to us. The military is hauling regular water in from other cities in their tank trucks and people can fill up jugs or whatever they have. It's really amazing to see what Americans can and will do when the chips are down."

Louise thought a minute and said, "You know, Jim, I'm not a vengeful person, but I can't help thinking that Saddam Hussein needs to be taught a lesson for his deeds. This whole thing is really stupid if he ever looked at our history. Nothing we have done would ever cause anyone to think we would back down from our convictions because of a terrorist stunt like this."

"That's pretty puzzling until you consider that this Saddam fellow always seems to me to be a big blowhard moron," laughed Jim. Continuing he said, "He's certainly paying the price now from his lunacy. After the Stealth bombers took out all the radar installations we sent in waves of Cruise missiles and regular bombers. The President's plan to level anything in Iraq that could have anything to do with the military seems popular. When our forces were strengthened enough the military pushed the Iraqis to the center of Kuwait and Saudia Arabia and squeezed the life out of them. Saddam even sent some of his fighter planes up to engage us and he lost almost his whole air force, just like the first Gulf War. You know, the President is so popular now I think he will certainly be our President until his two-term limit is up. He could almost be elected king with his popularity. But then I thought the same thing about President Bush and look how that turned out."

Louise smiled and said, "I'm just glad you and I will be around for our full terms."

As Team 4 was crossing the channel on one of the ferryboats the two men scanned the shore and the other ferries.

One of the men pointed at the ferry heading for the mainland and shouted, “Look, on that ferry. A Blazer. I can’t see the license plate. Pull over when we get off and I’ll use the binoculars.”

They pulled over to the side and the man crawled on top of his car and peered toward the other side with his binoculars. As the Blazer drove off the ferry and headed for Aransas Pass the man could clearly see the license plates. It was Rick Blaze.

The man jumped down, grabbed the cell phone and called Larry.

“Larry, I found them. They just left Port Aransas heading toward Aransas Pass. I guess they’re going back to Austin. They are in a black Chevy Blazer with the license number you have. Do you want me to go after them?” said the man.

Larry replied, “No, we can catch them easily. Meet us at the airport. We’ll be landing in a couple of minutes.”

All three teams met at the airport and Larry barked out instructions. “I want to be there when we catch him so I’m changing the team structure. Ed, you take Wayne in the plane and Hal will come with me. Team 3 will remain the same. I’ll be Team 1 and Ed will be Team 4. Team 4 will guide us from the air. Team 1 and Team 3 will each take a car. Everybody put on their radios and tune to channel 3. Now, lets go.”

They all scrambled to their vehicles.

“Dad, come in. Are you there?”

“Yes, Davis, I can hear you. Can you see us?” Rick asked.

Davis replied, “Yes, I can see you fine. We saw something else. Just as we left the airport a white Cessna with a red stripe was on its approach."

"I guess we have to assume it was Ed and Larry," said Rick.

Davis answered, "We don't have to assume anything. I could see its call letters with the binoculars. It was NQ3446. It's them all right."

"This may be good news, actually," said Rick. "They may spend a lot of time in Port Aransas looking for us."

"I sure hope so," replied Davis.

Rick thought for a minute and said, "Let's keep an eye on them for a while. Go up to about 5000 feet and do some wide circles. Let me know if they go back up. Watch them for about thirty minutes and then catch up to us."

"Okay, sounds like a good idea."

Twenty minutes later a frantic voice came on the radio.

"Dad, Dad, they are coming. They're right behind us so just listen. The Cessna took off and is coming this way. I flipped through the channels and heard them talking on channel 3. It seems like there are two cars and the plane. I think Larry is in one of the cars. We saw two cars, one white and one red, driving toward you at a very high rate of speed. They know you are in the Blazer and where you are. I guess they are going to use the plane to spot for them. I don't know if they have figured out we are using their radios, but we had better watch what we say."

Rick said, "Okay, I got the message. Get out of their way and let us deal with them. I may take some side roads and try to find cover. Keep us in sight if you can, but stay away from their plane. Do you understand?"

"Yeah, we understand," said Davis.

"What do we do now?" asked Kathy.

Rick replied, "I don't know. I didn't think they would find

us so fast. I'm going to try to elude them until I think of something better."

"I think it's time to break out the Glocks again," said Nate.

"Yeah, no argument there," replied Rick.

Rick turned off the main highway and kicked the Blazer up to 80 miles per hour. That was the best he could hope to sustain on these roads. He instructed Kathy to get the map out and navigate. She was able to keep him from hitting any dead ends. They drove for miles, never hearing the plane or seeing any cars. As he came to an intersection he could see two cars up ahead. A white one and a red one. They were waiting for him. He had been a fool to try and outrun an airplane. He jammed on the brakes and whipped the Blazer around, heading back the direction he had come from. The two cars came to life and began chasing him. They steadily gained on him, using their superior cornering ability to close the gap. The two cars were almost as one, steadily getting closer. Rick could now see Larry's scowling face in his rear view mirror. As Nate leaned out the window and pointed the Glock toward the closest car Rick saw something else appear in his mirror. An airplane. But it wasn't Ed; it was Mack and Davis! What were they doing? Rick asked himself. He said a quick prayer for their safety.

"I'll second that," said Kathy.

Rick realized he must have said the prayer out loud.

"Nate, don't shoot. You might hit the plane. It's Davis and Mack," Rick yelled.

Kathy was turned to the back, making sure Nate had heard Rick's warning. A chill went through her when she saw Larry's scowl. Rick returned his attention to the road just in time to brake hard for a sharp right turn.

Mack swooped in from directly behind the two speeding

cars. The Blazer was just about to a sharp right turn in the road. The timing had to be almost perfect. He was about three feet above the lead car and still descending.

Davis yelled, “I’m ready.”

Mack dropped the plane almost to the pavement only about twenty feet in front of the car. At just the right moment Davis opened the plane’s side door and dropped the two smoke grenades onto the road. A wall of smoke went up just before the curve. Both cars braked hard and tried to judge the turn. The first car turned too hard and spun several times, sliding through a barbed wire fence and into a field. The second car continued almost straight through the turn, flew at least fifty feet in the air and hit a tree dead-on before it landed.

“What the hell do you think you are doing?” yelled Rick through the radio.

“Mack and I thought it was too dangerous to have smoke grenades in the cockpit of an airplane so we decided to chunk them out,” laughed Davis. Continuing he said, “We’re going to circle around and see what happened. I don’t think either car can follow you.”

“Okay, let me know the status. We’ll continue toward the main highway,” said Rick.

“Man, Rick, those kids of yours are something,” said Nate with an admiring tone.

“Those kids of *ours* are something, Mr. Reilly,” scolded Kathy.

“I stand corrected, Ma’am.”

A couple of minutes later Davis came back on the radio. “Dad, one of the cars went straight through the turn and hit a tree about five feet up on the trunk. The motor is now residing in the trunk. I don’t think we have to worry about anyone in that car. The other car went into a field. The two men are out, but they and the car are tangled up in barbed wire. I think they'll be able to pursue, but it'll take a few minutes to get their car going again."

Rick firmly said, "Davis, you need to get out of there. Ed is somewhere close in his plane and there is no telling what he might try. Get up high and into some clouds if you can find any."

"Too late, Dad. He's coming at us. Mack just spotted him coming from above. I see him now. It looks like he's going to try to force us down," yelled Davis.

"Turn away! Maybe he will break off and come after us," ordered Rick.

Mack turned away from the direction Rick's Blazer was heading. Ed turned the same way, still bearing down from above. Ed's dive gave his plane additional speed, which Ed expertly used to maintain his course toward the top of Mack's wing. Just as Ed's wheels were about three feet above Mack's plane, Mack dropped the flaps all the way down. This was like throwing an anchor out of a moving boat. It caused Mack's plane to slow dramatically. Ed shot past and was so surprised to miss the plane that he almost hit the ground before he recovered. Mack immediately raised the flaps and climbed for the clouds. The two airplanes were virtually identical so neither had a speed or maneuverability advantage. Ed's Cessna had recovered and was climbing right behind Mack. Suddenly a bullet went zinging through Mack's right wing tip. It didn't do any structural damage, but did get Davis and Mack's attention.

Davis yelled, "Two can play at that game."

He picked up his newly acquired Glock pistol.

"Wait a minute," said Mack. He leveled the plane off and Ed pulled in right behind them.

"Are you crazy?" said Davis, "Now they have an easy shot

at us."

Mack replied, "I don't think so. I doubt that they are crazy enough to shoot through their own propeller."

Davis said, "Okay, now what? Just stay in front of them and see who runs out of fuel first?"

Mack thought a minute and said, "That gives me an idea."

He told Davis his plan and they decided to try it.

Mack started, "Get a coat hanger from our clothes in the back. Straighten out one end. Push your door open and stick the coat hanger up into the valve I use to see if there is any water in the wing fuel tank. The fuel should come out and blow back. If we can get enough to blow on Ed's plane the hot engine or a spark might catch it on fire."

"What if it doesn't work?" asked Davis.

Mack replied, "Well, we won't be able to outrun them in the plane, but we can put down in a field and outrun those old geezers on foot."

"Then let's hope this works. I don't like the backup plan very much," said Davis.

As Davis drained the right side fuel tank Mack tried to be sure the stream of fuel flowed onto Ed's plane. The tank emptied out and the boys waited for something to ignite the fuel. Nothing happened.

"We need a spark. Just one spark," yelled Mack.

An idea hit Davis and he said, "One spark, coming up."

He opened his door and aimed the Glock directly at the spinning propeller directly behind them. He repeatedly pulled the trigger causing bullets to ricochet off the spinning prop. Each ricochet caused a spark as metal met metal. The front of Ed's plane burst into flames and the Cessna began to careen wildly about as Ed struggled for control of both the airplane and himself. He tried to get on the ground as fast as possible, but the speed just caused the flames to increase. Ed couldn't see through the flames and plowed the airplane into a group of oak trees. His fuel tanks ruptured and the ensuing ball of flame left no doubt as to the possibility of survivors.

Rick saw the flames as the plane went down. His stomach turned as the flames shot above the trees in the distance. He could not tell which Cessna it was.

Suddenly the radio crackled, "We did it! We knocked those bastards out of the sky."

"Davis, are you and Mack all right?" asked Rick.

"Yeah, Dad, we're fine. We don't have much fuel left. We emptied one tank out on their plane and ignited it with a bullet off the prop. Mack says we need to land in about twenty minutes. Give us a minute while we get our bearings and find somewhere to land and hopefully fuel up."

"Okay," said Rick, "look at Beeville. I think it will be your best shot."

Rick turned and looked at Kathy. He could see the fear and concern on her face and figured his looked the same way.

"I need to stop this," he said.

Kathy replied, "We've had too many close calls. Also, we are leaving death and destruction all over. I need my family to be safe. You need to do whatever it takes to make that happen. I'll stand behind you, whatever you decide to do, but I want Davis and Mack out of it."

Rick knew she was right and said, "I'll get you all somewhere safe and take care of this problem. Let's get the plane fueled up and back in the air before the other car can find us. Without Ed spotting from the air, they're just driving blind, trying to guess where we are going."

"Dad, you were right. Beeville is the closest landing strip with fuel. We can just barely get there. See you in Beeville."

"See you there, son," said Rick. He turned to Kathy again and said, "Those boys are something else, aren't they?"

"Chips off the old block, I'd say," she said.

Rick grinned kind of sheepishly and said, "They are, aren't they?"

"I hate to change the subject, but Johnny law has a bead on us," Nate said from the back.

Rick looked in the rear view mirror and saw a black-and-white highway patrol car with its lights flashing.

He said, "I can't believe this. I guess someone saw the chase and reported us. I wonder if he knows about the other cars and the plane?"

Nate answered, "If he don't know now, he will shortly."

"Rick, you have to pull over. You can't run away from the police now," said Kathy with a sigh.

"Not so fast, Kathy. Me and Rick don't give up easily," interrupted Nate.

"If you have a plan, Nate, let's hear it fast. He's gaining on us," said Rick.

"I was thinking that maybe you and Kathy could bail out and leave me to deal with the friendly police," explained Nate.

"I can't leave you to take the rap all by yourself," Rick grumbled. Then he said, "Someone come up with a better plan."

After a short pause Nate said, "Okay, my plan wins by default."

"How are we going to bail out without the highway patrol seeing us?" asked Kathy.

"We'll have to get very creative," Nate offered.

"We need to get some space between him and us," Rick

said.

"Just let this old Blazer do what it does best. Head through that field toward the red barn," Nate barked.

Rick whipped the wheel around and crashed through the fence. He slowed and dropped the Blazer into four-wheel drive and bounced across a ravine and through the field, weaving around trees and cactus.

They watched as the highway patrol car followed. It slowed considerably as the driver encountered the ravine. He tried to take the ravine at a forty-five degree angle, slid sideways and got hung on a log.

"That's our chance," yelled Nate. "Drive through that barn and I'll drop you all off."

Rick floored the gas pedal and said, "Nate, get my survival pack and the weapons bag. You can't be caught with that stuff."

"Good thinking, Rick," agreed Nate as he gathered up the bags.

Rick barreled into the red barn and skidded to a stop. The doors flew open and all three jumped out.

Nate chunked the two bags on the ground and held out his hand. "Maybe you can get your old buddies at the FBI to help me out."

Rick grabbed his hand and sadly said, "I hate to leave like this, but I guess it has to be. I'll get you out."

"It has to be," said Nate calmly.

Kathy ran up to Nate and hugged him. Without saying anything she turned to Rick with a lost expression.

"Come on, Kathy, we need to hide," Rick said as he pulled her toward the hay bales in the corner.

Nate jumped into the driver's seat and waved as the Blazer burst out of the barn. He headed out the farm's driveway and out onto the highway.

"Now that's a true friend," observed Kathy.

"It sure is. I feel horrible about letting him do this," Rick replied.

"I know. So do I, but he really wants to help you. I think he knows you have unfinished business," said Kathy.

"I certainly do and first we need to get out of here and find the boys."

"Do we have the radio?" asked Kathy.

"Yeah, it's right here, but we need to be careful. The police can certainly listen in if they find the right frequency," Rick replied.

As they walked through the brush away from the barn they could hear the highway patrol car spinning its tires, trying to work free from the log. After another minute the sounds changed and they could see the patrol car moving across the field and toward the red barn.

"Maybe they won't find Nate," said Kathy hopefully.

"I'm sure they have a description of the Blazer with every law enforcement agency in the area and they all know about the wrecked car and the plane crash," Rick said solemnly.

"Yeah, you're right. It was just wishful thinking."

They crossed several fields, avoiding open areas and the highway.

After about a half-hour the radio crackled and Davis said, "Dad, mom, we're all gassed up. Where are you?"

Rick thought a second and said, "We're waiting for you to pick us up. Right where you left us."

"Come again?" said Davis, realizing that something was wrong.

"When you are ready, fly back to where you left us and

pick us up," repeated Rick.

"Okay," was all Davis said.

"What was that all about?" asked Kathy.

Rick answered, "I think he understands to fly back to where they turned away from us and headed for Beeville. I want to be very careful with what we say on the radio."

"Well, how are they going to find us and pick us up?"

"Details, just details," scolded Rick.

After another thirty minutes they could hear the Cessna's engine.

"Circle until I see you," Rick radioed.

Shortly the Cessna appeared overhead and Rick said, "Mark this spot and find a pickup place."

"Okay," was the reply.

"Go north one quarter mile to spot," said Davis.

Rick and Kathy walked as fast as they could and saw the Cessna circle twice and then touch down on a flat grassy field. The plane swung around to the south and headed toward them. When Mack brought the plane to a stop Rick put the two bags in the cargo area and he and Kathy climbed in. Mack throttled up the engine and began to accelerate. The fully loaded plane did its job as it lifted into the sky.

"What's going on?" asked Davis and Mack together.

Kathy related the story as Rick pondered their next move.

Mack turned to the rear and asked, "Where to, Dad?"

"Back to Port Aransas. We need to pick up Mom's car there," replied Rick.

"Wow, we haven't gained much ground, have we?" said Mack.

"Not much. Not much at all," said Rick sadly, thinking of Nate's plight.

# Chapter 38

Larry yelled, “Get this damn car going. We have to catch them.”

Hal Jones was the other man. He and Larry were cut and bleeding from wrestling the barbed wire off the car. Larry was so mad he looked like he was going to pop.

Hal said, “Larry, we aren’t going anywhere right now. The left rear tire is shredded. I’m going to start changing it. Why don’t you go check out the other car?”

“Yeah, okay, I’ll go check them out. I’m really getting sick of that damn Blaze family. They’re going to pay when I catch up to them, every one of them,” Larry muttered as he walked up to the road and surveyed the scene.

The other car was compressed into about one-half of its normal length. The tree trunk was scarred about five feet up, pinpointing the place of impact. The rear of the car had dropped to ground and the front still leaned against the tree. Larry ran over to the car and saw two lifeless bodies. A sense of rage swept over him as he looked at his co-workers. They weren’t really friends, but they were associates, part of the team, and he vowed to avenge their deaths. For the life of him, though, Larry couldn't really think of anything cxtra to do to the Blazes beyond what he had already planned. The rage passed a bit as his training began to kick in. His mind began to assess the situation and one thing was certain. The local sheriff's office would have someone out here quick and he didn't plan to be here then. He also wondered where Ed and his plane had gone. Probably to chase down the plane that had sent them off the road. Larry figured it had been the same plane that had come to Rick's rescue on Lake Travis. The thought of Ed forcing the other plane down brought a grin to Larry's face. Perhaps the revenge had begun.

Hal yelled, "Larry, let's go. I got the tire fixed."

Larry ran over and got in the car. As they drove onto the road Larry filled Hal in on the loss of the two men. Larry got on the radio and called Ed. He received no answer.

"Probably out of range," he said. Continuing he said, "We won't know where Blaze is until Ed gets back. Let's assume he's heading to Austin and continue toward there. Ed should be able to pick us up shortly."

They consulted the map and shortly returned to the main road. As they drove along Larry continued his efforts to raise Ed on the radio. After about a half-hour they saw smoke and emergency vehicles out in a field.

"Head over there," Larry commanded. "Let's see if that is Blaze's plane."

As they got closer it was obviously a small plane. Finally they could see it was a Cessna, probably a 172. They were using the same plane as Ed used, Larry thought. Larry began to turn red as the rage returned. He could now see the red stripe on the white plane and the NQ3446 on the fuselage. The cockpit and engine sections were burning completely and Larry knew he had lost two more associates, one actually being a friend. He and Ed Richter had been through many scrapes together and it pained him deeply to lose Ed. They had headed for Port Aransas with four teams of two men each, eight well-trained men. Now, he and Hal Jones were the only two left. How was this possible? Who was helping Rick Blaze? The FBI? The CIA? None of them would let Rick Blaze out to fend for himself. For a brief instant Larry Thomas thought about giving up the chase, giving up on his orders and passing on the $100,000 bonus. Larry had never given up on a mission before and his code of honor would not let him give up now, but he did have a level of uncertainty unfamiliar to him.

He turned to Hal and said, "Let's get out of here, partner. We've got a man to catch."

Larry could see the bewilderment in Hal's eyes.

"Come on Hal, we are going to nail this sucker and have a nice vacation. A nice *long* vacation. Let's head to Austin and regroup there."

Mack landed the Cessna at the Port Aransas airport. They got out of the little plane and hugged each other, oblivious to any onlookers. The Blaze family was all together and safe, at least for the moment.

Rick looked at the Cessna and said, "This seems like a mighty fine plane, Mack."

"It really is," exclaimed Mack. "Although it does have a bullet hole in it."

Kathy gasped, "They actually fired on you?"

Mack said, "The bullet didn't do any real damage though."

Davis replied, "Yeah, they were real serious about getting us down. But I think we had both skill and luck on our side. When they began firing on us Mack pulled right in front of their plane. They couldn't shoot at us through the propeller. That's what gave me the idea to shoot through their prop to cause a spark to ignite the fuel."

Rick said, "That was quick thinking for both of you. I'm proud of you two. I've managed to put you in some sticky situations and you have shown great skill and smarts. I have promised your mother that I would get the three of you out of danger and that is exactly what I'm going to do. When we leave here I'll take the car and you three will take the plane. I'm going to finish this thing with whoever survived the car wreck. At least we've narrowed the odds."

Davis knew his father was completely serious about continuing alone and decided not to challenge him. He said, "Where do you want us to go?"

"I want you all to decide that," Rick replied. Continuing he said, "If I don't know where you are I don't see how they could know."

Mack said, "How will we communicate? We need to be able to contact each other."

Rick thought a minute and said, "Yes, Mack, we need a way. We can do it through the newspaper, the classifieds. Let's use the Dallas paper. We should be able to find it most anywhere. Put an ad in the boat section. Use our boat for the text-say 1952 Chris-Craft Commander, 42-foot, no engines, fixer upper and give a phone number I can reach you. If I need you to contact me I'll run the same ad with my phone number. Putting no engines and fixer upper will discourage most people from calling about the boat."

Kathy said, "We can use that plan, but if I haven't heard from you in a week all bets are off. I'm coming looking for you."

Rick laughed and said, "Fair enough."

Kathy said, "I have one other concern."

"What is it?" asked Rick.

"What about police? Even with Nate taking the rap for now we are leaving quite a trail of bodies for the police. They won't just say I guess they were killed for some good reason and leave us alone."

"You've got a point there. I don't know if we have really left much of a trail, but they will be holding Nate. I think it's time to call Bill Whetland again. Maybe he can help get rid of these guys chasing us and get Nate off the hook," answered Rick.

"I think that's an excellent idea," said Kathy.

They loaded up the plane with Kathy's bags and hugged again. Rick watched as the Cessna gracefully rose into the sky and his family was again separated. He knew it was best this way, but he could only know they were safe if they were with him. But if they were with him, they would not be safe. The irony of this was almost overwhelming to Rick. He called the local taxi service and got a ride to Kathy's car. He got into the vehicle and drove to the ferry, not sure where to go or how to find the remaining men.

As he drove in the general direction of Austin his mind wandered through the events that had unfolded in his life lately. The danger was something he was not used to, but at least he had experienced the same feelings when he was dodging the Mafia and the FBI in Chicago so many years ago. But Kathy, Davis and Mack had never been involved in anything close to this. Rick was amazed at how well the three of them dealt with the predicament Rick had gotten them into. Kathy was cool and calm and, as always, his sounding board and reality check. Rick could not imagine where and how he might have turned out if he had not met Kathy. Even though their personalities were actually quite opposite, their morals and beliefs were always on a parallel course.

On top of all that, she had given him the best two sons in the world. Rick treasured his relationship with Davis and Mack because he was usually able to be their friend as well as their father. That could be a tough balancing act, especially if the boys tried to take advantage of the friendship side of the relationship. But they rarely did and so Rick had really not cultivated many close friendships with men his age. He preferred spending time with Davis and Mack to getting out with other males. He didn't need any male bonding activities since he was so secure in his relationship with his kids. They seemed to enjoy his company and even listened to his advice a fair percentage of the time.

Rick did have a close friend who had two daughters about the same age as Davis and Mack and he marveled at the difference in the two households. His friend's life revolved around the women and Rick's revolved around the men. He guessed that was just playing the numbers, but he tried to remember how hard it could be for Kathy, especially when most conversations eventually moved to discussions of sports or computers, no matter where they started.

A report on the radio brought Rick back to the reality of life at the moment.

The newscaster said, "Government sources are still being tight-lipped about the extremely fast development of a neutralizer serum for the poisoned water supplies. They are now saying that the serum was in existence before the devastating terrorist attack. Informed parties are saying that we, the American people, were extremely lucky that a connection was found that enabled the serum to be identified and located. Our sources are getting word, although this is not confirmed, that one person, a private citizen, was able to infiltrate the plot by Saddam Hussein and led government officials to this serum. This person has not been identified and no law enforcement officials will comment on this report."

Rick's chest swelled with pride. He really had pulled this off. He had saved peoples' lives. Now, if he could just save his own it could be a storybook ending.

# Chapter 39

"Hello, this is Rene."

"Rene, Larry here."

"Larry, I hope you're calling to report the death of Mister Rick Blaze."

"No, I'm afraid not."

"Didn't you catch up to him in that Port something or other?"

"Well, yeah, we did catch up to him and his family," said Larry.

"Well, what happened?" Rene demanded.

Larry replied, "We don't know what happened to Team 2. I'm assuming they are dead. Team 4 ran off the road, hit a tree and both were killed. Ed and Wayne were in Ed's plane. It crashed and they burned up. Hal and I are all that is left. We will continue the pursuit."

Rene yelled, "What's so hard about taking out a bunch of amateurs? I gather your cars and planes did not just crash by themselves. Are you saying this Blaze fellow is able to best you every time you confront each other?"

"So far, yes, but he must have professional help from the people with the plane. They seem to be quite capable as well," replied Larry. After a pause Larry said, "Are you going to put anyone else on this?"

Rene scoffed, "No, it's just you and Hal. The others don't choose to be part of the team anymore. The government knows I'm behind the water poisoning and is closing in. No one wants to be around if they get the proof. I'm making arrangements to leave the country. It won't be easy because they are watching me for just that reason. You take care of Rick Blaze, get out of the country and meet me at the France Company headquarters. Your $100,000 bonus will be waiting for you."

"Yes, sir. I'll stay here until Rick Blaze is dead. Hopefully that will be soon. I'll let you know what happens."

"Hi, Bill, this is Rick Blaze," Rick said.

Bill Whetland replied, "Hello, Rick. How is our secret national hero?"

"I'm okay, but I've had some close calls. Rene Charlton apparently thinks I should pay for my intervention. He has sent at least eight men after my family and me. They held my family hostage to get me."

"Your family, are they okay?"

"Yes, I took care of the kidnappers. There were two of them. The others caught up to us on the road. Two of them in a car were killed and two others in an airplane were killed. I'm pretty sure at least two more are still after us. I have two problems-one is to keep my family and me safe and the other is how to deal with the dead guys. I don't know if they can be traced to us, but I'm not used to leaving a string of dead bodies around. It's especially bad for someone trying to hide from the Mafia."

Bill said, "From the sound of it, the Mafia should be glad they've never caught up to you. I can't tell you it is okay to go around killing people, but I know you don't have much choice. Would you consider coming in and letting the FBI protect you and your family?"

Rick replied, "No, but I would agree to having a FBI agent help me deal with these guys."

"Sorry, Rick, the FBI won't send someone over to be your partner. You're a civilian and there are rules that are taken very seriously here."

"Okay, I'll think about it. What's going on with arresting Rene Charlton? I haven't seen anything in the papers about it."

Bill replied, "No proof. We can't pin anything on him that would stick. We have to be happy at this point that the situation turned out as well as it did, thanks to you. At last count there were almost no deaths due to the chemicals and the wave of anti-Iraq sentiment is raging. The military regrouped and hit Saddam with everything it has got. Even though all the attacks had to come from our aircraft carriers and missile ships until we got Saudia Arabia and Kuwait back, it's still turned out to be a very one-sided war. Our Stealth Bombers went in at night and knocked out all the radar capabilities in Baghdad and along the Iraq border. Every time they turned on a SAM radar a missile destroyed the location. The Iraqis never knew what hit them. All of a sudden bombs just started falling on them. They had bragged that their new radar from China would detect the Stealth airplanes, but obviously they were dead wrong. That Stealth stuff still works."

"That's great," said Rick, "but right now I need a Stealth car to stay alive."

"Look, Rick, I can probably keep the heat off you for the

bodies. We owe you that, but I can't protect you unless you come in. At some point you need to trust the FBI. We really are very capable."

Rick replied, "I'm not at that point yet. I guess I'll just have to keep doing this on my own."

"Rick, think it over. Stay in touch. Someday, when you fully trust me, I would like to get to know you in your current life. I really would like to know you better."

"Okay, I'll stay in touch. Also, Bill, I have one other problem."

Rick could hear the sigh as Bill asked, "What's the other problem?"

"Well, an old friend was helping me and I'm pretty sure he was picked up driving my Chevy Blazer around south Texas. I'm afraid he'll have to answer for the things I've done," replied Rick.

"What's the name of this friend of yours?"

"Nate Reilly. He put himself at risk to help me stay free."

"I'll get one of the agents to check out any arrests in south Texas. No promises, though," said Bill.

"Thanks, Bill. I owe you a lot."

Rick called into his voice mail at Austin Executive Suites. Scrolling through the messages he was relieved that most were from long distance and copier sales people. One message did stand out. It was from Linda in Operations.

"Rick, I know you're doing something important, but I did want to remind you that it is past time to do our invoices and get them sent out. If we don't mail them in a couple of days it's going to be hard to get our money on time. Let me know if I can help you in any way. Bye."

Rick had completely forgotten about doing the invoices. In

fact, he had forgotten about almost everything that concerned his business. He didn't know what to do now. He had a business to run and some killers on his tail. They didn't know where he was going, but he had been heading in the direction of Austin. They probably would stop to regroup and check in with the boss when they discovered the loss of the plane. Rick figured he had at least several hours in Austin before his pursuers would get there. Of course, Rick thought, there could be some already there. There was no telling the lengths Rene would go to in order to pay Rick back. Rick determined that he could get to Austin as quick as possible, do his part of the invoicing and get out of town well before any of Rene's men could get there. He cranked the car up to eighty and called Linda.

"Linda, this is Rick. Thanks for the message about doing the invoices. I'll be there in about an hour and do my part immediately. It'll take about an hour and a half so you can be ready to finish up your part and get them in the mail tomorrow. I really appreciate the way you all have held down the business the past couple of weeks."

Linda replied, "No problem, Rick. We know whatever you're doing is really important."

"Yeah, it really is," said Rick.

"Oh, by the way, Rick, Henry Hadford keeps asking about you. I just thought you would want to know. He seems to be really interested in your whereabouts, but he never wants to leave a voice mail for you."

"Okay, I'll check with him when I get in, Linda."

"Rick," Linda said, "I think he offered me a bribe to tell him where you are."

"Oh really? What makes you think that?" asked Rick.

"He said there could be something in it for me if I would

give him the information," Linda answered.

"What did you say to that?"

"I told him I still didn't know where you were. I would never tell that slime anything," Linda sniffed.

"Good girl. Henry is up to no good, but what could be so important that he needs to get to me right away?"

"I guess you'll find out when you see him," said Linda.

"Yeah, I guess so. Anyway, I better go now. See you shortly."

Rick hung up and began to think. He needed a new plan and his mind was blank. He could either keep running from his pursuers or set a trap to nail them. Setting a trap appealed to Rick, but he knew he could not just lay in wait and shoot them. He just didn't have that in him, at least not yet. Maybe it was time to let the FBI help him. After all, he was being hunted down, just like he had feared for twenty years. It just wasn't the people he thought it would be. Risking being found by the Mafia seemed down on the list of his problems right now. It would be great to lead his pursuers far away from his family so he tried to come up with a way to bait them, with him as the bait. An idea began to form in his mind, but he needed a way to lead the two men into the trap. He needed a way to feed information to the men, but how? Would they have left someone in Austin to watch for him? Someone with Worldwide Water Solutions?"

Rick dialed the office again.

"Austin Executive Suites, may I help you?" answered Sandra.

"Sandra, it's Rick."

"Hi, Rick, what's up?"

"Has anyone else from Worldwide Water Solutions been around the office lately?" Rick asked.

"No, they all skedaddled when the problems started," Sandra said.

"Okay. Has anyone else been looking for me?"

"Just that Henry Hadford. He always asks about you these days."

Then it hit him-Henry Hadford. Henry was a sniveling runt of a man who never got along with Rick or his staff. He was always griping about little things and trying to get something for nothing. Why would he be so interested in Rick's whereabouts? Henry would care only if there was something in it for him. Larry could have easily recruited him to be the in-house snitch and Henry would be too stupid to be subtle about it. It made sense to Rick, but that didn't mean it was true.

"Rick, are you still there?" asked Sandra.

"Yeah, Sandra. I was just thinking about something," said Rick.

"Anything I can do to help?"

"No, not now anyway. But thanks. See you soon."

The more Rick rolled the idea of Henry Hadford being a snitch around in his mind, the more it made sense. Rick spent the next fifteen minutes devising a plan. Then, he picked up the cell phone and called Linda again.

"Hi, Linda, its Rick again."

Linda said, "Hi, Rick, what's up?"

Rick replied, "I need you to do something for me that won't make a lot of sense right now."

"Sure, what do you need?"

Rick said, "Go tell Henry Hadford that I'll be in the office in about three or four hours and that I'll check in with him then."

Linda replied, "I thought you would be here in about an hour."

"See, it didn't make a lot of sense did it?" Rick laughed.

"No, but I'll tell him," she replied.

"Thanks."

Rick dialed another number and Bill Whetland answered, "Hello."

"Hi, Bill, this is Rick again. I think I have an idea that will lead the bad guys to your men."

Bill replied, "Let me hear it. Just remember that I'm retired and can only do so much myself."

Rick said, "Okay, I'll remember that. I think I have a way to feed information to the men. If it works I could lead them to Chicago and into some kind of trap with your men."

"What kind of trap are you thinking about?" asked Bill.

Rick said, "I don't really know. Something with me as the bait maybe. Get them for attempted murder or at least some kind of weapons charges."

Bill replied, "You know, Rick, they may have permits for their guns."

"For silenced Glocks?" asked Rick.

"No, not for silencers. We can get them for that at the minimum."

Rick said, "Okay, then, is it a go?"

"You'll have to work with Robert on this. I think I can get him to take it," replied Bill.

"All right. I can deal with that. I'll call you in a little while if it still looks good."

Rick pulled into the parking lot of the building Austin Executive Suites was in. He took a deep breath and walked into the building. The can of pepper spray and the stun gun in his pocket did little to ease the apprehension as the elevator opened on his floor.

"Hi, Rick," the two receptionists said almost simultaneously.

"How are the best receptionists in Austin today?" he asked.

"We're fine. You've sure been gone a lot, Rick," said Mary.

"Yeah, I've had some stuff to take care of," responded Rick.

"What kind of stuff?" asked Sandra.

"Personal stuff," said Rick.

"Well it sure has been exciting around here with all the Iraq mess," said Mary.

"Yeah, I even heard that Austin was supposed to be attacked," said Sandra.

"Oh really? I guess we just lucked out then," replied Rick.

Rick walked back to Operations and said to Linda, "Hi, Linda, did you get the message to Henry Hadford?"

Linda said, "Yes. He was really interested, but then he just waived me out of his office and started to dial his phone. He's a real oddball."

Rick replied, "He sure is. I'm going to check the phone room to be sure everything is okay, then I'll be ready for invoicing."

Rick walked into the telephone room and tore off the last few pages of the printout of outgoing long distance calls that went through the telephone switch. The printout logged the calls by the number dialed, time, length and the phone extension it was made from. Rick highlighted the calls made from Henry Hadford's phone. There was one call made after Linda had told Henry of Rick's arrival. Rick picked up the phone in the telephone room and dialed the number.

"Hello, this is Larry," a gruff voice answered.

Rick instantly recognized the voice as Larry Thomas.

"Larry, hell, what are you doing with Billy Don's phone?" Rick said with his best redneck accent.

"You got the wrong number," Larry said and hung up.

Rick grinned slyly as the pieces of his plan began to fall into place. He put the printout in his pocket and headed back to Operations. Rick quickly and perhaps a little carelessly entered the invoicing information into his computer. He always did this part of the job himself because he wanted the invoices to be as accurate as possible. Hopefully all his attempts at accuracy would cut him a little slack now if he made some mistakes in his haste. It was hard to concentrate on the task at hand when Larry Thomas was bearing down on him again. Rick wrapped up the job in an hour and quickly sifted through his large stack of mail. The trashcan quickly filled with junk mail, leaving a small stack of real mail to be dealt with. Seeing nothing that he couldn't put off for a few more days, Rick left his office and walked down the hall to Henry's office.

He walked in and, trying his best to look and sound very nervous, said, "Ah, Henry, Linda said you wanted to see me."

"Not anymore, Mr. Blaze. I already worked out my problem," said Henry stiffly.

"All right, if you need anything else just let me know. I'll be in Chicago for a few days and hopefully after that I'll be back for a while," Rick said.

"Where in Chicago? I know the city pretty well," asked Henry, trying to sound sincere.

"I had a little incident at an executive suite there that I need to make up for," said Rick.

"Which one?" asked Henry.

Rick said, "Just one I do business with sometimes. I've got

to go now."

Rick turned and walked down the hall. He ducked into the telephone room and checked the switch position of Henry's phone. It lit up, indicating that Henry was making a call. Rick quickly connected the telephone serviceman butt-set to the terminals of Henry's phone line. With the butt-set on monitor Rick could hear the call without Henry hearing him.

Rick heard, "Hello, this is Larry."

"Larry, Henry Hadford here. I have some new information. Blaze is here now. I just talked to him. He's leaving shortly and going to Chicago. He said he was going to take care of some unfinished business at some executive suite in Chicago. He didn't tell me which one, but he did say it had something to do with some incident, as he called it."

Larry said, "Good, Henry. This information has earned you five thousand dollars. Do you think he suspected you were prying him for information?"

Henry replied, "No, he just seemed pretty nervous and antsy."

"Good," Larry said, "I'll be in Austin in about an hour. If I catch him there it'll save me a trip to Chicago."

Henry asked, "Hey, Larry, can you tell me why you are after Blaze?"

"Not yet, Henry. You'll know when it is time."

The line clicked dead and Rick removed the butt-set clips. He needed to get out of there quickly and head to Chicago. He gave some instructions to his staff and headed for the car. Rick decided it would be too risky to fly out of the Austin airport and it would be possible to bump into Larry at the Dallas-Fort Worth Airport, so he decided to drive to San Antonio and catch a flight out of there.

# Chapter 40

On the way to San Antonio Rick's thoughts drifted to his family. Where were they? Were they safe? Rick knew that logically they were safe because Larry was after him and no one knew where his family was, not even himself. Trying to take his mind off his family for a while, Rick called Bill Whetland.

"Hello?"

"Hi, Bill, this is Rick," said Rick.

Bill replied, "How's your plan going, Rick? Can we help?"

Rick said, "Yes, you can help now. I don't have a complete plan, but I did find out that Larry Thomas is one of the men still after me and that he had paid off one of my business associates to keep track of me through my office. When I figured that out I used the guy to inform Larry that I was going immediately to Chicago and that I had some unfinished business at Oakwood Towers Executive Suites. I monitored a call from this man to Larry and made sure the message got through. Larry is hot in pursuit."

"Oakwood Towers Executive Suites," Bill exclaimed.

"There was a story on the news the other day about some kind of disturbance there. Something about a man with a gun and another guy pulled the fire alarm and no one was ever apprehended."

Rick said, "That was me and Larry. I barely got away."

"You really amaze me, Rick," said Bill.

"Thanks, Bill. I guess I need to level with you about my current situation. I know I can trust you and Robert," replied Rick.

Bill said, "I'm really glad you are beginning to trust us."

"Okay, here it is," said Rick. "As you know, I changed my name to Rick Blaze and I live in Austin, Texas. I have a wife, Kathy, and two sons, Davis and Mack. My family is hiding out somewhere, I don't even know where and I really want someone else to know my secret in case something happens to me or them."

Rick explained his system for finding his family and Bill said, "All right, Rick, I've got all I need to know for now. Excuse me if I sometimes call you Randy until I get this all clear in my mind."

"Sure, Bill, you can call me either one for a while," Rick replied.

"So when are you going to be here, Rick?" asked Bill.

"I don't know exactly. I'm going to catch a flight out of San Antonio as quickly as I can."

Bill said, "I talked to Robert and he said he'll be glad to help. I'll get him to meet you at the airport when you get off the plane. Just use your real name on the ticket and Robert will know when you will arrive."

Rick replied, "It'll be good to see his face when I get off the plane. I'm tired of doing this alone. I'm afraid my luck will run out."

Bill said, "Rick, I don't get the impression that there is

much luck involved in this. I think you have just plain out-smarted these guys."

"Maybe, but I still will like having some help besides my wife and kids. I'm scared to death one of them will get hurt," replied Rick.

Bill said, "Relax, Rick, we can take care of this. It's what we do best. Say, I just talked to the agent who was tracking down your friend in south Texas. He can't find any one who has Nate Reilly in custody."

"Really? That's odd. We all assumed he would be apprehended."

"Well, our information is pretty good. See you in Chicago," Bill said, glad that he could give Rick some good news.

I wonder what in the world Nate did or if he somehow ran into Larry and was dead, Rick thought.

An hour later Rick pulled into the parking lot at the San Antonio airport. He used the bag he had commandeered from Larry to combine his survival pack and some of the items from Larry's bag. He decided he should not carry guns or the smoke grenades with him. Rick then walked through the San Antonio airport, checking with each airline for the fastest way to get to Chicago. By now it was seven o'clock and Rick was getting tired. It had been quite a long day. He was almost relieved when the ticket clerk told him the first flight to Chicago left at nine-thirty in the morning. He left the airport area and found a small hotel several miles away. Rick laid down on the bed to rest and immediately went to sleep.

Larry and Hal rushed into Austin Executive Suites, hoping to catch Rick Blaze at work and finish him off then and there. Their disappointment was clearly evident when the receptionist said Rick had left an hour ago. As they drove to the Austin airport

Larry cautioned Hal to keep his eyes out for Rick or one of his partners. They had been very resourceful and clever in their actions, Larry related. Finding no flights leaving until the morning, Larry and Hal booked the earliest flight. Then they checked the airport for signs of Rick and, finding none, went to the bar for a couple of drinks. Larry took a break from drinking to give Rene a call.

"Hello, Rene, this is Larry."

"Hello, Larry. Have you disposed of Rick Blaze yet?"

Larry replied, "No, not yet. We do have a line on his current movements and are in pursuit. How are things going for you?"

Rene said, "I lined up a way out of the country. The FBI came in with a search warrant, but I hid in the secret room. We need to be careful with what we say on the phone, no details. Even though my security people say it's secure, I assume the FBI is trying to tap it."

Larry said, "My flight leaves in the morning so Hal and I'll catch up to Blaze and finish him off. Then we'll leave the country. I'll check in later."

"Yes, Larry, you do that. And Larry, this time try not to screw up!"

Fortunately, Rick awoke the next morning at his normal time of seven. This gave him plenty of time to get ready, especially since he didn't have a change of clothes. He had meant to take care of that last night. At eight he was ready to go. Still wishing for fresh clothes Rick kept an eye out for a store that was open this time of morning. Nothing was open besides gas stations and convenience stores. He resigned himself to looking scruffy today. After parking he entered the terminal and headed to the gate. He stopped at a newsstand and bought some magazines. After the airplane was in the air, Rick got up and walked through the plane, looking at all the faces. With great peace of mind he sat back down in his seat, confident that no one on the plane was a danger to him. Rick laid his head back and began to think about his family being reunited, going to the lake and just having a great time. His thoughts turned into dreams as he dropped off to sleep, something he was still short of. Rick jolted upright when the plane touched down in Chicago. After the plane reached the terminal, Rick walked slowly up the jet way to his gate, wondering what was in store for him in Chicago. His eyes brightened as he saw Robert Whetland standing outside the gate. Their eyes met and Robert waved briefly, causing Rick to feel a little more secure than he had for quite a while.

"Hi, Rick, good to see you. I'm really proud for your success with all the yahoos from Worldwide Water," said Robert.

Rick replied, "Thanks, Robert, it's good to see you, too."

Robert said, "I have a car outside. Let's go see if we can come up with a good plan."

Robert Whetland told Rick that his FBI team would like to draw Larry to a location that innocent bystanders would not tend to be involved. Therefore, they felt that a small motel would seem reasonable to Larry and a fairly secure location for the team to keep Rick safe and apprehend Larry and his accomplice. The Northern Inn was the location Robert had chosen for the operation. It was about ten miles from the airport, fairly secluded for a motel and on the edge of the industrial district. The only problem was getting Larry to show up there.

Rick said, "I think I can lead him here through the Oakwood Towers Executive Suites."

Robert replied, "Yeah, Dad said you had slipped Larry

information that you were going to the Suites. I hope that was the right place to choose, since, according to Dad, the last time there you caused quite a commotion."

Rick said, "Well, there was a commotion there, but I like to think that Larry caused it. After all, he was the one who pulled a gun."

"That brings up a good point, Rick," cautioned Robert. "Messing with people who have guns is dangerous. It's not like in the movies where the bad guys always miss."

Rick replied, "That's why I'm dealing with you now. I'm afraid my luck might run out. I really want this guy off my back and I want to see my family again."

As they drove on in silence Rick thought about one more idea he had been kicking around.

He said, "Robert, I need a favor before Larry gets here in Chicago. I have to take care of some personal business and I need a computer and a fax machine."

"You can use the ones in my office," said Robert.

Rick replied, "I really want to use a neutral site, like a Quick Print or some other copier service. It'll take less than an hour and is very important."

Robert said, "Okay, but we need to take care of things at the Executive Suites first."

"I agree. Let's go over there now, then I can take care of my other business," replied Rick.

Rick and Robert walked off the elevator and asked for Beth Newly, the manager of Oakwood Towers Executive Suites.

"Rick, get your butt in my office and explain what happened the last time you showed up here," said Newly.

"Easy, Beth. There won't be any problems this time," replied Rick, hoping he was telling the truth.

"I certainly hope not. I'm still getting pressure from the owners to explain what happened and the police really want to know who was involved," said Newly.

"No problem, Beth," said Rick. Continuing he said, "I'm really sorry for the fire drill and everything. I also appreciate you keeping a lid on my identity to the authorities. This time I would like for your staff to let someone find out where to locate me. This person is heading to Chicago now and will show up here at your office soon thereafter. This is Agent Robert Whetland of the FBI and he's actually in charge of this operation."

"Am I in any kind of trouble?" asked Newly.

"No, not as long as you continue to help Mr. Blaze and myself," responded Whetland.

Newly said, "What can we do? You know, Rick. I have to admit it was kind of nice to have some excitement around here."

Robert Whetland said, "Ms. Newly, all we need is for your staff to accidentally let this Larry Thomas find out where Rick is staying and to keep this plan secret. Can you help us with that?"

Newly asked, "Sure, no problem. What do you have in mind?"

"We were thinking about leaving a piece of paper with my motel name on it laying out where Larry could see it when he asked for me at the front receptionist desk. If that doesn't work, I would like for you to help him, because I messed up the place before or something like that," said Rick.

"I think Rachel can help us with this. She's a pretty good actress when she wants to be," answered Beth. "Let's go talk to her," she continued.

"Rachel, Mr. Blaze and Mr. Whetland here have something they need you to do," said Newly to her receptionist.

"Sure, Beth, what do I do?" said Rachel.

Rick said, "A man by the name of Larry Thomas is going to come in and try to find out where I am. We don't want him to know we're giving him the information, so we need to make it seem like he did it himself. He'll be looking around, trying to notice anything that will help him find me. What I want to do is have you leave a piece of paper with my name and the name of the motel I'm staying at written on it. Tell him you can't give out that information when he asks, but leave the paper in plain view. He will most likely see it. If he doesn't, Beth will come out and help. Can you do it?"

Rachel replied with a laugh, "No problem. He'll think he figured it out all by himself. Can you tell me what this is all about? Is he wanted by the law?"

Robert Whetland leaned over Rachel's desk and flipped out his badge, "Rachel, this man is dangerous and we're trying to deal with him. Your help will be invaluable. He won't harm you or anyone here if you don't mess with him. That's as much as I can tell you."

"That's good enough for me," Rachel chirped.

"Great," said Beth.

Rick handed her a piece of paper with his name and the Northern Inn written on it. She laid it to the side, but still in plain sight. Rick and Robert left the Executive Suites and drove towards a Quickie Print location close by. Robert stopped and let Rick out.

Robert asked, "How long do you need?"

Rick replied, "Oh, about an hour will be enough."

"All right, Rick, I'll be out in the parking lot, catching up on the sports pages."

"Thanks, Robert. I really appreciate this."

# Chapter 41

Rick walked into the Quickie Print with an idea. If the idea worked his life would be much simpler. All his current troubles would go away. Rick rented a computer station for an hour. Fortunately the computer had Word software loaded on it. He was familiar with Word because that was the software he used at Austin Executive Suites for all the word processing that Linda did in Operations. Rick quickly typed out the body of the letter. It was short and to the point, only about a half of a page. That was the easy part. Next, he scrolled through the graphics files until he found a graphic perfectly suited for the letterhead. Rick imported the graphic into the letter and moved it around until he was satisfied with the position. This had to look official and professional. The heading was accomplished with the centering tool and a larger bold font type. Rick pulled out his pocket calendar and retrieved the phone and fax numbers he needed and typed them under the heading. Now all he needed was a closing and that was accomplished quickly. Rick ran spell check and printed out the document. It was exactly how he wanted it. Glancing at the clock

Rick saw he had spent about thirty minutes on the document. He was right on track.

Rick went to the counter and said, "Could I borrow a Chicago phone book?"

"Sure," said the person, whose name badge said Neal.

"Thanks," said Rick as Neal lifted the heavy volumes onto the counter.

Rick paused and looked around to be sure they were alone.

He said, "Neal, I need a favor. I have to fax this document out to about twenty people. It is very sensitive information and I need to send it myself. Is there a fax machine I can use myself, maybe somewhere private?"

"We aren't supposed to let customers use the fax machines," said Neal.

Rick responded, "I would be glad to kick in an extra fifty dollars to you or the company, whichever is appropriate."

Neal replied, "Fifty bucks, huh? I could really use an extra fifty bucks. I tell you what. We have an old fax in the back. We keep it plugged into a phone line just in case all the ones out here break. It's over in a corner and you would have some privacy."

"Excellent," exclaimed Rick.

"Okay, follow me," said Neal.

Rick followed Neal into the back room, lugging the phone books and his document. When they got to the fax machine Rick set down his load of books and handed Neal a fifty dollar bill. Neal grinned and walked off. Rick flipped through the phone books until he found the listings for the Chicago police precincts. He began dialing each number from the fax's phone, asking each precinct for its fax number. Next he wrote down the name and phone number displayed on the fax machine. He pushed a few buttons on the fax to get into the programming mode. Using the keypad Rick punched in the company name and the phone number he wanted the receiving machines to record. The name and number would be displayed at the top of each fax transmission and Rick certainly didn't want the recipients to know the fax came from a Quickie Print in Chicago.

Starting at the first fax number he had written down, Rick progressed through the list of about thirty numbers, sending the document without any cover sheet. It took Rick another thirty minutes to complete the job. After the last fax was completed Rick again went into the programming mode and changed the name and number back to its original setting. He scrolled through the other programming options until he came to the activity report. He pressed the start button to print out the activity report, thus wiping the information out of the fax machine's memory. As he walked back to the front Rick walked by a shredder and fed the activity report in.

"All through, Neal," said Rick. "How much do I owe you?"

Neal figured up the bill for the computer time and the per fax charge. It cost Rick another fifty dollars, but if this worked it would be the best money Rick had ever spent. As he walked back to the car Rick saw that Robert was just starting to come in the Quickie Print to check on him.

Robert looked at his watch and said, "One hour and fifteen minutes, Rick. We need to get situated at the motel. Larry and his partner could be here at any time."

Rick replied, "Okay, sorry it took a little longer than I expected, but I really needed to take care of that business. After all, I have a life to get back to when this is all over. That is, assuming that Larry doesn't have his way."

"Don't worry, Rick, we'll take good care of you," said

Robert confidently. They got into Robert's car and headed to the Northern Inn.

When they came upon a mall Rick said, "One more favor. I really need a fresh change of clothes."

"You do look pretty frumpy and wrinkled. I guess we can spare a few minutes at the mall. I haven't heard from Beth at Oakwood Towers yet," replied Robert.

They entered the mall and Rick was happy to see the GAP and Old Navy signs right away. He bought a couple of pairs of jeans at the GAP and two shirts at Old Navy. One more stop a J.C. Penney's got him stocked up on socks and underwear.

Larry and Hal pulled into the parking lot, scanning for signs of Rick. They went into the building and up the elevator. Larry walked directly up to the receptionist's desk of Oakwood Towers Executive Suites while Hal hung back, observing the reception area and the adjoining offices and hallways.

Larry said to the receptionist, "Hi, I was supposed to meet a business associate here in Chicago, but my assistant over there lost the paper with the addresses and phone numbers on it. Fortunately, I was able to remember this place's name. The man's name is Rick Blaze. Do you know anything that might help me track him down?"

Rachel said, "Mr. Blaze is scheduled for some meetings here over the next several days."

"Is he here now, by chance?" asked Larry.

Rachel glanced at her status sheet and answered, "No, he's not here now."

"Can you tell me where to reach him, like where he's staying?"

Rachel said, "I'm sorry sir. I'm not allowed to give out that information."

Larry was expecting this response so he was not looking at Rachel. Instead his eyes were scouring her desk for any information he could use. Long ago he had developed the ability to read upside-down, a talent that often proved invaluable in just such occasions. Larry's eyes caught a piece of paper on the corner of the desk. It said: Rick Blaze, Northern Inn.

"Oh, I understand. I'll try to catch up to him later," Larry said.

Rachel replied, "Can I tell him you came by?"

"No, I really want to surprise old Rick," said Larry slyly.

He turned away and walked to the elevator, signaling Hal to follow.

As they went down the elevator Larry said, "I got it. He's staying at the Northern Inn. We will nail him there."

They got into the car and called information on the cell-phone. After locating the address on their Chicago map Larry and Hal sped toward their prey.

Sergeant Mario Ritolli of Precinct 17 scanned the incoming faxes. One caught his eye. The name on it seemed familiar. As he read it his mind was working furiously to recall the details of long ago. Finally it all came together. Ritolli read the fax again to be sure he was right. Yes, he thought, this information would be worth a lot of money to the right people. And he knew the right people. Ritolli was already on their payroll, but this was certainly worth a bonus. He folded the fax and put it into his pocket, being sure no one was looking.

Ritolli went to the file room in the basement where the archived records were kept. His mind kept jumping to how he could spend the money he would soon have. First, he must be sure of his information. Ritolli smiled as he pulled the file and flipped through it. He was right. After replacing the file, he quickly left the Precinct building and drove a short ways away to a pay phone. His hands were sweating as he dialed the phone.

A voice answered with a gruff, “Yeah?”

“Joey, it’s Ritolli. I got some info for you,” said Ritolli.

Joey replied, “Spit it out. I ain’t got all day.”

“I know where to find some one you’ve been looking for a long time. What’s it worth to your people?” asked Ritolli.

“Who is this person?” asked Joey impatiently.

Ritolli said the name into the receiver.

“Yeah, that’s worth a lot. I was beginning to think we never would find him. I think I can get you an extra ten thousand for that, Ritolli.”

“Come on, Joey, with what this guy did, I was thinking more like a hundred grand for this kind of info.”

Joey replied, “Okay, Ritolli, I think I can get that for you. It’ll look good for both of us to nail that guy. Now where do I find him?”

Ritolli gave Joey the information from the fax and said, “When can I get my money?”

Joey said coldly, “When we nail the bastard.”

# Chapter 42

When Rick and Robert Whetland pulled into the Northern Inn they were signaled over to room 125 by several of Robert's fellow agents. There appeared to be a total of six agents in three cars, including Robert's. Robert gathered the men together inside room 125 and began to fully explain his plan. Robert and one other man would stay in the room with Rick and the other four outside, pairing up in two cars. Rick was not so sure Larry would find them and just barge in to kill Rick. Robert replied that Larry was a pro and if it were too easy he would get suspicious. A little bribe would get him the information he needed from someone at the motel. Robert reasoned that by this time Larry would be pretty anxious to get the job done and the direct approach would be most likely.

Robert said, "Now everyone who's staying in the room must put on one of these bulletproof vests. Rick, I want you to stay in the back. All we need is your voice if he knocks first. We will be in radio contact with the other agents so we'll know when they are coming. Any questions?"

"Do I have time to change clothes? That new stuff isn't doing me any good in the bags," said Rick. "Besides, I probably don't smell good enough to be in a small room with some of you guys," he continued.

One of the other men said to Robert, "Let him change, Robert, please."

They all laughed and Robert said to Rick, "Change your clothes, but don't take a shower. They could be right behind us."

Everyone shook their heads and began to move to the positions Robert had indicated. Rick put on the new clothes and felt better immediately. After Rick put on the bulletproof vest he felt bulky, but safer. After an hour Rick began to get antsy. He had never been very good at sitting around and this was magnified by the danger of the situation. Rick looked around and saw how cool Robert and the other agent appeared to be. He wondered if the coolness was real or if they had just learned to act this way.

Robert's cell phone rang. All Rick heard was Robert saying, "Thanks, you've been a big help." Turning to his agents and Rick, he said, "Larry's got the information."

Now the waiting seemed endless. Minutes dragged on like hours. Even the agents began to fidget and pace around the room.

Suddenly the radio crackled. "Robert, two men are going into the office. I think it's our guys."

"Roger, I copy," replied Robert.

Rick noticed the two men began to tense and were obviously ready for the action to start.

After about ten minutes the radio came to life again, "Robert, the two men and a third man are approaching the room. The third man looks like the motel clerk. You know, kind of mousy. You're going to have to be careful with him."

Robert got to his feet and snapped, "Rick get in the back.

Duck into the bathroom if there is any trouble."

The two agents moved to the front of the room, guns drawn.

The radio went off again. "They're at the door, but the clerk is in front and the two others are right against him. We don't have a clear shot."

There was a knock on the door.

Robert nodded to Rick, who said, "Who's there?"

"Housekeeping," came the answer.

"Okay, I'll be right there."

Robert started toward the door to unlock it when Larry kicked the door, sending Robert sprawling back. Something rolled into the room. Rick recognized it as one of the smoke grenades that Larry's bag had contained. He wished he had thought to tell Robert about the grenades. Rick started toward the bathroom as smoke filled the room. The smoke and the presence of the clerk paralyzed Robert and the other agents. Larry pulled an UZI 9-mm auto pistol out from under his jacket and began to spray the room with bullets, most of them at chest level. Rick saw Robert and the other agent go down and then was jolted backward by two bullets hitting him square in the chest. The two bullets had gone through the sheetrock walls and even though the bulletproof vest stopped the bullets, the force knocked the wind out of Rick.

He could hear Robert say, "I'm hit."

There was no reply from the other agent. Rick could see daylight as the door opened completely and he began to fear the worst. Suddenly, he could hear shouting from outside.

"FBI, put down your weapons," said one agent.

"You have nowhere to go. Don't make it worse," said another.

Rick could see the three figures in the doorway move and

the UZI opened fire again. Since no bullets were coming his way, Rick reasoned that Larry was firing on the agents outside. Now, the sound changed, like it was in stereo. Both men had UZI's, Rick realized. He also noticed no return fire. The clerk was a human shield, a very effective one. The yelling outside stopped and Larry and Hal began running to their car, dragging the clerk with them. Rick ran to the doorway and saw a red Taurus driving off and the clerk lying on the ground. Rick expected to see the FBI cars in hot pursuit, but they weren't moving. A closer look revealed the flat tires and shot up radiators and the agents lying on the ground, possibly wounded. Rick turned his attention back into the room and could see the other agent sprawled on the floor, not moving. Robert was trying to get up, but blood was running down his shoulder and arm. Suddenly, it hit Rick. It was he and Larry again. Rick was tired of being the pursued and decided to turn the tables.

He ran over to Robert and said, "Robert, give me your gun and car keys. I have to follow them. Everyone else is out of action."

Robert winced and said, "Here are the keys. I can't give you a gun. Just follow and call in your position on the radio. Be careful. Don't be a hero."

"Right," Rick said as he grabbed the car keys and sprinted toward the car.

He hesitated at the door and returned to get his survival pack. He dashed out the door and around the corner to the car. Fortunately, because of its location the car had not become a victim of the gunfire. Rick glanced down the highway and saw the red Taurus heading south. He sped through the parking lot and into the street. The tires squealed as he bounded across the north lane, skidded through the median and finally was heading south. He decided to catch up slowly and maybe he could surprise them.

After fumbling around for a minute he located the radio and microphone.

With the mike button depressed Rick said, "This is Rick Blaze. I'm in agent Robert Whetland's car. I'm in pursuit of a red Taurus on Highway 94 South. There are some wounded agents at the Northern Inn. I'll keep you posted on my position."

He ignored the incoming transmissions so he could concentrate on keeping track of the Taurus. Larry and Hal were obviously trying to stay within the speed limit so as not to attract any attention. Rick figured this meant they had not detected him following them. Rick reached into the survival bag on the front seat and removed the pepper spray and stun gun. He slipped them into his pocket. When the Taurus started moving over to the right-hand lane Rick deduced that Larry was about to get off the highway. This could make it much harder to follow. It was time to do something.

Rick gritted his teeth, put his right foot to the floor and closed the gap to the Taurus. He moved all the way to the left side, using an eighteen-wheeler to block the view of his approaching car. At just the precise moment, Rick wretched the wheel to the right and drove into the rear bumper of the Taurus at a forty-five degree angle. Keeping his foot on the floor Rick forced the Taurus off the highway, across the access road and through a chain link fence surrounding a long-deserted factory. The two cars skidded through the parking lot, locked together and bouncing wildly. The Taurus plowed into a light pole, stopping it immediately. Rick's car crunched further into the Taurus' trunk. Rick was a bit groggy from the collision, but forced himself to move.

He had no idea what Larry and Hal were doing and he certainly didn't want to wait around for them. He spilled out the driver's side door onto the pavement. The Taurus' left door was still closed, but he heard the other door open. Peeking above the door Rick saw Hal stand up and look at his car. Rick's eyes widened as he saw the silenced Glock 9mm pistol come up. He ducked down as two bullets whistled through the side windows and right over his head. He tried to think of something to do. All he had was his stun gun and the pepper spray and he could not think of any way to get close enough to use either one. Hal bent over and began to edge around Rick's car. An idea flashed into Rick's head and he turned the stun gun on. He laid on the ground so he could see the approaching man's feet. When he saw the ankles bend forward Rick knew that Hal was leaning against the car. He thrust the stun gun against the metal car door, being careful to keep away from the car himself. He heard a yelp and a thump as Hal hit the ground, stunned by the voltage.

The left door on the Taurus began to open and Rick scrambled around to the other side of his car. Hal was slowly rolling over and Rick kicked him viciously in the head and Hal slumped to the pavement. Larry heard the sounds and turned to run away from the confrontation. He probably figured it was the FBI after him, not Rick Blaze. Rick watched as Larry kicked in a rotted door and entered the old factory. Rick looked at Hal and was convinced he was out for quite a while. Picking up the Glock 9mm, Rick decided to pursue Larry although it was against his better judgment. He looked in his car and saw his bag in the front seat. Rick reached in and grabbed his survival gear bag and ran to the door Larry had entered.

Would Larry wait just inside the door to ambush him or would he try to get away? Rick wondered.

Unable to decide, Rick hesitated a second, reached into the bag and pulled out an emergency roadside flare. He broke the flare and as soon as it ignited Rick chunked it through the battered door.

Shots rang out as the flare hit and rolled across the floor. Larry is definitely an ambush kind of person. I should have known that, Rick thought. Searching for an option, Rick spied another door at the other end of the large building. He sprinted to the door, staying low as he ran. The door gave as easily as the one Larry had kicked in, the years deteriorating both equally. Rick dove through the doorway, rolled several times and came to rest behind some barrels.

Rick pulled his flashlight out of the bag and checked the clip in the Glock. The gun was down to six rounds and there was no more ammunition to be had. Rick took a deep breath and carefully worked his way towards the other end of the building. After every few steps he would stop to listen for sounds of Larry moving, but either Larry was sitting still or moving very quietly. Rick decided his best approach was with one wall of the building against his back so he slid along the wall ten feet at a time.

He had moved about seventy-five feet when he began to sense another presence. Careful listening revealed a noise some twenty feet ahead, next to some kind of large machine. Rick pointed the flashlight directly at the spot and turned it on momentarily. He saw a figure dash by and before he could get a shot off the man was out of view. Cursing under his breath for not being quicker, Rick was startled when two bullets came flying just past his head. Larry had gotten a fix on Rick's position in the instant the light had been on.

I've got to be more careful. Don't underestimate him, Rick thought.

After listening for sounds and hearing none, Rick began moving along the wall in the direction he had seen Larry move. Rick thought he saw a movement and fired two quick shots. He instantly knew there was little chance that he had hit anyone. The shots had been fired out of nervousness and not towards a definite target.

Only four shots left, thought Rick, I can't risk wasting anymore.

Suddenly, Rick heard a roaring noise and turned to his right to identify it. A cart loaded with some kind of metal scraps was approaching him at an ever-increasing speed. Instinctively, Rick fired right into the cart, but it kept coming. Rick's mind flashed with the realization that his shots were not only using up his ammunition, but were also giving away his position. The cart was about ten feet away and obviously being pushed by Larry. It was moving much too fast to be rolling on its own.

Rick tried to decide which way to roll and how to avoid the bullets that would certainly be coming in his direction. He jammed the Glock into his belt and at the last second glanced up and saw pipes running overhead, about eight feet above the ground. Using the muscles he had honed in hours of basketball with Davis and Mack in the driveway, Rick leapt high. He grabbed one of the pipes and swung his feet up, barely clearing the pile of metal on the cart. He dropped back to the floor and pulled the Glock out. Firing as he ran for cover, Rick avoided shots being fired at him, but the cost was all but his last bullet. Trading stealth for distance was Rick's immediate plan as he sprinted away from the cart. A couple of shots rang out just behind him as he covered at least fifty feet in a hurry. Rick was now the pursued again and he had no choice, having only one bullet left. His mind was spinning as he desperately searched for an idea and suddenly an image leapt into his head. If only he could move to the back of the warehouse quietly enough to buy a little time, Rick thought his plan had at least a chance of working. He crept around equipment, staying low and watching for anything on the floor he could trip over.

Since no shots were coming his way, Rick felt he was moving undetected. Shortly he approached the area he had originally entered. About twenty feet away was a wide semicircular trough about six feet long. He had noticed the trough when he had first entered the building and it now had given Rick an idea. He ran over to the rusty old device. It was made of at least one-quarter inch metal, plenty thick for Rick's use. With a burst of strength Rick stood the trough on its end. He rummaged through his survival bag and pulled out his rain poncho. The jagged edges of the trough's side held the poncho in position. Rick spied a bucket and hung it from the top edge. Next he pulled an aluminum reflective blanket out and placed it behind the poncho and bucket.

All he needed now was something to lure Larry to the trap, although the noise he had made would have him approaching quickly. Rick grabbed the combination battery and solar-powered radio and turned it on, keeping the volume low. He picked a station and turned it up just a little. After placing the radio behind the trough Rick backed away and hid off to the side, making as much noise as possible as he moved. Larry's relentless urge to pursue was to be his downfall, Rick hoped.

As he sat to the side with the flashlight from the survival gear at the ready Rick could hear noises as Larry approached. He saw a faint outline as Larry followed the sound of the radio. Just as Larry was about forty feet away Rick turned on the flashlight, pointing the beam at the trough. Larry reacted instantly as he saw the outline of a man silhouetted in the reflected light. He fired ten quick rounds into the poncho. The bullets had another target in mind as they ricocheted around the semicircular trough and returned in the direction from which they had come.

Larry stood perfectly still, stunned to be bleeding through several bullet holes. He dropped his gun and tried to stagger away.

Rick stepped out and said, “Good shooting, Larry. You just blew your own ass away.”

Larry turned and faced Rick. He was livid as he recognized Rick’s taunting voice. As he made a desperate dive for the gun, the wounds and perhaps the anger became too much and Larry Thomas sunk to the ground, never to bother the Blaze family again.

What irony. Felled by your own bullets, thought Rick.

Rick walked through the door to the parking lot, lugging his bag with him. He had placed the Glock at the bottom of the bag so he would not have to explain to any authorities why he had a silenced pistol in his possession. He could see several cars pulling into the parking lot. Rick waved, hoping they would know he was one of the good guys. The cars stopped and six agents got out, guns drawn. As they swept the area with their weapons Rick saw Hal had regained consciousness. He stood up and instantly was noticed by the agents.

One of them yelled, “Put your hands up and walk slowly away from the car.”

Hal began to raise his hands, but suddenly dove into the red Taurus and came out with one of the UZI’s. Rick was about fifty feet behind Hal and so far was unnoticed. He reached into the bag and the first thing he felt was a can.

As Hal started to fire at the agents, Rick ran forward, gave a yell to distract the gunman and heaved the can of Wolf Brand Chili straight at Hal. Hearing Rick screaming caused Hal to spin around. The UZI barked several rounds and Rick felt the now-familiar feeling of being driven back as two bullets hit his chest. Hal took the can of Chili directly in the face, causing him to drop to the ground in a heap. The agents were all over him, putting an end to the danger.

Rick rolled over on his side, moaning with pain, but

thanking God for bulletproof vests. He had not removed the vest and that had saved his life. He would be quite sore for a while, having taken what felt like four sledgehammer blows in the chest in the last hour. A car screeched to a halt right beside Rick and Robert Whetland climbed out.

His shoulder was bandaged and he was still a little unsteady, but he rushed to Rick and said, “Rick, are you all right?” Without waiting for an answer Robert yelled, “We need an ambulance over here.”

Rick sat up and replied, “Robert, I’m okay. This bulletproof vest has saved my life twice today. I’m just pretty sore in the chest area. You know, Robert, I might have to ask for one of these vests for Christmas this year.”

Robert chuckled and said, “Keep that one. You’ve certainly earned it. Now tell me. What have you done with Mr. Thomas?”

“He’s inside that door over there. He just couldn’t take it anymore, so he shot himself,” said Rick.

“He committed suicide?” asked Robert incredulously.

“Not exactly. I guess I kind of tricked him into shooting himself,” Rick said with a grin.

“I’ll be damned, Rick, I don’t know what to think of you sometimes,” replied Robert.

“I don’t know what to think of all this either, Robert. So do you think it’s over or is Rene Charlton going to keep after me?” asked Rick.

Robert answered, “My personal feeling is that you’re safe, now. We’re closing in on him. We searched his office but couldn’t find him, but we will soon. There’s very little activity at Worldwide Water Solutions headquarters. Most of the rats have jumped ship. But I must warn you; people like these hold grudges for a long time. I’m not sure you will ever be safe unless we can get him behind bars."

"So all I have to worry about is the Mafia and Rene Charlton for the rest of my life?" asked Rick.

"I'm afraid so," said Robert solemnly.

Rick perked up and said, "Well maybe things will turn out okay. You just never know."

"I hope so, Rick, I really do. Are you ready to get out of here? We can go back to the office and take your statement. And by the way-thanks," said Robert.

"For what?" asked Rick.

Robert laughed and said, "For destroying my car. I was ready for a new one."

They got into one of the cars and headed for the Chicago FBI headquarters.

After a few minutes Rick said, "Robert, can I borrow a phone? I sure would like to call my wife."

"Sure, Rick. I'll even dial the number for you," replied Robert.

"Well, I don't have the number, but hopefully that convenience store over there does," Rick said while pointing down the street.

"I don't get it. Perhaps you could explain."

"My wife is supposed to run an ad in the Dallas newspaper telling me how to reach her. It should have been in today's paper," explained Rick.

"I still don't quite understand, but how about if I just go to the store," replied Robert.

"Thanks."

Rick slowly moved from the car to the store and purchased the Dallas paper. His hands actually trembled a little over the anticipation. He found the Boats for Sale classification and quickly scanned the thirty or so listings. There it was:

*1952 Chris Craft Commander for sale, forty-two foot, no engines, fixer upper. 214-555-1233*

Rick dialed the number with Robert's cell-phone.

After a few rings Kathy answered, "Hello?"

"Hi, Kathy, it's me."

Kathy gushed, "Rick, are you okay? Is it over?"

"Yes, it's over, we think. Larry's dead and his last partner is in custody. I'm fine."

"Can we go home now?"

"Yes, but we have some thinking to do. We'll still have to be careful."

Kathy asked, "From Rene or the Mafia?"

"Both, I'd say. Unless, of course, something happens to get one or both out of our hair."

"Rick, do you really think that could ever happen?"

"Maybe so, maybe so."

"When are you coming home?" asked Kathy.

Rick looked at Robert and asked, "Robert, when can I go home?"

Robert replied, "Tomorrow morning. I'll fly you back in our plane."

"Kathy, I'll be home tomorrow, probably in the afternoon. When can you be in Austin?"

Kathy said, "I'll let Mack answer that."

Mack jumped in. "Dad, what's going on? Are you okay?"

"I'm fine, just a little sore. Say, when do you think you can get that old plane back to Austin so you can get back to school?"

"We can be back by noon tomorrow," Mack replied.

"Great, I'll be there a little after that. The FBI is going to fly me in on their little Lear Jet," said Rick.

"Cool, Dad. Say, Davis wants to talk to you."

"Hi, Dad. What did you do to Larry?" asked Davis.

"Well, to make a long story short, I tricked Larry into shooting himself," replied Rick.

"What about the other guy?"

Rick said, "He's in custody. He pulled an UZI on me so I chunked a can of Wolf Brand Chili in his face. I think he'll have a broken nose to remember me by."

"Wolf Brand Chili? Is that all you had to defend yourself?" Davis asked.

"Well, that was the first thing I pulled out of my survival pack. I just thought about the commercial, you know-How long has it been since you had a bowl of Wolf Brand Chili? Well, that's too long!" laughed Rick.

"That's really funny, Dad. I'm glad your arm is still in throwing shape. So what about the FBI? Weren't they supposed to do the apprehending?" asked Davis.

"Yeah, well, it didn't turn out exactly like that," said Rick. Continuing he said, "I guess I'd better go now. Tell mom that I'll call her at home and let her know exactly when I'll get to the airport."

"Wait a minute, Mom wants to talk to you again," said Davis.

"Rick, why is Davis asking about the FBI? Didn't they take care of everything?" asked Kathy earnestly.

Rick replied, "Well, there were some problems, but it worked out just fine."

Kathy asked, "Don't give me any bullshit, Rick. Did they shoot at you or anything?"

Rick winced and said, “Yeah, I got into the line of fire twice, but I had a bulletproof vest on and all I got was a bruised chest.”

Kathy erupted, “Rick, you told me you wouldn’t be in danger. The FBI was supposed to take care of you.”

“I know, but it just didn’t happen like we thought.”

Robert reached over and motioned for the phone, “Hello, Mrs. Blaze. This is Agent Robert Whetland and I just wanted you to know that your husband is a very special person. I readily admit we let him down today, but he showed the kind of initiative and drive that has pulled him through the numerous close calls he has had in his life. If you want to chew anyone out I guess it should be me, so go ahead.”

Kathy was momentarily stunned, but finally she said, “Agent Whetland, I appreciate your honesty as well as your assessment of my husband. Please put him back on the phone.”

Robert willingly gave the phone back to Rick, who said, “I’m sorry you have had to worry so much about me. I’ll be home soon and we can get back to our normal lives.”

Kathy said, “I don’t know about normal, but I’ll be glad to get back to our life together. I love you and I was getting used to you being around all the time.”

“I love you, too. Very much.”

“Well, then get your butt back to Austin,” she said, starting to cry with relief.

“I’ll see you in Austin tomorrow,” Rick replied.

# Chapter 43

Rene Charlton was getting worried. His employees were leaving at a rapid pace and his crack team of field personnel was being reduced to nothing by a nobody, just some guy with a knack for screwing up his plans. The last he had heard from Larry was that they had located Rick Blaze and were at the motel he was staying at. That had been several hours ago and there had been no word from Larry or Hal. Rene had to consider that they had failed again.

He dialed the phone and a voice said, "Hello?"

"Mike," Rene said, "I need to get out of the country immediately. Are you ready?"

"Everything's ready. Be at the dock at 11:30 tonight. We will take a small boat out into the ocean. There I have made arrangements to meet up with a freighter headed for Spain. You can make your own way from Spain to France," answered Mike.

"Good job, Mike, I knew I could count on you," replied Rene, relieved to be getting out of the United States.

"Travel light, Mr. Charlton," advised Mike.

"All right, I'll have only a couple of small bags. I'll be at the dock at 11:30, Mike."

"Yes, sir."

Rene decided to leave the office immediately. He was tired of hiding in his secret room. He gathered up a satchel of papers and began to shred the files he could not carry. This took about fifteen minutes and then he was ready to leave. Rene took the freight elevator down to the parking garage. On the way down he thought of Rick Blaze, the man who had ruined what seemed like a perfect plan. Rene vowed to get even, no matter how long it took. Anyway, it would be easier to wait a few months and then send someone after Blaze. His guard would be down and the revenge would come easily. The elevator doors opened and Rene walked to his car. It was a fairly new Lexus and Rene would miss the car.

No matter, he thought, I can always get a new one in France.

As Rene drove out of the parking garage he didn't notice the man staring at him. The man got into his car and followed Rene. Both cars drove to the highway and south to Rene's neighborhood. The man was a pro and Rene never had an idea he was being followed. Rene pulled into the driveway of his secret residence and pushed the garage door opener. As the door was opening he saw a car pull into the driveway behind him. Rene didn't recognize the burly man behind the wheel.

He drove quickly into the garage, almost scraping the car roof on the garage door. The door changed directions as Rene punched the control again. As the door closed he saw the man start to get out of the car. Rene breathed a sigh of relief when the door closed before the man could get to the garage. Rene heard the car start and was glad the man was leaving. But the car noise was getting louder instead of quieter. The car smashed through the flimsy wood garage door and rear-ended Rene's Lexus.

Rene turned to run, but the man said, "Hold it right there, Mr. Charlton. Or shall I say Mr. Flanagan? We have been looking for you for a long time. We always find our enemies and they always pay the price."

"I don't know what you are talking about. I'm Rene Charlton. I'm the President of Worldwide Water Solutions," Rene screamed.

"That's all I need to know," said Joey.

He raised the silenced Beretta and fired three quick shots into Rene. As he breathed his last breath Rene had a look of total confusion on his face. Joey waited a minute and checked for a pulse. Detecting none he turned and walked deliberately back to his car, got in and drove off.

As he pulled out of the driveway Joey said out loud, "That closes the book on Randy Flanagan. Mr. Carlucci will rest easier in prison knowing that rat is dead."

Joey was admitted to the prison visitors area. After a short wait Gino Carlucci came to his side of the booth.

They both picked up their phone sets and Carlucci said, "What's the good word, Joey?"

"I nailed his ass, Mr. Carlucci. Randy Flanagan is not of this world anymore. You can rest a little easier, I hope," said Joey.

"Yes, Joey, I can rest easier. Revenge always makes me feel better. Did you pay off the cop, that Ritolli guy?"

"Yeah, I gave him the money. He's really in our pocket now," replied Joey.

"Excellent, Joey. There'll be some extra dough for you as well," said Carlucci.

"Thanks boss," said Joey with a grin.

# Chapter 44

Rick and Robert spent several hours going over the events as they had happened. Rick was amazed at the paperwork required to document this case and as a small businessman he was quite used to loads of paperwork. The evening dragged on and Rick's chest was bruised and throbbing. Finally, the chore was over and Robert dropped Rick off at a hotel, one much nicer than the Northern Inn. Robert left two agents outside the room in the hall to reassure Rick that he was safe. Rick immediately dropped off to sleep and got the best night's sleep he had enjoyed in several weeks.

The next morning Robert Whetland picked up Rick and they drove to the airport. The Lear was in the air in less than an hour. Rick wondered why Robert came along on the flight. A highly ranked FBI agent such as he would be very busy thought Rick. After the Lear leveled off at cruising altitude Rick discovered the reason Robert had come along.

"Rick, I need to talk to you about something," said Robert.

Rick replied, "Sure, Robert, what do you want to talk

about? Basketball or football?"

"Real funny, Rick. Actually, I want to talk about Rene Charlton, or I guess I should say the former Rene Charlton."

Rick's heart seemed to skip a beat, but he tried to seem calm. He asked, "What happened to our friend Rene?"

Robert replied, "He was gunned down at a residence yesterday. We think it was a sort of safe house for him. There are no suspects. It seems the killer drove through Charlton's garage door and shot him several times at close range. The local police feel it was a professional hit. I just had a feeling I should ask you about it. Was I right about my feeling?"

Rick reached into his back pocket and pulled out a piece of paper. He slowly unfolded the paper and handed it to Robert. Robert's eyes widened as he read the document:

**WWW**

WORLDWIDE WATER SOLUTIONS, INC
13204 Water Street
New York, New York 10032
212-951-6432
212-951-6466 fax

To whom it may concern:

I am looking for a Bill Whetland. He was an FBI agent who worked on a case involving Randy Flanagan about twenty-five years ago. I do not think I need to conceal my identity after this long of a time, so I can tell you that I am Randy Flanagan. I went on the run myself and eventually ended up in France. I assumed the identity of Rene Charlton. Some trouble has come my way and I would like to talk to Mr. Whetland. I am sure he can give me some excellent advice.

My phone and fax numbers on the letterhead would be the best way for Mr. Whetland to reach me.

Thank you.

Sincerely,
Rene Charlton

"And just what exactly did you do with this letter? Rick," asked Robert.

Rick kind of grinned and said, "Well, I faxed it to about thirty Chicago police precincts. It seems like one precinct may have a connection to Gino Carlucci's people."

"I can't believe you did this. You did it at the Quickie Print while I just sat on my ass in the car, didn't you?" barked Robert.

"Yeah, that's when I did it."

Robert said, "That's one of the sneakiest, most low-down things I've seen in a long time."

"So are you saying it was a bad thing? It seems to have solved problems for both of us," replied Rick, beginning to get worried.

"It was damned brilliant. That's what it was," laughed Robert, "damned brilliant."

Rick let out a sigh of relief and said, "I guess I'm not in trouble, then."

"No, not this time. I'm just curious, what made you think of sending that fax?" asked Robert.

Rick replied, "Actually, it was a conversation between Larry Thomas and Ed Richter that was on one of the tape recordings I made. Larry was talking about how much I resemble Rene in appearance and apparently temperament as well. I guess I just filed that information away until it could be useful. It popped out when I was racking my brain trying to figure out how to take Rene out of the picture. When I thought about sending the Mafia after Rene the fax idea seemed like a logical way to throw out the bait. I think it points out that the Mafia has contacts inside the Chicago Police Department, but I guess that's not news to anyone."

"No, not really, Rick," said Robert. "It's pretty frustrating for us honest cops."

"Yeah, I bet it is," said Rick.

Rick called Kathy at the house, "Hi, it's me. I have some great news."

"You're already home?" asked Kathy.

"No, I'll be home at 2:00. The news is that Rene Charlton is dead. He can't hurt us anymore. Also, the Mafia is not a concern anymore," Rick blurted out.

Kathy's heart jumped as the message sunk in. She asked, "How did all this come about, Rick?"

"Well, it seems the Mafia got the notion that Rene Charlton was actually a certain Randy Flanagan and they sent one of their killers out to get the revenge they had waited so long for," Rick answered.

Kathy asked, "How did the Mafia get that idea? And why did they just happen to figure this out at such an opportune time for us? Wait a minute; this has Rick Blaze written all over it. What did you do, Rick?"

Rick laughed. After explaining he said, "As I hoped, there was someone on Gino Carlucci's payroll at one of the precincts. Rene was apparently trying to skip the country when someone tracked him down at his house and shot him."

"That's incredible, Rick. I never realized how clever you are," said Kathy proudly. "You know," she continued, "a month ago I couldn't have squashed a bug without feeling guilty and now I don't seem to feel the least bit bad about the characters you and the boys have disposed of."

"Yeah, I don't feel bad about them either. Davis and Mack are dealing with it pretty well, too," Rick replied.

"They're strong, just like their dad," said Kathy.

"We're a strong family, no doubt about it, and I'm just glad we're really off the hook now. We are safe," said Rick.

"Oh, Rick, we really are. I'm so glad. I'll be even happier when you get back to Austin," she said tearfully.

"I'm ready to be there. Be sure to bring Davis and Mack to the airport this afternoon," said Rick.

"I don't think wild horses could keep them away," she laughed.

"I'll see you then. I love you," he said.

Kathy answered, "I love you, too, Rick Blaze."

Rick hung up the phone and looked forward to tonight when they could stay up all night talking and telling their stories. Most importantly they would be a normal family again.

A couple of hours later the Lear touched down at the Austin airport. As it taxied toward the terminal building Rick could see Kathy and the boys standing with several men on the tarmac. The Lear came to a stop and Rick fairly pushed the door open and bounded down the short stairway. A tearful Blaze family reunion ensued and a great peace came about the family as they were all together again.

Davis said, "Dad, so you got Larry to shoot himself and the Mafia to kill Rene Charlton. Do you really enjoy getting other people to do the dirty work for you?"

"I guess so, Davis. It's better than doing it yourself," Rick laughed.

"Dad, do you think they'll take me for a ride in the Lear?" Mack asked.

"I don't think they'll take you up, but I bet you can look around the plane. It's pretty neat," answered Rick.

Mack ran over to the Lear and was talking to Robert. He

motioned for Davis to come over.

Kathy said, "After all the excitement all he wants to do is fly."

They turned as the Lear's engines came to life and the sleek plane began to taxi toward the runway. They laughed as they saw Mack and Davis waving out the windows.

The plane took off and Kathy said, "I have such a hard time keeping this family together for any period of time."

Then she seemed to remember something.

"Rick, I have a surprise for you," she said excitedly.

She turned and waved toward the car the agents were standing by. The rear door opened and Nate Reilly got out.

"Nate. Boy, am I glad to see you. Did the FBI get you out of trouble?" asked Rick.

"Didn't have to. I never got into trouble. It seems I'm as slippery as you are, my boy," replied Nate.

"But how did you get away? There had to be dozens of law officers after you."

"Let me ask a question," said Nate with a wink to Kathy. "How do you like the color red?"

"It's okay I guess. What does that have to do with anything?"

"Good, then you'll love your new red Blazer," laughed Nate.

"What the hell are you talking about?" said Rick with a touch of exasperation in his voice.

"Okay, I'll explain. I made it into a little town about ten miles down the road before anyone really got after me again. I found an old boarded-up house with a detached garage. The old garage door opened with a little work and I hid the Blazer inside. After a while I got the hare-brained idea to change the color of your car. I just walked over to the hardware store and bought some masking tapc, sandpaper, a roll of plastic and ten cans of bright red Krylon spray paint. I spent some time sanding and taping it because I wanted to do a really good job on your car. Well, also because I was in no hurry to get on the road again. Later that night I opened the door and drove your bright red Blazer back to Austin without so much as a second look from anyone."

"Why didn't anyone tell me?" groaned Rick.

"We like to have our little surprises, too, Rick," teased Kathy. "Anyway, we haven't known for long. I went by the office and he was there."

"Just looking after the place like you asked," said Nate with a broad grin.

They all laughed and it really felt good to be able laugh about something again.

Rick and Kathy put their arms around each other and watched the Lear swooping past the airport. They really were free of the past, from thirty years ago to yesterday.

# Epilogue

Two weeks later all was well with Rick Blaze's world. His family was safe and healthy, his business was back on track, both Mack and Davis had been treated very well about their excessive class misses by their respective schools, thanks to a few well-placed calls by FBI top brass. There were no Mafia or terrorists after him and he and Kathy had gotten a few days of vacation at their Port Aransas house.

American forces had driven Saddam's forces out of Saudi Arabia and Kuwait with a vengeance and had pounded Iraq even harder than in the previous Gulf War. The Iraqis had been warned that the bombing would resume if Saddam ever showed his face again. The world waited to see if Saddam was dead or if he would continue to be the thorn that infected the Middle East.

Rick was surprised when the doorbell rang because it was getting late, about eight o'clock. He went to the door and looked through the peephole. Rick was totally shocked to see Robert Whetland standing there next to a man who looked just like Robert. He swung the door open and welcomed the men inside.

"Rick and Kathy, this is my brother, Bennett," said Robert.

"Pleased to meet you," said Kathy.

Rick reached out and shook the man's hand.

He said, "I hope you haven't looked back and decided I'm in some kind of trouble."

"No, it's not anything like that," laughed Robert. He continued, "Actually it is quite the opposite. You see, Bennett here is a Deputy Director of the CIA and I, as you know, am a special assistant to the Director of the FBI. We have a proposition for the two of you. First, I need your promises that what I'm about to tell you will remain completely secret. You can't tell anyone. Agreed?"

Rick looked at Kathy and they both nodded and Rick said, "Agreed."

Robert continued, "There's a group of people, shall we say private contractors, who are employed by a top secret agency that works to bring the FBI and the CIA together. By cooperating instead of fighting with each other we have been able to accomplish many more things. One interesting aspect about these private contractors is that they are allowed and expected to operate beyond the law if that is what it takes to do their job. Our joint agency will furnish resources such as training, equipment, compensation and backup, but we can't be exposed to the public in order to get you out of trouble. We won't abandon you, but there is a point we can't cross to help you. We want the two of you to be a team working for this agency."

He paused and sat back in his chair, allowing the offer to sink in.

Rick said, "You mean you will give us a job to do and full resources to do it and we can get it done any way possible?"

"Basically, yes," said Bennett. He said, "Rick, my Dad and brother have been impressed with the way you and your family have handled the Worldwide Water Solutions case. You can do great things for your country in this program."

"Yes, but will we be killed serving our country?" asked Rick.

"That was my first thought, too," said Kathy.

"Well, I can't say there is no danger, because of course there is, but most cases assigned to you'll be money laundering, counterfeiting or basic surveillance involving wire tapping and conversation recording. You also will be well compensated for your efforts," replied Robert.

"Where would we live and do our work?" asked Rick.

Robert replied, "You can live anywhere you want and I think most of your work would be in Florida and the offshore islands like the Caymans. We knew you two liked boats so we thought a couple of wealthy yachters cruising around the area would seem quite normal."

Rick looked at the two men and said, "This is obviously something we need to discuss in private."

"Yes, certainly. Bennett and I will leave you now and let you think about the offer. How about if I check back in a week?" asked Robert.

"Before you go can I ask a couple of questions?" asked Rick.

"Sure, ask away," replied Robert.

"Was the group that got us into the warehouses in New York one of these secret agency teams? I thought it was odd that they didn't seem to follow the laws about breaking and entering and you didn't have a warrant," said Rick.

Bennett replied, "You were very perceptive, Rick. That was one of the teams, one put together just for that purpose. In fact, each team is different-with different talents and abilities. We pick the team for the particular job."

"My other question is actually a request," said Rick. "I would like for you to personally tell Agent Parker in the Austin office he should have taken me seriously in the beginning."

"Mr. Parker doesn't work for the FBI anymore," laughed Robert.

Rick replied, "Well, that takes care of my questions for now."

Robert said, "Great. I guess we'll leave you two now. I really hope you decide to come on board with us."

"That goes for me, too," said Bennett.

They got up and left the house.

Rick and Kathy sat in the living room and at first said nothing. Finally, Rick said, "Well, how about that, a job offer."

"Not exactly your everyday, run-of-the-mill job, I would say," replied Kathy.

"So, what do you think about it?" asked Rick.

"I think it sounds dangerous. We would be crazy to do anything like that. We have a good life here and I think we're safe from everyone now," she said.

"Yeah, but what do you think about it? Doesn't it sound kind of exciting and we would be doing something for our country," said Rick, seriously.

"Rick, I told you, I think it sounds dangerous."

"Didn't you kind of enjoy the excitement of nailing Rene and Larry?"

"No, I did not!" she exclaimed. "Well, not much anyway," she added.

"Aha, you did find it exciting," exclaimed Rick.

Kathy looked kind of sheepish and said, "Okay, it was exciting, but it was scary too."

"Well, I think we should at least consider the offer. Mack will be off to college and out of the house soon and we'll need something to do," Rick said.

"I'd been thinking more of taking up golf or tennis or something like that, not continually saving the country," Kathy said.

"Robert and Bennett said it wouldn't be real dangerous work," Rick confidently said.

Kathy laughed and said, "When did you start believing the FBI, Rick Blaze?"

They both laughed and Rick walked over to the sofa. He gave her a long embrace and said, "Why don't we just sit on the idea for a few days and see if it sounds better then?"

"Oh, all right, you win. We'll think about it," Kathy said, wondering in what direction her life was about to go.